BY
SILENT
MAJORITY

ROBERT BUSCHEL

A POST HILL PRESS BOOK

ISBN: 978-1-68261-056-5
ISBN (eBook): 978-1-68261-057-2

Cover Design by Christian Bentulan
Interior Design and Composition by Greg Johnson/Textbook Perfect

Post Hill Press
275 Madison Avenue, 14th Floor
New York, NY 10016
posthillpress.com

Printed in the United States of America

10 9 8 7 6 5 4 3 2 1

for Rita and Bradley

PROLOGUE

DANIEL CARLSON AWOKE FROM a dream—a few seconds later, he registered it as a nightmare. He exhaled hard confirming he was awake. The same dream. The dream was an emotion, not a scene. It was real. The dream did not forsake the laws of science. The dream was pure feeling engendered by an internal dialogue with himself. He thought about the recurring character in his life—the Silent Majority. The Silent Majority is the fear factor in Daniel's life. As much as he hated it, it was a motivator. On tough days he grew exasperated with it. He constantly has to disprove the obvious. He has to disprove its fiction it blasted with conviction. Admittedly, it's a lot of work.

The Silent Majority is a fact-denier. It wants to win to win. Win for power. At some level every day, it cuts into and attacks Daniel Carlson's character, optimism, views on policy and his desire to be revolutionary, important and different. The Silent Majority is unaware. It is unaware of others. It is a cancer. The immune deficiency yielding to the artificial forces that deaden the positive evolution of society. It is unaware of the host. It is not conscious of the whole. It is a silent killer because it represents itself as the whole, as America.

1

The Silent Majority is made up of the human that is defeated by an ATM, or the cell phone. It is the person that stands in the middle of the airport when everyone is getting off the plane, and obstructs the flow of terminal walkers making their way home. It abhors technology in the name of economic loss manifested in the form of displacing American jobs. The Silent Majority thinks it is special, different, represents the many, but it is only really a vocal minority. It is religious and exclusionary.

If you ask the Silent Majority what happens next when America is pure, one man, one religion, one culture, it fails to recognize it's not even what it thinks it wants to be. It does not realize it will continue to exclude, subdivide and be sanctimonious, based upon color, geography, heritage, new traditions and God. It is easily offended, and the offended has no recognition of the irony in the world or itself. The Silent Majority distorts. The Silent Majority is evil, and like God, many take its name in vain. "What's the matter?" Daniel Carlson asked himself. "What's bothering me today?" He asked *what's really the matter* often when he feels vulnerable after waking from this dream. Daniel remembered his dreams too often. He's been scared much too often. What does it matter? It matters because Daniel Carlson is President of the United States.

CHAPTER 1

American Royalty

THE FIVE O'CLOCK ALARM beeped softly, but loud enough to wake the President. President Daniel Carlson sat up in bed, rubbed his eyes with the middles of his fingers, and then turned the alarm off. The backup wakeup call from the White House operator rang. The President picked up, said "got it" and hung up. It was a tortured night's sleep. When he threw off the sheets and covers, his maroon silk pajamas were exposed. His wife, June, quickly snatched up more than her share of the covers. *She finally won all the covers*, Daniel mused to himself.

After putting on a robe, Daniel stared into the mirror and noticed the colorless face he had every morning before taking a shower. He felt calm and relaxed, but not ready to tackle the whole day. Usually his morning massage got him started for the day's events.

The President leaned down to the intercom by his vanity table and pressed the intercom button. "I'm ready," he said to the Secret Service man outside his bedroom door.

"Yes, Mr. President," the cool official voice replied.

"Oh, remind my wife's secretary that she is having lunch with the British Ambassador's wife again this afternoon."

"I will, Mr. President." The President released the button to the intercom and walked out of the bedroom.

The President opened the door to his wing of the residence. "Have a good day, Jasper."

"I will, Mr. President," the agent said and smiled.

Most of the three hundred domestic staff members and Secret Service agents assigned to protect Daniel Carlson were fond of him. The President knew all of their names. President Carlson had a superior memory. He was also an expert politician. Legend had it, he could memorize the order of a deck of cards after two glasses of scotch. But since becoming President, he did not drink.

After a short walk down the hall of the residence in his bathrobe, Daniel Carlson turned the corner and opened a door to the right. He looked up and noticed a Chinese woman in a robe with a painted smile on her face.

"Good morning, Mr. President. Do you need anything?" another agent asked.

The President shook his head. "No, thank you."

"I'll be outside."

The President walked into what was dubbed the *message* room, which was equipped with a hot tub and four flat screen televisions. Assorted magazines lined the table outside of the tub. There was special meaning and an inside joke to the name *message* room.

"Mr. President, I am Ying. I am going to give you your massage this morning." The woman's accented voice was languid and pleasantly exotic.

"Where's Bruce?"

"Bruce is not in this morning. I must take his place."

"I really prefer Bruce. No one told me about this."

"I'm very sorry, Mr. President. I will go."

"No, hold on," he said sincerely, remaining suspicious.

The President came up with the idea of the morning and sometimes-early evening *massages*. There he received Top Secret messages from highly sensitive sources, from both within and outside the country. These were so sensitive, no one else saw the messages except the President. This covert network wasn't shared with Congress nor tested in the courts. Even President Carlson, as popular as he was with the American people, wasn't sure if this type of "domestic monitoring"—spying on potential threats within the United States—only for the "President's knowledge" would have too many "flying quotes" to be believed or acceptable. He knew that it could end his Presidency, if it were ever exposed. The work that they did in the message room was critical to the President's ability to guide policy. The only saving argument or propaganda Daniel Carlson could think of if it were ever learned he sanctioned unauthorized and unsupervised spying, was proclaiming he was disrupting domestic terrorist acts.

One morning he read a report about threats by terrorists to concurrently detonate thirty homemade bombs at various major malls around the country. With that knowledge, he gave specifics to the FBI. The Director of the Bureau was curious about the President's source for the information. The Director was never able to figure out how the President knew more than he did about this particular plot—and it was critical information. The Director was convinced the President had a mole in the FBI. In the world of American bureaucracy, this bothered the Director, who was not appointed by President Carlson, but by his predecessor. Daniel Carlson didn't have to answer to the Director.

President Carlson developed the veiled system to contemplate issues surrounding national security and economic terrorism. Making an informed decision based on the best available truths made decisions easier. Other presidents had tried to reform the special interest lobby. Daniel Carlson decided to do it without Congress. The President believed this source of information was well justified. This morning, as he began most mornings, the President had a massage and received his message. One day a staff secretary wrote about the massage room but thought "massage" was spelled like "message." The pieces fell together and then some of the staff knew what the President was really doing in the Massage Room.

The President asked Ying for the code. She replied: "Stay the course." Carlson's suspicion subsided. Ying passed a note that was sealed in a plastic encasement. Daniel Carlson cracked it open with his teeth, and read the contents.

Urgent message coming tonight

After reading the cryptic note, Carlson lightly pushed the note into his mouth and chewed the rice paper on which the message was written. With one swallow it was gone.

"Not exactly a hearty breakfast," he said jokingly. Ying smiled demurely in response.

Carlson quickly disrobed without embarrassment and reclined face down on the heated table covered with thick white towels. Ying turned on the small television at eye level, which was pre-set for news. Then the Presidential day continued with news and massage therapy.

Thirty minutes later, Ying signaled the massage was done, left the room, and the President sat up and walked over to the tub. He slowly slipped into the 102 degree water, exhaling and allowing himself to float. He sat in his favorite seat, which had a rotating jet aimed at the lumbar area. It circulated the blood in the entire lower back, and released the lasting stress that doesn't go away with sleep.

Daniel then went to the small refrigerator in the corner and poured a glass of water and a glass of orange juice. He brought the juice to a lounge chair with a tablet loaded with a special version of the *Washington Post, Bloomberg,* and *The New York Times.* This special version didn't have the local news and advertisements, but focused instead on national news. The President's *attaché* prepared the special version for the President each morning going through section by section, before the President awoke.

In between articles, the President swallowed the juice in three gulps and read the first page. After ingesting the gist of the media's version of yesterday's events, he immediately turned to the editorials.

It's always a good morning when I'm not slammed in the editorials, he commented to himself. President Carlson wouldn't admit this aloud, even to himself, but his reelection was assured.

The President then turned his attention to the television. The news anchor of the hour was breaking a story about the Mayor of Spokane, who was arrested for possession of cocaine. Carlson sighed, and admitted to himself he wasn't shocked by these events anymore. He slipped on his sandals, left the room and returned to the residence master bedroom.

After the President showered and dressed, he joined the Vice President for breakfast in the Rose Garden, where they both had a view of the Capitol. A breeze cooled the outside, and the garden was beautiful in the spring. Gardeners worked diligently in the lawn to make it a show place.

The server nodded as he pulled out the chair for the President, who was dressed in a blue pinstripe suit with a yellow tie, which he'd insisted his valet tie in a half Windsor because that particular knot appeared less conservative and wasn't as tight on his neck. The table was covered with a white cloth that draped down to within an inch of the floor. The cutlery was fine Swiss silverware. The dishes were fine china, and the glasses were imported crystal. There were men on staff who stood around to attend to the President's requests. The Vice President was already seated and waiting for the President to arrive, as protocol required.

"Good morning, Mr. President," the Vice President said.

"Hello," the President greeted his personal attaché. He was a thin young man; age twenty-five, with horned rim glasses, and a grimace for a smile.

"Your tie is very conservative, Eyerson. Is blue the only color you have?" The attaché gulped.

"It's traditional, sir."

"Why don't you try and loosen up? Try a power red and only a single Windsor instead of a double. Everyone's going to think you're a stiff," he said with a smile. Eyerson relaxed and smiled back.

The President took the printed schedule from Eyerson's hand. President Carlson skimmed it: *Charles Mathews—campaign kickoff update; Presidential Daily Brief; State Department Meeting; Counter-intelligence meeting in the Situation Room; Lunch with British Ambassador; CID/NSA advisor meeting; Labor, Education, Environment (L.E.E. Core group) Depts. Meeting; "Kitchen Cabinet"— Golf; Chopper to Mr. Clineshaw in North Virginia with staff of Comm. to Re-elect; Veterans group— Oval Office; Dinner Banquet—Fundraiser/power meet; Campaign meeting.*

"Cancel the meeting at nine. I asked those people at defense to realign the AS1-Lion package budget proposal and he deliberately ignored me. Tell them to get it right, and then reschedule. Add nightcap with the Chief of Staff at 10:00 tonight."

"Very good, sir. You'll be spending the weekend on Star Island. Your children will be visiting," Eyerson said.

Vice President Jack Milner Adams suddenly chimed in as the attaché left them. "I'm surprised your son Alan has time for a family weekend outing. I've read that he's a highly coveted dinner guest and quite the ladies' man."

"Yeah, well you know. He's such a handsome young man with a lot going for him. Who wouldn't love him? We're doing so well in the polls; a weekend at home is the ultimate sign of strength. We're having the voters come to us. A rally at the home."

"On Sunday, Director Stone will be visiting you to discuss the final plans on the Bureau's counter-intelligence program projected for the new millennium."

"How do you think his strategy is coming along?"

"Basically, Stone sees it as what he coins, 'Third World Backlash.' His intelligence is telling him that Third World terrorist groups are still backlashing for a piece of the Middle East power pie. More human intelligence source development will be necessary, which means funding these human sources; however, not much special agent infiltration, like in the Hoover Red Scare days."

"What do you think? Is it a plan that even a dove would support?"

"These new eggs taste the same, but are better for the heart. All part of the Zen platform," the Vice President said in an attempt to joke with the President. The Zen platform was a media concoction. It was meant as a compliment. It referred to President Carlson's ability to be patient and not to force things—to be as cool as Calvin Coolidge. President Carlson went with the label. Carlson refined the term and defined it to include thinking about the long-term future of America. Adams thought Zen anything was silly.

Vice President Adams wasn't a *confidant* of the President. In fact, they only met at a debate when they were both seeking the nomination during the primary. Carlson needed the Texas balance. Texas, a big state, where Adams was from and Carlson wasn't. Ever since Carlson won the class presidency with his best friend in fifth grade, in the back of his mind he thought that the Vice President should be a friend. Adams, however, was the runner-up, and since he was the governor from Texas, he was a good choice for Vice President because it meant electoral votes.

A good vice-presidential candidate is meant to satisfy the second largest faction in the political party, and appeal to a constituency in another part of the country. Carlson thought he could turn Adams around, as Abraham Lincoln had once done by recruiting his rivals to serve in his cabinet. Lincoln's rivals reformed around their President and transformed into his best allies. They cried on the day of his assassination. Things were different back then, or Lincoln was a better leader. Carlson knew that Adams would be strong if President Carlson were tragically assassinated.

"I know you've mocked the tone of the Presidency, Jack, but it's what this country needs. The problems this country has been having are the same ones we've been having for more than twenty years. Stopgap measures and functioning by crisis will never lead to long-term health in the economy or education. These things are long-term investments. We'll have to look back in history in twenty years to see how education has failed to make a difference on today's generation."

"We have to press on with prayer and Intelligent Design," the Vice President replied. "These issues need to be dealt with."

"Yes, I've always tried to understand your views. I know we haven't seen eye to eye, but you've been a loyal party member.

When you're President, you can focus on that. However, America doesn't only care if we have prayer and Intelligent Design as part of the school curriculum. They care about health care, affordable housing, a decent job for their children. Most importantly, they don't want to pay taxes."

"The Silent Majority cares about prayer, Intelligent Design and a strong military," Vice President Adams with conviction.

Ugh, there is the nightmare again, President Carlson thought. Maybe he's right. "The Silent Majority is a false god. Besides, if a member of the Silent Majority lost his job, we'd see what he'd care about."

This was an ongoing debate the President had with himself almost every day and usually from the night before. Politics used the term Silent Majority. It was a monster, an entity, a character that must be referred to as an it, but was alive in the President's mind. Most fields of endeavor have a term that is used to guide actions one way or the other. In a theater, it's the audience. Producers can use the audience to make an actor do something, or make the writer change a line or a scene. A trial lawyer has to think about the jury. Very intangible. Who really can tap into what the Silent Majority wanted or demanded? How many politicians used the Silent Majority's name as a crutch?

"I suppose you know what you're doing. Unemployment has never been as low, and the economy is looking strong. HUD is making some serious progress in the inner city," the Vice President conceded.

"That's my area. The other stuff is your area. That's why I want you to handle the deficit battle, but after the election. I want to continue to focus on terrorism and employment.

Without much of a pause, the Vice President said, "I'll be happy to be a dutiful Vice President."

"You will, of course, report to the Chief of Staff about any progress."

"Yes, of course, Mr. President," Adams said as he looked down at his eggs and took another mouthful.

"Yes, good luck. It'll be good to have you around another four years," Carlson said with just a touch of sarcasm.

★ ★ ★

Daniel Carlson walked into the West Wing of the White House and into the Oval Office. Waiting on his desk was the Daily Brief, which outlined the gathered intelligence on the various global theories. As Carlson read, Lynn, his secretary, entered when he pressed her call button on his phone.

"Lynn, please get Alan on the phone." The President sat in his chair and waited.

"You can pick up, Mr. President."

"Hello, Alan. How are you?"

"Okay, Dad."

"You sound tired."

Alan sighed, "Exhausted. I have to finish these exams, and then take the Bar in July. It's a lot of work."

"Well, you're doing fine. I'm proud of you. Your mom just told me you were elected editor-in-chief of the Law Review."

"Yes, well, I'm the President's son," he said sarcastically.

"It's been a long time since law school. Can I roll a home movie for a moment? I remember when I was in law school. It wasn't easy. It was social life versus studying . . ."

"Harvard's for guys who couldn't get into Yale."

"Don't make me laugh." Daniel feigned a British accent.

"I want to do civil rights work."

"So do it. You've had the offers since your second year," Daniel replied.

"The President's son can't . . ."

"The President's son this and that. Do what you want. . . . Just don't become a ballet dancer."

"I don't want to be like my brother-in-law either. Getting a promotion at DMI because they think he has the ear of the President."

"How 'bout the FBI?" Daniel said with a smile. "They always want lawyers. If a certain member of my cabinet had his way you could spy on *North China, Inc.*"

Alan laughed aloud. "Right. I can't even jog from here to my car."

"You know it's all around the Hill that you're quite a ladies' man."

"Yeah?"

"Yeah," The President said with satisfaction. "I'll see you this weekend."

"Bye, Dad." As Daniel hung up, he felt good inside. He was confident that he gave his son everything—more than the boy's biological father probably ever could. He knew that Alan understood that, too.

Daniel studied some data and reports from CIA, DIA and FBI intelligence. CIA's seemed on target and DIA's was bizarre. He was pleased. The Department of Intelligence report seemed to have the type of conclusions that the President was looking for. It seemed as if the FBI was using CIA counterintelligence reports rather than the Defense Intelligence's. Daniel enjoyed the relationship the Director of the Department of Intelligence and the Director of the FBI had. They went to boarding school together. Sometimes he didn't like the way they worked together, however.

The compromise occurred when the President took office. Carlson knew that the Senate was done with the CIA, but the unpublished yet critical functions of the CIA could not be dismantled and reconstructed without risk to the county's well-being. The way the State Department washed the intelligence it received from the CIA, it was a wonder if the President ever could get it right. Turf wars created agendas. Agendas create wars. Wars create death. That was just bad. It was that simple to Daniel Carlson. There was good and there was bad. Finding out whether some action was good or bad may be murky. Some call the world gray, but it was not to Daniel Carlson. There were pros and cons, but the final answer was right or wrong.

"They're ready for you in the Situation Room, Mr. President," Lynn's voice said on the intercom.

* * *

In the Situation Room, the President sat with the Director of Central Intelligence, Roger Coltrain, and the Director of the newly formed umbrella agency the Department of Intelligence, Admiral Neal Zane. The new and simplified Department of Intelligence replaced the short-lived Department of Homeland Security—a failing testament to supposed sharing of a warehouse of intelligence. President Carlson had to start over. The major difference between the Department of Intelligence versus Home-land Security; the one that made the Department of Intelligence work: Budgetary control by the Department over every other intelligence agency. The CIA and others would share information or that agency could potentially fell the funding crunch.

This afternoon's topic was covert military assistance in China.

"The Finding is clear, Mr. President. The Chinese under-ground resistance, like the guerillas of Kuomintang days, needs arms support that we can do covertly," Coltrain said.

"How?" The President asked in a serious tone.

"The Japanese are willing to help us. All we have to do is put the money in a Swiss bank account. The Japanese accepts it as payment for the arms, and gets AR-15s to quell the North Wing factions."

"And SIGINT and other satellites tell us that the North Wingers are stockpiling weapons, Neal?"

"Yes sir. I believe that Roger's men are right on."

"We have to act now, Mr. President. Get the covert action in motion," the Director of the Department of Intelligence said. The President feigned thought and smiled.

"Gentlemen, let's wait for the vote in Congress."

"Sir, action is needed now. Let's get this started now, and when Congress votes, we'll already be in motion," Coltrain offered.

"When they vote against?" Daniel asked.

"We'll abort."

Daniel smiled and couldn't help but roll his eyes. In frustration, Director Coltrain stood up. "Better to ask for forgiveness than permission."

"I don't think it works like that," The President said. What will it think? What will the Silent Majority decide: is this an unjustified secret war, or a justifiable police action? It hates. It eats.

"Where do you stand, Mr. President? We seemed to have convinced the Vice President. Which way are you going to urge Congress to vote?" Daniel seriously considered this question.

"Let the White House Counsel and myself look at the findings. If it's a real analysis, I'll probably want a further review of covert action, perhaps overt assistance options. If it's a high shine job, forget the whole thing. I don't understand why you bring these things up to me now. You know I can't commit this in the campaign."

"We need to know as soon as possible, Mr. President. We want democracy to sprout in China. If we wait, my people tell me it will be perceived as weakness. With all respect, sir, weakness is not the image you want to convey in the upcoming election. You'll need CIA support to foster your image of strength."

★ ★ ★

Six men, including Daniel, walked into the Backroom of the White House, not dressed in formal suits, but in flashy golf attire that would make Lee Trevino jealous. These men did not have poor taste in clothing, but were superstitious—the multicolored dress socks and the pom-pom berets helped their game. These men were of assorted backgrounds of distinction. All of them were successful in their endeavors throughout their careers. One cannot plan with great care to be a part of the President's Kitchen Cabinet, which was created by the seventh President, Andrew Jackson, but must be distinguished enough, and be the President's friend.

These men now had the delight to sit with the President, before their golf game, in an undecorated room with only a round table, and talk like men in front of the television in their underwear who had a couple of beers. These men had uncanny power to be candid and influence the President.

The Backroom sessions had no stenographer. No aides advised the proceeding. No lawyers were there to discuss legalities. What was spoken of in these sessions wasn't spoke of ever again.

To the right of the President was Thompson, a distinguished artist and the most liberal of the bunch. Next, was Hesse, a former CIA and NSA man from the Cold War, now a retired CEO of a major computer company. He tended to be Thompson's political opposite. To the left of Hesse, Dr. Terrell, D.O. His view of the world was gray. He viewed men as generally idiotic. He was judgmental and quick to discriminate. To his left Marksman, a CPA. Cut-and-dry described his paradigm. The sixth, a psychologist, the noted Doctor Curley. He had a tendency to remind everyone of the realities of the world. Daniel kept quiet in these sessions, for the most part. For one, he wasn't asked to speak. Secondly, he didn't want to speak. These sessions could be very entertaining. His job, as he saw it, was to glean useful information, then translate it into a language Americans could use.

"Abortion," the President blurted out.

"Forget about the damn conservative, anti-abortion people who have no sense to keep other people's business alone," Thompson said.

"No, don't start citing case law, you goddamn socialist," Hesse replied.

"Perhaps states should be given even greater freedom. Allow some more restrictions on access nationwide," the President inquired.

"It's bullshit," Dr. Terrell said. "You have these women with a third world mentality, who keep pumping out babies like Curley smokes cigars, and it's a damn burden on the rest of the Goddamn taxpayers. This administration's policy has been right on the money. Don't loosen up on the right-wing conservative--"

"Most poor women don't have abortions, Terrell. Statistics show—"

Hesse interrupted, "Statistics, again. Not everything's a darn widget, Marksman. It would be wise for the President to consider more state autonomy on the issue. That's something constitutional. Go figure that, Thompson."

"Don't pick on Marksman and Thompson just because they haven't gotten laid in twenty years," Dr. Curley, offered. "Well that's excluding, Rosy palms." Curley laughed as he pointed to his palm. "Get it? Rosy palm . . .. Sociologically speaking, you need to have abortion clinics. Why? Because women are going to have abortions anyway—legal or illegal. Why not continue helping the girls who get knocked up from some shmuck who isn't going to help raise the kid? Not everyone is like the President. Most people don't raise kids they don't want."

"People can change their mind. Women and their mates have been known to change their mind," Thompson replied.

"Let me tell you something I've been saying since I've been a psychologist for some thirty-five years—behavior is consistent. It's goddamn consistent. These losers of society, the men that is, are going to raise these kids? Give the child a better chance in another lifetime."

"You don't leave much hope for man," the President said to Curley.

"Well, behavior can be modified. Patterned behavior is next to impossible to break. Why do you think I stayed in business for thirty-five years?"

"I'm tired of this issue," Marksman declared. "Let's go play golf."

★ ★ ★

The President came back from his golf game at a club in Maryland. He changed into a suit and walked into his secretary's office to pick up the mail.

"How was your game?" Lynn asked.

"82."

"Not bad. Guess who just called me?" She asked with her noticeable southern accent.

"Who?" The President wondered.

"An old college buddy of yours—Scott Witherspoon."

"Really? Scott Witherspoon," the President was happily surprised. "What did he say?"

"He's visiting next month with the whole family."

"Did you put him on the schedule? I want to see him. Give him tickets to anything he wants."

"It's done. I know who this guy is. You've only talked about him a thousand times. How long has it been since you've seen him?"

"Maybe twenty years. I still remember at one fraternity party. He grabbed this girl . . ..

"Watch it there, Mr. President," Lynn said with a smile.

"Oh, look who's talking. The woman who gets kicked out of the Tombs for being too rowdy. And you have to be seriously rowdy to get kicked out of the Tombs."

"That was twenty years ago. Working for a freshman Senator who was bound for the Presidency wasn't the most stress-free job around, ya know," Lynn responded.

"You had no idea back then I would be President. While you were . . ."

"Stop! The chopper is waiting for you." Lynn pressed a button under her desk and a Secret Service agent walked in the office. "Take the President to the chopper."

"Did he tell you where her top was hanging the next day?"

She laughed and said, "Bye."

"Write him a letter and tell him I'd be happy to see him. And try and fit him and his wife in for a dinner while they're here."

Lynn Palmer was a small town girl of Pensacola, Florida. She was with Daniel from the very beginning of his political career, from the first time he ran for Senator.

On a whim, the young Ms. Palmer was in town, saw the campaign office, and walked in. She was neither a Democrat nor a Republican and wasn't politically savvy. Three months into the election campaign, she knew everything and did everything to help her man get into office.

She was taking courses in typing and dictation at the local community college, but she developed into a person more valuable than anyone would ever expect.

Before she began work with the soon-to-be Senator Carlson, her self-image painted a picture of a school girl from a backward hillbilly town, destined to become a wife to a domineering husband.

Her image began to come into focus by the time she graduated from high school. She married her prom date, Tim Palmer, three months later. Tim, she discovered, after the fog of affection lifted on her marriage, was a heavy drinker, and he would beat her after a long night of binge drinking.

Later, the night that Lynn joined the Senate campaign, while she was tending to her baby, Tim came home from a long night with the boys. He was murmuring that there was no food in the refrigerator. When he turned to berate her for not keeping it stocked, she took a direct punch to her eye. She couldn't drop her baby to save herself.

The next morning she began to make a change. She restocked the refrigerator and was determined to keep it filled. Dinner was going to be ready on time every day. She wouldn't complain that he stayed out all night and didn't help with the baby.

She also went volunteering the next day with a black eye, and boy, did she hear from her co-workers. They said, 'Lynn get out of that house. You can't be a part of that sick mentality.' She promised that he would stop. She explained that he feels sorry the next day. All she would have to do is leave early from the headquarters and tend to the house.

One of the workers picked up her daughter, who was playing in a crib with other babies, "You can't subject this poor little girl to a childhood of violence." Lynn said she knew what she was doing.

On the eve of the election, for all of her hard work, the future Senator, through a memo, asked if she would be his personal Secretary in Washington, D.C.

That night Lynn watched the television with baited breath. She didn't discuss working as a secretary for a Senator with Tim. He didn't even know she was volunteering on the campaign. The election was a landslide. There would be a new Senator. Her man won.

Early the next morning, Tim staggered in from another night of drinking. She put him to bed quietly. He didn't notice the suitcases standing by the door. She dressed her baby and a car came early the next morning to pick her up and take her to the airport. Her career was launched and her freedom discovered.

* * *

The presidential helicopter was waiting to take the President to his meeting with Franklin Clineshaw, a wealthy contributor and friend of the President. Daniel waved off reporters who were waiting for him by the helicopter. It would be a twelve-minute flight to Mr. Clineshaw's estate in Virginia. Daniel stayed for almost an hour. Certain cabinet positions were discussed. On the trip home, Daniel called Lynn and asked her to write a secret memo to the Secretary of Defense and advise him that the Assistant Secretary should look for another job at the end of the term.

* * *

The dinner banquet was the usual formal affair. The food was excellent and the company boring. He greeted and spoke with the governors and the other guests. He let his wife do all the work. She did it well. However, just a few words and the charismatic President with a natural sense of humor made another two million dollars for the Committee to Re-elect. He brought it to his strategy meeting with his public relations team and went over the progress. Everything seemed to be going as planned. There were no hitches—re-election was almost guaranteed.

The President escaped at 8:45 and ran into his bedroom to change into his bathrobe. He walked into the massage room and greeted Bruce.

"Missed you this morning, Bruce," the President said.

"Sorry, sir," Bruce seemed a little disturbed about something. Perhaps personal family life, and the President didn't want to intrude.

"I have that pain in my neck again. Will you do that thing you do?"

"Oh, here's your message, and the code—*a thousand points of light.*"

"Thanks. You feeling okay?" The President opened the plastic casing. What he found was a shock. To his chagrin, the case was empty. Daniel was not bewildered, he was upset. This was never to be. If there was no message for the day, the code would signify "no message." It was especially odd because the morning message said there would be an evening message. This could only mean one thing—*his source is dead.*

The President was worried. Although he was tense about it, he knew the massage wouldn't help much. Ten minutes into the massage there seemed to be a ruckus outside the door.

"I must see the President immediately! I'm the—"

"I know who you are and the President sees no one while he's in the Massage room!" There was a loud thump against the wall. "Post 3 . . ." Instantly, a dozen Secret Service agents with shotguns and automatic weapons stormed the hall.

"Mr. President, get under the table, sir," Bruce said. He seemed to reach into a bag. The President wondered what he was grabbing. Bruce, Secret Service? Nah.

"No, wait a second." The President recognized the voice through the door. He opened the door. "What's the problem, Jasper?" All the President saw was two agents pressing a man against the wall.

"I'm the goddamn Chief of Staff!" It was the President's closest friend and confidant, Peter Spark.

"Let him go," Daniel said. The Chief of Staff fixed his suit. "Couldn't this wait until our nightcap?"

"Sorry to disturb you, Mr. President." The formal approach from Peter signaled something was wrong to Daniel. "I know no one is supposed to interrupt your massages, Mr. President, but they know. Do you hear me? They know!" Instantly Daniel knew that Peter had the answer to why the plastic message casing was empty. "They know, Daniel. We have a crisis on our hands." The two men locked eyes, and chills ran down Daniel's back. They both knew what had happened. Only days before the end of the first term of Camelot and the Presidency had just become a nightmare. Daniel had heard Peter's footsteps down the hall in his mind many times before. He knew what the steps meant. After all these years, Daniel never would've believed that it would ever be known—it was—and Daniel knew he would have to live with this crisis.

CHAPTER 2

Land of Rain

"Look here, buddy. This may be the last time we'll get American girls."

"In Jamaica?"

"Yeah, D.C. Let's face it, your career with women in college was below average. You were every girl's best friend. I, however, am Broadway Joe Namath hitting one or two receivers at every fraternity party. You need to build up your confidence. We need a place where we can get all the practice we need. The trip's a complete package—all you can eat and drink. We'll be bombed the whole time. I even hear that they let you smoke grass there!" Scott Witherspoon, Daniel Carlson's closest friend, said.

"Woah! I heard that stuff makes you crazy," Daniel said with a little nervousness. "I even read the North Vietnamese poisoned the stuff, to hurt American soldiers."

"Don't believe all that shit. Tell them you just graduated from Yale in political science and you're going to be an officer. And this is the last vacation you may ever have," Scott replied.

"It's true. We can get killed in artillery practice. The war is over." Daniel said with a smile.

"Forget about it, forget about it. Even without a war, we're tough. Are ya tough? You are. We got the Yale spirit. We ain't comin' back from Negril until we find two Cliffies and show them what fairies they've been going to college with the past four years," Scott nodded to show that he was proud of his plan of action. "Hell, tang is sweet, but here we won't be getting shelled at."

"The only thing I'm worried about is . . ."

"What? What could you possibly be worried about? Ya got to loosen up Yaley!"

"Well, I don't want to get any girl pregnant. I mean who needs the responsibility and I'll be going . . ."

"What are ya talking about? You're not going to get these girls pregnant. Besides, it's not like you're going to see these girls ever again."

"Scott! Are you nuts?" Daniel answered.

"Listen, D.C. Haven't you learned anything about sex in college? After you're done, take her to get a banana. You have to do it right away, though. That will slow the sperm motility rate."

"Who told you that?"

"My brother, read it somewhere."

"Sounds like your brother wrote it down on a sheet of paper and then read it back to himself."

"Are you with me my brother?" Scott asked raising his hands above his head.

"After all we've been through, I just want to say you mean a lot to me and I'm going to miss you during any future war we're sent to. . . . I am with you my Phi brother!"

"Woooh! Outta sight!"

Scott picked up his beer and shook it on Daniel's head. Both were dancing around Scott's apartment like a couple of college kids ready to embark on a sunny resort week in the place whose name means "land of rain," Jamaica.

The two college grads shuttled around the airport making their way to the immigration section.

"Two seconds off the plane and they have you plastered," Scott said as he staggered through the immigration line.

"He better not ask me any difficult questions," Daniel said as he laughed. "Free rum punch while you wait on line?"

"Is this great?! Did I lie?" As the boys made it past immigration, Scott put down his bags, pulled out a pack of Lucky's from his back pocket, and lit one. "Go on, have one D.C."

"All right, its vacation, right?"

"Yeah, that's my guy." A native in a red T-shirt approached the boys and said:

"Right, mon. This is your bus ride to the compound."

"Great!" They both said. A Jamaican brought their bags to the charter bus and told them to get Red Stripe beer from the man by the cooler.

"They give us free beer for the trip," Daniel said in wonderment.

"This is totally great."

Scott picked up a bag of marijuana from the guy who carried their bags to the bus. Before the bus left the airport the boys were asked twice more if they wanted to buy some "ganja."

The trip from Montego Bay Airport to Negril was more than an hour long. The boys were in a constant state of fear as they were whipped and shifted around the steep and narrow corners of the mountain. The fact that the driver was on the left side of the road increased their anxiety.

The people on the bus were from all over the United States. Everyone was chatting about what they wanted to do the most: sailing, water skiing, snorkeling, drinking. Scott made it really clear what he wanted to do the most. In fact, he couldn't conceal his laughter about a woman who said she was going to the resort for the purpose of sailing, exclusively. It seemed she had no idea that the place was for swinging singles. Daniel had a hard time concealing his laughter too.

The coast was mostly jungles. "Just like 'Nam, D.C." The water reflected the sunlight. All along the way there were villages, apparently impoverished. Daniel answered the question that he thought Scott was thinking. Cows and other livestock ran free throughout each village.

"The British just formed the West Indies Federation with about nine other British areas. Hopefully, that will help these people."

"Check out the guys with the dreadlocks," Scott said. "They're Rastafarians. They think they're going to be grabbed by their dreads and brought to heaven. Pretty irie, huh?"

"Where did you learn, 'irie'?'" Daniel asked.

"I'm not just some dumb preppie, you know. I know my *Patois*, the official dialect of the Jamaican people."

"Hey mon! We are here!" The bus driver said. "Your bags will be brought to your room."

"Wow! Look at all these trees. It's paradise."

"It's so humid, D.C."

"Ah, it's just like Florida," Daniel answered.

"Bar!" Scott's attention immediately focused on the large hut a hundred feet from the entrance, covered wall-to-wall with bottles of alcoholic beverages.

"Let's go!"

The young graduates were intoxicated for the remainder of the day as they toured the grounds with a helpful blonde co-ed. The nude beach and Jacuzzi surprised Daniel, but it sounded good.

As the sun was about to set, the boys went to their room to change for dinner.

"That girl Karen is kind of nice," Daniel said.

"She's all talk, Daniel. I'm surprised you didn't pick that up. You're not here to be her best friend."

"She spent the entire day with us. You don't think she likes one of us?" Daniel said.

"She was with us for protection. You have to change your vibe. She knows that she can fend you off. You just have to change your attitude and maybe she'll come around. Meanwhile, I think we should split up for dinner. I need to put in some time with that sure thing, Mary." Scott asserted.

"Uh, she's disgusting. The one with the chubby cheeks and the freckles?" Daniel usually wasn't this blunt or opinionated, but a day of being tipsy-to-drunk had left his defenses down.

"You know what she can do with those chubby cheeks, Daniel?"

"I've finally figured it out. Why you get so many more girls than I do. I've always said, what does Scott have that I don't? More charm? Better looks? More money? What?"

"Yeah, what's your answer?"

"You've got . . . lower standards."

"Fuck you," Scott said as he threw a pillow at Daniel from his bed. "Hurry up, I'm losing my buzz."

★ ★ ★

The resort offered activities around the clock. The disco remained open until five o'clock in the morning. Food was presented throughout the day. Daniel took advantage of the new activities he never had a chance to pick up at Yale. He learned how to play squash, European style. He mastered the fine art of sailing a little boat. Daniel also had a workout on the trampoline. He didn't realize it could be such a cardiovascular exercise.

The two boys met up for dinner that evening to discuss their day's adventures.

"You know I've always wondered what a massage felt like. I just got one. After I went sailing and snorkeling I went for the rub down. It was great, just great," Daniel said.

"Cool! Just screwed Mary in the hot tub," Scott said, half drunk, half stoned.

"Well, I hope you don't have a disease. A couple of my new friends just informed me that you were Mary's third victim since she got here three days ago."

"I'm wounded. I thought it was my charm," Scott said half kidding, half seriously. "Listen, you met that guy, Bob, right? I asked him to set you up with a sure thing. I think you ought to. You're going to Southeast Asia and frankly, I wouldn't want you to die a virgin."

"Who told you I was a virgin?" Daniel demanded.

"Don't worry about it. It's not what's real it's what everyone thinks. He knows a girl that saw you and liked you. She thought it would be neat to be your first. Decide tonight at the toga party."

* * *

The disc jockey was playing a mixed version of "Saturday Night Fever" and everyone was trying to disco and keep his or her toga on in the midst of the cool smoke-filled room.

"Can't believe they're still playing this old shit," Scott said. "The lights are neat, though. Hey, there's Bob."

Daniel began to think about what Scott said about what was real versus what others think. Daniel locked on and deconstructed the logic of why the remark was stupid, but considered Scott was right. It is the way things are, not the way they ought to be. Why must we consider the others when it is about only the individual. Daniel struggled with these thoughts for long moments, almost losing the mood engendered by his surroundings.

Bob, a tall, lean, muscular blonde, with a pencil-thin mustache. He had a lit joint in his hand, and walked over to Daniel and Scott.

"Hey, cool, Bob." Scott said.

"Here, want a hit?" Daniel half smashed, looked at Scott and said, "What the hell." Daniel inhaled deeply and burst out coughing. Bob and Scott laughed.

"Try again," Scott said. Daniel again sucked in deeply. "Hold it. Hold it. Slowly breathe out. Look at the lights man."

"Wow!" Daniel began to laugh. "Holy shit, let me hit again." Daniel was a little braver and inhaled even deeper. "Wow, I'm kind of light-headed, dizzy." They laughed even louder. The laughter was contagious, but Scott couldn't control himself.

Suddenly a voice came over a loud speaker, "Whoever's smoking the ganja has to put it out. We can get in a lot of trouble." The comment made all three boys laugh.

"Come on," Bob said to Daniel. "Let's go get laid."

"I see her. Okay."

"Yeah!" Scott gave a big kiss on the cheek. "Tell me every-thing." Bob and Daniel left the disco and walked off to the beach together. Daniel would finally come into his own.

CHAPTER 3

After Vietnam

IT HAD BEEN A few years since the goal of *containment* was announced as the foreign policy of the United States. The fear of Soviet encirclement lingered well after American forces had been deployed to Vietnam to protect Southeast Asia from the Communist insurgency—freedom and justice for all in the world. Uncle Sam wants you! Now, Uncle Sam didn't want you in Vietnam. It was over. But, Daniel Carlson ran to fulfill his calling, his duty, as an American. Scott Witherspoon went back to a local army recruiting station in Connecticut and Daniel went back home to Florida. It was the perfect time, but Daniel needed a war. Well, Daniel didn't need a war to cling to, but the voice inside his head told him, serving his country was what was required. It was what was expected of him. By whom? He had not named this voice, this force, this ghost that gave criticism. The ghost-character was not a ghost from the dead, it was an apparition that navigated his path. Proper young man, Yale, the Army, and beyond—his is the path for Daniel Carlson. Daniel remembered his grandfather, his mother's father, proudly serving in World War II. It was a

well-defined war that made his grandfather a man in his grandfather's own eyes, and everyone else's.

After filling out eight pages of vital statistics, the young graduate stood in line in boxer shorts and an undershirt, waiting for
an Army doctor to examine him. The wait was long. The line
moved slowly. But the waiting made the experience all the more
exciting. The anticipation was strong. With his college degree,
Daniel was counting on leading troops into battle as an officer. It
was prestigious to serve one's country. To come back as a hero—
the applause, the parades. Daniel began to sing in his mind, *I
love a parade.* A couple steps forward and then, *Over here, over
there, send the word, send the word to beware, cause the yanks are
coming, the yanks are ...*

"Next!" Daniel stepped up. "Name?"

"Daniel Carlson." The man began writing. "No, Daniel's my
first name."

"Last name, first. First name last. College?"

"Yale. Uh, yes, sir."

"Move along, college boy." The soldier didn't even register
let alone express resentment. Daniel moved to another line, for
more waiting.

Daniel's psychological exam seemed like a breeze, but who
really knows? Part of being crazy is not knowing you're crazy.
Right? Well he hoped so. He didn't want some penciled in bubbles
to thwart his progress as an officer. Yesterday's crazy could be
today's insightfulness.

Yes sir, Lt. Carlson, Daniel heard in his head. *Well it's hi, hi,
hee in field artillery. Over here over there ... Oh, already sang that.*

Daniel passed the vision test. His vision was better than
20/20. ... *Off, into the wild blue yonder.* I can't sing that. *Anchors
away ...* Forget it.

Finally, the last stage of the tests—the physical. Everything seemed to be in order. After all, Daniel was an athlete and in fine shape. He waited to receive final approval from an attending military physician. He noticed the doctor walk in, and his pulse began to rise.

The doctor was military, but not dressed in a uniform. He wore a white lab coat. The doctor's name—Thelvious Comsky, the son of Polish immigrants of World War II. He was a little over five feet and had to look almost directly up at Daniel.

"You know I visited Yale once," the doctor said.

"Really?"

"Please sit on the table, Daniel. Tell me. Are you anxious to serve your country?"

"Yes. Very. Wouldn't you be? I mean, aren't you? I want to volunteer." Daniel replied.

"Yes. I am. What I'm trying to say is that there are many ways to serve. Which would you like?" Dr. Comsky pushed his glasses back up on the bridge of his nose. He waited for Daniel's answer.

"I would like to lead a group of men into battle. As an officer," Daniel blushed as he listened to his own words.

"Daniel, then I have bad news. Well, you didn't think you would have problems with your knee? Your cartilage has degenerated. There is some hope in new technology called arthroscopic surgery. You won't be able to lead a group into battle. I'm sorry."

"What?" Daniel said in shock. "I was a varsity letterman at Yale."

"I know. A runner, right? I can see from your X-rays. Can you run anymore?"

"Not as fast as I used to but—" Daniel's voice cracked, "A leader is a leader."

"Daniel, you can lead. But the troops need someone physically capable as well. Your X-rays don't lie." Daniel looked down at the floor. It was hard for him to comprehend.

"I can be physically able. I'll work at it. Persistence!"

"It's not a matter of conditioning. The sad thing is, the more you work out, the more damage you will do to your knee. You'll need to have surgery one day." Daniel noticed the slight Polish accent that the doctor had acquired from his parents.

What does the stupid Polack know? They piss in a fan to take a shower. You can get a one-armed Polack out of a tree by waving. Commie, Soviet puppet. Scum of the earth. Cong sympathizer.

"I can do! Give me the chance. Please, Doctor, I can show you. Anything," Daniel pleaded.

"Please, son. There are other ways to serve without so much risk to your life. Not everyone can be a fighter. A boy of your intelligence . . ."

"I can do all your tests, Doctor!" Daniel stepped off the table and looked into the eyes of the Polish doctor. Daniel stared intently. He noticed the hairs the doctor missed shaving. The doctor took a deep sigh and would do as Daniel wished.

"Come here, son. Squat down." Daniel leaned against the wall and slid down to a level as if he were sitting without a chair. The doctor watched Daniel's balance intently. He could see Daniel suppress the pain by watching his face.

"You can't do it. Son, please, the pain is not worth it. Stand up."

"I can do it," Daniel squeaked out. *Commie, Comsky. Deny the Army a good officer. Cong. Commie, Comsky, Cong.*

"Can you bend forward?"

"Yes."

"Go on. Do it." Daniel leaned forward. The pain in his left knee was unbearable. He reflexively dropped to the floor. Still, he persisted. He was a soldier. Pain is gain. If this was the worst pain he experienced from the war, then he would be lucky. Daniel's face reddened. He began to sweat from the pain.

As Daniel collapsed it was the biggest disappointment in his life—he couldn't hold out. Couldn't hold on just a little longer. He was a quitter. The result—no glory, no service. For the first time in his life Daniel didn't get what he wanted. Something he had his heart set on. Tears welled up in his eyes, but he did not want to show anger or sadness. He could at least act like a soldier with discipline and honor here. Daniel stood up. He took the medical report from the doctor, saluted him, and walked out.

Weeks later, in the mail, Daniel received a letter from the Army. He wanted to pretend to show no concern, but he couldn't lie to himself. He was mostly apprehensive (what kind of assignment could he get); and, eager. He opened the letter slowly. Maybe, the Army reconsidered.

There was only disappointment. He was rejected. The Army didn't even need him for supply. He just couldn't get through basic training. What would everyone think? Who was everyone? Only his mother would be happy. Her dream came true. There was no one home at the time, so Daniel gave up on the notion of Army discipline and cried. In the glimmer, a moment of honesty, Daniel felt relieved.

The disappointment consumed Daniel for months. The picture Daniel drew in his mind was defaced by the very entity that asked him to create it. All the propaganda, the recruitment effort asked Daniel Carlson: *what could I do for my country*? His country bluntly answered, not much. Daniel knew he could do more.

CHAPTER 4

Three-L

THE FIRST YEAR THEY work you, the second year they scare you, and the third year they bore you. The same formula seemed in place with Daniel Carlson's law career, which was well into his third year at Harvard. He finally got over his emotional defection from Yale, and made the prestigious Law Review, the highest law school honor society. He was beaten out by his best friend, Peter Spark, for editor. Spark delegated most of the responsibility to Daniel as assistant editor. In the end, though, it was better for Daniel. Spark was a few years older. He was hired for a part-time position through the Pound Placement Office clerking for Atkins, Hoffman, Young, Baker and Lewison. Spark convinced Daniel the experience would be good for the sole purpose of ruling out the private practice of law in a national firm that had more than three hundred lawyers. Daniel wasn't particularly excited about working for a private firm—in all honesty he wanted to teach—but that was where the money was and he could litigate cases as well.

Daniel maneuvered himself to do work in the litigation department. His research skills were comprehensive, and he could write well. He honed his oratory skills within the past two and one half years in law school in intensive mock trial sessions.

The firm had just begun filing motions on what had been dubbed, the "Blackwell" murder. A homeless man murdered in Roxbury and dumped into the sewer. It took a basket, rope, and five men to pull the John Doe out of the sewer. It also took a week to identify who was the victim. As a replacement name, a detective in the Boston PD named it the Blackwell murder.

This case had no glory and no media coverage. A murder of a homeless man in Roxbury was common—and even less news. Atkins Hoffman et al. agreed to accept the *pro bono* case by the Suffolk County Court. They would defend the suspect, another homeless man, Michael Mandell. Daniel was assigned to help a lawyer interview Mandell that afternoon.

Daniel Carlson and Peter Spark left a Law Review meeting and started walking toward the Harkness Commons.

"That's great. So, he is not going to testify?" Peter asked.

"I would think we'd have to."

"So you're going to do it. You're selling out your best buddy Peter to go work for a private firm. After all we've been through—Property, Evidence, Trial advocacy with Zimet."

"Don't give me that through-the-trenches stuff. I haven't decided that I'm going to work for Atkins. Besides they haven't made me an offer."

"You know they're going to offer you a position, Daniel."

"But I like litigation, what's the big deal? This has been a confusing time. I don't want to miss any opportunities. However, it seems that if I take one option all the options disappear for the rest of my life. Nobody wants used merchandise. Once you commit to a track, you're on that track."

"Well, you wouldn't necessarily kiss teaching goodbye. You could always pick it up once you're successful enough to live off a teacher's salary. As a man in the heart of government, you could do that. As you know, my vote is for Senator Bratton. Make it the best with Bratton," Peter joked. "He's coming to HLS."

"Yes, and I told you a thousand times I'll hear him speak."

"I'm going to introduce you to him," Peter said. "Think of the opportunity. Do you want to get guilty men freed? Or—"

"Lie, cheat, and steal from the American public?"

"Pick your poison, Daniel."

As the future attorneys walked outside the Harkness Commons, they saw a motley crew of vociferous antiwar demonstrators. Most of the marchers were undergraduates protesting the war in Vietnam. In 1972 public sentiment was turning against the war. A dozen students were marching in a circle with signs. As Daniel and Peter walked by the demonstration one of the protestors yelled at them: "Don't allow the murderers in Vietnam to continue their rampage!"

"We're not. The Americans are fighting the Viet Cong and trying to stop those murderers," Carlson yelled back.

"Let them be Daniel," Spark said.

"I'm talking about the Americans. The American soldiers are the murderers!"

"What did he say?" Daniel asked Peter. He was in disbelief and was stopped in his tracks.

"Daniel, forget it man," Peter said.

Daniel walked over to the skinny man who was holding a sign.

"The Americans aren't the murderers. They're fighting for a cause. And if you weren't such a girl," Daniel flicked the man's pony tail, "you would get off your ass and help them."

"I burned my draft card, pal," the protestor said almost nose to nose with Daniel. Another female protestor walked beside him.

"More like rolled it and smoked it," Daniel replied. Peter laughed right in the protestor's ear. "I was in the Army for three years, man," Peter blurted.

The woman said, "You were a fucking baby killer! Baby killers!"

"Yeah! Murderer! Pig!" The crowd chimed.

"I was in the reserves, bitch!" Daniel said as he poked the girl with his index finger to the top of her chest. More protestors gathered around them.

"And you! You support that Capitalist instigator of world terror, Senator Bratton," the protestor slapped Peter's campaign button on his chest, with the palm of his hand.

"Lick me, pal," Peter said as he punched the guy to the left of the protestor who insulted him. The battered protestor was shocked and hurt, and fell to the grass. The woman then kicked Daniel Carlson in his bad knee and he screamed. He hurled back and punched the chief rabble-rouser in the nose. A major rumble ensued. Daniel and Peter were flailing their arms and kicking their feet. It was two against twelve, and Daniel and Peter were doing well. After three minutes of rolling around, every protestor was getting their turn.

Finally, the university police arrived. Daniel Carlson and Peter Spark, the newly invented activists, ran and occasionally looked back. Peter took the lead. Daniel had problems keeping up. They ended up ducking into an empty classroom in Langdell Hall. The men laughed while they caught their breath. Both were laughing in between inhales. Peter turned and tried to make out the reflection of his face, which had a strongly noticeable scar from his eye down to his lower jaw, in the window. Daniel never asked how he got the scar. He detected Peter was very sensitive about it.

"So, what are we going to do about the cops?" Daniel asked.

"Fuck 'em. If they ask, we'll say that they started it."

"That's a little bit of a lie."

"So? There were over ten guys, versus two. Who are the cops going to believe, law students or some stoned hippie fucks? Don't worry about it, man. I'll take care of it."

"Well, you got to admit, that was fun," Daniel said with a smile.

"Good friends bail you out of trouble. Great friends are with you when you're in trouble." Peter replied.

* * *

Carlson, dressed in a three-piece suit, entered the office where he worked. He followed Barry Farkis into the interviewing room. Farkis was a hardworking attorney in his mid-thirties who had thinning brown hair, and was about to be considered for partnership with the firm.

Carlson and Farkis walked into the small suite where the client, Mandell, and his assigned social caseworker were waiting. Farkis was surprised that Mandell had taken a shower and looked somewhat presentable in the issued orange jumpsuit. Carlson had a legal pad ready and eagerly awaited the questioning and strategy session.

"Mr. Mandell, this doesn't look good for you. Witnesses saw you and the deceased arguing hours before the murder. Do you know what the deceased means? Anyway other witnesses said that you owned the knife that the victim was murdered with. It also has your fingerprints all over it. However, I think I can work on a plea agreement." Farkis said this in a way that made it seem it was well rehearsed and well thought out. Farkis' whiny voice along with the waving of his hands, decorated with many rings and a gold Rolex (which he didn't earn but was given) made it seem that he was anything but sincerely concerned about the case.

"Wait a second. I think I want another attorney," Mr. Mandell said to his social worker.

"Mr. Mandell under the circumstances taking this case to trial will ensure you do at least twenty-five years."

"You're not even goin' to listen to my side of the story? You're supposed to be helping me, man. But if you have better things to do than I'll take my chances with a public *pretender*."

"I agree," the social worker said. "We appreciate the court assigning this case, *pro bono* to your firm, but if you won't pursue this case vigorously, and give Mr. Mandell the process he deserves as a citizen, and as a black American, and as a homeless person, whose rights are constantly abused in this—"

"Alright! Take a breath," Farkis said. "This is not a racial issue. It is not a homeless issue. I'll be happy to hear Mr. Mandell's explanation. And if he wants we will go to court with his defense. Satisfactory? Good. Start anywhere you like." Farkis rolled back his sleeve and looked at his watch. He then put his hands in his lap. Daniel turned and raised his eyebrows.

"Okay. This is what went down. I lent the son of a bitch my knife. I mean I lent the deceased," he paused on the word, *deceased*. "Somebody else must've killed him. I was just minding my own business, all day long and next thing I know the police is harassing me. Telling me I did it. Harassin' me. Sayin, 'You the spade with the blade.' They were looking through my stuff, where I live. And then they brought me to jail."

"With all due respect to everyone's race and shelter status. It sounds weak. How do you explain the fight earlier? And your prints are all over the knife the police say was a match."

"I fought with the man. But we fought all the time. I never threatened him or nothing. Ask anyone."

"Mr. Mandell, when you say fight, does that mean you argued verbally, or with physical force?" Daniel asked.

"We were just talkin'. See first, the man asked for the knife to build something. So I let him borrow it. In fact, that's what we were arguing about. I wanted it back. He was stalling me. The prints were on the knife and that's why they're pinning this on me. But it was my knife, so my prints should be on it. Their case is weak. They got nothing on me. No reliable witnesses. He used to physically fight with a man named Horace all the time. He could've done it. I swear it wasn't me."

Daniel Carlson wrote down some notes and on the top of the page wrote *Reasonable Doubt*.

* * *

The hall filled up with law students of every year. It's one of the few times all the students were together for some function. Most classes are segregated by year. No mingling allowed. This event was a special *Harvard* event. Judges from the community took their seats, along with University officials. Even Harvard's President Bok was in attendance. When a Senator comes to Harvard, particularly one of its own, it is a big deal. The man who would deliver a speech, as an HLS alumnus, was Senator Bratton. It was election season and the Senator was beginning at the base of his support—Harvard. Not that there were many voters from Florida there, but some alumni give money to the campaign just because Bratton is an alumnus. More importantly, Bratton was planning someday to run for President—the more name recognition, the better. Most importantly, it raised money for Harvard. Students were free. Everyone else, pay a little something, with a cocktail hour later.

Daniel sat next to Peter. Peter had a glow about him. Peter was so excited and proud that he was going to work for this great man. A Senator who worked closely with Truman, Nixon, and Kennedy. A man who could be President. He was proud that he would be an aide to the Senator after he graduated. The job was a risk, of course. It was contingent on the election results. But since Bratton was well-supported and, more importantly, an incumbent, Bratton would probably win.

Daniel's curiosity was peaking, but he was not about to abandon a future with trial work and one day a seven-figure income. Peter, however, had a not-so-hidden agenda for Daniel. Peter planned that Daniel would join the Senator's campaign. Every chance he'd get he would give Daniel the pitch. Since Daniel was from Florida, it would be an advantage with the Senator.

Peter's fiancée, Melissa, sat next to him. She was a lovely girl and wasn't necessarily cut out for a world of politics that Peter planned to be a part of. She also wanted to be a teacher. She loved kids and figured with Peter working as an aide, she would be able to be a teacher in a local elementary school. She would grade papers and plan a curriculum at night while she waited for Peter to come home.

Melissa came from a large family in a small town in rural Kansas. She went to Kansas University for her first year of college. Did well enough to transfer to Radcliffe College for women at Harvard. It was in her first year she met Peter. She was smart, in an academic way, but Peter knew things about the real world that she found very impressive. He was older and a war veteran.

Instead of being a lost soul, he went back to law school, at Harvard no less. She continued to work hard at being sophisticated. Slapping the rural out of her system. Cambridge being world's away from Lawrence, Kansas. Peter could be her ticket out of a simple and boring life. She was eager to help Peter find a place with Senator Bratton.

The Senator was in his fifties. He was a distinguished looking man still with gray sideburns. He spoke about the future of America. He recounted the great strides in Civil Rights and the worldwide fight against communism. He illustrated with great eloquence the plans for the future and his vision of the geo-political world. The Senator avoided talking about Vietnam or the Arms race, which was somewhat of a fiasco in the public eye. Finally, as a great strategic ending he declared that the men and women of Harvard should lead this great nation into the wondrous era of the future. Everyone rose to their feet and the Senator accepted the grand applause. Daniel could hear the background noise of protest outside the hall. The noise unconsciously inflamed him.

Peter introduced Daniel to the Senator after the speech. Daniel accepted an interview that Peter set up with one of the Senator's aides for the next day. Daniel was keeping the options open. He was nervous about the range of choices. Yet, he was taken by the idealism that Senator Bratton displayed. Government can make a difference. Some of his classmates had to take the one job that was offered. He could make the choice, rather than the choice be made for him. Freedom can be so stressful.

★ ★ ★

Daniel, who thought about the interview he had with Senator Bratton's aide, was a great storyteller. He had a relaxing nature about him. Someone spending ten minutes with Daniel would have an affinity toward him at the end of the talk. Some felt it was because of his wit and his ability to turn a phrase. Others felt it was his boyish smile.

At the end of the interview, the aide assured a position to Daniel assuming Bratton wins the election. Daniel thanked him for the offer and said he would need time to think about other job options. Daniel really had his mind on one thing.

What Daniel was excited about was the upcoming trial on the Mandell/Blackwell murder. Instructed to go directly to the courthouse, Daniel skipped a day of researching and writing. He was finally going to take part in a trial. He was going to help a man who Daniel legitimately believed was not guilty. The hours of research and preparation would all culminate into a glorious display of articulated evidence and supposition. Daniel also personally researched the avenue of thought that the search by the police of Mr. Mandell's personal belongings was an invasion of his privacy, and needed a search warrant. That idea was quickly dismissed as liberal bullshit—too progressive—by Barry Farkis.

Barry Farkis had a reputation of being an excellent speaker. His skills would be pit against a less experienced lawyer from the Suffolk County District Attorney's office. Daniel dressed in a three-piece suit. With his briefcase in hand, he noticed Farkis talking to the D.A. as Daniel approached, Farkis walked away from the D.A.

"Come on, I'll give you a ride back to the office," Farkis said. Daniel followed behind him.

"What happened? Continuance?"

"No, plea agreement."

"Plea agreement?"

"Yeah. Got the guy three years," Farkis said with satisfaction.

"Three years. The guy had a great case. What the hell is this? I worked for hours!" Both men stopped walking.

"I know. Good job. It got the guy a deal. I'm the lawyer. I decide whether we have a good case or not." Farkis began to walk again.

"What bullshit! Did Mandell agree to this?"

"He got three years for a murder. He'll be thrilled."

"He's getting three years for nothing—he's innocent. He shouldn't have taken it. I'm going to tell him to withdraw his plea."

Farkis stopped in his tracks and pointed his finger at Daniel.

"You'll fuckin' do nothing of the sort! I'm not going to tell Mr. Lewison that you even suggested such a thing. If you so much as give him change on the street I'll see that you're fired." Both men were nose to nose. The ultimatum was clear in Daniel's mind. He had the opportunity to back up his idealism. Daniel was going to put his money where his mouth was.

"Fuck you, drive by yourself. I'm taking the T!" Daniel said, as he stared intensely into his supervisor's eyes.

"You'll see, Carlson. The guy will be grateful that I'll get him three meals a day and a place to stay for the next maybe three years. Oh no, he might get out in two and a half years, if he lives that long," Farkis said with a laugh.

Daniel didn't mull over his decision. The facts were on the table and he was able to decide. Daniel skipped going into the office the next day. After a few beers at the Harkness Commons he typed up his letter of resignation, called Senator Bratton's office, and accepted the position in politics with his friend Peter Spark.

CHAPTER 5

The Anderson House

DANIEL CARLSON, THE NEW Senator's aide, fit into his small but pleasantly decorated office at the office of Senator Terrence P. Bratton, in the traditional Rayburn Building on Capitol Hill. Carlson had a couple of framed pictures and some indoor plants that he got from the neighboring Senator's office. Carlson's desk was small, but he made room for a picture of his mother's face standing alone. The picture was fuzzy due to its age. Black and white. Her neck was slender, carrying a necklace that held a charm that resembled the hand of God. Her picture was in a frame, along with a family photo of her, his father, and himself, outside of their home in Florida.

Daniel's first assignment as an aide was to compose rhetoric, formulate ideas for legislation, and garner support for a civil rights package in the name of Senator Bratton, in honor of the late President Kennedy. Daniel never had the opportunity to meet President Kennedy. He sat three rows directly above President Ford at a Harvard/Yale game. Daniel could hardly contain his excitement or focus on the President because Daniel was sitting next to Chief Justice Warren Burger. The Chief Justice looked at Daniel in a fatherly way. Chief Justice Burger reflected on the day when he was on the Law Review at Harvard. The Chief Justice knew that all Harvard Law Review graduates had the potential to be leaders of America, so he returned the respect to Daniel.

"Maybe you'll be a Justice of the Supreme Court someday, Mr. Carlson." It sounded a little like the Chief Justice was encouraging a child. It was a little hokey, maybe patronizing, Daniel admitted to himself, but he liked the compliment. Daniel wouldn't repeat it, but knew the Chief Justice was right, his resume was right. Daniel was surprised that he had that thought. Daniel thought it was arrogant and unseemly to have those thoughts in the past, but recently he felt that keeping an internal pep talk would be acceptable.

"I hope someday to hold the qualifications and respect in the legal community to be one, Mr. Chief Justice," Daniel replied respectfully with half a smile.

Daniel couldn't remember the score of the game. He recalled that Harvard had lost. However, Carlson did not—lose that is. He glowed for a week after the game. A friend of Daniel, who was in the stands at the game, took a spontaneous photo of Daniel and the Chief Justice and the then-Deputy Chief Secretary of Defense and him, which Daniel hung on his wall in the office.

Senator Bratton and Jack Kennedy were as close as a President and a Senator could get. They didn't see eye-to-eye on many issues. But, it didn't matter. There were basics they did agree upon. Kennedy relied on Bratton for Southern support on the Hill. Senator Bratton believed in the President's quest for desegregation and the creation of jobs for the black community. The Bratton Bill was the essence of the Senator's mission as a Senator. Daniel felt extraordinarily fortunate to be working for Bratton. If Bratton led his legislation through Congress successfully, it would send a strong signal to the Party that Bratton should be considered for the Presidency himself. Therefore, Senator Bratton was pulling all the strings he could, exerting all the influence he could muster. He voted for bills he wouldn't normally support in order that certain senator's would owe him a favor when his bill came up. It had all the right ingredients: the cherry on top of what would have been a Kennedy supported sundae. It would have support from the Northeast, minority support, and Bratton's Southern influence. All this ambition for the brass ring had Daniel Carlson working late into the night.

This evening, Daniel was busy working late on coordinating the latest aspect of Bratton legislation with members of the Presidential staff. Daniel had a knack for understanding what the people wanted. Carlson's job: listening. He read the popular press's interpretation of civil rights groups but understood that's what is was, the popular press's interpretation. He enjoyed meeting with dignitaries and speaking with senators and Presidential aides. He was developing the art of persuasiveness, nudging commitment from semi-reluctant power players.

That day was particularly special. Daniel was on another spiritual plane because hours earlier he had met with Correta Scott King, the widow of Dr. King. Daniel recalled the way Dr. King spoke when he was younger. The "I have a dream" speech was one of the most inspiring. No matter which political party, equality for all is America. After listening, Daniel just wanted to get up and dance. Daniel privately made notes on Dr. King's oratory skills. It seemed that Dr. King would speak in simple language. But his words would create vivid pictures. His words would be short memorable phrases. Daniel felt Dr. King liked him, but understood that was part of Dr. King's personality and mission to recruit support. Daniel Carlson was sincere and would suggest

Dr. King's ideas in the composition of civil rights legislation. He had to force himself to stop work on the project, to dress for a formal reception on Massachusetts Avenue for the Ambassador of China.

Daniel unwrapped the tuxedo from the cleaner's plastic and examined the outfit. His parents had given him the tuxedo as a college graduation present. His father said that a Yale man would require a tuxedo. Boy, he was right. If Daniel Carlson had to rent a tuxedo for every formal event he had to go to, it would cost him ten percent of his salary.

Daniel dressed slowly. He looked at himself in a mirror behind the door to his office. He walked with extra stature in his tuxedo, as if he were wearing a cape. His eyes ran over the crisp turns in his collar, lapel, and sleeves. Tonight he wore a black bow-tie. Then he slipped on his onyx cufflinks. He looked handsome and he knew it. He ran his fingers through the side of his head and he was ready—ready to meet the Ambassador of China.

The Anderson House was an old wood house. The design was intended to be homey. It was filled with many rooms with an upstairs full of more rooms. It transformed into the perfect location for politics. Politicians can mill about and have little private conversations in any of these rooms. Daniel entered the House and stopped at the door to look around. He recognized the usual faces but his attention went to a pretty blonde server who was carrying a tray of spinach quiche. After handing his invitation to the decorated Marine at the door, he walked over, double time, to the blonde. He grabbed an appetizer and dipped it into a sauce that he could not identify but looked sweet. Peter immediately approached him.

"Come on. Quit stuffing your face and say hello to Bratton. He's speaking with the Ambassador." Daniel thought that he would be able to speak to a couple of lightweights before he would actually meet the Ambassador. *Good strategy*, Daniel thought. He quickly slipped a napkin out of the fingers of the server and wiped his mouth.

Strategically, the two men maneuvered into Senator Bratton's eye. The Senator was surrounded by several dignitaries from China that neither of the two could identify. China was an important player to America. China is the key to American stability in the Far East. Japan is the key to American stability in the Far East. It all matters. Senator Bratton said China would have an enormous economic influence over the next thirty years. Only a strong relationship with Korea, Japan, and China could ensure safety and tranquility for the United States. Daniel didn't quite understand why. He thought Europe was the key to stability of democracy in the world. Bratton knew better. His mastery of foreign policy and international relations took a backseat to no one.

Peter smiled at Bratton. Bratton gave a look of acknowledgment. Bratton liked showing off his young *protégées*. It gave him a chance to brag—a chance to hear himself talk in a grandiose manner without getting into trouble, commitment wise. He knew his boys were smart and intelligent, with bright futures ahead of them.

"Ah, Mr. Ambassador, let me introduce you to my aides. This is Daniel Carlson and this is Peter Spark. Daniel is very smart. He writes many of my speeches for me, a brilliant young man. I don't know what I'd do without him." Daniel knew he was laying it on a bit thick, but loved it anyway. "Daniel studied law at Harvard and grew up in Florida, where you will be visiting soon." Daniel greeted the Ambassador and his wife.

"Here, also another Harvard graduate, Peter. He is my right hand."

"You've compiled quite a collection of right hands," the Ambassador said.

"Yes, and both so attractive," the Ambassador's wife said.

"Behave yourself, dear. We don't want the Americans to have a bad impression of us." The Ambassador and the Senator laughed. The Ambassador's daughter's eyes widened toward Bratton.

"This guy, Peter might be a Senator someday. He has what it takes. Don't you think?" Bratton referred his question to the daughter. She and the Senator locked eyes and she smiled. He smiled back.

"I think this one has what it takes, too." She pointed to Daniel. Peter was annoyed by the comment. Stay ten-steps behind, Peter barked in his mind's voice.

"You stay away from this one," the Ambassador said referring, to Daniel.

"It was a pleasure meeting with you," Daniel said and slightly bowed.

The Senator excused himself for a moment and walked with his men over to the champagne table. Each took a glass.

"The Ambassador's daughter really likes you, Peter."

"Yeah. It's worth a shot," Peter said. Daniel just smiled, and took a sip.

Americanized Chinese music was played. The ambiance was very elegant, but the people were not very warm.

Suddenly, Melissa, Peter's date, approached them. She slapped Peter sarcastically.

"Peter, I wanted to meet the Ambassador."

"Oh, sorry, honey. I only spoke to him for thirty seconds anyway."

"Did you see his daughter's dress? Very authentic. Loved it . . . really hated it." she said with a laugh. Peter smiled.

"I didn't notice, but Daniel did. Oh, you remember, Daniel," Peter reintroduced.

"Of course." The two shook hands lightly. She smiled at Daniel. She was impressed by him since their first meeting and thought Daniel was a good influence on Peter.

"I want to introduce you to a friend of mine I came with. Her name is June. Maybe you'd like to go out with us after this party is over?"

"Don't force her on him."

"I'm not. She's my friend. How bad could she be?" Daniel thought Melissa was impressive as well. Her presence was soft yet had a certain strength. She was short but her high heels compensated. She was studying for her Master's in Education at George Washington. Daniel was jealous and impressed with that fact. He remembered Melissa, and liked her. She was also someone Peter could be seen with in public and fit his image. Daniel thought, how bad could her friend be?

"Okay. I'd love to meet your friend."

"I'm going to steal Peter for a while and we'll catch up with you."

By the shrimp server, a man in his forties approached Daniel. He was a conservative-looking man. The message his look depicted was stoic. His hair was cut close to the sides of his head. He wore silver wire glasses that had circular lenses. He smiled briefly at Daniel and asked him questions without introducing himself.

"You're Senator Bratton's aide, aren't you?"

"Well, one of them," Daniel said with a smile. The man swallowed his shrimp and then continued.

"He's told me a lot about you, Daniel. He thinks you're the one who will take his seat one day."

"I don't think I understand."

"You know, you're working on the civil rights legislation that will naturally lead Bratton to the road of the presidency. There'll be a vacant seat in the Senate, you know."

Daniel smiled and was flattered. Bratton says that about everyone who works for him.

"Well, there are elections, you know," Daniel politely mimicked the man's speech pattern.

"I'm Austin Hesse. And I'm not a bullshitter. I'll leave that to the old *machers* in Florida. Bratton has told me you're the man and I just wanted to meet you." Daniel thought this white bread wasp sounded funny forcing Yiddish into a sentence.

"What makes you so sure?" Daniel didn't know what to make of this guy. "I was told Peter Spark has the Senator's support."

"I didn't mean to upset you. I know you're loyal to your friend Peter."

"What do you do, Mr. Hesse?"

"Daniel, we're friends. Call me Austin. I work for Central Intelligence."

"Really?"

"Sure thing." This man intrigued Daniel. With his seamy background and strange approach, he didn't feel totally at ease with Hesse.

"What kind of work do you do for the Agency?"

"I'm officially retired. However, I work in the Directorate of Operations, in an advisory capacity. . . .Politics is a hobby."

"Well, it was very interesting to meet you. If there's anything I can do for you, give me a call at Senator Bratton's office," not willing to continue the conversation with a CIA man. Daniel was still relatively new to the job and still wasn't sure what he could discuss freely or what to keep under wraps.

"Oh, just continue being who you are, Daniel. You see, I know about Peter. Look out for him. He's a good friend to have, but he can be sneaky."

"I've always found Peter to be a loyal friend."

"Well, it was nice meeting you, Daniel." The two shook hands and parted.

Daniel saw a woman staring at him through the corner of her eye. She was an attractive woman who was busy talking to someone else.

"Hello, Daniel. Great party, huh?" Daniel's friend, Laurence Thompson said.

"How's that civil rights stuff? I'll help you hold off those conservatives."

"I'll keep you in mind. How's your Senator doing?"

"Fine. I have to keep him in line every now and then. If I don't, he'll turn into a goddamn fascist."

"Who's that girl staring at me over there? —Don't turn around now!"

"Can I look, now?"

"Slowly." Lawrence began to turn.

"That's June Ware. She's kind of a professional socialite."

"Then you approve."

"She's nice. Her husband was killed in Vietnam. She's friends with Peter's girl." The name rang a bell in Daniel's head.

"Her husband was on active duty?"

"A real hero, from what I understand." Daniel just stood there in silence almost jealous. "Say was that Austin Hesse that you were just speaking with?"

"Yes. What do you think of him?"

"He's a spook from the Pickle Factory. The Pickle Factory is another name for the CIA."

"I know," Daniel said

"You never retire from that line of work. But he's okay as far as right wing war mongers go."

"That's the nicest thing I've ever heard you say about an Eisenhower Republican."

"Why don't you go over and introduce yourself, instead of copping stares?"

"I will."

"See you later, Daniel."

After two minutes of awkward staring, Daniel decided to approach her. He took two glasses of champagne. As he walked closer to June, his mind blocked out the music. His heart rate rose. He was becoming more acutely interested with every step. She had such an atypical past compared with everyone else in the room. He no longer could hear the music. He was infatuated with the fantasy that she created. What Melissa and Laurence Thompson had created. Daniel added his own hopes to the fantasy. She was striking and provoked interest. She seemed to be handling herself well with the person she was speaking with. He was close enough.

"Hello," she said.

"Hi, Daniel Carlson. Champagne?"

"Thank you," She took the glass from him and looked from his shoes up to his face. "Have a light?" As gawky as he felt he had to answer in the negative. A gentleman to Daniel's left overheard and produced a lighter.

"I'm June. Melissa's friend."

"I know."

"How did you know?"

"People tell me things." Daniel gave her a wide smile.

"Do they?" She knew he was flirting with her.

"Let's get away from this noise. Would you like to go for a walk?"

"Sure."

The two left the main area and walked around the balcony of the House.

"Washington is such a pretty town, it's amazing what really goes on there," June said to make conversation.

"Oh, what goes on there?"

"It's so bright and honest on the outside. So shady and spooky on the inside." Daniel didn't respond. June thought he would be interested in talking about his job in an idealistic way as a response to her definite jab, but he did not.

"Do you have any family in town?"

"No. I do have two children," she paused for a reaction and then continued. "My husband was killed some time ago in the war."

"Boy and girl?"

"Yes. Did someone tell you that? . . .Connie and Alan."

"Have any pictures?"

"Yes." She sifted through her purse to find her picture wallet. "I never thought I would be showing these at this event. You really want to see my children?"

"Yes." June finally found them and Daniel studied each picture.

"They can't be that old." Daniel really meant it.

"I was a young bride."

"They're beautiful."

"Thank you."

"I didn't get a chance to serve in the war." There was no answer from June. There were some noticeable tears welling up in her eyes.

"Why would you want to serve? In a war that nobody wants to fight. Good men are lost for no reason! You're too smart for that Daniel."

"My country needed me," Daniel said without trying to sound too corny.

"Your country needs you alive. I can see it in your eye. You're going places. You can be a Congressman or a Senator." Daniel blushed. "No. I'd never run for office."

She didn't believe him. "You never know when the bug may hit you, Mr. President."

"Right."

"I want to say that I planted that seed in the back of your little ambitious mind. No one will believe me when I say that I started you in your career in politics, but I'll know."

"I don't want to talk about it."

"Okay."

"What do you do?" Daniel asked.

"I organize social events for Senator Bishop from Iowa."

"Ah, yes, Senator Bishop, Republican. That's good. You know I've always wondered what it would be like to have kids. Do you enjoy it?"

June was relieved that she didn't have to be the first to mention her children. It's usually an invitation to end the conversation to a man. Although, it was a good tool to get out of one too. In this case June was interested, so it was good that Daniel already knew about them, but didn't politely smile and walk away. She was not rest assured yet. She was dealing with a fledgling politician.

"I don't enjoy raising them on my own. But I love them. I just got Alan out of the terrible two's. So now I can keep a sitter."

"I'm an only child. Never had children."

"Well, I'll let you babysit sometime."

"Sure. I would like to meet them sometime."

"Really? That's remarkable. I meet a guy and when I tell him I've got kids I can't remember which way he ran."

"Well, you just don't want any guy. You want to take the chance with the right guy. And the right guy uniquely fits the kind of person that you are, right?"

"Yeah. You're right. You're not a stereotypical aide."

"How's that?"

"These parties are times when aides meet and maneuver in the world of power. And here you are asking me about my kids."

"Like I said, the right guy uniquely fits the kind of person that you are, right?

* * *

My first year out of formal schooling was awakening. While many issues in school can be resolved with an overwhelming sense of orderliness in the law, it doesn't translate in the real world in the same way. The reason it doesn't translate well is the fact that real people are involved—people in strange circumstances.

I could talk about the law to legislators, but all they want and wanted are results. On more than one occasion a Senator has told me to keep unconstitutional language in a bill because it would take several years before that legislation would be declared constitutional. But that is not the only pressure I had been feeling.

Senator Bratton had hinted that he favored me as a legislative aide. I wasn't happy about that. I felt he was more of a father figure, and the aides were his children so to speak. I didn't like the fact that he favored me over Peter, especially since Peter brought me into the Senator's organization. The Senator also felt he could shape other areas in my life.

In a not so subtle fashion Bratton told me it would be wise to find a wife. I thought his candor was a form of humor, but it wasn't. A serious politician needed to create a finely tuned life. Each area of my life had to fit the mold. By fitting the mold I could enter the system, by entering the system I could change it. Do you see how I fell off the track? About a month later it all fell apart or, fell into place.

Daughter v. wife?

CHAPTER 6

The End of An Era

CLEAR AND QUITE SHOCKING. Senator Bratton's picture was next to a front-page investigative article.

SENATOR BRATTON HAS LIAISON WITH
AMBASSADOR'S WIFE

Leinwand, from the newspaper *USA Today*, broke a story about the State Department having new insurmountable hurdles to clear because the Chinese Ambassador to the United States and Senator Bratton were at odds over the Ambassador's wife. Sources claimed the Ambassador was outraged with the situation and labeled it as a clear violation of diplomatic protocol.

A picture of Cho Ming, the Ambassador's wife, was printed on the opposite side of the article. There was something about publishing a picture in an article describing the scandal. It was something about, *the cameras*. The cameras made life. It put pictures with names and made the stories, fiction or fact, become real, alive, ring with truth. When the cameras offered a reaction shot to the scandalous news, the public instantly forms an opinion on guilt or innocence. Most of the time the deliberation turns up the guilt. Because guilt is easier. It requires little effort. Frankly, it is more fun.

The only picture the *Post* had of the Senator was on file from a British embassy party from last month. Since it was the weekend, Senator Bratton was home in Florida and probably just learning about it. Or some spy that Senator Bratton had at *The Post* called to tell him that the article was going to be printed. This was devastating. What was worse, the political devastation or the personal? The political. He could always straighten it out with his wife. She knew the rules of the game—an unspoken agreement. It was that damn silent majority that wouldn't forgive. The silent majority—God says. . . .

What to do? First, start with a scotch. Then the Senator called a friend in the Party. A friend? A person in the know. The one in control. After a long talk it was decided what had to be done. Daniel and Peter waited outside the Senator's door until he arrived. They didn't know what to think, but they wanted some answers. Didn't Bratton realize that other people's interests were at stake?

Senator Bratton walked into the office. The secretary glanced up for a second and then continued typing. Senator Bratton smiled at his men and waved them to come in. They followed but neither of the men knew who was supposed to start talking first.

"I suppose you read the article already?" The Senator asked. "Well?"

"Shit, Terry, it was a stupid thing to do," Peter said, not hesitating to use his embattled boss's first name.

"All right. What's happened is done. It wasn't smart. I took a chance, and I got caught. That simple. It happens all the time."

"So what's it going to be?" Peter asked.

"I'm going to apologize for the appearance of indiscretion at a press conference that's going to be in five minutes. See how it plays. It's the '80s. Why do leaders have to appear perfect?" At that moment Daniel realized that Bratton was having sex with the wife of an Ambassador. He was embarrassed he was that naïve, even to himself. Still so young and idealistic in thought, Daniel didn't understand why Bratton would need sex outside his marriage. Daniel didn't realize Bratton didn't get sex inside his marriage. Peter, however, was never so gullible.

"Damn, you know how it's going to go over? You cheated on your wife—end of story. You committed adultery! We're screwed hard. Damn! If I would've known about Leinwand two days ago, I could've taken care of this," Peter exclaimed. Bratton cut him off with a wave of his hand.

"Listen, I fucked up. Literally. It's doesn't have to affect me politically."

Daniel began to think. He was an advocate even in this moment of discovery that his boss was human and fallible.

"Isn't there a way around it? Go out there and say that Sherry forgives you. The revelation has brought you closer together. And now you will be able to serve your constituency with a new outlook on life, an outlook free from burden, and strong family support," Daniel said it as if he were giving the speech for him. Daniel was loyal and instantly was acting as Terrence Bratton's lawyer. All of the men remained silent for a moment.

"Not bad, Daniel." The Senator laughed and wrote something down on an envelope that he took out of his jacket pocket.

"Oh, bullshit. Only an evangelist could get away with some bullshit like that, Terry," Peter said. "Look what you've done. That whole civil rights package is right down the drain. The Presidency! Your dreams!"

The Senator felt the ice in his veins. "I'll have Senator Sparling takeover the civil rights bill as his own, if my apology doesn't work. I'm the only one in trouble here. Now quit criticizing me, and back me like good aides."

"We can fight this, Terry," Peter said. "Why don't you deny it? Who can prove she slept with you? Some reporter has a picture of you at a public function. Rumors are flying? That's evidence?"

"I'm going to see what the reaction is to the whole thing. Peter, I know it's ridiculous. I had sex. The woman had a big mouth. Her husband's an Ambassador." The Senator smiled. "Should it ruin my career? Did sex with Cho Ming affect my ability as a politician? As an administrator? Shit happens." The Senator laughed again. "Good headline, right?"

"How can you joke at a time like this? Jesus, don't you know there are other people whose lives and careers are at stake as well?" Peter demanded.

"Don't get overdramatic, Peter. It's just not smart to lie about it. We're in a new era. Nixon spoiled it for all of us. Do you know how many Senators have girlfriends? More do than don't. I picked one who's an Ambassador's wife, and says it happened. Scandal! Don't worry my boys; I'll discuss your future after I have lunch today. I promise I haven't forgotten who's important. If the polls reflect forgiveness, we're still in business. If not, then we'll talk. Daniel, call the Ambassador's office and see if we can smooth this thing out and let bygones be what they're supposed to be." Daniel Carlson wondered how he was suppose to do it. He certainly wouldn't talk to the Ambassador directly.

The Senator ran his fingers through his gray, curly hair. He got up and buttoned his dark blue jacket. "Come watch the press conference." The Senator closed the door to his office behind him. The three men saw Sherry Bratton sitting in the waiting room. She stood up. She was an attractive woman. Very sophisticated looking. Daniel had thought she was sweet and almost sincere, but didn't know her very well. Peter barely talked to her. He would send Melissa to do the job.

She was dressed in a black blazer and a formal silk shirt underneath. The Senator grabbed her elbow and said, "Why are you wearing black? This isn't a funeral."

"Oh, shut up, Terry!" She said aloud.

All the cameras were there, surrounding the front steps of the Rayburn building. Senator Bratton's attorney stood beside him when he approached the microphone. His wife stood one step behind his left shoulder.

Daniel and Peter watched the Senator with anticipation at the bottom of the steps. Daniel empathized with the Senator. He, too, feared that one day he might be talking to the cameras apologizing for something of a personal nature. A free press doesn't mean that it should interfere with personal lives, public official or not. If it affects the public, it's fair game. If it doesn't, get lost. Yet others have said it is the cost of being in the public eye. Nevertheless, Daniel sided with his first thoughts.

The Senator approached the microphone. "Good morning, ladies and gentlemen. I have a brief statement to make. In yesterday's *news* I was accused of indiscretions concerning the wife of the Chinese Ambassador to the United States. I would categorize the relationship I have with this woman as one of encouragement and friendship. The appearance of our relationship could be misconstrued and I take responsibility for that. However, I do plan to continue to serve my constituency.

Yesterday's story has brought my family closer, and allowed us to air-out family issues. With this new enlightenment, I will now serve as a stronger man. The people of the State of Florida will know a new Senator. A Senator with new courage, and new avenues of ability and freedom to serve the people of Florida, and this great country." The Senator felt a sudden jolt of tension. He felt a lack of confidence. Tunnel vision set in and he almost got dizzy. "Thank you for your time."

Sherry Bratton felt her husband's weakness. She took one step toward the microphone. She spoke clearly and projected her voice with confidence. She was the wife. She was supposed to protect her husband.

"My husband is a wonderful man. He has been my husband for more than twenty-two years. Through the ups and downs we have remained a family. His children love him. I love him. And most importantly, the people in the State of Florida love him. I'm not a woman who'll just follow her man around. I'm not a weak woman. I'm not a woman that just sings *Stand by Your Man*. If I weren't happy with Terrence, I would be gone. He's a wonderful man. And, if he tells me that he has been faithful, then I believe him. He's a wonderful Senator, who enjoys the confidence of his people. He's sponsoring a very important civil rights bill that will ensure freedom and civil rights for all in this great country. We must dismiss this nonsense and let a great man continue his work." She dropped her voice. Sherry was done speaking. She smiled confidently, and she performed well.

The Senator, with panic in his heart, bolted toward the front door of the Rayburn building. The cameras followed. The media recognized a collective sense of miscommunication between the couple. Wait a second. Did Peter put her up to this unplanned denial? Bratton was dizzy.

"Senator, are you saying you didn't have an affair with the Ambassador's wife?"

"Senator, what will happen with the civil rights bill?"

"Is that a denial, Senator?"

"Please, some questions, Senator!"

* * *

Daniel was left at the bottom of the steps. He gazed and wondered at the whole spectacle. He knew that the Senator was hurting more than he let on. He knew the jokes in the office were a shallow defense mechanism to ease the tension. How did that gaff happen? A public relations nightmare. Who knows how the cameras will reveal what they captured—the less disclosure, the worse chance of a positive spin.

One o'clock rolled around and the Senator was back from a private three-martini lunch. He got wind of what the newspapers thought of his quick getaway that morning. Like a suspected criminal, you run, you're guilty.

Daniel and Peter were waiting nervously inside Senator Bratton's office. They didn't speak at all. Peter was hoping that the Senator had a good lunch meeting because his career plans required it. The job satisfied every itch he had, the policymaking itch, and an executive's itch. To one day work for the President of the United States. Peter Spark's power would be expansive.

The Senator walked around his desk. He had a look of pain on his face. This was not good news.

"Well, fellas, I'm finished." The Senator took a deep sigh and tears began to well up in his eyes. He lost his sense of humor. Like a child he succumbed to short-term gratification and didn't account for the long term consequences. "I'm going to finish out the term but—" The Senator looked down at the floor. " . . .I'm not going to seek re-election."

Daniel and Peter sighed in disappointment. "We're going to be dragged down too, aren't we?" Bratton looked at Peter and ignored his comment. He looked at Daniel and continued to speak.

"You have dreams and goals. You get tempted by human urges. It's stupid. I've tried to do some good. I did some good. I tried to be an apolitical politician. But it's impossible. Ends justifying the means. That's the way it is. Don't let any self-righteous idiot tell you otherwise. You have a goal. If you have to make a deal, maneuver, do it. It's avoiding the appearance of indiscretion. That's it. It's not the indiscretion by itself. You see what I'm saying?" Daniel heard the Senator, but wasn't taking in what he was saying. He felt sorry for him. All right, he was stupid. What did he do, though? He got nailed for something that gave the appearance of wrongdoing. So fuck him. So fuck me. Daniel wanted to know the underlying reason for failure. Why did Bratton do it? Urges, that was nonsense.

"My relationship with my wife wasn't a loving sharing giving anymore. It was like a contract. A partnership agreement. It was a contract with the terms created by trial and error, by penalties and rewards, which kill the romance and intimacy, the drive to want to be together through love," Bratton said.

"Isn't that compromise," Daniel asked. Bratton nodded.

"But the distinction between love and business is blurred. I didn't want to make deals with my wife. I suppose that now that I fucked this woman I'm not a great speaker or as politically astute anymore. And if I weren't caught, now that really crystallizes the issue, no one would know. You see? It wouldn't matter. I mean Jesus Christ, I'm not on drugs. I'm not dangerous. I didn't take money. Something like that would be inexcusable. I mean at least the old equipment still works. You'd think the American people would like that."

Peter chimed in. "Terry, you know the rules."

"Yeah, what do you care? I'm just your fucking ticket to Congress or the White House, right Peter?"

"Goddamn it! I fuckin' trusted in you. I believed in you." Peter stood up and yelled. "I was about you! I wasn't using you. I was for you. You broke the contract, asshole. I was always a hundred percent loyal."

"Yeah, you really helped with that cloak and dagger stuff with that—" The Senator stuttered. Daniel shifted in his seat, flustered. He didn't know what Bratton and Peter were talking about.

"I did that for you. You asked me to do something. I bear responsibility for my mistakes. For my actions. Now you have to. What the hell did you tell my wife to deny it for? That's what fucked it up you idiot!"

Senator Bratton turned his attention to Daniel. "Learn something here Daniel. Don't work for a man you admire, you'll only be disappointed when you learn that he's human. Okay, Peter, you want the straight deal. Sit down. I just came from a lunch with the head of the Party. They want Daniel to be the next elected Senator." Peter was in shock. Daniel was very surprised but he was elated. "And I agreed. Good news, huh, Daniel? I know it's a shock to you, Peter."

"No, Peter should have the support of the party," Daniel said. His elation withered away.

"Save your breath, Daniel." Peter responded. "Why? Why did you sell me out? What the hell? You know it was my turn. You led me on like that."

"He's right, Terry. Everyone knows that you promised him," Daniel said.

"They don't think you'll have public appeal."

"What?"

"Public appeal, it wouldn't be with you. It's irrelevant. That's what the hell I've been talking about, which you weren't interested in hearing at all. I feel bad for myself. But I feel worse for you."

"I, I, don't understand. How the hell would they know? What am I too curt? What is it? I speak well. I've got a beautiful fiancé. What the fuck is it? Do I have B.O.?"

"It's the goddamn scar, Peter! People are ignorant. You look like a goddamn terrorist. You're the fuckin' elephant man."

"Jesus, Terry. Take it easy. That's a huge overstatement," Daniel said.

"It's the constituency. It's the ignorant voters." It's the Silent Majority, Daniel thought. "Your career would best be served as a statesman. There's no voting, you'll just need an appointment."

Peter stood up and ran his fingers over his scar and muttered, "This is what I deserved." Peter stormed out of the office. There was a dramatic pause. Bratton and Daniel were alone. The mood in the room dropped.

"Daniel, you want to be a Senator? It'll take a lot of commitment."

"I'll have to think about it, Terry."

"Well the opportunity will sink in and you'll come around. I know you better than you know yourself. It's time that you get married to June. She's a lovely woman cut out to be a Senator's wife. In addition, you should adopt her children. You'll be a wonderful father. I know you care about them. As of the end of next month you will be moving back to Florida. I'm relieving you and Peter. You both will be working out of the U.S. Attorney's office. You'll be involved in major criminal litigation. You'll be working for the Justice Department for the next five years, 'til the end of my term. You'll work on some cases, get on some charitable/political boards, stay involved, and get some name recognition, the party will support you and you'll win."

"What about Peter?"

"He'll come around and eventually get involved in your campaign. He'll have enough experience by the time your campaign comes around. When you win, you'll make him your chief aide. Just remember Daniel, keep your dick in your pants. Play things right and I think you'll be on the road to endless possibilities. You'll have a chance at the Presidency like I once had."

Daniel, still naïve, looked at the Senator and felt the Senator was gazing into a crystal ball of hope, and not forecasting any political reality.

* * *

Daniel Carlson hadn't spoken to Peter Spark in a day. But Daniel knew that he would see Peter at the formal affair scheduled for that evening. Daniel hoped with Bratton, Peter would come around.

At the moment, Daniel was worried about June. Daniel was comfortable with June, and he loved her kids. He asked her to consider marrying him the night before. At first, she was excited. Then they discussed adoption of the kids, moving to Florida, and running for Senator. This took her by surprise. They spoke all night over dinner. She wasn't sure about the adoption or moving to Florida. The whole package seemed to be questionable to her.

Daniel revealed some deep things about the way he thought, his plans, for the future, and his past. He felt it necessary so she knew exactly what she was getting. Dating is dating; marriage is a partnership of a different kind. He didn't want to give June surprises after they were married. She wanted to think about it. Daniel felt that she would give her answer at the party.

A political party doesn't have the same connotation as a regular party for a birthday or wedding. Basically, a formal party had some dancing, a lot of drinking, but again, not much warmth. The purpose is to gather people together to talk—network—make deals.

Tonight's party was in honor of the independence of Argentina. Daniel made the usual rounds and exchanged some pleasantries with some of the people he knew. From the corner of his eye he saw Peter standing off in an area that was being used as a dance floor.

Peter and Daniel locked eyes. They stood and stared at each other. Peter took the first step toward Daniel. Daniel walked toward Peter. Peter smiled and wrapped his arms around him, and gave him a quick squeeze. The strong smell of scotch was on Peter's breath. He was really drunk.

"The American public wants you to blend, Daniel. Blending allows you to walk around and be liked by everyone. Blend to obtain general acceptance. Once you've mastered general accep-tance. You can move onto the next level *public acceptance*. Public acceptance is reserved for a few, and only for a short time. But you Daniel, must decide whether you will go to the next level and strive for public acceptance. You must sell something when you decide to want it."

With a sigh Peter Spark said, "Fuck it, I'll help you. We'll move to Florida, and have a great time. We'll prosecute some mobsters, right?" Daniel smiled. Peter was hammered but Daniel knew Peter was right. There was a sale. What was he going to sell? The day Daniel decided to be more than generally acceptable and strive for public acceptance, is the day Daniel Carlson decided he had the makings of a President.

Daniel then saw June at the other end of the room. His killer instinct honed. One down, one to go. Daniel excused himself from Peter. He walked toward June who was drinking champagne and talking to some State Department official. She was pretending not to notice Daniel, but it was obvious that she was trying not to notice. As Daniel walked toward June, Melissa Spark grabbed him by the arm.

"Daniel, can we talk?"

"Sure, Melissa." Daniel noticed her black dress with thin shoulder straps. Daniel always liked Melissa, but felt bad for her at times. She often took verbal or silent abuse from Peter. Now it seemed that she wanted to have a heart to heart.

"June and I spoke. I think it's wonderful that you asked her to marry you. We had a little *tete a tete*. I hope you're not upset."

"No. I figured June might talk to you about it."

"Daniel, I think you guys will come together. I think you have a lot going for you. You're bright and handsome, and have a gift of speech. You're a really special guy, Daniel. You could make any woman happy. And those kids, they love you. I wish Peter would take the time to give us that kind of happiness. I wish he would be a father. It's not how much time you spend with children, it's an attitude. You have the right attitude to be a great father." Melissa ran her fingers through the side of Daniel's hair. She was drinking the same scotch Peter was drinking. "God and you're going to make a great Senator. You are, Daniel. A suave, distinguished Senator. Mark my words." Daniel was blushing.

"Thank you, Melissa. I'm going to try to live up to your expectations. I think Peter will be great too. He has a wonderful woman."

"Come let's dance. I think it's exciting that we'll be moving to Florida. Will you tell me about the cases you're going to be working on?"

"Sure."

"Because, I don't think Peter will talk about his work at all. It's some strange way of his." The lights dimmed at a song change. Melissa slowly put her hand to the back of Daniel's head. She pulled his head down toward hers and kissed Daniel on the lips. "You have a wonderful future ahead, Daniel. I'm glad I'll get to be a part of it." At the end of the song the lights turned up, and Daniel smiled at Melissa. His opinion of her went up just like she wanted.

The man from the State Department left the conversation with June. Daniel walked over to her and took her elbow. She smiled.

"Hello, my dear."

"Hi."

"You look wonderful. Uh, would you like to dance?" Daniel felt nervous. More nervous than when he approached her the first time they met. The mood was romantic. He felt like a fifth grader. The band had a string quartet. The band was playing familiar classical music. And in a moment, June took Daniel's hands and looked him in the eyes and said:

"Daniel, I'll marry you. And I want you to be a friend to my children." Gazing into June's eyes, Daniel smiled.

"I want to be more than a friend. I want to be their father."

CHAPTER 7

Behind the Cross

*Should I ever divulge or cause to be divulged, any
of the secrets of this order, or any of the foregoing
obligations, I must meet with the fearful punishment
of death and traitor's doom, which is death, death,
death, at the hands of the brethren.*

FLORIDA IS HOT, and it's not a dry kind of heat. It's 89 degrees, and it feels like 99. The sun is bright and anyone can feel the heat from the sun directly upon one's face—directly upon one's face. Everyone drove a car. Daniel and Peter moved to Miami. June and a graduate student were sharing a place together in a *make due* apartment on Sunny Isles Beach, a small unincorporated community near Miami Beach. Melissa and Peter had been married a year and her family helped a little each month so they could afford a place with room for another child, who hopefully would be on the way soon. Peter's parents had both passed away by the time he was eighteen.

Everything was going according to schedule. Daniel was involved with various political clubs and benevolent organizations. This was a good start to get into the mainstream of politics. What Daniel and Peter were hoping for was to create or find a major case to get them name recognition so Daniel could go into the next Senate race strong. A young face getting involved in elderly residents' politics was accepted. Every now and then some member of an organization would die, just due to old age. Even the self-centered curmudgeons who redefined themselves to a level of great importance allowed Daniel Carlson to lead by having a leader like someone they knew—like Bratton.

It was the end of a long Friday and Peter was in Daniel's office with his feet up on Daniel's desk. Peter was smoking a cigarette. He thought that the job as a DOJ lawyer was a stepping-stone, but he was on a different mission from God. Some of the young Assistant United States attorneys plainly threatened anyone who went against them. Particularly, the assistants involved in drug enforcement. Public opinion painted the picture of the defense attorney as the unscrupulous one defending the immoral. Guilty by client. Who the lawyer's client was reflected on the lawyer. A month in the Justice Department and Daniel thought differently. Peter and Daniel weren't naive; they were just surprised that the intimidation tactics were all so above board. For example, a defense attorney who continually caused difficulty to their boss suddenly found he and his family were being audited by the IRS. Daniel didn't use those tactics.

Daniel learned to love litigating and prosecuting. He already helped another senior U.S. attorney round up some New York mob bosses who vacationed in Florida and used the phones, giving jurisdiction to the local United States Attorney. The hours were endless; but, Daniel was on a plan. With Daniel's tireless efforts, the U.S. Attorney for the Southern District of Florida was now on the bandwagon, ready to help Daniel in his campaign for the Senate. Each day Daniel's ability to blend increased, and Peter marveled. Admittedly, Peter was jealous. It was just odd that the roles between Peter and Daniel had reversed. Peter was the handler and Daniel was the master. With Daniel's charismatic personality and help from a couple of party members, some of the higher-ups in the Justice Department Organized Crime Task Force were looking for the big case. Miami was a growing town in the late seventies. Fidel threatened to dump tens of thousands of Cuba's *undesirables* on the shores of Miami. With an increasing population, crime was sure to follow. With weather like Las Vegas, the crime would be organized. A crime issue was waiting. The plan was great, but some party members were getting a little itchy.

Peter continued to smoke a cigarette as Daniel spoke on the phone to Elana Goldstein, a local Dade State Attorney. She worked with Daniel Carlson on the organized crime cases. She was told to reduce sentences on State cases, and agreed not to prosecute others, in exchange for *cooperation* from witnesses who testified in the federal trial. Peter smiled as he listened to Daniel's side of the conversation.

"No, I don't think I can meet you for dinner tonight to discuss this new case with you." Daniel looked up and smiled. "I know that you think it's a big one. You think every case you have is a big one. You're a twenty-eight-year old gung-ho prosecutor and you're supposed to think that every case is a big case. The case that's supposed to break open your career. The case that will shock America. I'm not making fun of you. I have plans already . . . Don't you have anything else to do on a Friday night? . . . We'll talk Monday . . . Okay, at lunch. Yeah, bye!" Daniel tried to speak with a tone of control for Peter. If he didn't, Daniel knew he would get twenty-questions from Peter.

Elana Goldstein was born in Brooklyn to a middle class Jewish family. When she was eight, her family moved to Miami Beach. Later, she was awarded a full scholarship to law school at the University of Florida, as one of the first women to attend that law school program. Elana Goldstein was a lawyer rich with idealism. She was attractive, with ebony hair and thick eyebrows that she thinned almost daily. She was feminine and had to tone it down in the world of law in which she worked. She was unique among even the few woman lawyers in Florida. There was a judge in the local courthouse who would ask a woman lawyer for her Bar card before she addressed the court, and that was on a good day. On a not-so-good day, he would ask her: 'Are you a lawyer or a suc-retary?' " in a thick southern accent.

Goldstein dressed in dark-colored business attire every day. This was part of the no-nonsense business-first image she liked to portray. She fostered that image because she was one of the only woman in the prosecutor's office outside of her boss. She virtually had one chance of moving up, because she was a woman, even though the State Attorney was the first woman in that position. She needed a big case. Elana Goldstein still demanded respect from the people she worked with. Daniel gave her that respect without her having to fight for it. He got teased about it by others, but Elana adored him for it.

"That girl wants you, Daniel," Peter said.

"Give me a break, Peter. Don't you have something better to do on a Friday?"

"That girl wants a piece of the next Senator from Florida."

"All right, maybe she kind of likes me but not because of that. I'm nice to her. I listen to her talk about her aspirations."

"Right. She's not power hungry," Peter said sarcastically. "She likes you for your good looks. You're telling me some over-achieving little Jewess isn't dying for a powerful political man to give her a leg up? And maybe more than just a leg. Hey, maybe she thinks she can be the second woman State Attorney."

"She says she likes me because I laugh at her jokes."

"And—" Peter said to probe for the real reason.

"She says I've got this soft quality that most men are afraid to show."

Peter laughed. "What a fucking wimp. You'd roll over for that girl."

"That's not true. In fact, Lana was a real pain in the ass when it came to getting deals on the La Cosa Nostra trials."

"Ooh, you've got a pet nickname for her. Does she call you, Danny?" Daniel nodded his head with disgust.

"Shut up. All right, so we're discussing wiretaps used and all that other legal admissibility stuff. So she says that the public telephone taps done by a couple of Miami cops prove that Dante Marcoigne was running numbers games across state lines, as well as commercial prostitution operations. So she's going on and on about these taps and what they have on tape and blah, blah, blah, and then I said, 'What about Katz?' So she says, 'who's Katz?' Like he's an attorney." Peter dragged on his cigarette and smiled.

"Now, I wasn't trying to make her feel stupid, but I guess word didn't get down to the prosecutor's office about Katz, even though the case is about twelve years old. So she was going on and on about these taps. I mean these two detectives who have this thing for Elana work overtime monitoring these taps." Now, Peter started to laugh. "So a couple of the other lawyers start to laugh. She's getting mad. I can see it in her face. She finally says, 'Who the hell is Katz?'

"I said, *Katz v. United States*. It's a Supreme Court decision. It says, 'Use of electronic surveillance without prior authorization cannot be justified on grounds of hot pursuit.' Since the detectives didn't get a warrant for the public telephone, we couldn't use it." Peter nodded and ashed his cigarette. "So she says, 'What about Lewis?' Everybody's laughing now. She's so red; I think she's going to burst into flames. Then I said, 'We're not laughing at you, we're laughing with you— if only you were laughing.' Well that did it. Everyone was hysterical at that point. Man, she didn't talk to me for days after that."

"So, what does she want from you now?" Peter asked.

"She's babbling about some trend she sees in these murders of eight young men in the last three years. I don't get it? I don't think she gets it?"

"See, she wants to drag you into some local affair so she can be with you. I can't believe you don't see it."

"What do you suggest I do about it?"

"Bang the crap out of her, Daniel." That's something Scott Witherspoon would've said in Jamaica, Daniel thought.

"What about June?"

"Don't tell her. Besides, you can use her to get you votes. She'll work for you because you're fucking her and she'll get you all your Jewish votes in Miami Beach. Your dick can single handedly get you more votes than any other part of your anatomy."

"Look where that got our mentor," Daniel retorted. Peter immediately sobered up and became angry on the inside.

"I'm only playing with you, Daniel. Don't count Goldstein out. She might just come up with that winner we've been looking for. You'll have the Margoines and whatever. Oh, and I told Melissa that we would go see a movie tonight after the Party meeting."

"Yeah, that'll be fine. We wanted to see that new one that came out, *Once Upon a Time in America*. Law. Crying. Fun for the whole family."

Peter enjoyed some of the people at the meeting, but Daniel was a natural at working these people. He was good for a joke or a favor. He would know some of them were phony but he did his job with a certain flair. It was still strange to Daniel that Peter wasn't the candidate—all in the wave of a hand over a two-martini lunch, with a bunch of big wig party members and it's done. "No, no, Peter wouldn't be right," Daniel envisioned the meeting with Bratton and the party leaders went. So much for having a people's candidate.

Daniel was getting better at Peter's instructions. "Hi! Hi!" Daniel would say brightly to everyone. He had almost a photographic memory when it came to people's names, which was a huge plus. Nothing looked worse than when a friend has to whisper the name of the person standing in front of you. Everyone knows what's going on. Nothing shatters the bond that the voter has with a candidate than the knowledge that the candidate doesn't know who the person is.

These parties got boring at times, but every now and then a purse would walk up to Daniel and pat his inside pocket and say, "I've got a blank check with your name on it when you start the campaign." Who knew who could or would deliver? Daniel just had to be nice to everyone until the truth was revealed. Everyone has to toot their own horn. Some were serious. Some were full of shit.

★ ★ ★

It was 12:15 on Monday afternoon and Daniel met Elana Goldstein in the coffee shop of the federal courthouse.

"So, Elana, what's on your mind?"

"Will you take a look at these cases?" She handed him a large stack of case folders dated from the present to the past seven years. Daniel smiled sweetly but turned his head as he shut his eyes.

"Elana, what am I going to do with you? Murder's a state crime. I don't have time to help you on these things as much as I'd like to."

"Listen, I know that you're busy. I don't give away my tough cases. I want you to look at these and tell me what you think. I think there's room for something federal. I need resources and man power that the State Attorney's office doesn't have."

"Elana, we worked well on the Marcoignes case—"

"Don't give me the tap dance Daniel. I hear that crap all day long. I'm going to you because you're the only one who would give me the help I need. Since you have such insight. You'll get the benefits of my labor. Right? Right." Daniel shook his head in disbelief.

"I know your agenda, Senator. Trust me. Just do your job and help me with this as a favor. You'll see that doing your job as an end instead of a means to the Capitol you'll get there a lot faster. I'll back you up and you know I'm not lying. This town is Jew heaven. You think they want some *shaygets* representing them. They'll vote for some do-nothing Berkowitz if you don't have a Jew in your corner." She grabbed his face with her hand and squeezed his cheeks. "I can mobilize the condo-commandos you schnook." She said schnook with such a distinct Brooklyn accent. It was quite enticing to Daniel. She was asking for his help, but in his heart Daniel knew he was really manipulating her. How could he say no? Even though there has never been a Jewish Senator in the State's history, she made her pitch so well.

"What a golden nugget. Copy that and sign it for me, I'll put it on my wall."

Daniel resumed, "I'll look at it sometime this week. But no promises. I mean I've got bosses too. I can't just dish out federal manpower if there's nothing in it for us. Marcoigne was a good example of what's okay."

"If this is like Marcoigne, then I can get your help?" She asked. Daniel answered, yes.

★ ★ ★

At the end of a long Friday, Elana Goldstein wandered into Daniel's office on the Third Floor of the Federal Building. With her hand on her hip, she smiled in anticipation.

"You know what links these eight cases together? Acid." Elana said.

"It's late Elana, I have to go to a Rotary Club Executive meeting," Daniel replied.

"Save your bullshit meeting. This is about justice."

"Then save your riddles. I can't think right now, it's been a long day. What's acid?"

Elana answered straightforward, "Muriadic acid, like the stuff you use in your pool or to clean tile with. There were traces on all of these victims." She strategically scattered the pictures on Daniel's desk to show the gruesome remnants of departed lives. Eight black males, twenty to twenty-five years of age, and that's where the similarities ended. "All were intelligent."

"So. Does that amaze you?"

"Just something that makes me wonder. Yet, with the acid on their bodies."

"There's no time frame these murders were committed. Even if they were murders. Look here this guy, it could've been suicide. And there are a thousand pools in your neighborhood alone.— I've really got to go."

"One agent. Please, someone," Elana pleaded.

"Begging is not like you." He put on his jacket and started to turn out the lights in his office.

"You're the only man I couldn't stand to put his balls in a vice. But I will if I have to. One investigator. I need access to FBI resources. . . .What kind of a club meets on a Friday night?"

"It's a social occasion. . . . I'll give you one agent. And only for a week, max."

* * *

Elana Goldstein sat at Daniel's desk and they ate Chinese food out of the box while they discussed her case. Between bites she spoke:

"I was right. You're going to be so happy you signed on this case with me."

"I haven't really signed on," Daniel said with a smile.

"You'll see. This FBI agent you gave me said there was a link. He's coming any minute and he'll surprise us both."

Suddenly a young man, age twenty-five, entered Daniel's office.

"Can I help you," Daniel asked.

"How ya doing, Brad Lefkel, FBI." The young agent waved a bound report that was in his hand.

"How's it going? I don't think we ever met. I'm Daniel Carlson, Assistant DOJ Attorney."

"Hi, I'm Elana Goldstein, Dade State Attorney's Office."

"Yeah, you're the one I spoke to on the phone," Lefkel replied.

"I didn't realize you were so young," Elana said.

"Yeah, I hear that all the time," he replied with cockiness to his tone. "As the young guy I get the shit assignments." Elana lost her smile. Daniel smiled. "I try and turn them into something we can prosecute."

"What do you think on this one?" Daniel said.

"I think you have some coincidences worth looking into." Elana regained her smile.

"Sit down. You want something to eat?" Daniel asked.

"No, just ate. The acid on the bodies of the victims seem to draw them all together. It's an anomaly that almost suggests that the culprits wanted to be discovered, but never were. Here are the results of our computer analysis of the acid burns. The bodies themselves would've been better, but they're long gone by now. Rotted. You get the idea. It appears that when the bodies were found the acid dripped. The computer analyzed the pictures and removed what it thought were drippings. I thought it would be a neat thing to program. Well, with my keen intuition, and expertise in crime scene investigation, this is what it spelled out."

Brad Lefkel pulled out the pictures of the eight murder victims that were found in rural areas off the long stretch of road called Tamiami Trail. Outlined in red were the letters AKIA, on some, and KIGY, on the others.

"Great. What does it mean?"

"Well, Mr. DOJ Attorney, it means AKIA, A Klansman I am. And KIGY, Klansman I greet you. Reads like an initiation into the club."

"Incredible," Elana said. Her excitement was building.

"Klan, in Miami? Aren't we a little south of the South?"

"Expanding markets," the young agent replied. "You're not from Florida, are you? Anyway, there are parts of west Miami that cock fights and cow tipping are the highlight of a Friday night."

"What's the motive for choosing these victims?" Daniel's interest was piqued.

"Don't know. None were in any radical black organizations, like the Panthers."

"You see, the victims being black wouldn't be much of a motive in court. How could we continue an investigation into the perpetrators?" Daniel asked. Elana was beaming with excitement. She enjoyed being right and the opportunity to work with Daniel.

"The Klan is pretty unified down here because they're looking to expand into new territories as a reaction to Johnson's and Martin Luther King Civil Rights laws. The major group is known as The Power. A man by the name of Forest Bedford is known to be the head of the group."

"Didn't you have something to do with those civil rights laws, Daniel? You should be taking this stuff personally. What does he do for a living?" Elana asked to facilitate the investigative process in the hopes of getting Daniel more interested.

"He's a real-estate developer."

"Continue to investigate. Let's bring some of these *Power* guys in for questioning, if we can. Let's try and dig up a motive. And good work, Lefkel."

"Now, I like this guy." Elana Goldstein said.

Agent Lefkel accepted the manufactured praise and said, "I'll keep in touch."

At that moment Elana turned and said, "This is murder, Daniel. And we're getting involved.

* * *

On any other day Daniel wouldn't have been convinced to go with Elana Goldstein anywhere, let alone some place off the beaten path to get a glimpse at what the Klan was all about. But she got him all psyched up. It was a Wednesday night and business was slow at the office. Peter saw the political possibilities and also told Daniel to pursue this Klan thing. Peter had a growing confidence in Elana as the ticket to the Senate. His money was on her to find the case he could exploit for Daniel's benefit, so he could secure the party's nomination. Daniel got in Elana Goldstein's car and was following her lead. Where, he wasn't exactly sure.

"I don't want to sound like a wimp, but what do you plan to do when we find these Klan guys lighting a bonfire in the Everglades?" Daniel asked.

"We'll take some pictures," Elana said holding up her 35 millimeter.

"What's in the basket?"

"Some sandwiches and a couple of sodas."

"What is this a Klan picnic?"

"Hey, I'm not into long boring stakeouts. I'm a prosecutor. And I didn't eat lunch."

"Where's Lefkel?"

"He's got paperwork to fill out or something. Let's go. He told me about it. What's the worst thing that can happen? You're the Arian. It's me they want," Elana said flippantly.

"They'll probably make me sign up."

"I think white's your color. So what? I'm driving. We're going for a ride."

Elana and Daniel arrived at a very rural setting dressed in casual clothing. She parked her car off the road. They were twenty miles outside of downtown Miami. The sky was clear. The sun was setting and it would soon get dark.

Daniel was getting nervous. He could feel his palms sweat and his pulse rise. Very often, Elana denied the fear she felt. She was a feel-the-fear kind of woman, and did it anyway. The unconscious barriers that were in ambitious women were worn away with years of practice.

She brought along the camera and the picnic basket. Daniel thought it was Elana's way of being sneaky. To lure Daniel on a date. A part of him was feeling that there wasn't going to be any Klan meeting at all. Elana was getting Daniel nervous as part of some elaborate seduction thing. First, make him nervous. Then with some wine and food, some stars and fresh air, he'd relax. Then he'd be vulnerable. Elana thought to bring a picnic basket along in case they really did get caught by some roving lookouts. They could have a legitimate reason for being where they were and the camera's purpose was to photograph their romantic evening.

Elana and Daniel walked for about a mile into the woods. The massive amount of tall, thick forestry was awesome. Most big cities didn't have one tree very close by. As they walked they could see where the trees ended. It was a sudden stop. Then there were grassy flat lands.

Daniel stopped three hundred yards from the end of the row of trees. Elana took Daniel's lead. She too could feel the urge to stop. She told Daniel to squat down. She produced a camera, which had a telephoto lens.

"This camera is great. I can bring in the picture as if it were right in front of my face. Look, go in the basket. They're binoculars."

"Hey, what's with the champagne?"

"It's for effect. If we get caught, we want to be believed. What romantic couple would have a picnic without wine?"

Daniel looked through the binoculars. All he could see was one R.V. in the distance, and a truck with a trailer.

"What do you see?" Daniel said.

"The same thing you see."

"What do we do now?"

"We eat. There's nothing going on." She began to unwrap a sandwich.

"How did you get this information from Lefkel?"

"He just told me. Said he couldn't do it himself. But, if some ambitious members of the Dade State Attorney's office could recruit some help—"

"He doesn't know that we're out here?"

"I left a note on my desk telling them where they could start looking for our bodies if we don't show up for work tomorrow." Daniel rolled his eyes.

"Great, what would June think?"

"Who cares? You'd be dead." Elana began to crack open the champagne.

"This is a good brand, huh?" Daniel said.

"That's good vintage. It isn't a cereal."

"Right. I knew that."

"Here's to the cutest Senator in the State of Florida." The two toasted. Daniel wondered if this girl was working him. Shouldn't he be working her?

"Thank you, Elana." She was glad he didn't make a funny or whimsical remark to her toast. She liked a man who could take a compliment as well as give one.

"You know, I hope we don't have to make a run for it anytime soon. I'm almost drunk." Elana laughed.

"I can't run either." Daniel said.

"There aren't that many accidents related to drunks driving. I mean, if you don't speed. You won't get a ticket. It happened to my uncle once. He was drunk after my cousin's wedding and a cop made my aunt drive home. —Straighten up, look!" Daniel drew his binoculars.

"Wow, there must be thirty of them. Look, more are pulling up." Elana began snapping pictures. "You can see faces with this lens."

"Let's wait. They're not doing anything."

"Look, they are starting a fire."

"It's eighty degrees out."

"I'm telling you it's ritual. —Let's go kill some Jew, and some niggers," Elana began to sing.

"You're strange."

"One Jew over here. Hi." She sang aloud.

"Cut it out! Jesus. —Well wouldn't you know." Some men began to emerge from the trailer with Klan garb on. Elana continued to snap away.

"Unpack another roll of film for me." The fire began to grow. The night added a brilliant contrast to the flames. "Let's move in closer. I'm losing the faces in the dark."

"Can you get a picture without a flash?"

"Yeah, it's special film."

"Jeez, not so close," Daniel whispered.

"Just a little more."

"Lie flat." They both were on the ground. Daniel threw his tie over his shoulder, and stared through his binoculars. "I didn't know they let women in the club."

"Somebody has to wash the sheets," Elana answered. Daniel enjoyed the fact that Elana wasn't always so serious, but he lost his sense of humor with every hard beat of his heart.

The environment seemed insipid. Just a bunch of people in white sheets singing gospel songs.

"Wait. It's just getting started," Elana said. "There's Brett Forrest. The Grand Wizard of the Miami Klan."

"Who's the starting Center?"

"Shh. He's going to speak through a megaphone."

"*Miami, Miami is not going to be like Jew York.*" Some applause was heard. "*No, we must keep Miami from becoming the hell hole of desegration that other growing cities have become. My question to you lovely people is this: Do you want your children growing up in the wrong colored schools?*"

A woman came out of the trailer holding a baby in her arms. The baby is dressed in a tiny Klan outfit. The "awes" could be heard from the people. She stepped up to the megaphone while Brett Forrest held it to her mouth.

"*This is my baby, Christopher. And he ain't going to grow up with New York values. Growing up in nigger schools. Touching nigger children. No, this boy is going to have Southern values. He's going to lead the charge. If he has to die for it. Because we all have to fight the war. Mothers included. The war is getting them Federal Bureau of Integrators exposed and destroyed. So decent white folk can live in peace.*"

"Hey!" A voice rang out.

"Oh, shit. Get up!" Daniel said.

"Stop right there!" Two men yelled from around some nearby trees.

"Run! Run!" Elana said leaving behind the picnic basket. Their hearts pounded as they sprinted with all their strength.

"Don't turn around, just run!" A shot was heard. Probably from a shogun. Daniel could swear some buck shot whizzed over his head. "Hurry up. Get in the car!"

"Do you have the keys?" Elana asked.

"Shit! You don't have the fuckin' keys!" Another blast was heard.

"I've got them! I've got them." She opened her side and hopped in the car. She popped open Daniel's lock, and they sped off, but not without a trunk full of buckshot in it. They escaped alive.

* * *

Elana pulled up to Daniel's apartment. They both felt they could breathe again. She turned the engine off and smiled.

"Bet you never had a first date like that before?" She began to laugh. So did Daniel. He could still feel the sweat on his finger as he held his head in his hands. Daniel went to unlock his seatbelt and realized that he never buckled it. He slouched down in the seat and sighed.

"How did I ever get involved in this with you?" Daniel loosened his tie.

"Here, why don't you tie your ties like this?" Elana reached over and unwrapped his tie. She re-tied it in a half Windsor knot.

"My grandfather would tie it like this. It gives the appearance of confidence because it's a relaxed kind of knot. It'll help you breathe. It's not so tight around the neck." Daniel liked the way the knot felt and decided that he would wear it from then on.

"Daniel, tell me about June."

"What do you want to know?" Daniel didn't like this type of conversation from someone he felt was infatuated with him.

"You never talk about her. What does she look like?"

"She has blonde hair. She's cute." Daniel nodded that he was finished.

"That's it. Say that you love her. Describe what type of person she is."

"She's a lovely girl. She does a lot of charity work in the community and she cares about me." Daniel didn't like being quizzed about June.

"Where did she go to college?"

"She never went to college." Daniel shifted in his seat.

"She's been married before?"

"Yes, and she has two wonderful kids, Alan and Connie. I love them. I think they're wonderful. They really love me too. Alan wants to be a pilot and Connie wants to be a Barbie doll model." Daniel smiled. Elana pressed her lips together.

"You'd make a wonderful father, Daniel."

"Thanks." Elana reached over and kissed Daniel on the lips. He was shocked at her boldness.

"Can't you just steal the kids and be with me?"

"Whoa, Elana." He smiled and looked away to break the tension. "You're a beautiful girl. And I mean that. You have a very compelling personality. Despite what you may think sometimes I like working with you. I have June. I can't have someone on the side."

"I don't want to be on the side! You make me happy. I enjoy watching you. I love the way you work. I love how you struggle to be a good guy in a slimy political world. You think you can make a difference." Daniel blushed. "Don't marry this girl just because she would be a proper wife. I know I care about you much more than she ever could."

"I can only say this and you probably won't understand. I'll never be able to make you understand. I can only love June the only way I know how. She can love me. I'd never be the man you'd want me to be."

"We'd learn and grow and adjust. I know we could work out. Why make yourself marry someone I know you don't love?"

"June is right for me."

"You don't act like you're in love. You're marrying for politics. My brother got engaged last year. His fiancé is the only thing he talks about. He talks volumes and volumes about how much he loves her."

Daniel smiled. "That's wonderful. Talking about June is just not my style. Doesn't mean I don't love her."

"Woman's intuition."

"Maybe you just are blinded by your feelings." Again Elana kissed him slowly, pushing her tongue into his mouth. Daniel didn't resist but he didn't respond. She pulled away. She looked him in the eyes. He was pale and speechless. Her heart sank. She sensed he was vaguely repulsed. At that moment, she knew she couldn't even be the side-woman.

"Maybe I was wrong. Just go. I mean it. Just get out of my car, please. I'm sorry I was leading myself on." Daniel opened the door and quietly left the car. He didn't look behind.

* * *

Peter Spark didn't want to know how Daniel and Elana Goldstein got the pictures of the Klan rally, but knew that they would make some great front-page newspaper photos. He prepared them for a press conference.

Brad Lefkel was taken off the "Acid Murders" because of his rookie status. Four veteran FBI agents were assigned to look into the motives of the deaths, and the U.S. Attorney for the Southern District of Florida, Alex Giulianti, took charge of the investigation. Months later what turned up was a terrorist white supremist group, linked with the KKK, was categorically killing "uppity blacks."

One case, in 1960, Horace Medford, a black man joined an insurance company. Horace was killed, and the business was burned to the ground. In 1961, Jack Roosevelt, a *Herald* reporter wrote a progressive protest editorial about what he coined as *Hate Crimes*, and shortly after was murdered. Later that same year, Dr. Poindexter Manis, a college professor of Sociology, at the University of Miami was upgraded to associate professor. In 1962, Cory Rand, a successful businessman moved into an apartment on Brickell Avenue. A realtor named Eric Berman, in 1963 encouraged several black families to move into white neighborhoods, was murdered. He was the only white person in the group to be murdered. A local minister of a Baptist parish, Reverend Nathaniel Reed pressed to have the murder of Cory Rand investigated further, and was murdered himself. The last death was a young attorney, Stephan Mills, the first black with the Dade County Public Defender's Office and was killed after the announcement of his first promotion.

For political purposes U.S. Attorney Giulianti, offered up the microphone to Daniel Carlson, the lead attorney who would prosecute the case.

"We sought and received indictments on several members of the Klan group called The Power. Including the leader of the group, Brett Forrest. This group is responsible for several deaths that Mr. Giulianti has spoken of and much more. This type of professional and systematic assassination is part of the destructive force that destroys the civil rights for all Americans.

"This case would not have come together without the help of Elana Goldstein, Dade State Attorney's Office, and Special Agent Brad Lefkel of the Federal Bureau of Investigation. Thank you."

Brad Lefkel tipped his imaginary hat at Daniel in appreciation, and left the courthouse. Elana was also waiting in the corner of the courthouse. Daniel approached her.

"I just wanted to thank you for your work on this case."

"Thank you." Elana sealed herself off from her hurt feelings. "I enjoyed working on it. Thanks for giving my office some of the credit."

"Listen, I really miss our friendship. You haven't really called me about your end of the case. I got approval for you to be loaned to the DOJ for this case."

"I thought you were busy. I have a tendency to be pushy."

"I like your pushiness."

"You know, listen, if you're buttering me up to work on your campaign—"

"No, I'm not. I meant what I said. Please don't be hurt. I really love our friendship. I wish romantic feelings toward you wouldn't interfere."

"You're ambivalent. I thought you were totally not interested."

"How could you think that? I have very strong feelings for you. It just wasn't meant to be."

"I can accept that, Daniel. Let's still be close."

"I'd love it."

"You looked really good during the press conference."

Suddenly, reporters surrounded Daniel again.

"Do you believe that this case, if you win, will make you a likely candidate for your old boss' seat in the Senate?"

Peter responded, "Assistant Department of Justice Attorney Carlson hasn't confirmed any plans to run for the Senate. His main concern is to prosecute these criminals to the full extent of the law."

"This case is definitely a landmark for civil rights in the DOJ. Since this is obviously your peak what other case could there be that could top it? What will be your next case then if you don't run for the Senate this time around?" a reporter asked.

For months preceding the trial, Daniel Carlson gave interviews to reporters and columnists throughout the State. He waxed poetic about the plague of racism in light of the birth of civil rights legislation. In one of those interviews, Daniel coined the phrase *disgracism*, when describing the phenomena of racism turning violent.

★ ★ ★

It was March, and that month was filled with memories of death, for Daniel and the children. The temperature was cool and breezy enough in Florida to sit under the white gazebo in the backyard. The day signified the anniversary of Daniel's mother's death and the harbinger of the anniversary of his uncle's death, which was in a few days. Daniel was thinking about them, especially his mother. He lit a candle that lasted a week for each of them. It was his family's unexplained tradition. His mother did it for her parents, and Daniel just thought it was a nice remembrance.

Sitting and drinking tea with the children seemed strangely formal, but it was a good way to spend time in silence. Alan and Daniel were dressed in suits, and Connie, a pink dress. It was Sunday, and they had just come from church. Daniel didn't feel comfortable in church outside of being with the children. June was elsewhere after church, raising money for some politician running for a congressional seat in Dade County.

Daniel would concentrate on what the minister says in church, he was an animated speaker; charismatic, a politician with his own agenda. Sometimes a seemingly narrow-minded hateful agenda. But he, like everyone else sitting there, turns off his brain and just sits. Daniel didn't feel the spirit with the minister. It was, on the other hand, the right crowd who attended the church. Church is a good place to see people or better yet, to be seen. The Silent Majority goes to church. He could see them there. Now, Daniel Carlson was a church-goer. It translates to a good character. June and Daniel agreed on a Presbyterian church, even though he was raised Episcopalian, and she, a Catholic. June explained it as she felt religious but didn't really want to do formal religious rituals outside of putting up a Christmas tree or making an Easter dinner. She privately referred to herself as *C and E* Christian, Christmas and Easter. Subscribing to certain religious events was another of June's contradictions, according to her. She thought it made her interesting and complex. Daniel didn't want to go round and round about the hypocrisy and the logic of religion.

But his thoughts were focused on his mother, and his sight was hazy as if in a dream. He looked down at the children he would soon adopt, and took a moment to appreciate them. They responded to Daniel's stillness. Alan asked him if anything was wrong. Daniel told him his mother died on this day many years ago, and he couldn't believe he lived so long without her. Alan understood, with a compassion that most children feel, an unforced empathetic comprehension.

"Our daddy died this month too, Daniel," Connie mentioned.

"And Uncle Sammy too," Alan volunteered.

"Imagine them all at a tea party—Dad, Uncle Sammy, and your mom, Daniel. What do you think they would talk about?" Connie wondered aloud.

"That's stupid, they wouldn't talk about anything, they wouldn't even know each other," Alan was put off by Connie's break with reality.

"They are polite people. They would introduce themselves. Daniel's mother would serve the tea, and Uncle Sammy would pass around the sugar cubes. They could talk about trips they've taken. They could talk about us, and how proud they are that we've grown up to be a lady and gentlemen. They would be most proud of Daniel. That he will be a Senator."

Daniel thought about having tea with his mother, and he ached to have a conversation again with her. She was the anti-majority. She was the voice of reason. He replayed one chat in his mind. He was unusually concerned for a child about what he would become. It was in the kitchen of the family home. Daniel was twelve years old, it was lunch time on a Saturday, and the phone finally stopped ringing for his father.

"Daniel, special boys like you don't do things they don't want to do," his mother answered the question, "What if I have a job I don't like? I want people to listen to me. I could teach them about things they don't know. I know how things work. I think that could be fun."

"Then you could be a professor. You need to go to a lot of school for that. But you like school, so that will be fun," Daniel's mother said. Daniel believed her for years after she said it. Daniel didn't know the Silent Majority yet. Daniel was a precocious child. He could do anything. Passion could lead Daniel's way. But she, his maternal angel, along with her foresight, relocated to a loftier plane, and the honest communication he had with himself led him to the disappointing conclusion—he couldn't believe her anymore.

CHAPTER 8

The Making of the Man

S O DECISIONS HAD BEEN made and the wheels were in motion. *Send D.C. to D.C.* versus Phil Taylor who is *Taylor made for the Senate.*

Phil Taylor was excellent for politics. He had a law degree from Florida State University. He was tall, with Robert Redford looks—bright blue eyes and light blonde hair. His family had an estate on Long Island and also a house in the country in northern Florida.

Strategically, about ten years earlier, Phil's father shifted his son's citizenship to the State of Florida to run for the Senate. Phil Taylor was a toy for special interests. If he won, he won on the coattail support of others. If elected, then so be it—but Peter had a trick or two up his sleeve before it would all be over.

A wedding could easily be turned into a campaign event. So a wedding was held for Daniel and June. Daniel hoped for the best of both worlds. He would work in Washington and frequently commute to his constituency in Florida. At least that was the plan. In the meantime, he was pleased the Klan case was over.

He finally did get to try a case. He got a real education on politics within the government while working for the Department of Justice. Daniel was glad that he had a chance to serve there.

June ended up hating Florida. What woman with straight hair would? Wanted to spend most of her time in more sophisticated places like New York. The humidity is overwhelming. But she had accomplished something great. She planned to make Daniel Carlson great. Her ambitions ran high. In her mind, she was an idol-maker. Her lust for a powerful influence was intense. Every step down the wedding aisle was a step toward greatness, not a step forward but a step up.

Because Daniel loved June's children, he would continue to raise them as his own children even though their father wasn't able enough to handle raising them. Their real father dropped the responsibility, dropped out on life. At least that is how June put it.

June's choice of a first husband was poor. He was a poor boy, with a rural upbringing. June said Tom Ware was killed in the war. In a sense he was killed by the war. He ran off after the Vietnam war; leaving all of the responsibility of the children with June. Daniel did not question her deeply on the subject. At this point in politics, he didn't have to. Daniel was resolved, no matter where he would end up in the world of politics; he would always be a good father. Even though he hadn't been there since their births, he felt blessed they were in his world. Connie was wearing a smaller version of the bride's light-pink dress. Alan was wearing a tuxedo that matched the groom's tuxedo.

John Carlson, Daniel's father, wasn't completely satisfied with June as a choice for a wife. John Carlson convinced himself he was a good father, but it wasn't true. He thought he looked out for the best interest of his son. He took Susan Carlson's father's small fortune from bootlegging, and developed it into a strong nest egg for generations of Carlsons to come. Susan Carlson was an only child whose mother died when she was a little girl. Daniel knew little about his grandfather's illegal activities. John Carlson used the money as a weapon over Daniel. But Daniel gave up on the money after college. Daniel paid for law school himself, and that infuriated John Carlson—but got his father's respect at the same time. Regardless of the family fortune, John Carlson made his living as a doctor. He was one of the only non-Jewish cardiologists on Miami Beach. John Carlson secretly resented his Jewish partners, but never spoke openly with Daniel about it. He never spoke with Daniel openly about anything. Once Daniel announced that he was running for the Senate, he was the father of a future Senator, and that was better than being Jewish.

Peter wasn't the only one nudging Daniel into the world of politics, Daniel's father had a helping hand. All those years of financially supporting incumbents, John Carlson was happy Daniel was finally getting his turn for Party support. John Carlson didn't like the fact June had children either. He didn't have anything against the children personally. He didn't really know them, nor did he make an effort to. He wouldn't get close to children that were not his son's. The family legacy shouldn't go to mutts. It just didn't seem right.

Politically, it was acceptable, if not laudable—instant family. It's American. If Daniel were divorced, that would be a different story. Politicians need to have a strong family life. To let a family fall apart through divorce was unacceptable. It was the '70s—leaders had wives. It was radical enough that Daniel waited so long to get married in the first place.

June's children weren't the only objection. June was a small town country girl, without an upbringing of any sort. The in-laws were almost embarrassing to be introduced to the distinguished guests. The father drove around with a pickup truck with a gun-rack, and went bowling twice a week. Not a total loss, John Carlson thought, they would probably be a hit campaigning upstate with the country folk.

Starting out running for Senator was incredibly ambitious. Daniel had a young distinguished career, but was only approaching his mid-thirties. Luck can play a part in politics. With Bratton out and the opposition also fielding a young candidate, there would be opportunity for Daniel to succeed. His father's money and contacts in the business community would help Daniel. Republican or Democrat it's good to have *the purses* backing you.

Daniel's mother was Susan Carlson. She was also a protective woman in a passive-aggressive way—a soft-spoken lady. Her job in life was that she served in her community doing service-oriented projects, an active community member. She was a lovely looking woman. Daniel had only good memories of her. But a long life for her was not meant to be.

Susan Carlson died of breast cancer when Daniel was in his third year of college. He was called home at an out-of-town track meet. Their home on Miami Beach was never the same without her. In her death, Daniel deified her. She was the woman that protected him against her father. She was the floor. The thin blue line of protection from the emotional abuse meted out by John Carlson.

Daniel remembered asking his cousin, when he was young, what it meant to be dead. Years later, when his mother died, he remembered what she said, "You don't eat. You can't brush your hair. You just lie there and don't move." But it was much more than that. The things that annoyed Daniel about his mother, when she died, endeared her to him. She was his refuge from the judgmental world symbolized by his father.

Susan Carlson would've liked June. Susan Carlson liked everyone. If Daniel picked her, she would've loved her. June's children would've had another grandmother too. Susan never did any harm. Her love for her family was deep and seemingly endless. The male Carlsons would remember it for a lifetime. Perhaps that's why Daniel waited so long to get married; or, perhaps he just waited. For sure that is why John Carlson never remarried. Susan was a tough act to follow. And, John Carlson was difficult. All plutocratic, high society standards of John Carlson removed, John Carlson looked at June and didn't see Susan. Since she wasn't, she was subject to the criticisms of John's insurmountable standard.

June dreamed about getting an apartment in Georgetown for all four of them. She wanted to send the kids to boarding school, but Daniel overruled, and would enroll them into a local private school. The children weren't props to him even though he knew he would be criticized for doing exactly what he was doing. And, they weren't British. There was real and unreal in Daniel's world. He wouldn't be an unreal father. So his idealistic self said.

Peter was the best man and Melissa was June's matron of honor. Daniel and June were both happy that they were at their sides. Peter was happy for Daniel. He was satisfied that Daniel was finally getting married. Politically, it was good to be married. There was only one President in history that was single. Irrelevant it seemed, but Peter was particularly sensitive to the relevant irrelevancies in politics. Nonetheless, still believed that Daniel had to stay on track with the profile of a sharp political man of the future. Peter would be responsible for Daniel's future, and vice versa. Symbiotic relationships can be dangerous, however. Emotionally, one will be hurt when the other doesn't meet the first's expectations. Such was the risk, but both were willing to take the chance. In politics you dance with the one that brought you. That's why picking who you brought to the dance was critical to a career. They enjoyed working together. Daniel and June grew to be friends. Peter and Daniel grew to be true friends.

The ceremony was special. Connie was the flower girl and Alan was the ring bearer. John Carlson's estate was decorated lavishly. A cool breeze helped make the outdoor wedding a pleasure. Many of the guests were strangers to June, and some even to Daniel. Somehow even weddings can be politicized. The right people need to be invited in order to feel like they were intimate with the candidate. These people were judges, businessmen, and other politicians, all with big purses. They were always known as, *the purses.* Democrat or Republican, though it was a rule that Daniel would try to evade, override, and circumvent a truth in politics. He who controls the purse of the leader, controls the leader. Only the deft leader could control the purses. It's called power.

As the minister recited the matrimonial vows, Daniel looked into June's eyes. At that moment, and for the first time, he fell in love with June. He took her hand and held it. For all his faults she accepted him. It was seemingly unexplainable why it appeared that Daniel sought acceptance of any type. She was willing to put their differences aside for a lifetime. Daniel liked to believe that she meant she had an unconditional love for him.

Clarence Terrell, a friend of Daniel's, packed him some pornographic tapes as the couple entered the limousine bound for Miami International Airport. The new couple were bound for a two week tour of Europe sponsored by Daniel's father. The support was necessary based on, Marksman, Daniel's accountant's assessment of Daniel's financial outlook.

On the way to the airport Daniel continually kissed June on the cheek. She smiled and said she enjoyed every moment of the ceremony. She, like Melissa, would be suitable and ready for a life of politics. The only difference between June and Melissa, is that Melissa would tolerate Peter's life in politics, and June would thrive on it. June slid his hand up her wedding dress and moved up her inner thigh. She then said: "We're going to have a great time."

* * *

Back and refreshed from a honeymoon in Europe. Daniel walked into his new office, Campaign Headquarters. Signs and posters were already made. A photograph of him was perfect, and was somewhere on every piece of campaign literature and propaganda. He greeted everyone. Many were working hard to spread the name recognition of Daniel Carlson. He smiled and waved. He told everyone they were doing great and he was about to join them in their efforts.

Peter beckoned Daniel into his office to discuss strategy.

"Hello, Daniel. How was the honeymoon?"

"Fantastic. I had a wonderful time. June really enjoyed France and Italy."

"Wonderful. I'm so glad. You're going to have a great life together. So let's get going."

"Great," Daniel said recognizing small talk and fun time was over.

"Early strategy is our *puppet* propaganda. *Taylor is made for taxes*. We have everyone coming up with colorful slogans. *Taylor made for* . . . I mean we have cartoonists working at the *Herald*, at the *St. Pete Times*, all over. We gave them a lot of food for thought. We start with lofty goal outlining. Until we come up with concrete support and plans. We put him on the defensive. We'll talk about Space, how we're really the ones who are tough on communism and crime. We'll say that while he was smooching special interest butts, we were fighting crime with the Justice Department. When he finally turns around and attacks us, it will be too late. He will look like a last minute whiner. Trust me, I know the campaign firm he hired. While we're making solid proposals to rectify these ills, he'll still be saying your Senator Bratton's boy. Since Bratton is stepping down, everyone will still like him. We kind of deny that you are a Bratton boy, and then we get the best of both worlds. That, along with a mini-scandal or charge late in the campaign and I'll say we'll be taking the next flight to D.C. Lastly, I believe we should hire Roger Rock as a campaign consultant. He really has a handle on polls and all that statistical stuff. He would be an asset," Peter concluded.

"I don't know. What about his reputation? It's not the best. I don't think we should risk it," Daniel said. What Daniel was really concerned about was Rock's reputation as a negative campaigner. Rock was the grand-master of opposition research also known as *the smut peddler.*

"We're going for the progressive campaign, right? I think it should all start today. Listen, the guy's business is his own. Not for us to pass judgment," Peter responded.

"I don't know. Image is everything. We have to with Bratton's coattails. I don't think our image can handle—" Daniel said.

"Daniel, Bratton told us to try and sever ties with him as best as we could."

"He's supporting us publicly."

"Daniel, you're being naive. I love the guy personally. But let's distance ourselves from him okay. We have to sell you as a person with his own mind and own ideals. Otherwise we're going to lose major support in the party and we'll have to fight for the nomination. That's just what we need: a weakling in the primaries. We have one. Bob Fielding is very close to running. I want to concentrate on Phil Taylor; we're going to attack Phil for being a pawn of the special interests. You must have solid ideals, which Terrence did, and we share. But we have new ideas, and a separate agenda. Okay?"

"I hope you won't sell me down the river, if I mess up, Mr. Prosecutor."

"Don't you think you're being a little sensitive?" Daniel replied.

"No, I don't. If you want to know the real truth, and I'm going to tell it to you straight." Daniel shut the door on the campaign workers. "Since we're breaking each other down psychologically what would you say to the idea that you're compensating for your scar."

"What! What the hell are you talking about?"

"Hear me out."

"This is personal bullshit," Peter yelled.

"Man, you're my friend. I got to clear this in my own mind if I'm to know you're with me."

"I'm your best friend. I'm going to be your campaign manager. We're going to win this election. Then you're going to make me your special counsel. Understand? I'm with you!"

"Tell me what happened. Since Bratton cut the legs out from under your career, you haven't been yourself. You've had the scar since I've known you. How bad could it be? Did your mother hit you with an iron or something?" Daniel asked. Peter smiled. Daniel had no idea. Peter wasn't the type of man who would get a scar like that as a child—or worse doing something childish.

"No. My mother never touched me. What I'm going to tell you is personal. I wouldn't exactly call it a skeleton, but I wish you wouldn't repeat it, ever. In fact, after I tell you I don't want to discuss it, okay?"

"Yeah, sure."

"Fine, Daniel. After I tell you, you decide whether you still want me running your campaign." Daniel gave a quizzical look, but nodded to continue. Peter's state changed immediately to a somber state and he spoke in a solemn tone.

"When you were hoping to join and instead started counting canned fruit, stateside, I was in Saigon. I was with the Naval Intelligence Service. To make a long and sad story short, I got cut by a piece of exploding glass and shrapnel. One of my buddies was killed in the explosion. He was covering a drop for me. You know, an intelligence drop. Well, it was a set up. It was meant for me. I ran to the site when I heard. Right after I saw he was blown to bits, a second device went off. For the rest of my life I have guilt on the inside and guilt scratched down the side of my face. I guess it cost me a career in politics. You're lucky you never went, Daniel. It changed everyone who did." In the speed of a thought, Daniel believed it was Peter who was the lucky one to avoid the career in politics. Daniel dismissed the thought and went back to the conversation.

"I never knew you were in the war."

"Not something I talk about."

"So, is your real name Spark?" Daniel asked.

Peter laughed. "Yeah, it is. But once you're in an Intelligence service you're connected for life."

"So that's what Bratton was talking about in his office," Daniel just pieced together, and then out of self-preservation and ambition dismissed it. Peter didn't respond. "We're going to win this election. Then in the near future we're going to show the American people what progressive thinking is all about. You're going to be a powerful politician. Americans are going to love your scar."

"Wait, Daniel. I just want to help you. I'm not looking for any growing *kumbaya* experience from this."

Daniel took a moment to think.

"Okay, I'll be the front man in this two-man band. And since we're rapping about skeletons, I think we better talk and decide whether you want to continue to help me." Peter raised his eyebrows. "Let's go for a walk."

"Whoa. I thought I had sensitive stuff. This really must be sensitive stuff."

"Well, you have experience in it. What I'm about to tell you should never be talked about, and nobody else knows. But if it ever came out, I'd be finished permanently. It would bring you down too, if you're with me."

"Unless you were Adolf Hitler, I'm always going to be behind you. We're a team, right?"

"Right. Let's go for that walk then."

CHAPTER 9

Primary Education

Daniel Carlson sulked on the inside as he delivered the same speech over and over. He had to deliver it with the same gusto each and every time. He had to sell the same speech, with day-to-day modifications. It was the stump speech. It was boring. What he had to do to become Senator, made him forget why he was doing it. Daniel felt he was losing himself in the process. He felt he was being handled by Peter, by Senator Bratton, and by the party. It wasn't about Daniel Carlson being the best man, it was about him being the man who fit the position. The man who fit the role. The man the Silent Majority wanted on election day. Daniel Carlson pounded Phil Taylor with the criticism Taylor was a puppet of his party's powerful. At the end of the campaign, Daniel Carlson felt the same. With the victory, however, came benefits, if Daniel Carlson wanted them.

* * *

The cheers of victory were still ringing in Daniel Carlson's ears. Senator Carlson from Florida. Daniel took the morning to think about some of the people he would bring on the staff and who would be his advisors during the next six years.

Elana Goldstein wouldn't be on staff with Daniel in Washington. Surely, she would remain a confidant. Her guidance was accurate. Her understanding of him was deep. She was his friend. A friend that didn't give him lip service. She would pump his ego when he was down, but always demonstrated her honesty when she was asked, or wasn't asked her opinion.

"So, are you going to remember us small people in Washington?" Elana Goldstein asked.

"Maybe as small as you, but no smaller," Daniel said sarcastically.

"Another politician who can't relate," she snapped back. Daniel sensed she was somewhat serious.

"What are you saying?"

"I'm saying don't forget the reason why you did this. Go to Washington and fight for the good guy. You'll see big business interests are going to jump all over you because you're a freshman Senator. Take you out to dinner, give you gifts. And the people are going to make passes at you all day long—they're called lobbyists."

"Elana, I'll remember. I can resist. I'm not a virgin to all of this."

Daniel threw himself into the chair at his desk and put his feet up on his desk. He was sad to be leaving his job at the Department of Justice, after a leave of absence. The fact that he had to leave his favorite chair behind triggered a feeling of nostalgia.

Elana stood at the other side of the desk. She stopped packing Daniel's belongings away and listened to what he had to say. "My father of all people, probably inadvertently, made me empathize with the working man when I was in high school. One weekend he asked me to type something for him—something work related.

I forgot to do it. I was a kid and had better things to do than that. Well, he yells at me like I've never been yelled at. He made Peter look like a concerned educator."

Daniel likened his father to the evil aspect of the Silent Majority. Do what we know is best, not what you think is right. You're logic fails because you have no experience. Sympathizing with others is no way to live. Daniel was young. He was stubborn.

"He decided to teach me responsibility. If I say I'm going to do something, damn it, I'm going to do it. My father decided that life was too easy for me, so he cut me off. And I don't mean just my allowance. He took away all spending money. Wouldn't let me withdraw from my savings account. No credit cards in those days for a kid my age. I couldn't drive my car, which included going to school. A friend wasn't allowed to drive me either. I had to walk. He forbade my mother from making my lunch. My mother would slip me a couple of dollars so I could buy something at school. I considered that welfare. I had to stay away from the house until six o'clock, when dinner was served. Then I had to leave and couldn't come home until ten o'clock at night. This included weekends."

"So what happened? Did you rebel?" Elana asked.

"But I didn't eat dinner. I either sat there or didn't come home. It was a war of wills." Daniel secretly wished he had such clarity today. He was scared that he would not be able to fight the current of the Silent Majority in the Senate. He had some power. But, would he have to get along with the Silent Majority?

"I didn't care after awhile. I started an afterschool program and tutored kids in the neighborhood. I had a couple of kids whose parents couldn't afford my fee, so I gave them a scholarship. It turned out I like teaching and I was good at it. That was one of my happiest times. I learned that not everyone learns the same way. So, I would come up with different ways of teaching the same thing. It helped me and them. My hope was to be able to do that during the campaign—teach. But that didn't happen much. What it turned out to be was advertising. I'm hoping things will be different."

"When did the standoff with your father end?"

"My mother couldn't handle it anymore. He was punishing her. She told my father she wouldn't allow him to cut me off anymore. It was six months before the whole thing ended. Then my father didn't want me to tutor anymore. I did. We didn't speak my entire senior year of high school," he said.

Daniel harkened back as a victorious warrior. He beat his father's will. But will he be able to defeat the new father in his life? The father that didn't know best. The father that was a petulant child.

"It was then you discovered you had remarkable powers of understanding," she said. "And now you taught me that so do I." Elana then tossed a thick edition of "Corpus Juris Secundum" that hit Daniel dead on his chest. He yelled out in pain. Elana answered, "For instance, I know that hurt like hell."

"Very funny. Now get back to work."

* * *

Daniel was ushered into the ballroom as the sound of his name bellowed through a microphone. He didn't know the man who announced his presence but the man pretended to be a close friend of Daniel's when he entered the room with June.

"I would like to thank you all. I want to thank everyone in the campaign who helped me." Daniel adjusted the microphone. "Immigration reform is critical to the foreign policy issue of this country. Lady liberty proclaims the words of freedom. To accept the tired and the weary—the huddled masses longing to breathe free. On my agenda is to have sound immigration reform. If we do not, one day we will have people from oppressed lands perishing on rafts and climbing ladders to travel to this land. Let's be prepared. Imagine the horror if we had to turn freedom seekers away. To come here with a yearning for freedom and a will to succeed only to have freedom's doors be closed. Join me in support of a home-land in America for all those who want freedom."

With loud applause he stepped down from the podium and began to shake hands. He dared not give out a comprehension test to anyone on his remarks. They would fail miserably. This was a victory party. All those present had their own agenda to be pressed. Perhaps they would throw support for Daniel's bill if he supported theirs. Daniel's power account had no credits.

He thought that the *word* power he commanded was an act of courtesy. It was not. It was on an account to be paid at a later date. As a freshman Senator he was owed very little on his power account. In six years a Senator can run up a tab.

On the Senator floor, a visitor, Elana Goldstein, spied the able freshman Senator Daniel Carlson speaking. Two minutes were yielded to the Gentleman from Florida. Daniel spoke: ". . . My colleagues. Whenever a bill like this is introduced, it threatens a system that we all know very well. Something Americans all over the country expect, either as supplemental income or in some cases—some very sad cases—as sole support in our later years. Yes, Social Security is a pillar, an establishment in our Amer-ican system of government." The Senate chamber boomed with Daniel's resoundingly energetic voice. It echoed sweetly—slightly off the top domed ceiling.

"Even to entertain any alternatives to a system so accepted . . . a system that is America, in good times and bad. We must not vote for this bill—the domino that sets a momentum against the very established economic pride of our country. Thank you." Daniel turned to the President of the Senate and said, "I yield the rest of my time to the gentleman from Iowa."

Senator Carlson overcame his fear of speaking in front of the Senate. He was so adept at speaking, yet feared that once he was a Senator, he would be considered a fraud. He saw the podium as all his fears erected into one symbol, one revealing symbol: that he was an imposter. That he was nothing but a school teacher. The best he could do is teach an occasional civics lesson. Ironic that his fear was the one thing that could've made Daniel live in happiness.

The first time he had spoken on the floor of the Senate, Daniel quoted Andrew Jackson. The quote was about courage. Really, the quote was for himself, but it worked in quite well with his speech. This is the first time he had a chance to overcome what was developing as the inner demon of the Silent Majority. And it appeared that the vote before the speeches were going one way, however, when the votes were counted at the end of the day, it mysteriously went Daniel's way. He didn't really go out on any political limb. A Senator from Florida giving a speech about protecting social security was predictable. A real challenge would have been a speech about proposed reform to social security. But Daniel Carlson knew that he couldn't even bring up the subject or risk being thrown out of the party. Was it just political reality, or reality? Or was it something more insidious. Something that would make Daniel spring up from his sound sleep to wonder if he is selling out his spirit's purpose.

Daniel quickly glanced up and felt Elana's presence. He loved his friend quietly and from afar.

CHAPTER 10

Secondary School

D ANIEL WAS NUMB AFTER a long day of walking and lobbying for his free trade/immigration to Cuba bill. A bill he was trying desperately to get through Congress. The fear of *being ahead of his time* has Daniel motivated to work harder to communicate his ideas. The novelty of being a freshman Senator has worn off. Work was starting to feel like work. Yet, Daniel took pleasure in knowing that he was firmly in place in his job for the next six years. After the first election, the second is much easier and so on. Each time out was much easier, unless you fell into scandal or lost favor with the Silent Majority.

★ ★ ★

Daniel entered the Florida home and the house was quiet and empty. It was a welcome change. The quiet made it seem like there was an end to the contained nuclear reaction, which was the schedule he kept for the past three weeks. Three weeks of constant meetings and receptions, and luncheons. He felt like he didn't get a blessed thing done.

Daniel was depressed. The visit to his mother's grave wasn't the best exercise for his mental health, but he felt he had to. It was the only way he could get away from his aides. No one wanted to go to a cemetery unless absolutely necessary. Besides the only voters that were there were the voters that helped put Eisenhower in office. It was the only way Daniel could commune with his increasingly vocal minority. The little voice inside his head that said go ahead and do the right thing. Be who you are. Comfort is correctness, in logic, and certitude.

As Daniel turned up the stairs he heard a noise coming from Connie's room. He couldn't figure out what type of noise it was. It sounded like a wail or whine. He heard the phone slam down.

He knocked on her door. "Who is it?" Connie sounded annoyed.

"It's your father."

"Oh," she replied. Daniel opened the door slowly. He saw Connie was crying. Her hair was messy.

"Who'd you think it would be?"

"I thought it would be Mom—making a big deal about something."

"Well, it's me. What's going on? You want to talk? I think this is the first time we can in a long time. Poor kids are growing up not even in front of my eyes." Daniel embraced Connie. Then they both sat on her bed.

"I just got into a fight with a friend. It wasn't really a fight. And it isn't just a friend," she said crying into her hands. The number sixteen popped into Daniel's mind and he realized that's how old Connie was. He hoped it was something important only to a teenager that she was crying about.

"Was this friend sort of a boy?" Daniel asked.

"Yes," she said with a sigh of embarrassment.

"You got into a fight with a boyfriend?"

"Sort of." Connie fidgeted with her hands in her mouth. "You see when you, Mom, and Alan were away in Washington last week and I was here by myself..."

"You had a party?" Daniel tried to make light.

"No, Dad!" she whined. "I kind of went out with this guy Jeff. He wasn't really my boyfriend but we went to the movies and then we came back here." She paused to check if her father was catching on and getting angry. She couldn't detect anything so she continued. "We came in and sat down by the couch and started kissing. Then we went upstairs," she held her breath for a moment. So did Daniel. "And we had sex." Connie released her breath with a sigh. She glanced up waiting to see her father's reaction to what she had just told him.

Daniel thought for a moment. He wasn't shocked. He hoped that Connie wouldn't be so open to her mother. He came up with an outline of what he wanted to say. There was no point in shaming his daughter, but he wanted certain values inculcated into her head. When he thought *inculcated* he meant *beaten*. He understood what had happened. She slept with a boy while getting carried away on a date when the parents weren't home. Now the boy wants nothing to do with her.

Daniel took a deep breath. He wasn't comfortable discussing sex with Connie but knew that she could never go to June.

"Do you know if you're pregnant?"

"No, I'm not."

Daniel sat, leaned his back against the bed post and put his feet up on the bed.

"Girls and sex are a mystery to boys. Kids your age have been interested in the opposite sex for quite some time by your age, but haven't been able to do anything about it. It's hard to kiss a girl goodnight if your parents are in the front seat, right?" Connie listened.

"Now that boys have cars, and parents let children stay home by themselves, opportunity sometimes comes faster than the children are ready."

"I didn't mean to take advantage of the situation, Dad. It just happened."

"I don't mean to say you took advantage of me. But were you fair to yourself? You slept with a boy you didn't know very well, and entered into a risky relationship, and now this boy doesn't want to remember your name, right?"

"He won't even talk to me on the phone anymore," she said.

"Do you deserve that kind of treatment? That boy was to some point interested in you, but unfortunately you could've been almost any girl. A lot of boys get pressure to have sex even before they're ready. Most of the time it is from their fathers who live vicariously through their sons' conquests."

"You mean he told his father!" Connie realized.

"Maybe."

"How can I get him to talk to me again?"

"Forget, Jeff. Write him off. He doesn't want to show you respect for whatever happened; he doesn't deserve you." For a split second Daniel heard himself speak in the voice of his mother. "You are gorgeous. And high school is a tough age to believe that you're wonderful. But trust me, send this guy Jeff a cool breeze his way, and he'll do one of two things: go away, or not leave you alone. Either way you'll get over him." Connie started to cheer up.

"You really think so?"

"It's politics. Just like I do every day. You don't have to be ashamed of what you did. Just realize that you got what every boy wants. And I don't just mean sex. You can offer the real you. And that guy will be very lucky."

"Why is there so much pressure to do it? I mean when did you do it, the first time?"

"Well, I was older than most, but it's a different type of pressure for boys. And there is a double standard. Boys become men, but it's not the same for girls. I think girls are probably ready at an older age than boys. It's a complicated emotional issue even as an adult."

Connie hugged her father. He thanked God he had a relationship with June's children. He was wondering whether to tell her not to have sex again until she was older. He felt guilty for going away, and not being at home. How could he have let this happen?

"Do you know for sure you're not pregnant?" He couldn't help but ask again.

"I had my period," Connie answered. "I know getting pregnant would hurt your career in politics." Daniel was hurt by that comment.

"I think it would hurt you. Would you want to raise a baby at your age? Worse, would you want to have to have an abortion?" Daniel was inspired to walk away from politics for life, if it meant being there for his family. Why he didn't say that to Connie he regretted moments later.

"I don't think it will happen again," Connie offered.

"It's not like promising never to stay out late again. It's a heat of the moment thing. It could happen again, and you need to know that. So you're better prepared to deal with it using your brain instead of your emotions."

Connie appreciated this sage advice as best as she could for someone who was lying about what was the real problem. She couldn't even tell her father what was eating at her. Connie laid out some facts that would distract and explain why she wouldn't be herself in the weeks to come. Connie was protecting Daniel from a political nightmare, which he would have to live with if the press ever found out what she did. Connie thought Daniel, her father, was worth the protection.

Suddenly the telephone rang and delivered even more news. Doctor John Carlson was dead of a heart attack.

★ ★ ★

Daniel began dealing with his father's death. It was always in the back of his mind, creeping to frontal consciousness from moment to moment. A man who was an adequate father. Whose best thing he ever did in life, and didn't know it, was to marry Daniel's mother. He's gone and Daniel was morose for different reasons. He wished they could've been closer. Probably like every child, regardless of how a father has treated him. Children are programmed by some instincts to seek the love of his parents, even the bad ones. Daniel knew he never could get closer to his father.

John Carlson could only understand so much. Even though John Carlson was a man of science, he was quick to accept that this is the way it is, and Daniel must adapt, rather than attempt to change. The man could only forgive to a certain point. He never could've accepted Daniel unconditionally. Daniel concluded: thank God I pleased him by being a Senator. It was nice having him pleased with me, no matter how fleeting. Daniel reluctantly conceded his father was a member of the Silent Majority. The vocal disgruntled. A man with so much fortune could still conclude, the government was against him, the system was plotting against him, and everything he did for others turned out to be the ungrateful. Some fathers can never be pleased. With those instincts to seek love is the child's ability to con himself into thinking he can please the unappeasable father. Daniel was having difficulty coming to terms. John Carlson's tombstone would be in place, and Daniel was taking time out to visit his grave tomorrow.

★ ★ ★

Daniel wore a coat, even though it wasn't very cold. He enjoyed putting his hands deep into the pockets and pressing down hard. He walked out alone to the middle of the graveyard. No one else was there. It was quiet. Only a cool breeze rustled the flimsy branches of neighboring trees.

Daniel liked the way the gravestone appeared—not too gaudy. He never liked the overdone gravestone; or, the whole overdone funeral ceremony. The person's dead—what's to gain by lavish funeral processions? It must be to prove to the world, this is evidence I loved my father. Or worse, "Dad, are you pleased now?"

Daniel looked down at the grass, unable to stare directly at his father's grave. He felt ashamed. Like the irrational belief that a child can please the unpleased parent, Daniel had a belief about the dead. He believed that after death the spirit becomes omniscient. The Great Education as he called it. A person dies and all the questions he asked or didn't ask on earth are answered. It may be a childish theory, unable to be proven or disproved; still, it was Daniel's belief.

"Hello, Father. You got a nice tombstone, didn't you? I miss you. I feel we can be closer now, Father, now that you're gone. It's sad that it had to be that way, but I know that it was best this way. So now you know. You know the real me. You know the pain that has been encapsulated in my viscera for what seems like an eternity. What do you think of me now? Do you still love me?" Daniel paused to sob some more. "I'm still a Senator. I'm a powerful man in spite of, huh? I still love you. Hopefully with your education you've learned understanding. I hope you can forgive me." Daniel wiped the tears from his eyes and spoke about a more lucid topic.

"So you're with Mom now. That must be a bonus about dying last—you get greeted by such wonderful company. I still wait for Mom to yell something to me at the front door of our home. I'm so happy that I'm sad when I don't hear her voice. I figured that over time I might forget things about her. I still remember everything. I can still hear her voice, Father. I can't forget it. It's wonderful. I'm jealous you get to have her to yourself. I can walk around and smile and say innocuous things like: 'Hi, hi, how's it going? Real great to see you.' I function just fine to the onlooker. But they don't know my pain. All I have is my children, now that you're gone. I wish peace to your soul—rest well." Daniel placed one rock that was in his pocket, on top of the tombstone, turned to the right, and placed another stone atop the tomb bearing the name, Susan Carlson. Another family tradition.

CHAPTER 11

Phalange

STEVE VANN STARED AT his shoes and his watch wishing that he had a cigarette to smoke, but promised his wife, Johanna standing beside him, that he would quit. The blond man with a ponytail stood impatiently with his wife in a crowded corner of the airport in Beirut—the jewel of the Middle East. Steve swore a life of PTA meetings and a steady job if he would just get out of the Middle East. Steve was willing to make a deal with God or the Devil, he was desperate and only wanted to take the plane to Paris, Paris to New York, and New York to Miami.

Johanna could only be described as sweet to those who knew her. She had no enemies, had no desire to define herself through making enemies. Her slicked back black hair and plump structure didn't advertise the beautiful harmless creature she was inside. She only wanted to be loyal to her family. Her son was home in Miami, and she was with her husband in the middle of the ruins, the eye of the swirling storm of religious love.

For in this hurricane of Jesus versus Allah remained another war. A war that left Johanna asking why she would be so loyal to a man who was, in the eyes of the law, a drug dealer. The answer came easily, in her eyes, Steve was a caring husband whose only crime was that he had an anarchist streak within him, and still was a holdover hippie from the seventies. He was egocentric and cocky, and she couldn't help resenting him for getting caught with so much marijuana. Steve made a deal, but not with God or the Devil.

Steve Vann traveled with Johanna to Beirut and set up a heroin deal with some men of considerable power in the region on his own behalf, and perhaps on behalf of others. Both Steve and Johanna knew Lebanon well. They were both students at the University of Beirut for many years before the tragedy. Steve was comfortable with the deal. He wanted to plea out his arrest—get credit for time served and some supervised release. He was not just working for himself, however. Steve worried about his son at home. He prayed that his mother was taking care of Alex; that Alex was getting to school on time, getting enough to eat.

Steve cursed silently to himself that the flight had been delayed again. He didn't feel right about the whole deal. It wasn't in and out. There were a few more men with guns, and grenades; some extra assurances that they would check him out, to see if he was who he said he was. "The Americans talk too," they assured Steve. That's what made him nervous. Who in Washington would casually leave his file in plain view on his desk for the wrong person to see?

There wasn't law and order in this neighborhood. These men have killed and would kill again to make a point to the rest of the people who dealt with them. There were no courts. One could get away with murder, bury the body in the sand, and that was it. Unless one was protected by the government of the United States, say a confidential informant of the DEA—but only if the United States government wanted to admit it.

The Phalange militia acted against Steve Vann because a friend he introduced to them owed $1.5 million. Steve vouched for him by merely introducing his friend; therefore, it was Steve's fault. He would have to pay. As always, it was hot in Beirut. It wasn't much cooler inside the airport. Nine men dressed as Arab soldiers, with their faces covered, wielding AK47 assault rifles walked into the airport, and marched Steve and Johanna out without much of a fuss. They were afraid to scream. No one in the airport seemed to notice even though the gunmen were carrying machine guns. In the Middle East if you wear some type of uniform and carry a rifle, you blend. They were transported in a VW van that would match Steve' aura, but his karma became distorted and irregular.

Steve and Johanna were kept alive in captivity for 19 months. There, in a sealed building in Beirut, they stayed hoping they would be freed. They were eventually released—scarred and traumatized, hoping that the day would be realized that their release was mishandled by the U.S. State Department. Their lives were left in peril because the DEA failed to come to their defense; denying that the Vanns were working on their behalf. Their day in court would come. They expected vindication; as Florida residents, they went to Senator Daniel Carlson for justice.

★ ★ ★

It was almost two years earlier on a cool winter night on a long stretch of highway in northern Florida. Steve Vann was ironically playing country music and enjoying it. With his unsophisticated model radio, country was the only music that came in clearly.

Steve Vann had left Jacksonville nearly two hours earlier and the sun was dipping into the horizon tracing a fiery pink skyline of beauty. The set traced a sun that could only be experienced through sight, one that a camera couldn't replicate. In an instant, the peak of beauty faded away.

Steve was cruising exactly at the speed limit when he noticed the Florida State Trooper behind him. His heart rate rose but he commanded himself to remain calm—he wasn't doing anything wrong.

Steve regretted his last thought when he saw the blue lights go on atop of the police car. He hoped that his tail light had malfunctioned, he would get a ticket, and that would be the end of it.

The trooper approached Steve with his hand on his gun. By the time the police officer told Steve to step out of the car another trooper arrived.

When the first trooper got finished examining Steve's license and registration three more officers pulled up on this lonely stretch of highway. Steve was concerned about all the attention. He got tense when he saw a sergeant approach him.

"Mr. Vann?" The sergeant said. "We would like you to open the trunk of this here vehicle."

Steve Vann was an intelligent man and knowledgeable about the law. "First, I'd like to know why you stopped me. I mean don't you guys have an old lady to walk across the street?"

"Well—"

"Then I would like to see your search warrant," Steve said clearly and in a moderate tone.

"Well, Mr. Vann. The Sheriff up in Jacksonville just arrested your friend you just visited and he said that he sold five pounds of marijuana to you. That's our reasonable suspicion for stopping you. And this search warrant here," the sergeant showed it to him, "says I can impound the car and search for the drugs if you don't oblige."

Steve wanted to disappear, vanish. He opened the trunk of the car and the block of marijuana was in plain view. It was over. He was placed under arrest and the State had first dibs on interviewing him, but not for long. Vann was part of a drug network that the federal government was interested in.

★ ★ ★

Peter sat at the edge of Daniel's desk with his feet up smoking a cigarette. It had become a Friday evening ritual the two confidants enjoyed. It allowed Daniel to see a soft human side of Peter. The end of the week was the peak of exhaustion for both men. Peter would relax and let his guard down. He would trust Daniel not to reveal his compassion to anyone else in the political world.

"What is on your mind?" Peter asked with sincere concern.

"I'm sort of disturbed with this letter I received from Congressman Beecham, about Steve Vann. Have you read it?"

"Yes, I read it just before you did."

"Do you believe the DEA could do such a thing, Peter? Leave an agent of theirs out in the cold?"

"Wait, an agent? More like a cooperator, right?" Peter corrected. Daniel nodded, yes. "Well, what we know is this: this guy is a drug dealer who was trying to beat a long prison sentence by helping the government. The question is whether he was acting on their behalf on his last trip—the trip he was abducted."

"You didn't answer me," Daniel insisted.

Peter waited. He thought some more, and answered: "Yes, I believe they could do such a thing. But you have to realize that he's already free and we would only be hurting the government. His lawsuit is asking for $40 million."

"You see, that disturbs me that you would think a government agency could abandon someone they asked to work for them. No matter who it is. How would you've liked it when you were with them?"

"My boys in the Navy would never hang me out to dry like that!" Peter said emphatically. And Daniel noted Peter's use of the present tense.

"I want you to check it out. Make some inquiries at DEA."

"I will, but I don't think it wise. I'm not going to make a lot of noise about it."

"Sometimes you just have to do what's right, Peter, and forget about how it looks." Daniel's resolve was immovable. He came to terms with the fact that he would not be a teacher; he was way off the track. Since that was clear, he was just going to do his job as he saw it—idealistically—no ambition, no quid pro quo to powerful forces that be. He waited to see how long that could last—and whether it could really work.

★ ★ ★

Peter ran into resistance to his inquiries from the agency and other politicos. The Republicans wanted to step up the war on drugs and this kind of publicity would hurt the effort.

Deep inside Peter's heart, he knew that this was killing his own ambitions for Daniel Carlson and a run for the Presidency. This issue is all that the Republicans or Democrats would need to assassinate the stupidly idealistic Senator. Senator Carlson is against the War on Drugs. Even Peter wasn't that fired up about America to buy that nonsense. But the American people were. Yes, the Silent Majority was all about America and drug-free America.

Peter didn't want to know or help Steven Vann. But how could Peter undermine Daniel's benefit to keep Daniel's best interest at heart. The debate within Peter's heart ricocheted through his gut. This values dilemma was never in his programming.

After intense thought, Peter reminded himself he worked for Senator Carlson. Senator Carlson was his friend. He wanted to make Senator Carlson the most powerful member of Senate, if not President. Peter set a priority on friendship over ambition. This surprised him, but he took comfort in his decision. With that resolve in mind, he picked up the phone and dialed.

"Hello, Code name Cottontail," the voice on the phone said.

The voice was British. The voice could have said, 'Bond, James Bond,' and it would be eerie. Instantly the voice flashed the picture of his colleague's friend. It was a tall lanky man's, with dark hair, and circular plastic dark-framed preppy glasses.

"Hello, Berger," Peter replied.

"Not playing the games anymore, Peter? How can I help you?"

"My conscience has given way. I do need to know if Steve Vann was an agent of the DEA and if his release from Lebanon was mishandled."

"This is for the Senator?"

Peter hesitated, "Yes, it is." Peter quickly added, "But the favor is for me. Still, within the boundaries of the group's agreement."

"Yes, I guess it is Peter. But you know my position with the agency. You're asking a lot. You'd be jeopardizing my job."

"Where are your loyalties? You took an oath to the group. And by the way, you'd be doing the right thing."

"What would you do, Peter? If you had to make the choice of being loyal to the group or to your Senator?" Peter didn't answer the question but he didn't ignore it either.

"Nothing will come of it if the DEA's version is accurate. It's a fifty-fifty shot."

"No, it's not. Vann was a shithead who put a lot of agents in harm's way. But he was given the shaft in Lebanon. Are you on a secure phone?" Berger waited. "Take down this number 12-244-45-129-9899A. That file will shed some light."

"Thank you, Mr. Berger."

"I don't think you're helping anyone, Cottontail."

★ ★ ★

Peter sat in his chair and was smoking a cigarette on, again, another Friday evening. Daniel had grown accustomed to the secondary smoke, and even admitted he enjoyed it because the smoke came from Peter.

Daniel knew that Peter was having a difficult time investigating Steve Vann. Daniel also knew that Peter was the only one who could get answers. Even a Senator would get a run around from the intelligence community, unless he had subpoena power. Senators and reporters were lumped together and were the reason for cover-ups. "We're all ready to go to the press with the information, Daniel."

"I want to thank you for giving this case your all. I know it was difficult. I'm surprised that you haven't drilled me for jeopardizing my minute chance for the nomination for the Presidency."

"I'm doing it now, Daniel. We don't have to do this. Steve Vann was kind of an asshole. I don't think he deserves forty million dollars in a federal lawsuit."

"The money is not what we're suppose to decide on," Daniel said in a stable tone. "This isn't about Steve Vann. It's about government making good on what it says. It's about doing the right things for the right reasons. Not the right things by accident."

"We lost the railway stimulus bill because of this. Just the rumor has alienated you with even the most liberal faction of the party. Perhaps we can save it. The House version could—" Daniel interrupted.

"I think we've made a decision. I've asked our old boss, Giulianti to take Steve Vann's case on a contingency. Which he was happy to do as a favor."

"Giulianti is in private practice now, huh?" Daniel nodded. "Do you know in Vann's file it says that billionaire H. Cal Remington raised two million dollars for Vann's release and the government squelched it?" They both smiled. "You know rumor has it that he wants to run for President." They both smiled wider.

"What we must do now is rely on the people to demand their rights. And a Bill will come through in the future." Daniel's voice dropped. He knew he was kidding himself. Only destiny could create what he had hoped.

* * *

The news had hit the front page of every major newspaper in the country. Senator Carlson received fifteen phone calls from various bureaucrats from the DEA asking how he knew about the DEA file. He would return none.

The press called Daniel Carlson a hero Senator and Steve Vann said Daniel Carlson was the only honest man Vann ever dealt with in the government.

Peter walked into the Senator's office. "I just got the results of a party poll and you're not going to believe it. Sixty-five percent of the public approved of your inquiry and the poll concludes that you're the most popular Senator next to every-one's hometown Senator. The percentage of people who were in favor of an upscale on the War on Drugs has remained intact.

Effectively eliminating the argument, you hurt the War. And, this is the best part, Cal Remington has said that he admired your gutsy move and thinks you're the material that leaders should be made from. Can you believe it? That's not all, the House is debating their version of your railway stimulus bill right now. Can you believe it?" Peter said raising his hand in the air for Daniel to slap.

"No," Daniel said shaking his head. "I can't believe it."

"You just need one more issue to play off of this publicity," Peter said. "We woke up the dormant sixties radicals and stole an issue back. Now you own *honor* in government. The government can't lie. We own that now. Government for the people belongs to you, and we have to hang onto it."

"The whole theme of government for the people and by the people belongs to me now?" Daniel said.

"Yes, and everyone else will want to co-opt the theme and make it their own. We have to stop them or force them to see you in order to perpetuate the theme. See, the Right has school prayer and anti-abortion firmly entrenched in its back pocket. From time to time, the issues become hot. When it's close to an election where the *conservative right* need to mobilize and energize the Christian right, the smart strategists try to get those issues hot again. You got the radicals that don't usually vote because they've been lulled or frustrated into apathy to want to vote again for a moderate like you. You can be President, Daniel." Peter smiled.

Daniel listened at what he thought was Peter's wishful hyperbole.

"What do we have to do next then?" Daniel said in an effort to amuse Peter.

"We need to milk this for what it's worth, and then we need some real luck. But your enemies list has just grown. They hate you for stealing from them." There was a collective shaking of heads by powerful members of both political parties. Daniel Carlson was just blessed or charmed. He was untouchable.

CHAPTER 12

Days of Reckoning

Senator Carlson remembered the day quite clearly. It was one of those pivotal days where a decision was placed squarely before him, and that choice changed Daniel Carlson. Throughout his life, Daniel always regretted his decisions after the fact when he listened to that Silent Majority. He had made another's mistake. He should've listened to his own voice. At least if it was a mistake, it would be his, and he could live with that. The frustration of living with the advice of people who claimed to know what's best for him was an unquenchable knowing inside of him.

After two terms in the Senate, Senator Carlson was ready to leave. It would be a great and honorable voluntary retirement. In his heart, Senator Carlson always wanted to be Professor Carlson. Senator Carlson was quoted during a personal interview, "I like leading and teaching, and that's what I would really like to continue doing after I leave the Senate." Teaching is what Daniel felt he was all about. Daniel called a fellow Senator's son-in-law, Ted Hand, at the University of Miami. President Hand offered

Senator Carlson a position. What University wouldn't want a two-term Senator and lawyer as at least a distinguished visiting professor? One that was being considered for the Presidency of the United States.

"You know, Edward, I've given this a lot of thought, and I want to accept the professorship. I can't wait to teach," Daniel remembered saying.

"I'm sorry, Senator. My father-in-law says you're going to be the next President of the United States and a faculty position can wait," Hand replied.

"Well, I'd have to run for President—party primaries and then a general election. I'd just as soon pass. This is what's best for me."

"What about the party? With all due respect Senator, don't you think you owe the party you're loyalty? The majority of Americans that believe in you?"

"I owe myself loyalty. I've done all the required soul searching, and I'd like to know that I'm going to be a professor at UM before I give the party leaders my rejection."

"I think you should decline running for office first, and then we'll talk." Daniel, realized that President Hand was withdrawing the offer entirely. Hand wanted nothing to do with making powerful politicos upset with him and UM, for luring a potential President away from the White House. "Check it out with everyone else first, and then get back to me, okay?" Later Senator Carlson learned that one of his biggest contributors, a software company in Simi Valley, promised a five million-dollar trust to the computer-engineering department, if Senator Carlson was not a professor at the University. Senator Carlson didn't get what he wanted because he wasn't a better blackmailer. He could've gotten another software company to setup a ten million-dollar trust for the school. But instead, Senator Carlson checked it out with everyone else first.

★ ★ ★

Agent Brad Lefkel knew he was due for a change in geography when he was assigned to the Washington, D.C. office headquarters. It was a promotion of sorts. He got a pay-grade raise, and would be conducting public corruption investigations. Public corruption investigations were given to career agents. The Bureau didn't think Lefkel was leaving. Better stated: he didn't have ambitions outside of the Bureau.

However, what Agent Lefkel didn't quite understand was why he had been assigned to watch Senator Carlson. Lefkel remembered Daniel Carlson from Florida. It had been years since the two had seen each other. Carlson was an ambitious Assistant U.S. Attorney from the DOJ, and politics made him a Senator. Lefkel just didn't believe Carlson was being investigated for corruption. There remain certain consistent truths about every politician, but Daniel Carlson wasn't a criminal. Lefkel pondered the shades of gray between political corruption and being a criminal. Carlson was well shy of the line.

Lefkel also knew he had to be especially careful at his surveillance because Carlson knew him. This increased the chances of being detected, or *made*, in Bureau parlance. What are the chances Lefkel could come up with a story about why he was in a parking garage at the precise moment Carlson was getting into a car? It was delicate. The Bureau administration was highly secretive about this assignment. If it was helpful the surveillance agent know his target, why didn't they explain why? If it was helpful, then Lefkel needed to know why it was helpful. It didn't take long before Lefkel knew that Carlson had political enemies in the

Bureau. Who and why was a chess game of a different level than Lefkel was ever interested in comprehending.

Another reason this was fishy was because Lefkel wasn't with another agent, although this was a low-risk surveillance. What if Carlson walked right up to Lefkel's window and said, "Hey, what the hell are you following me for?" It's not like Carlson would get violent. What operation would be exposed is another question. But why Lefkel was alone, in Georgetown at 5:00 pm waiting for Carlson to come out of Georgetown Park mall and walk into the neighboring garage was a mystery.

This couldn't be protective surveillance either. The Senate had its own police force. The Bureau has rules regarding protective surveillance, like your protectee has to know he's under protection. Another rule is that the agent protecting the protectee has to know he's on a protective detail. In addition, if there are death threats, the Bureau has an obligation to tell the target the Bureau believes the target is the focus of death threats, and should take precautions, or allow the Bureau to protect him.

The surveillance logs Lefkel had to fill out were target logs, not protectee logs. This made no sense. Why wasn't Lefkel being trusted with any information about the investigation? Was this investigation even legitimate? The Bureau is bureaucratic, but rogue investigations? That's not conceivable.

In a moment of lost thoughts, Lefkel thought *Chinese*. Definitely Chinese. Wide-face, moved like the wind. Lefkel instinctively snapped two pictures with a zoom lens camera. Lefkel got out of the car and just began running across the parking lot. It was just a feeling. An urgent feeling like he was missing a bell's deadline. This guy didn't belong. He was too close to Carlson. He was dressed like he was trying to blend, but he looked like a tourist trying to not look like a tourist. Carlson didn't acknowledge the man. In that moment, Lefkel noticed a moon-like tattoo on the man's left hand. Carlson wasn't there to meet this Chinaman. Flashes of incomplete theories flashed through the agent's mind as he bolted into a full sprint. It was something about the Chinaman and Carlson.

A solid cylindrical pointed weapon, a sleeve arrow, slid out of the cuff of the Chinaman's shirt. His hand had a decorated moon-shaped tattoo. Daniel Carlson didn't even feel this guy behind him. Nothing. He was just that slight. Nothing abrupt about any of the man's movements. He was inches away from Carlson. He pulled back ready to thrust as Carlson began to unlock his car door. Carlson didn't bring a driver. He was alone. This was shoot or don't shoot situation. Lefkel didn't know anything except his surveillance target was about to be shanked from behind. A target that he knew but didn't know why he was following—for a reason he didn't understand why he was following him. What the hell! A Senator was about to be killed and the FBI knew it—that would be the story in two weeks when the dust settled. Inadequate information, inadequate time to think, that's shoot, don't shoot. Lefkel was not as slight as the Chinaman. *Bang!* Lefkel shot his snub nose revolver. He crouched down in a good *Weaver* shooting stance. Lefkel hit the Chinaman right in the mouth, and the bullet when through the back of his head. *Splat* the bits and fragments of blood, skull, and brain, sprayed behind on the concrete wall of the garage. No one stood behind the Chinaman. The bullet lodged in the concrete wall behind him. The man fell funny as he dropped to the ground. This wasn't a movie western's drop to the floor. It was a sick and morbid death drop. Both he and Carlson knew the guy was dead on the way to the ground. The sleeve arrow slid out of the Chinaman's hand. Lefkel said, "FBI" in a quiet, low tone, left over from the prior split second decision not to shoot before he shot. Lefkel was in shock.

Lefkel then looked at Daniel Carlson. Carlson noticed it was a face he knew. He heard Lefkel say, "FBI." In that moment, Carlson saw Lefkel's younger face in his mind, and then recognized him. Senator Carlson was sweating. He realized what just happened, what was about to happen, and he was dumbfounded. Carlson then asked Lefkel, "Brad? What were you doing here?"

* * *

Peter learned of the assassination attempt, and after he was relieved that Daniel was not hurt, he loved it. Senator Carlson was a hero because a Chinaman wanted to kill him, and Daniel survived. Carlson was now an authority on international relations. It was better than being able to see Cuba from his backyard. Any perceived weakness in foreign policy was gone. Senator Carlson was Presidential material. He could win. Peter Spark knew how to ensure a win, if Daniel got past the primary.

* * *

Senator Daniel Carlson went to his office at the Rayburn building after a sleepless night. His body felt the strain of pressure that welled up inside of him. His chest was tight. While in bed, the night before, Daniel had an extreme case of heartburn, he thought it even might be a heart attack. In time, the burning pain in his chest subsided, and he opted not to wake June to tell her. It was the dream again. The Silent Majority speaking to Daniel in his dreams. Daniel knows there is no real way out. He was a hero. America wants a hero as President. He survived his own personal attack. The fact Daniel didn't serve in the Army will be an attack that would fall flat. Daniel was a leader worth killing by America's new enemy. The Silent Majority likes getting behind a hero that America's enemy wants to kill.

In the morning, Daniel skipped drinking even decaffeinated coffee, he felt wired enough. Daniel kept analyzing himself. He always felt he was his own psychologist. He didn't have to ask what's the matter. Today, he couldn't defuse the neurotic thoughts that were causing his anxiety. His secretary Lynn had the morning paper already on his desk. There he viewed a picture of himself on the front page. Seeing his picture in the newspaper always triggered a surreal episode in Daniel's mind. Today's picture was large. The caption: *The Day of Reckoning is Near—Senator Carlson of Florida expected to announce whether he will throw his hat into the ring as the fourth candidate for the Republican Party's nomination.* The accompanying article suggested that he would be the front-runner if he entered. However, many Republicans already declaring support for other candidates defensively stated that "D.C.'s" candidacy would make little difference to the race as a whole. Both sides referred to Daniel Carlson as a RINO— Republican in name only. Both sides were secretly nervous that Daniel's positions on immigration, education, and social services were downright compassionate and middle. Now, some foreign agent had wanted to kill him. It almost seemed like Peter Spark had planned it.

Daniel resented people who called him D.C., especially people who didn't know him. It was a cute nickname for very close friends to use. His mother called him that when Daniel was a little boy. Where did these people get off being so familiar? They did it only to show disrespect—as if he were a pesky little boy who needs to be shown attention. Peter told him that in politics he would have to get over the fact that people called him *D.C.*

His resentment wasn't enough of a reason to run for the highest office in the land. One doesn't win the Presidency out of spite. After all, if he won, he would still have to lead the country.

Daniel was never that ambitious. It always appeared to him that the Presidents-elect, Democrat or Republican, go into office with idealism and a plan. Then the real powers that exist take the new President into a sealed room and tell him how it really is. "We're in charge, you're the pawn. Do what we say and you won't get hurt." Daniel never wanted to lose that idealism. The vocal minority must not be silenced. He tried to maintain the spark of optimism through every season.

The power of a President is awesome. He is head of state and domestic policy. He controls the foreign policy of the country. He can veto any bill that the Congress brings to him and call a press conference with ten minutes notice. He can and would be on television every day of the week. The privacy in life is all gone. The world would know his whereabouts every day of the week. In the next four to eight years, every word that he said would be scrutinized and construed toward the negative at every opportunity.

The children, they were becoming mature adults. Connie just graduated from Syracuse with a degree in communication. Alan would be finishing in a couple of years at Daniel's alma mater, Yale. He wanted to spend more time with them. As President, he would be lucky to spend any quality time with them once a month. The Secret Service would have to be assigned for the children; they would hate it.

Daniel then fantasized about being an active President. He would want his hand in just about everything, at least everything that interested him. He would be busy. He believed the children could handle the routine. Time with June wasn't a consideration; he knew how she felt about being the First Lady. She would love it.

Campaigning. That's a different story altogether. The days would be from five in the morning to near midnight nonstop. He would hire Peter again as chair of his committee to elect. He did the job for the past eighteen years. Peter wanted Daniel to run since the day Daniel Carlson became a Senator. Peter always wanted to be President himself. Daniel could do it for Peter instead.

The thing about campaigning that scared Daniel was the digging—the investigations. Everything was so personal. Everyone tries to get something damaging about your past.

"Show me a man who has never failed and I'll show you a man who hasn't done anything."

Daniel had a political corollary: "Show me a man with a clean background and I'll show you a man who hasn't done anything." Daniel wasn't worried about the pot smoking or something like money to the contras. He just didn't like reporters and investigators poking their noses into his business. These personal investigations led to attacks. Then the candidate had to defend himself against these attacks. So he counter-attacks. Pretty soon the election is about imaging and not about substance. What does this candidate stand for? The *toothpaste* literature doesn't help much. So when the debates turn into image warfare, the country loses because we have a President who never defined any real course for his administration, only a better image.

This was the time for Daniel to run for the Presidency. He had enough experience and wasn't too old. The American people need someone to look up to. He was a true leader. He led by example and pushed policies of good merit through the Congress. His personal life was exemplary. He just feared the probing.

After completing that thought, June was escorted into Daniel's office.

"Guess who I just bumped into at breakfast?"

"Who?" Daniel asked, but already knew.

"The chairman of the party, Norman Stratford, three of his aides, and his wife."

"Wow. I bet you liked that," Daniel said, masking his understanding of the chairman's motives behind the breakfast meeting with June.

"They want you to run for President, Daniel." Daniel didn't answer. "Daniel, did you hear me? President!"

"I heard you, June. He's having breakfast, lunch, and dinner with five other guys this week, and he wants them to run too."

"They told me that behind every good man was a good woman. So they asked me to use my influence and get you to save our country." The chairman knew just what to say to June. "We've discussed this before, Daniel. I think you would make a great President. And of course, I would make the best First Lady this country has ever seen. I think you should run!" She was almost breathless. The idea seduced her. Daniel never saw her so excited before. Intoxicated was the better word.

Peter Spark walked into Daniel's office. He asked June if he could talk privately with Daniel. She knew Peter would convince him. Daniel promised he would think about her opinion.

"Good morning, Senator," Peter said enthusiastically. Daniel was waiting for Peter's report only. He was in no mood to banter. "It looks good. I'll know by the end of the day if everything is okay. I think you'll be able to run."

"Is it that you can't find him, or you don't think anyone else will be able to find him?" Daniel asked.

"Both. We're okay. People knew you were Presidential material in your second term in the Senate. If they haven't dug it up by now, they're never going to."

"I wish I could just talk about it."

"Not a chance. Nobody would understand." Peter was almost annoyed. "You have a chance to run for President and win. You have an obligation to yourself and to your country to run."

"What do you think they'll come at me with?"

"They won't be able to for a while. I mean some crazy Chinaman almost just killed you because of what you stand for. You're bulletproof, for the moment. Of course, they'll ask you about the drug use. They'll make a big deal about that. It'll blow over. I don't think they'll find out about the Israeli money. And basically they'll say you didn't do enough as a Senator. And that you were a flip-flopper. When they do, we'll kill them on that."

"Maybe I should think some more," Daniel said.

"Senator, it's been five weeks. Everyone in the press has been waiting for you to declare. I think you should do it." Peter got closer to Daniel. He sat on his desk. "You have the chance to become one of the most powerful men in the world. You can implement the vision you've wanted to have your whole career . . . since Harvard. When that snotty defense attorney told you justice didn't matter. Well it does here. You want to know why? Because this is the Goddamn United States of America. And Daniel Carlson is the President of this country and things are done a little differently here than in the rest of the world." Peter could tell that Daniel was eating his flag waving up. "One question? If you could avoid the campaigning, just instantly be the President, would you want to do the job?"

"Yes," Daniel said instantly. Daniel recognized the duality in his own character. He would be happy as a teacher. He would also be happy as the Leader.

"I'll get you elected. You just listen to me. It'll be like old times. Send D.C. to the White House! Then as President, you can do as you like."

"Okay, Peter. I'll announce as expected." Peter couldn't believe that it was that easy. He was impressed with himself.

"Very good, Daniel. I look forward to it."

"Good day, my friend." Daniel said and smiled.

* * *

What is the motive for the party coming to a candidate and asking him to run? Daniel pondered this question continually throughout the last five weeks. They obviously think they can control me. They'll learn. I'll spank anyone who gets out of line. The party needs me. If they want to get me, they'll have to pay me in respect.

"Lynn, send out the press release and call a press conference in Florida." Daniel said confidently into the intercom.

* * *

A few close friends of Alan Carlson's fraternity gave Alan the high five at 12:00 a.m. as he was leaving the party. They gave him the cheer for his father, who decided to run for President, but more importantly, he was leaving the party with a very attractive co-ed who was coveted by every man in the room. Her name was Karen and she had long blonde hair down to her roots. Her blonde eyebrows confirmed the fact that the color was natural. With her pale blue eyes to match, Alan knew for sure that he was getting a California girl to go back to his room with him.

Actually, Karen looked like a girl from the sunny west coast but was from Binghamton, New York. Her father was a powerful person in the real-estate market and in the Republican party of New York. Her father now and again was asked to run for office, but nothing serious. He was a man who liked accumulating power behind the scenes.

Alan had been chasing Karen all semester but never seemed to get anywhere with her. He even tried to appeal to her father's need for power once. Alan had met him on a parent's weekend at Yale. He approached Karen's father and informed him that his father was indeed a Senator from Florida. Karen's father knew of Senator Carlson, but since he was from Florida and could do nothing for the real-estate power master, he was impressed but not seduced.

Tonight was different. Alan Carlson was the son of a candidate for the nomination for President of the United States. Now he possessed significant influence on a man who could one day be the most powerful man in the free world. This influence aroused Karen. Alan was right; he could appeal to her sense of power, like her father's. She hung on Alan all night. She danced toward him in a way that was indisputable, she wanted him. He too could be part of a legacy. The legacy that develops around a powerful family. Alan Carlson, the son of a President. He would be very powerful someday.

Thoughts of this kept Karen drunk all night. Alan helped by filling her glass with the spiked punch. He loosened up and danced with her in an overtly erotic way. He didn't care what the onlookers were thinking. This would be the last night that he could act crazy. He would have to put on a show for the media, or political spies, who would seek to discredit his father through him.

Karen slurped Alan's tongue into her mouth, in lasting kisses on the dance floor. The disc jockey, who was a friend of Alan's, lowered the lights on the dance floor to give him some sense of privacy. She pressed her chest against his body, hard. Karen wiggled her pelvis slowly up and down his body, knowing she was making him horny. After she caressed the inside of his thigh during a slow song, Alan could no longer stand being at the party anymore and guided her off the floor and out of the fraternity house. He sang her a romantic song as they crossed the grassy sports field on the way to his room.

Alan opened the door of his dorm room. He led Karen into the dark and shut the door behind him. She went for the light switch but he grabbed her hand gently, and made her rub his crotch on the outside of his pants. She massaged him as she sucked his bottom lip softly. Karen was impressed with his size, but she wouldn't go further: "Not until you make the phone call."

"Okay," Alan replied. But first, Alan went to his desk and picked up his electronic dictaphone, which he found with some help from the moonlight that cracked through the blinds. He turned it on and said in a semi-drunk state, "Let the record show that Ms. Karen Dansky has consented to come up to my room, Mr. Alan Carlson, son of the President to be, and by her own volition has consented to have sex in my room. Is that correct, Ms. Dansky?"

"Yes. But only after you make the call." Alan clicked off the dictaphone and tossed it on the desk.

Alan took off his sweater and unbuttoned his pants. He sat on his bed, and fixed his pillow behind his head. Alan waved his hand to Karen to join him on the bed. She took her sweater off. She was magnificent. She wasn't wearing a bra and she didn't have to. Her breasts were awesome, like a nineteen year old girl's usually were. Her nipples were dark and large, taking up almost half the diameter of her breast. She smiled at Alan as she crawled onto the bed and rested her head on his crotch.

Alan then picked up the phone that was on his night table and began to dial. He waited for a ring. Karen heard the click through the phone that someone had picked up on the other end. She unzipped his pants as Alan said, hello. She licked and sucked his belly button as he continued to speak.

"Congratulations, Dad. —I'm proud of you. . . . I'm glad you decided to run." Alan had to pause for a moment while Karen worked her hand into his underwear. "So what finally made you decide to run? . . . Uh huh, right." Karen now had her mouth around Alan's hard penis. She was moving her head up and down, and slightly side to side. Alan was having a tough time concentrating on what his father was saying. "Dad, I want you to say hello to a friend of mine. She wants to wish you good luck."

Alan handed Karen the phone. She took it from him while still massaging his cock. "Hello, Senator Carlson. I'm Karen Dansky. We met at a parents' weekend once." Daniel convinced her that he had remembered her. "I just wanted to wish you good luck. I know you're going to get the nomination. It's just all so exciting! My father, Daryl Dansky, is an officer in the New York State Republican Party. I know he's going to support you. All right, good luck again. Here's Alan."

Karen continued sucking and Alan picked up the phone again.

"What? Secret Service? I don't need any of that. I suppose. Alright, fine."

Daniel ended the conversation by saying, "Oh, and Alan. Don't forget to use a condom."

"Right, Dad. Thanks."

Alan had difficulty hanging up the phone. He groaned loudly. Moments later Karen jerked her head back quickly as Alan came intensely. This was a wonderful day.

CHAPTER 13

Footsteps

O UR PAST HAUNTS US in moments like these. When we're asked to reflect and determine what would be objectionable to others. The objectionable actions, solicitations, and foibles in our lives make us always regret. But why? None of us thinks we are doing anything wrong at the time we do it. Yet, the present looks back on the past with a relentless unending scrutiny. The scrutiny can wreck futures. The people do the scrutinizing. They pass judgment. Don't judge me! Ridiculous. We make judgments all day long. From the time we wake up, select our clothes, until we decide what time to go to bed. These are judgments. And, the Silent Majority judges too. Their judgment is random and sometimes stupid. At times, they can be curiously insightful, if inspired. In short, it remains a matter of luck which way a President will be selected.

The Carlson family, committed to helping their father, was asked to reveal the scandals in their pasts to a stranger. The strange man was Roger Rock. Rock was in charge of investigation strategy of Daniel's campaign. He needed to prepare the responses in the event the opposition's *investigations* turned up any of the personal scandals. Rock assured each of them that he alone would know the facts of each event and he would never reveal them to anyone. Still, it was difficult to rehash old memories. Painful ones, that were deep and repressed, had to be dug up and shared. One note that Rock left with the family: He would not reveal the secrets even to the other family members. Each one of them had to schedule a private meeting with him. With that promise, Rock expected all secrets, even if nobody else in the world still alive can possibly know about the event. He was saying that no such an instance existed, and he must prepare for every possible image destroyer. The opposition cannot get ammunition to use with the Silent Majority.

Alan looked straight up at the ceiling in bed the morning after the meeting with Rock. His breathing was long, shallow, and hesitant. He scanned memories of grade school that were excusable but disturbing. Instantly, his thoughts went to high school. He delayed the thought of one major incident for which he was ashamed. The major footstep in his life that left the most remarkable print. At first, scared to roll the film from the beginning, he forced himself to recall, for his father. Thinking about your footprints is one thing, telling Rock about them is another. Too much shame.

The house was hauntingly big. A place where a stranger could get lost. Inside it was arranged like a museum. Tonight the parents were away. The whole decor was changed by the music that was being played. It was somewhat loud, but it didn't preclude speaking at normal tones. Beer and mixed drinks were plentiful. Alan had a light beer in his hand. He liked fitting in. He felt comfortable with something in his hand. Alan had a tendency to fidget, but with a beer, he was completely confident, from his hands to his painted smile. Liquid courage.

Cynthia saw Alan making small talk with Lee Travis. Lee, apparently excited about something, spoke rapidly as perspiration ran down his face. Alan tried to get excited about what Travis was talking about, but he couldn't quite follow the story; Travis was very drunk. Travis was the nerdy type. He spent most of his time at school researching for debate tournaments, as school presented little challenge. He was speaking quickly, desperate to keep Alan in a conversation with him. Perhaps a girl would see Travis with Alan and think they were close. That would be prestigious and appealing to others.

"Alan," Cynthia called from atop the stairwell looking straight down. He looked up and smiled, feeling the buzz of his second beer. She waived him upstairs. Alan slapped Travis on the shoulders and turned to walk away when Darren Kingsford, the prep school quarterback, who was closest to a hero as the team had, yelled to him. Kingsford was tough off the field, outclassed on the field.

Alan looked up again, enjoying his buzz and smiling slowly. He appreciated that Cynthia was saving him from the drunken stumblings from Travis. He lifted one finger to her to say "one minute," and then he walked to the other side of the room, close to the stereo.

Kingsford was six foot three inches tall and appeared large in his football vest. He was sweating beer, trying to cover the pain of being sacked four times earlier that night. Kingsford put out his hand and Alan smacked it in a gesture of approval.

"What's up, man? Tough game tonight. Almost had 'em," Alan said. Kingsford pursed his lips then let out a fake laugh.

"Not even close. I'm lucky there were no scouts out there for me tonight. Thirty-five to three, that fuckin' sucks man." Alan realized he couldn't console Kingsford. It was a lousy exhibition of football, and Alan couldn't even make up a bright side.

"Hey, man," Kingsford slurred. "Cynthia wants to do us all tonight." Alan's curiosity was aroused.

"What?" He spoke softly.

"She wants you start the train on her."

"What does that mean?" Two other guys around Kingsford laughed. Alan shifted his stance in his defense. Like who the hell ever heard of *training* someone. "Like what is that the new word for the week?" Did any girl in her right mind want to have more than one man in a night? Women are supposed to be the monogamous creatures, and men, the wolves on the hunt.

"No man. Training. She wants to screw us all." Kingsford waited for Alan's reaction. Alan squinted his eyes in disbelief, not sure he could take Kingsford seriously. He enjoyed the fact that Kingsford, one of the most popular guys in school, even was talking to him. Alan felt he never really was in with the football crowd. But Alan had a following of his own. He was in charge of the intelligent preppie crowd, the ones who were most likely to succeed. His group was popular, but in a different way. The girls who liked the more refined characters, the ones who could see a little into the future and know who was going to be something other than a real-estate broker living off of Granddaddy's trust went for Alan and his crowd.

"I'm telling you man, she wants us: Me, you, Davis, and Hopkins. But she wants you to be the first." Kingsford spit the *s* and the *t*.

"Uh, say it, don't spray it!" Alan said. Kingsford pushed Alan to regain his honor. Alan thought. *She wants to fuck us all?*

"That's right. But she needs a little convincing." Alan smiled at Kingsford's last sentence.

"She needs a little convincing. If she wants to screw my brains out, and she needs some convincing to screw you three, why do I care? I'm getting what I want." Alan thought he found his perfect way out.

"Because I'll tell Mr. Dieterson, you were the one who posted the German exam answers in the showcase a half hour before the exam. And considering you did it, and we know about it, you'll probably get nailed for it." Alan also thought that since he did it, Kingsford was probably right; he would get nailed for it. Dieterson was such a Nazi for lack of a better, probably no more accurate word. He ran his class like a storm trooper, embarrassing one after the other. He coddled the Aryans, it seemed, and *blitzkrieged* the other men and all the women. Steven Gold, the only Jew in the prep school, dropped out of his class after the first week, because Dieterson was such a pig to him. Alan could hear the slapping of the wooden pointer against Dieterson's knee. "Carlson, you cheated on the exam! *Der* are consequences for such behavior!"

"He'll never believe you." Alan said. The other two football rogues were getting frustrated. They were pacing and spinning about.

"Calm down," Kingsford said to his cohorts. Three of us we'll say we saw you," he said to Alan. "Do you think that it would look good if a Senator's son was suspended for cheating? Or getting a hand-job from Baker's fifteen-year-old sister?" Alan was sweating. "That's a crime isn't it?" Alan didn't reply. "You're the one who wants to be the lawyer. It's a crime isn't it? You're eighteen, she's fifteen. . . . Doesn't matter you were a senior in high school."

"I'll talk to Cynthia about it if it comes up. But no promises," Alan said looking for as many words that gave him space to work.

"Good. That's all we ask." The whole scenario was unbelievable to Alan. As manly and worldly as he thought he was, he didn't think training happened in the real world. Maybe in some very wild fraternity parties and pornographic films that happened, but in high school?

"How do you know she'll even go for it?"

"She's a hound, man. It was her idea. She's fucked everyone on the Sunset high football team. Tell her she should do it as a favor to you."

"Alan!" Cynthia called out. Alan just turned away from Kingsford and took two swallows from his beer. His legs were heavy and he drudged up the stairs to meet Cynthia. He forgot about Kingsford and his pals half way up, and smiled widely. Cynthia met him at the top of the stairs and embraced him. He squeezed her hard and smiled at one of her friends he didn't recognize.

"Oh, this is Rachel." Alan said hello and shook her hand. Rachel resembled a pretty girl's best friend. She felt above the high school courtship games and knew all about men at age seventeen. She was of no consequence, though. Rachel said, "I'll leave you two alone," and walked downstairs.

"Let me give you a tour," Cynthia said. She took him by his arm and quickly showed Alan her father's office. "He won't be using that until he gets back from vacation on Sunday."

"It's very Ivy league looking," Alan said. Cynthia showed him her parent's bedroom. All Alan could recall was that it looked brown, not what he thought a bedroom would look like. It didn't seem like much love could be made there. The carpet was shaggy, and very proper looking pictures hung on the wall that seemed to match the brown decor. Alan had the feeling Cynthia agreed, and she took him from the room.

On a table outside the bedroom was a shot of Tequila poured, but untouched. Cynthia reached down and then threw it to the back of her throat. With a sour swallow, she grimaced and squinted. Once it was down, she smiled and continued with Alan by her side. "It's not as bad as the first one," she slurred.

"It never is," Alan replied.

"And this is my room," she said and pushed him into the room. Cynthia shut the door behind her and flicked on one dim light. She took Alan's beer from his hand, went to the open window, and tossed it on the lawn two stories below. She shut the window, turned around, and smiled. "Lock the door," she said. He did. Cynthia ran into his arms and hugged him. Alan leaned down and kissed her with his open mouth. She grabbed Alan and pushed him to her bed. They kissed for a while until the point where Cynthia realized, she had to take the initiative. Alan was a bit nervous. He wanted to have sex with Cynthia but he didn't want to set her up for what Kingsford assured was next.

Cynthia took her pants off first and Alan noticed her lace powder blue panties. His mellow disposition from the beer did not override his desire. She made some comment about wearing them all day and how the sexy panties are uncomfortable. He ran his hands over her thighs. She lost all control. Cynthia took charge. She placed Alan on her bed like the next day's clothes and removed her blouse and bra almost simultaneously. Alan smiled, and could not believe his good fortune. She consented and she was the captain. Their destiny was at Cynthia's command.

Alan felt his clothes coming off. His eyes were closed, and he could hear the people downstairs, the music, and the football team. He repressed that thought. He would not be a part of that conspiracy. Why should he? It was the wrong thing to support. He would be true to his resolve. He had to be, that's what made Alan different from the others. The reason he is destined for greatness in his own right is his ability to be the shepherd and not follow the herd. His own code guided his course of action. Now he could enjoy the sex.

As Cynthia lowered herself on top of Alan, she moaned with accomplishment. She spoke the word *yes* and lowered herself more. Alan was patient. The light from the outside illuminated Cynthia's figure enough for him to enjoy her visually. She recoiled upward and came down hard. She established a rhythm that built the intensity, level upon level. Cynthia moved with self-possession and a knowing that she was making Alan enjoy himself. She didn't even have to ask. She could hear him.

The tension was building for both of them. Cynthia was moaning louder and relaxing. She became increasingly more comfortable with Alan. "Not bad for my first time," she said. Distracted, Alan's climax was delayed. After a moment passed, he reveled in the thought that he took her virginity. He participated more vigorously because of his discovery. Within moments, he climaxed, and Cynthia sprawled out on top of him.

Alan breathed deeply and was satisfied. Good guys occasionally get good fortune. Strange to Alan, he heard his father's voice tell him to stick to a path of conscience and you'll be rewarded in good fortune many times. When he's right, he's right. What better reinforcement could there be?

A few minutes later, after thinking of nothing for several beats, Alan wondered if he would have to spend the night here. He knew it would not be a good idea. For one, he wouldn't know how to act with Cynthia, and he wouldn't be able to explain to their parents why he was out all night. Alan knew he could explain it to his dad, but not to his mother. She automatically presumed that he was involved with drinking and general debauchery. Of course, he was involved in it; however, he didn't want to defend it to his mother. There are other teens who have problems controlling their drinking and their associations, but not him. He stuck to the code. His code kept him out of trouble, and allowed him to have a good time simultaneously. So there was no reason to defend it.

Alan's thoughts were disrupted by laughing and tapping on the door. It was Kingsford. "Go away," Alan said loudly enough to be heard, but not to wake Cynthia who seemed to have passed out on top of him. She was not asleep, she was out. Alan heard, "Quit hogging the bitch." The code, the code, he heard above the voice. Alan slipped out from under Cynthia undetected. He sat at the edge of the bed thinking in strobe. Thoughts fragmented in his brain. He knew how he would get home. Alan decided to give Travis the honor. He would be sober by now. The code said that he should call Cynthia tomorrow. He decided he would. It would make the entire affair honorable: love of two infatuated youths, rather than a lustful interlude with a regretful aftertaste.

Knocking, knocking, at the chamber door, brought a gust of evil into the room. Alan did not know how to escape. He thought of Dieterson. He looked out the window and realized that it offered no escape. The ground was too far below, for a safe fall.

Alan decided that he must confront the rogues at the door. He dressed and opened the door slowly, in an effort to communicate that quiet was important. Kingsford pushed open the door.

"Are you done with the whore?" Kingsford said.

"Shh, she's sleeping," Alan replied.

"Great, that'll be fine."

"Get serious."

"I am serious. I meant everything that I said downstairs, Carlson. Move it or you're going to get busted up." Kingsford pushed Alan into a wall outside of Cynthia's room. Alan became worried. He did not want to fight Kingsford. He did not want to be there and knew what would happen if he left. How could he?

"Listen, she's asleep; you'll wake her up." Alan took a risk and grabbed Kingsford from behind. He turned Kingsford toward him and said, "I spoke to her about it and she said maybe next week."

"Forget next week. I want it now!"

"Well you can't get it if she's asleep!"

"That's what you think. It really doesn't matter to me." Kingsford then stepped into Cynthia's room, and he became aroused. Alan grasped the back of his football jacket and yanked it hard. Alan yelled, "Cynthia," in hopes of waking her. She didn't budge. Kingsford broke free and laced his arm between Alan's leg. Lifting upward, Kingsford threw Alan over his shoulders. Possessed by the will of hormones, and a desire to accomplish his deed, he walked over to the stairwell. He leaned forward slowly, lowering Alan off his shoulders. Kingsford's friends neither aided nor obstructed their raging cohort. Alan rolled off of Kingsford's neck and head and fell about ten feet on his back. Stunned, he felt paralyzed. His head rushed, his body ached, and at the same time, he was grateful to be alive. It was more disbelief than anything else that controlled Alan's emotions.

Travis and two others ran to Alan's aide. Alan stood on his feet and told Travis to drive him home. He rationalized that his duty was done. He didn't care anymore. Alan walked out the door, as Travis happily led the way.

"How did you feel once you were home?" Rock asked out of curiosity.

"I swore off drinking, like most teens do. And I prayed that Cynthia wouldn't think I had anything to do with what Kingsford and the others did."

"Do you know for sure they all raped her?"

Alan winced and rubbed his hand hard over his lips. They didn't *take advantage of her*, they raped her. And he allowed it to happen.

"Look, Alan, I know this is a painful memory. But I'm not your psychiatrist. Just tell me the facts and I'll worry about the fall out."

Alan took a moment to think. He reflected on Rock's statement. "Yes, that's what I heard."

"And Cynthia, did she ever tell you about it or say anything?"

"No. It took me a few weeks to warm up to her again. I was really disturbed by the whole thing. She wanted to make-love with me again. I never gave her the chance. What's going to happen?"

Rock thought for a few moments, but wanted to give the impression he was pondering.

"Well, I think you're safe. If this didn't come out when your dad ran for the Senate, chances are the only people who know don't want to say anything. Kingsford and company aren't going to admit that they raped a girl in high school. And fortunately, Cynthia wouldn't want to deal with her rape so many years later. I think she liked you and wouldn't want to hurt your family's chances to get to the White House. Of course, I'll speak with her very discretely and straighten everything out. You may have to talk to her."

"Okay." Alan was relieved.

* * *

Connie thought for days about what she could tell Roger Rock. She wanted to tell him something so that he would believe that she was participating in good faith. She wanted to spice up the story about when she hit the neighbor's car and didn't tell. She would rather say nothing, justifying her desire by thinking it was nobody's business. Connie doubted that Rock would keep her information secret. If he was going to investigate the situation, couldn't the investigation leak the information? This worried her. She was not as trusting as Alan. Alan was always a *big mouth*. He would talk to anyone and say anything, if he was in the mood. She was sure that Rock knew how to get Alan in the mood to talk.

Connie wondered what Alan had said in his meeting. She liked hearing about how Alan got into trouble. It was a secret pleasure of hers since infancy. When Alan was in trouble, the heat was off her. She felt reassured and confident when Alan was what her mother was focusing on. She didn't want her mother's constant scrutiny on her. June examined whether Connie was *lady like*. Walking straight, speaking clearly, and always smiling. Connie didn't want to be a politician. Sometimes she didn't want to walk straight or smile. Connie learned. It was either smile before she spoke or frown from her mother's rebuke later. The promised result was a man.

The man that Connie married was not a politician, but a power broker in the defense community, at DMI. Conroy Hilton was a boy of privilege, prep schools in Europe, and West Point. He serves his pocket and his country. His upshot at DMI was due to his intelligence, his perceived relationship with the President, and his ingenuity and business prowess; however, not necessarily in that order.

Connie appreciated Conroy more than she loved him. That confession didn't bother her much. She valued stability and consistency in her life more than risk, adventure, and love. With Conroy's two-million-dollar a year income, she was in love. She offered that information as a segue to talking about what Connie should really discuss.

"I'm not a psychiatrist," Rock said. "I'm not going to counsel you on your feelings. I just need to shutdown any possible embarrassment to your father."

"Well maybe you should be a psychiatrist. I'm going to get anxious just thinking about some of the things I'm going to be telling you."

"Just relax and tell me. Everything is confidential like a psychiatrist. I'm extremely loyal to your father, which translates to being loyal to you.

"This happened such a long time ago. I don't see the point in me even telling you this." Rock paused and said nothing. He sensed she would begin. Connie could hear the footsteps rumbling through her memories—making its way to her consciousness.

Connie remembered she and her friend Jessica went into the girl's bathroom at school and put on makeup they both couldn't put on at home. Every fifteen-year-old girl in the sophomore year wore makeup, but not every girl had mothers like Connie and Jessica. That's what drew them together. The most powerful thing in common they shared was inflexible mothers on matters of etiquette.

Jessica's father was a Congressman from Georgia. He also was Republican, which made their friendship acceptable, if not encouraged.

"Gosh, Connie what did your dad say when you told your mom that you were too old not to wear makeup?"

"He didn't say anything. Sometimes he can be such a wimp when it comes to June. It's like she has this hold over him."

"My dad doesn't care. As long as it doesn't affect him, my mother rules. She knows what's best for his career, and all this Baptist way of life has put him on top and has kept me square."

"Not so square. You're dating Billy Kingsford."

"Yeah," Jessica answered.

"Does your mother know?"

"No way, I could never tell her. She would never approve of the jock type."

"You know that his brother Darren is Alan's age."

"Yeah, I know. You better tell Alan not to mention that Billy and I are seeing each other to my mother or I'll kill him."

"He won't. Besides I have more on him."

Class was the same old record played a little slower with each day that passed. Nothing really exciting except an occasional boy who may have looked longer than he should. She wasn't allowed to date any of them, and she didn't want to lead any of them on. After hearing over and over that boys want only one thing, she believed it. Connie wondered what was so good about the forbidden fruit, and Jessica already knew.

Jessica came over to Connie's house a few hours after school. Jessica's eyeliner was running down her face in streams of tears. Quickly, Connie ushered Jessica to the yard outside.

The yard was a five-acre stretch of grass and high trees. Carlson's property ended, but there was no fence separating the neighbor's property. To the eye, then, it was a vast grove.

Connie was excited by the idea that Jessica was upset about something. Something that Connie could get involved in, go to bed, and know it wasn't her problem. Funny how years later it has become Connie's problem.

The mood was somber, and a cool breeze was blowing. Jessica's focus was on the trunks of her trees and not on Connie's eyes. The sight of the trees was a more soothing vision. It was as if she were speaking to the trees and not to a person—as if it were not her problem, but a story. She began.

"I'm in very big trouble. I think I'd be better off killing myself."

Connie replied, "Don't talk like that. Start from the beginning." Her tone masked her hidden pleasure at the thought of having a really gritty problem to contemplate.

"You can't tell a soul. You have to swear."

"I swear. What is it? You're scaring me Jess."

"It's Billy."

"He didn't dump you did he?"

"No. I'm pregnant. He got me pregnant," Jessica sobbed.

Connie was shocked with sensory overload. She didn't know how to react. This problem was way over her head. Pregnancy was something that happens to girls in public schools, not Congressmen's daughters. "How?" Connie asked.

"What do you mean how, stupid?" Jessica regretted sharing this with Connie. If she was that ignorant, Jessica could not go to Connie. Jessica sought a woman with a level head, not some naïve school girl. Connie seriously didn't understand how she got pregnant? "I slept with Billy."

"You mean you had sex with him?" Connie said in disbelief.

"I knew I shouldn't have said anything to you."

"No, where?"

"Where did we do it? In my room at home. When my parents were away. His home, when his parents were away."

"What was it like?" Connie was fascinated. She couldn't believe Jessica was a girl *that did*.

"Who cares what it was like? I'm pregnant. This is no time to talk about sex. I don't know what I'm going to do." Jessica cried more.

"Are you going to tell your parents?"

"No, how can I? My mother would banish me to some boarding school."

"Does Billy know?"

"No. I'm not going to tell him. I'd probably lose him if I did."

"Well if he would dump you over this then he's not worth having," Connie said in her own mother's voice.

"Oh, he wouldn't know what to do either. All I need is a crazy person in my life to deal with."

"Are you going to keep the baby?" Connie asked. Jessica was relieved that Connie was not as innocent as she first thought.

"No, I need an abortion."

"A what?"

"An abortion Connie. You don't think I'm going to school nine months pregnant do you?"

"I don't know, it never occurred to me."

"I know, I never really thought about it either. Who plans these things? I'm fifteen years old. I'm the daughter of a Congressman. We wouldn't know what to do with a baby."

"So you're going to see a doctor by yourself? Can you do that?"

"No, I can't. I'm too young. Besides the doctor who would do it would tell my parents."

"You have to tell someone..."

Jessica shot back, "I'm telling you."

"How can I help you," Connie asked not as a friend but in disbelief. She wanted to know gossip but not be dragged into a tragedy.

"Connie, you need to be mature about this. You've always acted like a little girl, but in times like these you're going to need to grow up. Connie, you're going to have to do it." Connie was startled. Incredulously she answered, "You mean . . ."

"That's right, you're going to give me an abortion."

"How can I . . . I don't know . . . this is ridiculous. I can't give you an *abortion*." Connie whispered the word *abortion*. "I don't know how. I could kill you."

"I have a book. It's simple enough for a child to do it. I'm desperate. What would you do?" Connie thought. She didn't know what she would do. She never even thought about letting a boy see her naked, let alone question what she would do in the event she got pregnant. The adventure ensnared her, however, and Connie reluctantly said she would do it.

The next thing that Connie could remember was second period art class. Class was held in the portable classroom because second period was involved in a spray-painting project and the school didn't want anyone spraying in a good classroom. Connie was engrossed in her art like a good prep student. She watched Jessica out of the corner of her eye. The substitute teacher was gone from the room, and Jessica made her way into the supply closet. By stealth she captured the telescope brush-holder.

The brush-holder is a device with miniature hooks that can grasp. The hooks are normally used to grasp a paintbrush. The metal rod can be extended like a telescope so an artist can paint in high places. Jessica was ingenious; she had another purpose in mind. She collapsed the brush-holder into its smallest form and put the item in her purse undetected. Connie averted her eyes and pretended that she did not know why Jessica was taking the brush-holder. June trained Connie to think in innocent ways and Connie liked the way she thought even though she would never admit it to anyone including herself. Talking about rebellion was rebellious, but actually rebelling was not satisfying at all. Like a politician, talking about *change* is popular, but actually changing is not—until there is enough leverage. Leverage is the push that throws the recalcitrant actor over the cliff.

Connie wanted to remain friends with Jessica. She also felt that Jessica's problem was now her problem. Only together could she get over it. Besides, Jessica would owe Connie big for it. With these thoughts, Connie realized how much political savvy was inculcated into her personality. She would give Jessica an abortion, and she felt accomplished for it.

"And you did it," Rock asked, more for satisfaction of curiosity rather than to complete the story. Connie didn't realize that however, and she continued.

"She came over at the end of the day. I remembered it was raining and I had to do it in the rain."

"How did you do it? I mean, how did you know what to do?"

"Like I said, Jessica had a book and I followed it closely. I thought for the next week I should become a surgeon." Connie laughed nervously. "The operation was a success but the patient. . . ."

"She didn't die, did she?" Rock asked anxiously.

"No. Of course not. She got an infection and she became sterile."

"She went to a doctor?"

"Yes. Did he know why she got infected?"

"He didn't let on, according to Jessica. At least not to her parents. But she felt that he did, and was protecting her."

"You still in contact with her?"

"No. She went to college in Iowa and we lost touch."

Rock broke rank and told Connie what he thought. "It's kind of surprising that after such an emotional experience you two didn't keep in touch."

"I thought you weren't my psychiatrist, Mr. Rock?" Connie shot back. He remained silent. "She's married now. She adopted a baby Chinese girl. I think she's a lot happier than I am. She's got a baby. Her father pulled strings to get the baby. I heard he wanted a white baby for his daughter, but she wanted the first mother available. Anyway, he turned it around, and now having a Chinese granddaughter served his career. Isn't that sick?"

"You think her husband knows that she had an abortion?"

Connie didn't like that Rock cut her off. He was asking some very difficult questions. He should be tolerant of her guilt. But he didn't care. Rock had only one client, and his client was not in the room at the moment. Only if Daniel Carlson had a need to make his daughter happy would he do his best to make her feel better. To him, it seemed like a waste of time. Psychological counseling was nonsense. You just act, not feel. Respond logically, not emotionally, and the politically correct response will surface, and the negligible feelings will be repressed.

"Is that all, Mr. Rock?"

"If that's all then, yes, I'll check it out. Thank you."

"Okay."

"Don't tell my father."

"Why not?" Rock asked.

"I lied to him about this once," Connie conceded.

★ ★ ★

June walked into her family room and shut the door. She sat on a couch opposite Roger Rock. She was dressed as if it were a formal occasion. Rock was a man she felt she had to dress for. She looked at his eyes and immediately took out a cigarette and lit it.

"You're not a smoker," Rock said forthright.

"This whole dialogue is bothersome. I resent it and I don't feel very good about it. You're going to have to deal with my smoking?"

"I meant in public. The future First Lady does not smoke. It's a disgusting habit."

"You smoke."

"I'm not running for office, you are. The whole family is. And it's not what I think, it's what the public thinks. First Ladies don't smoke."

"First Ladies don't smoke," June said dutifully. She could say nothing else, he was right. She wanted to make it to the White House and knew that would be the climax of power. Where she would have the most influence. For what, even she had not resolved. June had no cause or pet project that she wanted to see furthered. The influence over others gave her a sense of security. An odd prioritization of values for a woman from the poor South. A priority of power number one makes a woman clawing her way up a silk curtain like a cat; but, instead of it being a game of adventure—the purpose of a cat—it is necessary for survival. With power as a need in June's life, surely she scratched the wrong rat along the way.

At first, June was reluctant to confide in Roger Rock, like the rest of the family. June, however, felt guilty. She was guilty in her mind. She told a couple of usual stories, linked to forgetfulness or laziness—not returning excess change at the grocery store. Rock grew impatient. June knew that this was not what he wanted. She needed some lubricant; she needed a psychiatrist.

"I'm your priest, June. You should tell me everything. Everything that will help your husband become President." Rock knew what to say next. "When Daniel is President, you will be able to bury these memories and do some wonderful things once you're tapped with authority."

June immediately complied. Her thoughts took her back to the early 1970s. She was June Wolfe back then. Tom, her husband returned from Vietnam less than a hero, as most soldiers did. While most wives pined away for their lovers or got their love elsewhere, she did neither. June didn't yearn for Tom or any other man. She moved on, financially and socially.

June and Tom had just leased an apartment in a suburb in Virginia, before he was called away to the Vietnam "police action." While Tom provided well for June financially, she wanted more from life than waiting for her husband to come home and offer to take her out. She wanted to *need* to go outside. "I have an appointment," she would love to say. Through a friend, she joined the staff of Senator Buckley of Alabama.

Her job at first was secretarial. The responsibilities grew as June demonstrated that she had a taste for the job. She had a sense of protocol. She knew how and when to be cordial; when and how to stall someone, without being too obvious. She also knew how to *send a message* to enemies of her Senator's camp; yet, she could remain undercover as the sweet office girl, able to revive her southern belle accent posthaste. She was creating exactly what she wanted in her life, even without her husband. This revelation was contrary to what she learned as a child; but that is how little girls from the country-bumpkin south think, not women of influence. June's mother, who was beaten by June's father, could think nothing else, until one day she died from a complete surrender. She lost all self-interest and only served her man. When June's mother didn't, she got thumped for it. June, instead of adopting a similar attitude, reacted to it.

June married a man like her father. When Tom was away in Southeast Asia, she discovered her opportunity to break free and live for herself. Like an overstretched rubber band, June couldn't recoil to the same position she used to be when Tom was the bread winner. Once she saw she could survive, she would never be dependent again—certainly not dependent on someone of Tom's caliber.

When Tom returned home, he told June to quit her job and keep house again. He believed he could get a job in the post office that would provide for both of them. When June told Tom that she was pregnant with Alan, he still maintained that he was the man, and he would provide for the family. In an attempt to convince Tom that having a job was good for both of them, she took him to an office social.

June took a big chance bringing Tom into conversational distance with her co-workers. He wasn't raised to know or even have an instinct for etiquette. Tom was working class. He wouldn't fit in. Tom also seemed more awkward than usual—since she remembered. June, however, was desperate to keep her job with the Senator, at least until Alan was born. She tried to make Tom feel comfortable, but all he could talk about was the war. Most of the people in the office were against the war, and were politically maneuvering to get the current administration to pull out of Vietnam. Tom became drunk and reacted with hostility to any contradicting point. June later learned at the end of the night that Tom wasn't only drunk.

June read about the symptoms in a magazine at work, but she was naive at first to think that Tom would've fallen victim to heroin. When she saw him in the bathroom shooting up the black tar into his veins she instantly lost all respect for him. She divorced any emotional commitment to him and their marriage. Now he was part of the gutter and she was from the Capitol. He was handcuffs and she was freedom. Where did he come from to think that she was his property, which he could do with whatever he wanted. How antiquated. She would no longer participate in it, for fear that she would die of the same disease her mother did.

June felt threatened, not with the idea of physical harm upon Tom's discovery that she knew of his addiction. Tom looked up at her from his squatting position next to the toilet. His arm was extended and he was tapping the last drop of liquid into his vein. He didn't react emotionally. He made the extra effort to shut the door so she couldn't see him complete the procedure. She wouldn't let it go.

"You humiliated me," she said through the door. She wanted a reaction and looked to bait him.

"Can't hear you."

She opened the door widely. "You humiliated me," she said with disgust.

"What a bunch of communist sympathizers you work for. They don't understand that I, and guys like me with the balls to serve, needed support from our country."

"They have a different view, that's all."

"I forbid you to work there."

"You can't forbid me, Tom!"

"I'm the man, damn it. I make the rules! Now shut the fuckin' door." The warm mellow feeling enveloped Tom as the heroin fully kicked in. He collapsed on the bathroom floor, the same place he was the night before.

How could June incite Tom if he passed out? It's no fun fighting someone who won't fight back. She wanted him either to be with her new life or out. June, deep in the pit of her ego, knew what she wanted. She wanted him out of her life. Her husband would sooner throw up on the shoes of the Senator, than say something appropriate. He didn't fit in. Tom was about heroin and she was about power, control, and influence.

The day had passed, and Tom had slept it away like every other day since he returned home. When he rose from the stupor, he was surly. He went to the refrigerator and stuffed food into his mouth, swallowed, then stuffed more food into his mouth. June gazed at him in disgust.

"What are you doing? "

"I'm fuckin' hungry."

"Don't talk to me like that!" June exclaimed.

"At work they may kiss your ass, but here I'm the damn Senator. I bet you would cook dinner for him. You're probably fucking him too."

"You sicken me," June rebuked. "Get out of here!"

"I take it back. I know you don't fuck, you fat bitch." Tom between swallows forgot June was carrying his son. He cared not to remember.

"Use a plate, pig."

"I'm done," Tom said as he slammed the refrigerator door. He walked to the bathroom to find his heroin, and inject more in his vein.

"Eat, sleep, and get high—you're worse than a dog."

Tom ignored her. His addiction made his procedure a mission. He opened the door to the bathroom and began to look around.

"Where is it, June?"

"I threw it out," she replied.

He immediately turned and charged her with force. Tom grabbed her by the throat and shook her head.

"Don't fuck around, June! Where is it?" Sweat oozed from his forehead. He was pale. His skin was thick like oatmeal. His blood ran cool. His breathing hissed when exhaling. Frightened, June immediately told him where he could find his stash.

"It's in the medicine cabinet," she eked through the portion of the throat she could open.

"Don't move my stuff, ever." Tom turned and moved back to the bathroom. He swung open the medicine cabinet door. He cracked the mirror door against the tile wall. June cried at the sound of the crash.

Tom's eyes were out of focus from the tears and cool wetness from his forehead that ran into his eyes. His stomach ached from the pounding onslaught of protein he just consumed. His thoughts remained clear but his hands would not cooperate.

He screamed out, "June, come here. You have to help me, I'm sick!"

"I'm not going to help you anymore. You can buy your own shit from now on. You can shoot the stuff up and kill yourself for all I care."

He cried, "I'm so sick, and nobody can help me. They made me sick in 'Nam. It was damn hell there. Every day you thought you were going to die. Escaping to the Caribbean is the only way you can survive. Please, I'll go to a clinic tomorrow. You have to help me get normal. Just normal." He collapsed to his knees. He looked up at June in agony. His grimace accentuated the thick stubble around his mouth. "Please June, for better or for worse, remember? I swear, on our baby, tomorrow I'll get some help."

June sensed that it was *hypo* talk. Tom wanted a fix and couldn't do it himself. She looked down at him and saw a weak pitiful man. He was dirty and unkempt. When once he was possessive, powerful, and ambitious, his spirit was dying.

June had the power and she made a decision to help. She edged her way into the bathroom. She wasn't afraid to touch him. She knew that he wouldn't hurt her if she was helping him get a fix. Tom wasn't a violent person, he was a drug addict, and he had an evil force pulling his strings. June resigned it as the devil within him. There was only one way to exorcize him.

June took the syringe in one hand, and the black tar heroin in the other. Instinctively Tom wrapped the rubber tie around his bicep to push the vein up in the joint of his arm. He filled the syringe with the usual amount. He looked at the syringe and he put in more. More, she thought, was too much. But she didn't protest. He added more tar to the heroin water mix. He pricked himself deep and quickly released the mixture into his arm. The warm numbness enveloped Tom's soul and he became relaxed. He was passive as a lamb—peaceful and kind.

Tom then tensed and regurgitated the last meal all over his soiled undershirt. This didn't bother Tom. This was part of the process. He felt higher than he ever did before. Lost in nothingness, he was on a vacation from the nightmares. The nightmares of everyday life, the world that hated him, which he thought were part of his inner-devil's dreams.

June stood up after Tom lost his lunch and walked away. She went into the kitchen and poured herself vodka straight. In one of the very few times in her life, she took a drink of the devil's nectar. She could hear Tom convulsing in the bathroom. She heard his body thump when he hit the floor. She knew he was in serious crisis. He injected too much heroin.

Coolly, after she waited twenty minutes, she picked up the phone and dialed for an ambulance. A few minutes later, the ambulance arrived. Tom was dead minutes after they examined him. There was nothing the medics could do. He was another bit of data in a statistic. Another dead vet. A shame for the woman of influence—but only for a moment in time. Now he was gone, it was a new life. A life of martyrdom. A capsized soul.

"Does Daniel know this?" Rock asked.

"No, I never told him. Do you think I can be framed as a murderer? Do you think I'm a murderer?"

"It's not for me to say."

"Okay. No one raised an issue at the time." Rock hoped no one would raise it again.

* * *

Roger Rock stood when Daniel entered his office at home. The two shook hands and then sat on the same couch in the corner of the room. Unlike the rest of the family, Daniel was not nervous. He had been primed for campaign politics, already had been elected and re-elected Senator so he thought there was nothing to worry about.

Daniel spoke about a time when his fraternity house was burglarized in college and he added some items to the police report that weren't actually stolen. For less than a thousand dollars in insurance money, Rock merely grimaced at the thought. Of course, Daniel spoke about the one time slip with marijuana and how he had regretted not maintaining his *political purity*. He was mad about slipping into the normal/human realm, not about the stigma associated with smoking marijuana. Daniel was never really against those smoking it. He was against smoking it only for himself. He knew it wouldn't be smart for him to smoke it. He violated his personal discipline.

Daniel decided years earlier that smoking pot is not healthy for his body or his brain. He betrayed the vocal minority. That to him offered him more disappointment today, then the liberating feeling he felt that night when he did smoke it. For he always reasoned, it's not what your personal rule is, it's whether you stuck to it. If someone said, no hamburgers, and then they ate a hamburger, then that person violated the personal integrity. Shame, shame on Daniel, who was not nervous but uncomfortable as he brought these thoughts into full focus.

Rock was intrigued by Daniel's comments about personal integrity. He asked Daniel to continue out of clarification rather than out of exploring possible exploitations by the other party. Daniel recalled his thirteenth birthday when he didn't invite his friend Lee to his party. Lee wasn't a close friend but a good friend of Daniel. He knew that he should've invited Lee to the party, like any good friend would. However, Daniel's class at school was small and snobby. A majority of the children in the class disapproved of or disliked Lee. Lee was a little effeminate, even at thirteen. Effeminate, was too sophisticated for thirteen, but Daniel saw it and Lee was persecuted for it.

Daniel always wanted to be above that but sunk to the common denominator when he didn't invite Lee because of his lack of acceptance by others. Daniel suffered pain, to this day for betraying himself and his friend. Lee wouldn't have done it to Daniel, in fact Lee didn't. Lee had a thirteenth birthday and invited Daniel to the party. Daniel attended the party and enjoyed it. At the end of the party, Lee's father drove Daniel and some of the other kids home in a large station-wagon. In the car was a bullhorn. It was used by Lee's father at work on construction sites. Daniel remembered walking out of the car and to the front door to his house. Daniel turned when he heard Lee's voice through the megaphone cry out with sincerity: "Daniel, thanks for coming to my party, buddy!" Daniel knew that Lee had forgiven him for not inviting him to his party, but Daniel never did. His need for acceptance outweighed the respect for his friendship with Lee, and it shouldn't have. It was not the only time that Daniel felt he betrayed himself. Daniel believed most of his life was a betrayal of himself, but within the confined framework, he chose not to violate his code.

That episode in Daniel's life inspired him to want to be a teacher. Teach people to stick to what they set out to do and be. Daniel's life calling was to be a teacher. He was a teacher. He felt it was a worthy calling. "Teach a person to fish, you feed him for a life time." But it never happened. It was all an act. Daniel however, was programmed to achieve. He achieved. Daniel also pretended to be in love with a woman whom he could barely stand. Not finally, Daniel was forced to deal with people he couldn't stand much—politicians. Within the framework, however, he maintained his code. He taught those he had to deal with—the young members of his staff and fellow members of the Senate. He was not in love with June, but he loved her continually for giving him children. Children with whom he loved so deeply it was the center of the pride he exuded daily. And the politicians had to deal with his lessons, which mostly were persuasive to the ones that cared even superficially for logic. Then if logic did not work, he spoke about his children. Thus, he had a system of internal personal integrity within a schema of personal betrayal.

So what did Daniel teach Rock at this meeting? Daniel taught Rock that he had the integrity to be the President of the United States, and in turn Daniel expected integrity from Rock, because come November 4th the election would be won or lost, but a transgression of integrity is a regret forever. If he convinced the American people that change in their thinking is required, then he would win. Progressive work was necessary. He was the forward thinking man for the presidency. Without ever ending improvement there would be stagnation. Stagnation is not standing still, but a slide downward. Americans had a tradition of being powerful. Daniel had a particular affection for that image too. It would require a change in thinking. A challenge to the rules that are the foundation of the Silent Majority will move the country upward, like a plane flying into the sun, to respond to the whirling wind of mediocrity, of sameness that forces a plane into a flat spin.

★ ★ ★

Peter shared the night's last drink with Daniel. Peter, who had his usual Scotch, and Daniel, a club soda, asked Daniel what he told

Rock. What were Daniel's footsteps? Peter was the only person who could comfortably ask Daniel that question. He wanted to know Daniel's secrets. Daniel told Peter that he had already known everything that would compromise the campaign. Rock told him that there was nothing for him to worry about.

Peter replied with a quick throat clearing and the conversation was dropped. "Did you tell him what you told me during our little walk after your honeymoon?"

"No, I did not."

Peter replied, "good."

CHAPTER 14

The Campaign

THE SENATOR WALKED INTO Crenshaw High School. He looked around and saw mostly Black faces, with a few Hispanic. So much for *Brown v. Board of Education*, Daniel thought. He didn't ask to be introduced and thought it more befitting to introduce himself. As Senator Carlson walked next to the stool that was left there for him to sit on at different intervals of his speech, a muffled but distinct voice cried out, "Whitey!" The hand over the boy's face was loud enough to be heard at the front of the room. Some people in the room were shocked. Most visibly, Charles Mathews and the teacher of the boy who said it. Daniel seemingly fielded the comment with ease even though some might have ignored it altogether.

"Whitey," the Senator said. "Whitey." There were releases of nervous laughter. Daniel surveyed his audience. Many of the students were smiling in anticipation. They were excited. Surely the Senator was going to address this outburst since he repeated it aloud. "What does Whitey mean anyhow?" Daniel meant it as

181

a rhetorical question but a girl in the audience raised her hand to answer so Daniel pointed to her.

"What Richard meant was that simply because you are white you should be dismissed without consideration," the girl said in a matter of fact tone. "I know this because Ricky is too stupid to read any literature about you, to find out what you stand for. And I apologize for him." Laughter erupted in the large classroom. Daniel felt decorum was pretty much out the door so he abandoned his prepared statements and said what came to mind.

"I think we might be a little rough on Rick. After all, Rick is a budding activist. And Activism is the cornerstone of democracy. What do I mean by that? Rick just started his career as a person who wants to stand up and be heard." There was continued laughter but most were locking onto the progressive Senator. "Rick needs a little work on his speech, though." Some sincere laughter was heard.

"He ain't Jessie yet." More laughter and some applause erupted. Then intense silence was detectable. "That's where the importance of education comes in. Education allows you to get to know the facts. How to find them out, and argue about them. That's where you make a change in the world. That's just not the white world either. I hope you don't think that I hired Charles over there because he has a black face. He charges too much. Unfortunately Rick, most in government, and the rest of the real world don't listen to people who aren't in a position to speak. With education and understanding comes the power to be heard. The power is with the pen, not with the gun. The power is with your mouth, not with the drugs."

Daniel stepped over the large blackboard and began to write. First, he wrote the number 1580 on the board. Then he wrote 3.95 on the board next to 1580. "These are the scores that I got in high school. I had a 3.95 average in high school and a 1580 on my SAT. I think they scored the SAT differently and now changed it back. But, a 1580 back then was missing one question. It was in math. I'm not really good in math. This may seem impressive, but I wanted to go to Yale. And I had a teacher in high school who hated me. Who wanted to see me fail as much as possible. He wanted me to go to community college." Some of the students laughed. Most of them didn't realize that he was making up the story. "His name was Mr. Bush. He would grade me harder than all my other classmates. He was old and couldn't be fired and really had it in for me. Some of you may not feel sorry for me with a 1580 on the SAT, but that score with my grades wasn't high enough to get into Yale. I knew I had to maneuver a way. So what did I do? I worked for a college professor from Yale the summer before my senior year. His recommendation to Yale gave me the boost that I needed." Daniel waited. He proceeded when he felt the students were ready to accept his point.

"You see, I was responsible for getting into Yale. I had to get the grades, the score on a meaningless test. I had to get around Mr. Bush, because he was out to get me. That is the whole point. I was responsible. Because there's always going to be someone or something that gets in your way. You have to work around it. Powerful influences will try and make you ordinary. Or worse, make you one of society's losers. When I say you have to take responsibility, I'm saying you have to make it all work for you. Don't complain. Get around. You have to slip and slide." The Senator bobbed and weaved to accentuate his point. "Make it all work for you by getting involved and take responsibility for what happens to you."

After the speech, the Senator began answering students' questions. There were many parents there as well. It turned out to be a civics lesson that kept the attention of the students and had an impact that was not to dissipate for a long while.

The questions from these students were as hard hitting as any of the reporters that Daniel had encountered. These people had not been dulled into content or given up hope. They demanded solutions to the problems in education. Daniel outlined some solutions to them.

Daniel spoke of a choice schools program. This could get bipartisan support. The program puts the concept of the free market into public schools. Public schools should advertise in middle schools. They should develop programs to attract a certain type of student through magnet programs in engineering, medicine, or the arts. Students shouldn't be forced to attend the school in their district. The choice schools program would encourage parents to get involved in the school their children attend because they chose it. If they don't like it, they can change where they go.

Daniel also elaborated on how schools squelched creativity in students. He offered new innovative training of teachers that would demand new approaches to teaching, that make it seem like a crime to discourage students. As an example, Daniel had everyone move their desks out of neat little rows and told them to sit in any way they felt the most comfortable. "If you're not comfortable doing what you're doing, you're not going to want to do it."

When Senator Carlson finished, there was loud applause. There were even a couple of dog-like barks. Then the Senator walked over to Rick. Rick stood up and rubbed his hands on his pants and shook Daniel's hand. He glanced at his teacher and then sheepishly looked at Daniel and said, "I'm sorry Senator Carlson. I didn't mean to play you like that."

"Rick, I'm supposed to talk to a few of your classmates about the school. I want you to be one of them and I meant what I said. Today is the first day of your life as an activist. What do you say?" Some classmates chimed in.

"Ah, DJ Slicky Ricky's gonna be advisin' the Senator."

"Yo, Yo, Ricky's gonna be the principal some day."

"I'll talk to you if you really want, sir."

"Come along then." Daniel looked at the boy's teacher and got a nod of approval.

Daniel and Rick had a thirty-five minute conversation about Rick's life and what he wanted from it. Rick was a typical inner-city kid who was raised in a single parent home. He bought into a handful of bad attitudes and beliefs, which Daniel and he corrected. Rick left with a feeling of hope, which gives a boy of a modest upbringing a chance to break out and be somebody. Daniel told Rick that they would be the same in a lot of ways. They would both dream, hope, and do for the rest of their lives. And one day they would die working to obtain a dream they never thought possible the day they thought about it.

Instead of alienating the boy, Daniel put Rick in charge of campaigning in his high school. Rick left with a box full of stickers, buttons, and other campaign literature. He walked away rappin' about the new President Carlson and how Senator D.C. is going to D.C. to shake the town down.

CHAPTER 15

I Have a Scream

WHENEVER THERE WAS A primary race where there wasn't an incumbent President, the field was wide open. Every Senator and Congressman from Iowa to California to Hawaii, thinks they have a shot. The race started with twelve. With Daniel Carlson in the race, a target of an attempted assassination and instant credibility, the race was now down to four. As Agatha Christie would put it: and then there were none. Today was a defining day, not by design, but all is unpredictable in love, war, and campaigns. Every day a candidate can say something smart, or worse, say something so stupid it devastates the candidate permanently. With the way media is becoming completely at large, one blunder can be repackaged and replayed over and over. Daniel Carlson had not made one, yet. Probably because he is himself, and he is a good person.

Every candidate falls prey to a blunder because the candidate gives a glimpse of truth about himself. Criticizes the British who are in preparation for the Olympics. He'll tell an off-color joke, or say the wrong thing in private, then it becomes public.

Then damage control must begin. Sometimes it works and sometimes it doesn't. Sometimes it's a fair destruction of the candidate, and sometimes it's just an accident. But, there are no accidents in campaigns. It's all image. Sometimes it has to do with which political party a candidate belongs to, but what is a voter to do when it's a primary? The randomness of selection increases. Does the American public collectively know what's best for it? Is it a mere accident if we have a good leader as President?

Today's Republican rally was on Daniel Carlson's home turf. The Party was determined not to let the State of Florida go Democrat, invigorating the electorate for the general election. So the next primary election event was in Miami, at the Miami Arena. The Arena is the old home to the Heat basketball team. At this point, it only served as a venue for concerts and other major events, like a Republican primary event. The last debate before the Republican primary. Very important. This is the last impression that the candidates can make. It can make all the difference.

The two running neck and neck were Dean Skipper and Daniel Carlson. Dean Skipper, also known as "Skip," was a businessman/Senator from Ohio. He had an MBA from Yale and an undergraduate degree from Ohio State. Skip was popular in Ohio. He was becoming increasingly so in the rest of the country. He was a war hero and exploited it. On background, Skipper's campaign has been leaking that Senator Carlson was a war dodger. Skipper was *in country*, knee deep in the rice patties. He lost his leg in the war. A *frag* grenade severed an artery in his right leg. It had to be amputated. The country thinks he's a hero. He, like Daniel Carlson, had credibility on international issues, because he got his leg blown off. Skipper thought he has so much credibility that he, through his campaign to elect, can attack Carlson for his lack of action in the war. Daniel was behind in the polls in his own state. It was only by two points, but that was a loss, considering Daniel was from Florida. His own state wouldn't reelect him as a Senator, but are willing to elect *another* Senator from a different state as President.

Daniel Carlson had been practicing for this debate. He had his quotes and stats down cold. He was a gifted orator and in his mind all he needed was a chance to be heard. The Arena was packed. There was media and thousands of people cheering, holding signs. High anticipation. There were many supporters of Daniel Carlson. *Send D.C. to D.C. D.C. for President.*

All the candidates were herded into one room offstage. It turned into a greenroom of sorts. All the candidates were very informal with each other. It was like being backstage at a play. The people about to walk onto the stage are different than the people about to enter onto the stage. Who they are behind the scenes not who they really are either, they are just different. Psych games are going on backstage. The front runners act like they own the world and are about to have the final showdown. The others act meek yet pretend to be optimistic. Their names are irrelevant, they have become unimportant. They become known as the *others*. One of the others actually asked if it was okay to take a donut. He was some Senator from a small State. He had a PhD. in economics. Still, no one cared what he had to say about the deficit or the economy for that matter. He just wasn't good at making people feel good. Worse, he was honest about economics. Lastly, he didn't look the part of President.

Daniel Carlson and Dean Skipper did. Dean Skipper fought in Vietnam. He lost his leg. Daniel Carlson didn't fight anywhere. He wanted to, but that's not enough. History doesn't play out the truth on such matters. Skipper was going to exploit it because he had a better story on the subject. He was a hero, and Carlson was an evader, whether he evaded with intent or not, he didn't fight, he evaded service. It would've been unseemly for Daniel Carlson to say something to Skipper directly about it. Besides, Skipper claimed innocence. He didn't know who was making those claims that Daniel didn't serve.

No class, Daniel thought. Daniel couldn't help but dream that he himself would be President, and there will be no room for Skipper in a Carlson White House. He went over the line. Daniel couldn't help but question the wisdom of a person who would attack a man who was almost assassinated by a foreign operative. Daniel couldn't understand why Americans understood that when he was first almost stabbed to death, but it is since forgotten or rejected.

The candidates were called to the stage. After some speeches meant to be warm-ups, the men entered the stage. The Stage was lit up with multicolored lights, like the start of a rock concert. Rock music was blaring. Balloons were everywhere. Daniel came out and noticed that it felt like a basketball arena. All the candidates waved like the Queen of England , like screwing in a light bulb. The people roared like there were really rock stars on the stage. The *diehards* were in the audience. The true believers. To the diehards, the men on the stage were better than rock stars. The ones who think that the man in the White House can make a difference. The country would be different. The country would be better if one of these men, and not a Democrat, were President.

It was not the debate that changed the landscape of the Republican primary, it was the after-debate. Daniel Carlson was smart and handsome. He had a great story. He fell in love with a widow, who lost her own love in a tragic death. He embraced her lovely children as his own. He was a man who accepted responsibility. A man who embraced leadership when others would reject it. When Daniel Carlson as a Senator stood up for a strong America against communist South Korea, he almost lost his life. So all the garbage came out. Daniel smoked pot after college. He didn't serve *in country*. What else can they attack him about. He was a prosecutor. He was a Harvard law graduate and inherited a Senatorship, from a scandal borne Terrence Bratton? Daniel felt thoroughly attacked as number two. Daniel's instincts to win kicked in when he heard the crowd. Daniel wondered if Skipper came to him and actually talked to him about whether Daniel Carlson, the man, wanted to be President of the United States, Skipper could have talked Daniel Carlson into dropping out. Now Daniel was hurt.

Daniel Carlson spoke to his constituents about his plans for the economy and foreign policy. His vision for America was lead by example. Keep America's house clean and encourage other countries to do the same. The major criticism is that Carlson's plans were too vague. What did that mean, lead by example? Carlson felt the economy was doing great. Don't tinker with it. Now is the time to invest in innovation. Research and development is the key to long term economic health. The whole world should be studying and learning here in this country. The whole country should be a research triangle of the world.

Out of all the messages that were accepted, this war dodger crap was getting some play. It was being accepted. Because in the world of politics, you say something over and over enough times, it becomes accepted as true. Daniel Carlson presented the doctor's report that showed he had a knee injury. He even was able to dig out high school track team records to show how he hurt his knee, but that wasn't enough to debunk the myth. The majority likes scandal and controversy. Bored with their own soap operas, a person says it, it must be true. If it's in writing, well then it's gospel.

Speaking well is one thing. But, not everyone listens to the speeches. The long debates turn into sound bites. The majority doesn't have the patience any more to delve into the issues. Daniel pandered in the past month, and he got off message. Roger Rock told Daniel to tell the majority what they want to hear, and Daniel went down in the polls and lost several states to Skipper. Daniel insisted no more pandering. He can't do it. He'd been lucky enough to make it in his career by saying what he really felt, and it worked. Even with Daniel's best, these men were running for the presidency. Good looks, a good speaker, and even a well-funded campaign weren't enough. The majority had to believe he was a president. It's an intangible. He needed a highlight.

Dean Skipper spoke of family values. Only he had them. Daniel didn't have family values because he didn't deal with families in business like Skipper did. Daniel was labeled a career politician. Manufactured by Senator Bratton like a blood pork sausage. Daniel Carlson wasn't in touch with the people. Skipper knew the people because he was a teacher for three years about twenty-five years ago. Then he ran for the local school board, and so on until the Senate. Skipper was a Christian. Skipper was so devout he talked with God. Skipper spoke in code to the fundamentalists. "I pray every day, which I lead this country toward fundamental values that we are meant to live by. . . . I live by a code given to us by our Heavenly Father. We all should live by that code; it's about responsibility and accountability. . . . It's who you consort with that says a lot about your character. I consort with the people, and my opponent was raised by a man who hasn't subscribed to the values of the Almighty."

Daniel couldn't believe that he was still meant to be paying for the sins of Terrence Bratton. Skipper Dean really scared Daniel Carlson. Scared is not an overstatement, because Daniel admitted to speaking with God on the campaign trail, but Skipper believed that God spoke back to Skipper. So when Skipper says that God will live in the White House if he's President, Daniel believed him. That little voice in Dean Skipper's head talks to him, and he thinks it's God talking back.

Daniel was nervous that Skipper did well in the debate, and that would be good enough to be close in Florida. Daniel feared mortification if he lost his own State in the primaries. Daniel's presidential bid would be over if he lost. There would be nothing but a repetition by Skipper of how he was more popular than Daniel Carlson in Carlson's own State. As the debate ended, all the candidates began the light bulb screw wave, as they approached the front of the stage. As a plant, Dean Skipper had a supporter come to the front row with her baby girl. The mother handed Skipper her baby for emphasis that he is the candidate of family values.

With his hands held high, with the infant in between, Skipper made a strong statement. *Family values! Family values*, he screamed! He smiled brightly. Skipper had it locked up. He was on message. Skipper turned slightly as he held the baby high. Again, *Family Values!*

Several people flooded the stage. Family members of candidates and aides went on the stage. A lot of fake smiles and congratulations. One of Skipper's aides went up to him with a bright smile and a slap meant for the back when Skipper turned. Daniel was standing next to Skipper when his aide appeared with the sharp show of confidence and approval. Daniel turned toward Senator Skipper when his aide came up behind him and slapped his arm because the aide yelled out *yeah*, in a sound of victory.

Daniel instinctively looked up. Skipper's arm slipped as it was hit, and lost hold of the baby. The baby facing toward the audience instinctively winced and then cried as he descended to the stage floor. As the baby fell, he grabbed the air with his arms. The baby's mother looked up from below the stage floor, in the first row, and screamed. The cameras were catching frame by frame as the baby was falling. Daniel reacted with shock. He reached for the baby and caught her with both hands. As he could not bend at the knees, Daniel bent at his waist as he grasped.

Without thought, and only out of a reaction, so that a thing, like a glass, wouldn't break when it hit the floor beyond the stage floor, Dean Skipper lifted his leg, to break the baby's fall.

But Daniel got the brunt of the quick leg lift, and got a foot in the face. When Daniel got kicked in his jaw, he moaned. The camera shutters opened and closed and captured the *as is* looks of both Senator Daniel Carlson and worse yet, Senator Skipper Dean. The baby was fine as Daniel put her close to his shoulder when he recovered. The country would notice Daniel's heroism and quick thought. Quick thought revealed true character. Daniel went to help the child and Skipper almost kicked her. The country learned for sure that Daniel wasn't lying about why he didn't serve in the military, he had a bad knee. The country also learned about Skipper's family values, and Skipper knew it.

Dean Skipper knew in that moment it was over for him. He didn't need a poll to know what the silent majority would think. Skipper looked at Daniel Carlson, nodded his head, grimaced to one side of his mouth, and conceded in what was the most sincere thing Skipper had said in months: *Best of luck, Daniel.*

CHAPTER 16

By Silent Minority

THE THREE MEN KNEW each other but didn't know that each was involved. Ben Bradford was in charge of recruiting the other two, and was allowed to communicate with them, but not reveal his identity. Bradford was recruited to help lead the other two into the group. Everything was very much on a need-to-know basis.

Eugene Poindexter Hawkins was one of the top computer programmers in the world. He was a software geek of the first order. Hawkins looks the part. He makes Bill Gates look like he should be on the cover of *GQ Magazine*. He has curly dark hair, black framed glasses from 1978. One would half expect a paper clip in the joint of the frame to hold an arm together. Hawkins really had a pocket protector in his white short-sleeved collared shirts. Hawkins demanded that he be called Eugene, not Gene. He was proud to be a computer geek. He knew the other two geeks, and they knew him. The other two disliked Hawkins. He was odd and stood for outlandish things. Hawkins was motivated by unusual motivators, but Hawkins was transparent. Bradford knew how to motivate him.

Hawkins liked knowing he could slink in and around the computer world and invoke his own justice, at will. He was not *Anonymous* he just was himself, anonymously or not. To prove a point, Hawkins hacked into the bank that held Harvard's Dean of Arts & Science's personal account, and made a generous donation on behalf of the Dean to the Wigand Foundation to buy computers for inner city schools. Hawkins did it because he took an Art history class with the Dean, the one arts credit Hawkins needed to graduate. The Dean made the mistake of giving Hawkins a B+. Harvard never found out how it happened, or who did it. The Dean of course couldn't ask for the gift back, and it ate the Professor up inside.

When the United States invaded Grenada and then traded arms for hostages with the Contras, Hawkins became perturbed and hacked into the Pentagon's computer, human resources section. For three months every general in the United States Army received half a pay check. The other half went to the AFDC school lunch program. The military never found out how it happened, or who did it; so Hawkins confessed. He pled guilty to an indictment filed in Alexandria, Virginia. After six months in a low-level halfway house he was released. The government on its own motion sealed and then expunged his record. The National Security Agency then recruited him. Everyone hurt by the half-a-paycheck gag did not forgive, however. Three years later a general who had hell to pay when his wife found out that he went to Fort Lauderdale with his mistress brought pain to Hawkins. Because his salary check was not issued by the government, the general had to pay by credit card, which his wife discovered when the bill came. The general lured Hawkins to a hideaway in Seattle, and the general got his revenge: Army training. Hawkins was paranoid and feared he could be lured again.

The whole set up for this meeting made Hawkins extremely uneasy. When you've been an arrogant computer geek for most of your life, you never know who might be pissed off at you, and want revenge. Bradford didn't worry. Hawkins would join the team, *the Geeks*.

The next techie targeted for the Geeks was William Goode. He was likeable enough, but only if you didn't work in the computer industry. Goode brought out resentment in other techies because he was all talent and no hard work. He was awarded a PhD in computer science from M.I.T. when he was twenty-two years old. He just had a flair for the computer. He was the ultimate cognitive computer scientist. M.I.T. didn't know what to do with him so they made him a professor. He taught so well that everyone got an A or B in his classes. This bothered the faculty because the professors insisted that a Bell curve must be used to evaluate performance. Professor Goode thought the Bell curve was stupid. You knew the material or you didn't. Why make a test harder than you said it would be just to make sure someone gets a C. When the other professors tried to make the prodigy's life difficult at the University, he responded in-kind.

Some professors in the mathematics department typed their exams on the computer and then printed them out. Goode published the answers to the chaotic math final exam via email to every student in the class. When the whole class aced the exam, a faculty summit was convened. An investigation was launched, but not a soul in the class revealed the answers were emailed before the exam, and not after, as was usually the case. Even a deep *meta*-analysis into the sending codes revealed the emailed exam answers were sent after the exam was administered. The whole faculty knew Goode was responsible, but not one tenured professor could prove it.

Professor Goode was tired of sleeping with female techies. He wanted hot girls. He referred to them as *straight girls*. In his mind, that took money. Not that he needed to buy prostitutes; he just knew that hot girls required entertainment money. He still dressed like a grad student, flannels over a T-shirt. So on a suggestion of a girlfriend he bought himself a *G belt* from Gucci on a whim. He couldn't believe a belt could cost so much money. He wore it around campus, and it made a difference. Women took notice off campus as well. Goode became hooked. With the clothes comes the car. With the car came the first hot girl. Then they loved him for his mind as well as his Beemer. Goode would join the Geeks because $10,000 a month continually was deposited into his personal savings account for the last year. He would at least have to show for the meeting.

The ostensible leader of the Geeks was Benjamin Bradford. He was motivated by the power. He was promised a position in the White House. Bradford was taking it all on faith because even he hadn't met the man behind the scenes. Money was showing up where it was needed. Bradford didn't know who was his benefactor, but he challenged his benefactor to prove his worth. Bradford had a friend that was a long shot for an appointment for judge in a suburb of Seattle. Not a problem. Within one month, Bradford's friend was appointed by the governor of Washington State. Bradford told his friend that he was going to make him a judge. That he had connections that can make it happen. Bradford liked the power of his unknown benefactor, and his word. In exchange for his friend becoming a judge, Bradford had to appear for the meeting of the Geeks, and make sure the other two would show up. Bradford kept his part of the bargain. He had to assure Hawkins that Bradford was involved. Goode didn't know Bradford was involved because Goode didn't insist on knowing.

Bradford never got indicted and never hacked into any computer for no reason even though he knew he could. He designed the software program that could do it. It's now the standard in the hacker industry. Hawkins would never admit that Bradford created the *Hackman* program prototype that is still used today, but Hawkins knew it. And Bradford knew that Hawkins knew it. Bradford also created the Dark. The Dark is where the few who were invited could remain, program, and hack under the cover. That's why among the Geeks, Bradford could be boss.

Bradford was benevolent and accepting but could be vindictive, however. Bradford hacked into the University computer once to change a grade. To get a student to secure an interview for a friend who wanted to be a professor at the University of Massachusetts. Bradford knew the student, Alfred Dias. Dias' father was Dean at U of Mass. Dias had real pressure to live up to his father's expectations. An A in advanced thermodynamics would be perfect. Bradford hacked into the computer and changed Dias' grade from a C to an A. Bradford told him that he spoke to the professor who was a close friend. In turn, Dias tried to get Bradford's friend an interview. It didn't happen. For some reason, Bradford's friend didn't get the job. Bradford was embarrassed, and didn't like that Dias didn't keep his word. Bradford responded by changing Dias' grade again, to a C–. When Dias learned the following semester his grade changed and for the worse, he confronted the professor. The professor didn't know Bradford, denied talking to him, and told Dias he kept the raw copy of the exam and he got a C–. The professor did his own computer check and it turned out the history on the software revealed no tampering and no history except the one entry of a C-. The professor told Dias to produce the hardcopy of the report card, but Dias had forwarded it to his father. His father didn't keep the report card and gave him hell for what Dias' father considered a failing grade in thermodynamics.

* * *

Bradford lived in Seattle since attending M.I.T, so he just drove to the designated location. He was the first one. It was in a warehouse district, and it was pretty deserted. All he could hear was a garage band in the distance. The main door was red and unlocked. He had parked ten spots away as directed. Bradford shut the door behind him.

"Stay where you are. Lock the door behind you."

Bradford did what he was told because he recognized the voice from the two years of phone calls.

"Relax, your eyes will adjust in a moment."

"I'm fine. You've gotten me this far," Bradford replied. "You know a lot about me, what about you?"

"No so fast. I've decided you will be the only one who knows who I am. And once you know who I am, you'll know what I do."

"I know what you can do. I just don't know why you are doing it," Bradford said.

"I'm trying to recruit you for a mission."

"What's the mission?"

"Whatever I say it's going to be. But for now I want you to research how to hack from remote locations. I mean not having a computer plugged into the wall."

"You mean wireless? We're there. Why would you want to do it from a remote location?" Ben realized who was talking to and figured it out. It would be tougher to leave footprints, and this guy doesn't want to get caught. Slowly, Bradford's eyes adjusted and could start to see who he was looking at. It was no one he'd ever met. No one that he recognized. "It's important that you tell me what you want exactly."

"I need you and your friends to be able to disrupt simple accounting software programs in progress. The encryptions will be difficult to read and alter. They will be designed by different companies, so chances are there won't be much in common."

"Which companies?" Bradford asked.

"Don't know yet. They're not even in existence."

"Do you even know if they're going to be in existence?"

"I have a good feeling they will be. I just know things about how society thinks. Which direction it wants to go."

Bradford was slightly amused by cryptic talk but was holding back on being annoyed. This person was right about a lot of things the last two years.

"How did you get my friend appointed by the governor to be a judge?"

"Does it really matter?"

"I just want to know why an extremely powerful man wants me and my friends to learn how to disrupt simple accounting programs with complex encryptions. Are you with the government?"

"I am to some extent. But I'm representing interest outside of the government."

"What do I call you?" Bradford asked.

"Are you in?"

"Would we be doing something illegal?"

"Yes."

"Would it be unethical?"

"Depends whom you ask? And what view point. For the greater good. It's moral. Ethical? That's questionable. But what you need to answer is, will you keep a secret until you die? I don't want to sound threatening, but you can't tell anyone that you even know me or what we're going to do. One day we're going to slide over the line, or not. I just want you to be prepared."

"I can keep a secret. No one talks to Eugene. And, as long as you pay Goode off you've got all three," Bradford said matter of factly.

"Go talk to them. Turn to your right. The connecting room Goode is in. Find out what he wants."

Bradford did what he was told. He walked into the next room and it was lit. Bradford shielded his eyes and saw Goode sitting in a chair in the middle of the second room of the warehouse. All they could hear is garage band music in the distance. The two old schoolmates talked for a few minutes, and then Bradford returned to the first room.

"Goode wants to be appointed to the board of Symantec, if this becomes big. Do you have the power to do it?"

"You oversold me, kid. We'll see where this goes. Until then, just tell him he gets the money he's been receiving on a monthly basis."

Bradford returned to Goode and then came back. Goode agreed. He felt good negotiating with a man who's been giving him $10,000 a month without ever meeting him. Goode trusted it. So Bradford went to see Eugene Hawkins and returned.

"You sure you want Eugene? He's an idiot. And he's temperamental."

"What did he want?"

"Eugene wants to know if you had him shot in the foot."

"What?" The voice was exasperated.

"That's what he said. He wants to know if you're General Speiser, and had him shot in the foot by a Chinaman."

"How long ago did that happen? Before you knew of me?"

"Oh yeah, long time before," Bradford replied.

"Tell him, no, I'm not, but I'll make sure that can never happen again."

"He also wants freedom for the internet."

He started to think Bradford might be right.

"What does that mean?"

"He said if you know about the wireless-internet encryption, then you're probably in the military and you're probably working for General Speiser."

"I'm not with the military," he said angrily. "If this project goes off like I think it will, General Speiser won't be shit to him. Okay. Tell him that. He has two minutes to decide or getting shot in the foot is not what he'll be worrying about."

At that moment, Bradford realized that this *asking* dialogue was not voluntary. He was in or he'd be out. So Bradford went back in to see Hawkins. Hawkins didn't moan and groan. Finally, Bradford returned and advised Hawkins was in. The voice told him to meet together about focusing on encryption research. They did.

Bradford came back into the first room. We're all set.

"Good," the voice said. He then handed Bradford three pieces of paper. Bradford couldn't read what it said in the dark. "There are encryption codes that need to be cracked. Hand one page to each of your friends. Let me know when they've been cracked."

"Okay. Should they leave now?"

"Yes, they can leave. I want you to stay so I can brief you to why we're doing this."

"You forgot one thing," Bradford said.

"What's that?"

"What about what I want?"

"What do you want?"

"I want to be able to do what you do. I want to be an influencer."

"You will be. Definitely."

"How will I know? I know you can give money and influence the Governor in Washington State. But what about beyond that?"

"Yes, beyond that. If this works out, you can work for me where I'll be working," Peter Spark said.

CHAPTER 17

Conspiracy Theories

T<small>HIS WAS THE LARGEST</small> gathering Daniel Carlson ever addressed. *Peter principle syndrome* surfaced in his consciousness. He felt like he was going to be exposed as the fraud. Who is he to dare to think he could lead a country? The greatest Republic in the history of the world. But the keynote speech began, as Daniel was behind the scene. "Tonight, I will have the distinct honor and privilege of nominating the next President of the United States—Senator Daniel Carlson." Applause—intense applause from thousands swelled in Madison Square Garden. It was an arena, a coliseum of political idealists, or dinosaurs stoned by the thick excitement. Daniel took in the applause and ignored the pain in his knee. He believed his fraudulent character for a moment. He could be President. How can so many people be wrong?

"This country's future welfare depends on the leadership of Daniel Carlson." Daniel listened from behind a curtain offstage. *Zealots.* Members of the herd, he thought. Cultish personalities bubbled to a peak. Even spectators of the media were overcome with the momentum of enthusiasm. Senator Dean Skipper continued, absorbing Daniel's glory. "He is our hope for our future; the future needs change; and Daniel Carlson is our man of change." A politically logical generic syllogism oozed with great ease from Skipper.

"The men in the White House tell a different story. They see the county in a different way than the rest of the people. They don't have to worry about whether millions of Americans will lose their jobs. They ignore those who struggle to pay their mortgage and those who provide an education for their children. They still believe they live in a glistening intellectual tower on a hill. They don't see the economic deterioration around us due to over-taxation." Daniel off to the side waited patiently and he too, through the permeating energy, enjoyed the raves. Daniel's knee tensed further with pain, but Senator Skipper spoke with no pain. He resolved his conflict, and was with the Carlson camp. Skipper knew the game and would benefit by playing ball.

"Tell the lies over and over and soon it will be true."

"No. No!" A person screamed.

"But what our children will know, despite what they hear from the White House is that there is little hope, even in America." Supportive boo's broke the monotony of the repetitive "D.C. to D.C." June glowed with pride from a distance, at Daniel's side.

"How can such a thing happen in the United States? Our economy is recessed, our streets are crime-ridden, and our children have fallen victim to drugs. This is because there's been a fundamental disregard for the other 99% of the country. The extra money from massive taxation hasn't trickled down to the rest so the American economy will grow and prosper again. Now the U.S. is no longer one of the largest creditor nations and producers of goods—it dove off the economic diving board and is falling downward. But in this global economy, there are no points for style."

Daniel could not help but nod. Nice turnaround on the top 1%, he thought. A flicker of hope ignited within him, and he decided to believe what he heard—that he was the man for change. Daniel looked around and noticed that no one was around him. His whole family was out of his peripheral reach. Focusing on his future, he again revisited the place where he left himself behind. The place where he ushered a young person into his office and spoke to them about whatever was troubling him or her. When Daniel would give a speech, it would've been a lecture about the law or the mores of society. How they as young people could change it.

Peter Spark was conspicuously absent, and Daniel wished he were there to hold his hand, in the spiritual sense. But Peter had more important matters behind the scenes to attend to. He was the bag man and he had more debts to collect.

★ ★ ★

Peter anxiously waited for the report from the Director of Central Intelligence in his office. His ties with Daniel and the Intelligence community opened the door to lead an operation on behalf of Daniel. It concerned the Chinese. Peter had no experience with the Chinese, and he was troubled by the apparent contrast in style between the old Soviets and the Chinese.

The Asian culture emphasizes shame over guilt. The Chinese could lie easier than be disloyal to the mission. Their upbringing presented a different challenge to the American Intelligence Community and Daniel's desires for more free trade. The Director walked into Peter's Office after he was announced. Director Yates' face masked the distress he was feeling. Contrary to the Chinese, he felt guilt and wished he didn't.

"At first this guy seemed perfect. I mean he fit the profile and everything. He spoke the right language. He was young and handsome, which was all that was needed." His voice was high pitched and explanatory.

Peter just listened to Yates. He was disappointed with the tone the Director used. It only meant one thing: he failed.

"All we got from our man outside the office was that he was talking with the blond man with the silver glasses. He had an effeminate voice. Nobody we've ever heard about before." The Director appeared downtrodden. Peter did not speak, but it was obvious that he was not pleased and that these kinds of failures fed Peter's obsession to control everything. "Would you like me to play the tape?"

"Yes, I would," Peter answered. Yates started the tape.

The tape began as if already in the middle of a conversation. "Are you good in the field of open law?" Which immediately meant to Peter as a question regarding the agent's stomach for killing. Rendition. What is illegal in the U.S. is legal somewhere else.

"Yes sir." The interview appeared to be going well. Nothing to worry about. Peter could sense that the boy was confident and poised for the next question.

". . . Are you good with technical equipment and the likes?" Peter looked down at the pictures that were presented to him on his desk. The young man, who was almost a boy, barely out of college sat adjacent to a desk in an undecorated room. He was Chinese and spoke English, Korean, and Japanese. His soft mustache was hair not thick enough to be considered whiskers. He barely had thoughts of his own. He was too new to the Agency for any independent thought. The harking to orders by an educated agent was rare, yet good for the brass.

"Yes sir." Suddenly, a gun came from behind this young man's head. He wasn't even given the chance to enjoy the coolness of the weapon against his temple. The man outside did photograph the tattoo strewn across the forehand of the man holding the gun. The man put a bullet in the young agent's head. The noise on the tape made the Director wince.

Peter stopped the tape himself. "What do we know from this?"

"We know very little. Tan could have been mistaken for a rival gang or a Mandarin agent. There is no way they could suspect he was with the Agency. But this is definitely a sign the Chinese think that Carlson will be elected President."

"He could have suspected. Did Tan say anything?"

"No."

"That's it. Just another star in the lobby of Headquarters?" Peter was genuinely concerned. Peter wondered about the boy and his mission that failed. Tan didn't expect to die for his country; otherwise, he would not have served. It just didn't seem right. What more is the fact that Daniel would suffer. That's all that Peter was left to be concerned about.

"What will you tell Carlson?" The Director asked.

"I'm not going to tell him anything. There is no point in upsetting him."

"What should we do . . . ?"

"Just continue with Plan B. We have to cover all contingencies. I won't have the next President's life threatened or his trade package by a bunch of foreign thugs. Find out if this group is really Chinese and then we'll know what action to take from there."

Peter wondered if this whole set up was really too easy. The tattoo of a crescent moon on the arm of the agent's killer. It stands out like a uniform. Not the mark of an assassin. But these assassins do not care if they are found. That is part of the message. The Chinese mob may have intended for Peter to know that it was they who wished to destroy Daniel's plans for the Presidency.

★ ★ ★

The older gentleman scrutinized the young man. They were in an empty warehouse in a Connecticut suburb.

"Assassination is not an option," the older man said.

"Does this group really have the power to do that?" The nervous one replied.

"You think I've been jerking your chain!" The older man barked. Even with the curmudgeon grimace on his face, the young man raised his concern.

"Well, we just don't like what the man stands for. I happen to like him on a personal level."

"This isn't a glee club. You knew what you were getting into. It just so happens that assassination is an option that cannot be accepted."

The young man approved the terms of membership almost a year ago. They were just refreshed in his mind again by his director's retort.

"You see, like Kennedy, his assassination prompted Johnson to get legislation passed that the live Kennedy couldn't."

The young man silently approved of that decision. He would hate to be the Brutus of the conspiracy. "This is something to consider when you have a proposed solution to a problem; you must take its consequences to the nth step. If you can live with them, then it's a wise option to take. If not, well then you can't do it."

"What do you want me to do?" He swallowed and focused on the wetness beginning to drip from his scalp to his forehead.

"Keep digging. Find out what it is. Everyone has at least a bone in the closet, the future President has his. Get somebody drunk, pretend you're not listening. You have the ability to find out what it is."

There was a long pause. The young man felt the squeeze inside his gut. The privileges of membership. There was really nothing for him to decide. He had to do it. He could take his time—just had to do it.

"I will take care of it, General Speiser."

"I expect you to contact me from school before the summer."

"Where will I find you?"

"Use the Pentagon number."

With that command, the neophyte returned to his battle ground.

* * *

The milieu was distinctly Ivy League. Legal encyclopedias and casebooks formed small mountains on the desk that separated Alan Carlson and his classmate Marcus Brutowski. The gold framed lamp, the traditional one with the green plastic dome shade, emitted a yellow glow that distorted the others faces.

Alan was quiet and pensive. His mood had mellowed and he was relaxed. It was a conditioned relaxation response triggered by the cool weather that swept over New Haven. Brutowski was from the Northeast and never associated a mood with the cold.

The two law students were studying professional ethics, a new course that was required for graduation.

"What bullshit this stuff is," Brutowski said. "We have to study this stuff for the bar anyway. I don't know why we have to take the course."

"It's just a bunch of movies, and now we have to memorize the code. Imagine if lawyers didn't police lawyers. We'd have a bunch of guys named Zeke who watch Matlock ruling on what was ethical," Alan retorted. Brutowski laughed at Alan's turn of phrase.

"Well I'm tired of this shit. Tell me how your dad's campaign is coming."

"It's going well."

"You have to help out in the entire social and campaign stuff, whatever it's called."

"This weekend I have to fly to California with my father. I get to speak at a young lawyers' luncheon and shake hands. It almost makes me want to study professional ethics, but I'll get a break from the cold weather."

"Any dirty tricks yet."

"Yeah, regular bullshit, we're used to it."

"Like what?" Brutowski eased Alan along.

"Like why my dad never really served in the Armed forces. They said his dad pulled some strings to get him out."

"Yeah, I heard about that shit," Brutowski yearned for more; his curiosity was great.

"Where did you hear about that," Alan inquired, half concerned.

"I read it in *Time* last week."

"Oh yeah? They got nothing on my dad. He ran for the Senate two times. You don't think they know about each day of his life on the planet."

"I suppose. I mean everybody's got something to hide," Brutowski's pulse rose as he found a great segue into the conversation he wanted to be immersed in.

"Yes, we had to discuss some of them with the campaign strategists."

"Really?"

"Yup," Alan was not happy that he released that information.

"What about your father?"

"He discussed whatever he discussed."

Brutowski noted Alan's closed answer. He dared to move on. He was careful not to cross examine, or appear that he was doing so. Regular conversation, that would be the key to his success.

"You don't know what he discussed?"

Alan replied, "Oh no. It's all a secret. He doesn't know mine, and I don't know his."

"Maybe you'll tell me yours later, over some beers."

"Yeah, in your dreams," Alan answered, unconcerned by Brutowski's prying. Alan thought he was a reliable new friend. He wasn't, however, going to play to his interest in First Family secrets.

"What did you think of the defense attorney whose wife was murdered, and didn't let any of his colleagues represent the man who murdered her?"

"What goes around comes around. He deserved to be sanctioned."

"What would you have done?"

"I don't know," Alan thought and became a little nervous.

"The guy did what any normal powerful man would've done. How could anyone just sit around and let a rapist go without punishment?"

The pause was thick and uncomfortable. Brutowski sensed it, but he didn't understand it.

"Maybe we should save this discussion for the beers too." Alan dismissed further conversation.

CHAPTER 18

Peter Spark

Peter Spark loved Daniel Carlson, because Daniel Carlson gave Peter Spark everything Peter needed to thrive. Daniel Carlson became Senator Carlson by his career history, breeding, and his ability to deliver a message by public speaking. Now, as a Senator, he had a voting history. Senator Carlson didn't play the favor bank like an adept politician. Most politicians don't do what's right, but do what's owed. How effective is the politician at figuring out whom he owes. Senator Carlson didn't do what was owed, but sought to do what was right. This made him unique and a political liability. On Daniel Carlson's bad days, he still held the conviction that even if he wasn't making a difference, he was trying to advocate for what he believed. So Daniel endured the state-by-state whirlwind tours where he advocated his *No child left behind*—for real speech. In Wisconsin, Senator Carlson gave his *Social Security: The train is coming* speech. Daniel Carlson emphasized medical research to stop breast cancer, a cancer that can be cured with a commitment of dedication and resources. Daniel believed that if breast cancer occurred in men more frequently, society would already have a cure. These speeches inspired Daniel to think about what government's role is in our society. Government must be the strong infrastructure, but not the foundation of society. This meant government should create opportunities for society so a strong economy, educated children, and health care for all can be the usual way. The United States should lead the world by example. Daniel Carlson resented the fact that children lived in poverty, weren't being educated and cared for, and yet the government considers it a victory when it sends a poor, uneducated, sick boy, who didn't have opportunities, to prison for the rest of his life. Pay now, or pay later, well America feels better paying later, second only to the plan of: do nothing until we're in a crisis.

Peter Spark didn't love Daniel Carlson because he strove for what was right, but by loyalty. Spark lived for the mission, needed the mission. His mission was moving Senator Carlson to increased power. Daniel let Peter Spark have his own independent power and authority. With that loyalty and love, Peter Spark made a promise to himself: to make Daniel Carlson President of the United States. That's why Peter Spark was willing to put together secret slush fund money of millions of dollars and spend $500,000 for an encryption code from BMI. BMI didn't know it, except for the employee who gave it to an agent of Peter Spark's. Peter gave it to Bradford, who in turn had the Geeks use it in their work, still not knowing exactly what they were being asked to accomplish. Peter Spark knew the *Geeks* would figure it out soon enough. The *Geeks* could access various large scale computer counters and the next step would be to alter their data from a distance without getting caught. At this point, having the encryption code to break into a specific type of computer, is like getting into a man's office and look around. There was still the matter of getting into his locked filing cabinet, and that was where Peter Spark wanted. Inside the filing cabinet, where Peter could really make a difference. Peter was grateful. When Peter felt grateful, he became a big tipper. For Bradford, Peter connected him to a high-level lobbyist in Washington State who got Bradford involved in politics. Bradford appreciated it very much and was building his political power. On a car ride with Dale Boatly an original employee and shareholder of Symantec hooked up one of Bradford's friend with a sizeable contribution for a State Senate race. Goode was given a promotion at BMI and was now in charge of the software development, remote link technology department. And since Hawkins actually was able to apply the encryption code from a remote location in a test exercise, Peter gave him a taste of the ultimate prize, revenge.

Peter knew a couple of guys from Naval Intelligence, specialists for this type of assignment. Peter knew the agent since he was a twenty-year-old operative in Vietnam, but the agent still had his good looks. The agent got to know General Speiser, and once the intelligence gathering on Speiser was done, the agent moved to his wife. Learned all about her, when she woke up. She jogged for an hour in her suburban Bethesda neighborhood. By the time she made her way home her General husband was already gone for work. She then showered and met a girlfriend for coffee. That's when the agent met her for the first time. Sherry Speiser's friend Suzie's car didn't start that morning, her battery was disconnected. The *AAA* guy figured out the problem within minutes, but it took him three hours to get there. So Sherry met the agent, a handsome man who knew how to talk to bored desperate housewives. It took only a week before Sherry invited the agent into her house in Bethesda. The General was away from dawn to dusk. She was ignored and she resented it. At this stage in her husband's career, Sherry was irrelevant. The agent learned more about the General than Peter even wanted to know. And besides taking her panties, he took a letter opener off the General's desk. It was a letter opener given to him by President Nixon. It was unique enough to convince the General that the agent was in his house.

General Speiser drove home from the Pentagon at 10:00 p.m. after a long day. On his way home, for seemingly no explicable reason, a man ran General Speiser off the road on Huntington Wilson Lane. The General was shocked and didn't understand what he had done to provoke this crazy driver. The slender man walked over to Speiser's car and helped him open the door.

"What the fuck is your problem!" The General screamed. The General noticed a moon tattoo on the back of the man's left hand. The calm slender man stared at the General and pushed him back to the driver's seat when he tried to stand up. The man was another *friend* of Peter Spark. His nickname was "Joe," but his real name was Han, Chinese. Han with a flick of the wrist elongated a telescopic *asp* baton and cracked the General across his left ankle as he pinned the General's foot to the asphalt with his own foot. Han was convinced he had broken the General's ankle, but had instructions to do more. Han took the General's letter opener and planted it right into his broken foot. The General was really screaming now. Han at last took out a pair of panties from his back pocket, which Han discovered had the monogram *SAS* on them, and tossed them. They landed on the General's lap. Han's last words, in a strong Chinese accent, before he sped off: "Clean up your blood with that." Peter granted justice for all, for Hawkins and Mrs. Speiser too.

CHAPTER 19

Election Day

EUGENE HAWKINS ALSO BECAME enamored with Daniel Carlson, but didn't know that he was working for Carlson up until this moment. What a joy of convergence that was about to occur when Hawkins realized that his work would make sure that the man he idolized was President. Hawkins, among his other obscure views, was for free internet and legislation for open source code for all online software. There was talk of taxing the internet and stricter intellectual property laws in the U.S. Having internal barrier chips in computers, which would send information to the government about usage on the internet. Hawkins thought it was Orwellian and intellectual obstructionism. No one understood the internet as well as Hawkins. Hawkins knew the world could communicate, market, express, and convey through the world of computers. With the right President, at a critical time, it could all be for the world to take. A marketplace of socialistic intellectualism. So Hawkins flew to Washington, D.C.

★ ★ ★

Bradford was sitting in the lounge area of the only place that had a really good panoramic view of the City of Fort Lauderdale. Reception was key by computer, and for whatever reason, Bradford determined, he had to be high. Within minutes, Peter Spark told Bradford on a cellular phone, you need high and facing the railroad tracks. Broward County's votes were being counted at a building on SW 6th Avenue. A local politician told Peter, who then told Bradford: "Go to the Tower Club."

The Tower Club is sort of a stiff place. A member has to be wearing a jacket to walk in. Bradford wore a jacket, but had a computer under his arm—a high-powered computer. Even the most fervent techie who goes to the computer-electronic trade show in Las Vegas wouldn't even know what was going on in Bradford's laptop. But Bradford needed reception. Tonight, Bradford was going to become a very powerful man. He knew Peter Spark as a grateful and powerful man, and Bradford knew what he was about to do. Daniel Carlson had no idea, because he was so close to winning or losing the presidency, that Peter Spark had lost his nerve. Peter wanted to win, was sure Daniel could win, but didn't want to leave anything to chance.

It's the same theory of the cold war. The Soviets had nuclear weapons; the Soviets were going to use them. Well Peter won the software wars. The Geeks discovered long distance election hacking faster than the Democrats, and now the Florida election will be won at the Tower Club. It's amazing, Peter Spark was extremely attuned to winning elections. He knew that Daniel had to win Florida. He knew Daniel had to be close enough in Florida that the number of electoral votes will tip in Daniel Carlson's favor to win in Florida and the rest of the country. Peter couldn't pick a state with too few electoral votes. He couldn't pick a State where Daniel was expected to lose by a large margin, because it would draw suspicion.

But thank goodness, Florida was great. Florida was still on the chad system. Peter had the chad software mastered. Broward didn't have the scantron system working; it had punch-out cards. It was perfect. Even if there was a recount, who the hell would know how or why the computers doing the counting were considering a vote. There would be no scandal, no indictments. But Peter didn't plan to get caught. Daniel just needed to win by enough, and that would be enough. Florida was an early return, it was all about Eastern Standard Time to send a message that this election was wrapped up, and yes, the Senator from Florida won Florida, despite all the media pundits trying to make it a horse race.

Bradford took the elevator to the top floor of some bank building that changes names so much even Peter couldn't get a straight answer on the name of it from the head of the Broward Republican Party. Bradford rode up twenty-eight floors. His ears popped as the silver elevator doors opened. He stepped out onto the marble floors. He walked through the heavy doors, not looking at the woman sitting behind the desk to the left. Bradford acted like he belonged and thought it would be sufficient. He was wearing an Armani suit with one of Goode's Gucci belts and Duchamp cufflinks. The receptionist didn't give him a second look.

It was a Tuesday, not a busy night for the club, but that could mean he would be noticed, and helped by someone from the staff. Bradford sat in a soft leather chair nearest the glass window that separated the inside from the outside. Bradford could see north as far as his eye could go. He noticed the bar on the other end of the room. The bartender dug into the ice bucket, and made a drink. Bradford looked around quickly and then opened up his laptop and began hacking; hacking into the Voting Executive Center—the VEC. That's where the votes were. *Bam*, there it was, right there on the screen, Bradford could watch the numbers of votes being calculated. Bradford was deep in thought.

"Would you like something to drink?" A waitress with a gray vest and bow tie asked.

"Oh no, I'll wait for the rest of the group, thank you." With a nod, the waitress was gone.

Bradford was clacking away on his laptop. It was apparent he wasn't getting past the first level of encryption because he wasn't getting a good connection. So, he stood up and the reception slightly improved.

Bradford walked out of the bar area and down the narrow hall, which was lined with wine- filled racks on each side. He looked down at his screen and saw that the reception was even better. A maitre d' looked at Bradford with a smile. He looked down for a moment to notice the open laptop in Bradford's hands.

"Can I help you sir? Are you a member?"

"Actually, I'm looking for Mr. Ferrero." Bradford replied.

"Oh, I haven't seen him yet," the maitre d' replied. "I don't see his name down with a reservation."

"I think he's just going to meet me for a drink. If it's not too busy in that corner, I was wondering if I can just take a quick look at the view. Please?"

"That'll be fine for a friend of Mr. Hamaway. But only for a moment."

Bradford was nervous he wasn't going to be allowed in. He walked briskly to the right, and noticed no one was there eating at a table. He didn't sit. He held the computer in his left hand and typed with his right. This was the spot. There was no better place in Fort Lauderdale for this type of reception. Within moments, the chad encryption got Bradford into the vote-counting machine. Daniel Carlson was sure to win in Broward County.

* * *

Ohio had an even more vulnerable system. The voting system in Ohio used a scantron code. Goode paid off the chief programmer at the company. It's the ultimate backdoor. No one in the whole scantron company knew about how to crack the code other than the programmer. Goode taught the chief programmer in graduate school, and they were simpatico. Simpatico plus money and alcohol, equals loose talk. The key to getting more votes for one candidate, the backdoor, is voting for all candidates in the first four races. Then in the fifth race, vote for the Republican and Daniel Carlson will get a boost in the number of votes by ten percent. Simple. Goode moved to Ohio and registered to vote. And William Goode voted. He voted for Daniel Carlson for President, once, but made it count many times.

* * *

Eugene Hawkins was dressed like a combat-ready photojournalist, complete with vest-jacket equipped with a large sleeve in the back of a jacket for his laptop computer. Hawkins turned in his black thick framed glasses and got himself a modern silver frameless German Luxor. He cut his hair like a Marine entering boot camp. Hawkins felt he was on a mission. He knew his mission was for a man he believed in. He knew Daniel Carlson was for a free internet and unrelenting belief for a national commitment to education, research and development in the field of technology.

Candice Kostinakas was one of Washington's best unknown known call girls. She never said anything about anyone. Discretion, a rare and perfect quality for a girl, and more particularly for this election night. Candice was a Greek goddess. She was five-foot-eleven. Long dark curls started from the top of her scalp and went five inches past her shoulders. Thick natural red ruby lips. Smooth fair skin. Perfect double-C breasts, also natural. She was smart and knew something about many different subjects. She could talk about the makeup of the Supreme Court, with surprising detail; it could make one wonder if she knew some of them. She could talk about the 1987 New York Giants. She could also talk about China, which was the only fact, that Peter Spark didn't like. But she was the best for other reasons. Peter still wasn't taking any chances. You could take her to a motorcycle bar or a ten-thousand-dollar-a-plate political dinner. She made every man feel she could be the perfect wife. She was so appropriate and didn't have to play a part tonight. She only had to get a room, do her thing, and be gone.

Hawkins walked into the lobby of the Watergate Hotel. She blended better than he did. Candice recognized Hawkins's description. She didn't know his name. He didn't say.

"Candice?"

"Yes."

"Did you get a key to the room?" Hawkins demanded.

"Yes, but there's a small problem," Candice said with some hesitation. She prided herself on details, and making things one-hundred percent perfect.

"What is it?"

"The suite you requested is occupied. Can it be another room?"

Hawkins, knowing he needed the best reception possible for his laptop said, "No, it has to be that suite." Candice didn't question why that particular suite was of such importance. With that response, Candice pulled out a keycard to the suite.

"They'll be gone all night. But my connection at the desk will call to the room if they come back early," Candice said.

"Good. Let's go."

Candice wrapped her arm around Eugene Hawkins's arm as they walked to the elevator. Once they were in the suite, Hawkins put his jacket on a chair and kept the computer in the back pocket of the jacket. The best call girl in Washington placed Eugene Hawkins on the suite's king size bed and connected to him like no woman ever had. She gave him a sexual experience that distracted Eugene Hawkins's thoughts about computers and an expanding internet for the first time in years. She was a pro. When she was done, she said: "Take the key with you, and don't be too long." With a deep sigh, Eugene Hawkins dressed and clicked on his computer. He was amazed that the chad software program worked so well and had to give Bradford credit for putting this whole thing together. Within moments, Daniel Carlson got a few extra votes and got the much needed electoral votes in Maryland, Washington, D.C. and Virginia.

In the post-coital resolution and election rigging, Hawkins celebrated in his mind, as he heard the door to the suite open. Hawkins's heart shocked into a panic. He closed his computer as he slid underneath the bed where he had just spent exhilarating moments. Where was the phone call from downstairs? Hawkins hid under the bed for hours. Hawkins figured out the two lovers inches above his head were running an undercover operation of their own. He was a Senator from Arizona, and she was his mistress. He knew Daniel Carlson was elected President before the couple lying on top of him fell asleep, and he could saunter out of the room undetected.

★ ★ ★

The election was too close for Peter Spark. There were rumblings about a recount in Florida. But the election wasn't that close. It was more than a one-percent margin, and under Florida law a recount was not authorized. Daniel Carlson had no idea what Peter was doing. President-elect Carlson was drunk with disbelief and the promise of power. Trumpets blared as Daniel Carlson walked into a party room at the Fontainebleau Hotel's convention center. Carlson's opponent was in no mood to be written in history's book as the man who made a legal challenge to an election. Richard Nixon knew he was robbed of his rightful place a term earlier, by a corrupt Kennedy campaign. He didn't want to be a part of a legal challenge to a Presidential election.

Daniel Carlson took to the stage and in that moment, as he walked to the podium and to the microphone he became the President of the United States. He transmorgraphied into the living leader of the free world. Daniel Carlson didn't look like a Senator. He didn't look like a man and was larger than his body. His family was behind him, June, his lovely adoring wife; his two children, which now America must accept as his own. "Ladies and Gentlemen, the President of the United States, President Daniel Carlson."

"Good evening!" The applause seemed endless. "I just spoke moments ago with my friend. And he has congratulated me as the President of the United States." The room erupted like the Beatles, with John, took the stage in a surprise performance. "Things are going to be different, and I mean it. I'm going to be a different President. I'm going to be thinking about you, America as if it were the last and only four years I can serve as President. I will act like I don't have to be reelected. I will be a true Republican. This is me. I will be a conservative economist while understanding there is a struggling working class that needs real opportunity to achieve. We level the playing field for all with education. We must prepare America for the future. If you trust me, I will be good for America. Thank you for your support." Daniel was convinced the Silent Majority had lost, and the vocal minority has won. Tonight everyone in that room believed in Daniel Carlson. He made others nervous, the type of people that don't like to be made nervous.

CHAPTER 20

The First 60 Days:
The President's Diary

DAY 1

I am the President! What a miracle that is! I continue to write in my diary for myself as notes for a memoir of the future, which I am compelled to write at the end of my term as President. But I made it a promise to myself, regardless of how I may spin, don't adulterate the truth in the future, for purposes known and unknown, I will write this journal with clarity and honesty.

The first day as President was incredibly heady. It is probably the last day I will ever feel just plain glory. The bands and the receptions—my hand is swollen and my forearm is strained from the endless handshakes. My head is ringing. I felt like a child who has stayed up all night with a new toy, and still wants to play, but beaten by exhaustion, succumbs to the gravity of fatigue and goes to bed.

I did do some constructive things today. I met with former cabinet officials from the last administration. I picked up a few hints from some wise men. I made a point to keep in touch with a few, on issues of upcoming importance. I also set up several appointments to speak with former Presidents by phone. Why repeat other people's mistakes? Instead of touching the stove for myself, and learning that it's hot, I'm going to get the most I can from others' mistakes.

It just dawned on me that I didn't speak with any Democratic cabinet members. Why shouldn't I? Behind closed doors, the old cabinet, as partisan as they are don't put on a show for the camera. They'll do it the second they leave my office, which is why I must be careful with these people, but they aren't all like Mafioso chiefs, of the Brando mold, who as skilled as chess masters can at first appear to aid my administration, and then months later manifest the mines that were laid in following their advice. I've learned over the years, and I have to rely on my experience, that everyone has his spin on issues. This isn't bad or good, just something that needs to be factored into a final decision.

One mistake is not having people around whom a President can trust. As I've known for years, most people in Washington have their own canoe to paddle. I've been toying with the idea and I really want to establish an informal cabinet like the one Andrew Jackson had when he was President. I just want a bunch of guys sitting around shooting the bull, giving me some honest answers. A group of guys who are older, wiser, and simply interested in seeing my administration succeed. I'll hold these meetings in a backroom in the East Wing.

I slept well for the first time in a long time. I think I have conquered my Silent Majority.

DAY 2

I think this was the longest day of my life. It was nonstop meetings and briefings. I didn't think I would even have time to write today. I have to pick cabinet secretaries and undersecretaries. I have given deference to some people because of their involvement with the campaign. I have to now appoint people to very important positions, and I don't know them very well, and then I have to trust them. I've learned about many agendas of many of the people who helped me get here. I barely won, and they act like the whole country gave me a mandate to do exactly what they or their little organization wants to get accomplished. Everyone is in their own little world. The Christian God Foundation has been bothering Peter to get a meeting with me. There is some prestige associated with meeting with the President within the first ten days of this presidency. Poor and happy Peter. The best decision I made was to put Peter in charge of it. I officially announced that Peter Spark would be the White House Chief of Staff.

DAY 3

June woke up this morning the same time I did. She looked at me after I got dressed in my Brioni blue pin-striped suit and said that I looked transformed into the President of the United States. I did look good, and I wanted to look sharp today.

Today, my speech writers have agreed that I don't have to regurgitate my inauguration spin off speech. Basically, the spin off speech is the key points of the inaugural address without having to repeat it. I can get into specifics and motivate my troops to push for the prescription medication bill. "No patient left behind." Things are going to have to change around this country. I really want to represent this country. I'm a Republican, but I'm not here to just make corporate America richer. That's not the Republican I want to be. I'm meeting with some CEOs of the six major drug companies today. They want to talk about government deregulation of prescriptions. I want to talk about Alzheimer's and breast cancer medication, HIV and reducing the costs of medication. It can't be profit at any costs. I want to stimulate research and development.

They actually had the nerve to ask Peter if they can have "Government relations" people in the room during the meeting! No lobbyist gets direct access to the President, ever. So, our first joke broke out at the West Wing today. Whenever the term "Government relations" naturally comes up in a conversation, the person to the right of Peter has to say, "lobbyist." No one really laughs, but we all pause to appreciate the moment. Business is going to change around the White House, and then the country. I've sobered up. Doing a good job as President is more important to me than getting reelected. I'll be a better Jimmy Carter if that's what's meant to be. The big difference between me and the last guy who was in the Oval office is: I mean it.

DAY 4

Budget talks are about to begin. I'm going to deliver a balanced one, so there is no talk of a balanced budget amendment on my watch. The round-and-round fighting that's going to go on is going to be crazy. I'm not keeping in a bunch of multi-million dollar programs so that some Senator can say he delivered home the bacon for his home state. I need a formidable budget for the foreign intelligence services. I just have a bad feeling we're behind. Learn much, take preventative steps, and avoid war. I got Peter started on proposals to revamp the whole intelligence community to eliminate the petty turf wars that exist among the agencies. I think the Director of Central Intelligence should have budgetary authority over all the agencies, and that would get everyone sharing information. I have different ideas about the military too. Yes, we need a big budget, but in times of peace, which is what I'm going for, I want the military to breed good will across the world toward the United States. It feels like everybody hates us.

On a pleasant note, Elana Goldstein agreed to accept the position of Deputy Attorney General of the Civil Rights division. She should be approved very quickly because she is a Democrat. Not much of a roar over that from the Party. I don't think they really care too much about civil rights.

DAY 5

It's only the fifth day as President, and the tension is unreal. I thought I had to put up with a lot of bull when I was in the Senate. Now all the bull is pointed at me. When I was in the Senate I always wondered what the hell is going on at the White House. Now, I'm wondering, what the hell is going on in Congress.

It was just a rough day. The opponents of change were particularly united today against my crime bill. This one attacks the root of crime. It will take twenty years to see a difference. What these opposition people need to understand is that criminals are not our enemies, they are citizens too, at least the legal ones. Instead of putting them in jail for three years, how about really concentrating on rehabilitation. A real restructuring of the whole corrections system. Educate the juveniles so that they will have new values. Make them have hope they'll live past twenty-five years old.

The opposition profits from the fear, and I resent it. They profit from the rage. Their counterproposal is more death penalty for drug lords. That'll work. It's never happened. The other brilliant idea raises the sentences for offenses. We have no room in prisons anyway. Besides, these bozos know we can only raise penalties for federal crimes not state crimes. What a bunch of empty rhetoric. I'm getting a massage.

DAY 6

I was speaking with a member of the armed services committee today. A general recently promoted was General Speiser. He was remarking about the good old days when research and development of the Star Wars program was making progress. I almost laughed at his sincerity. Wasn't the strategic defense initiative an utter waste? He didn't appreciate my lack of support. I think the only thing SDI was good for was bankrupting the Soviets. If we're going to spend that kind of money, I want some potential civilian spin offs. Call me a bleeding heart, but we should not be moving toward preparing for war, we should be preparing for peace. I'm not naive enough to believe that we shouldn't have a strong military. We must spend large amounts of money, because we need to spread democracy through a demonstration of peace. That is the only way that we can hope for peace in tumultuous regions of the world. No long draged out wars. Our foreign policy should be to stop atrocities and let countries deal with self-governance. Governments can't murder their own people. That's what we should be willing to fight for and die for. I was willing to fight and die for this country, no matter what they said about me during the campaign. I thought I died the day that doctor told me I couldn't fight for my country. But I didn't. It's better that I lived. I've done a lot of good since then. The world would've missed me if I had died in war. I was a tad too young to die in Vietnam. Let the other man die for his country anyway.

DAY 7

I flew to Florida today. This was my first trip as President of the United States. I've been on Air Force One before, but now, with all my ego, it is mine. It's the Oval Office in a plane. I could have surgery on the flight. It's amazing! I got a lot of reading done on the flight. I love that I don't have to wait for the plane to get clearance to take off. When I get on the plane, there's immediate clearance for takeoff. Heady stuff. If I need to talk to someone, that person comes along for the trip.

I hit four cities in Florida: Miami Beach, West Palm Beach, Tampa, and Tallahassee. It was good to see home. It's tough to tell if the country is ready for a new way of thinking. No one really wants to think that far into the future. The Asians see into the next quarter-century, and so should we. Enough with management by crisis. Education is key. Research and development is key for a competitive America. Republicans who want the profits through no regulation need to understand I'm the CEO, and we're investing know-how for the future. How are we supposed to beat China, Japan, and Europe if we just threaten trade tariffs? Be the best and we'll do the best. We say it, now we have to do it. But that's the big lie. Corporate America says we're the best, but doesn't want to train to remain the best. What Corporate America wants from government is to tilt the playing field. My response is: I'll give you the best equipment, you lift. I'll give tax breaks for development of poor areas, so that jobs can be created, but I just don't give something for nothing. Open a training facility, and then we'll talk. Teach these people how to read, write, and use a computer. I'm exasperated by our illiteracy in America.

DAY 8

I awoke at 3 a.m. today. A Korean airliner was downed flying over mainland China. By all indications, the airplane just crashed. I spoke to all the leaders in the region. I haven't been able to force myself to speak to the leader of China since I don't have enough for a murder conviction, but I have the sense that he tried to have me assassinated. He still vehemently denies it. Later in the day, the report from North Korean newspapers is that the plane crashed as retaliation from the United States. I know I didn't order anything. I asked Peter, and he said it really was just a tragic plane crash. Peter doesn't know it, but I can tell when he's lying. It's almost imperceptible, but his right eye slightly glazes over with a tear. I think it has something to do with how he got his scar on his face. Peter can control his breathing, he doesn't sweat, he doesn't miss a heartbeat, doesn't blink, but he can't prevent the neurological response in his eye. My guess is he doesn't even know it himself. I know I won't tell him. I accept Peter. He is my friend, but I know what he thinks about and what he wants. I'm going to Camp David tomorrow for the first time.

DAY 9

Camp David is an incredible getaway. I spent the morning with the foreign affairs staff. We are preparing for a meeting with the South Koreans at the White House. Then a few weeks later the Palestinians. I took a long lunch, 11:00 am to 1:00 pm. I was able to read on a hammock. It was wonderful. I was able to take a nap. I woke up from the nap and realized America needs to aide in the peace process for two reasons: It's the right thing to do; and, America will compete better in peaceful regions of the world.

DAY 10

We secretly got the Ambassador for South Korea up to Camp David today. We snuck him in without any press noticing. After really getting a look around the campus today, I wouldn't understand why Castro wouldn't want to sneak in and spend some time. But the real coup is getting the North Korean envoy in as well. The two of them talked alone for a while, and then I came into the room. Peter had a strange look on his face the whole day. He doesn't believe in the whole negotiating process between the Koreans. He says the world and particularly the intelligence services don't understand well enough that Asian cultures will lie about their feelings and thoughts as a matter of honor. Their cultures are honor-based cultures, not guilt-based cultures like in the West. Practically speaking, national pride is more important than being fair and honest. So today's promise can be completely disregarded, because they have an agenda that protects their national sense of honor. I am more optimistic. I must defuse the airliner fiasco. I trust the plane just crashed. But what is the truth and what is perceived are two different things. The Silent Majority lives. Facts are facts. Yet, I must defuse perceptions.

DAY 11

I think I've been photographed more in the last eleven days as I was in the entire campaign. Everything I do seems to be photographed. It was fun at first, but it gets a little wearing. I have my own White House paparazzi. Everyone who shakes hands with me wants a picture. A picture communicates something. Prestige. In my mind, I'm just a teenager, who has big dreams for America. I'm a child in a very adult job. Making decisions in a moment that can affect the world. Three years from now, or ten years from now, I can learn that I made a very bad decision. How do I know if I'm doing the right things? I wake up in the mornings in fear. I feel depressed and sometimes angry that I'm in this position. Who put me here? Why am I here? What am I suppose to accomplish? I talk to God, but he doesn't talk back to me. Some Presidents enjoyed a blissful ignorance. I know how much I don't know when I make a decision. I know it can all go wrong, and a lot of it is about how much luck, divine intervention, and a momentum set a long time ago pushes things in motion. I don't want to go to war. There is great pressure to make war happen. I hate those that want war to happen.

DAY 12

I spoke to a special counselor in the White House. He's a counselor to the President who happens to be a psychiatrist. I guess the President can't speak to a psychologist, because we're all suppose to have it all together, all the time. Tony Soprano can see one, but I cannot. I learned that visiting Florida a few days ago triggered my melancholy. The warm weather of winter in Florida. The salty air off the intracoastal. I've been thinking of the first time visiting my father's grave. It was internally tumultuous.

I think that it's only part of the answer. In a few days, I have to finalize my decision on whether I'm going to send a Navy Seal team into Jordan to help the Israelis blow up the beginnings of a nuclear power lab. I have lots of confidence it's there. We just can't get caught. Congress will be pissed off. The rest of the Middle East will be angry. The oil people from Texas will be mad. I'll be fine if I just don't get caught. Peter is telling me not to tell the Congressional leadership, and let the Israelis do the damage and take the risk alone. Peter is good about not sugar coating his views behind closed doors. I think that is part of his Naval

Intelligence training. Say it like it is and then advocate once all the information is out there.

I don't want to leave the Israelis out on a limb by themselves. The Israelis' role in American history has been *crazy as the Americans want them to be*. They do what we don't have the guts to do by ourselves.

DAY 13

I woke up again in the middle of the night. The Israelis scrapped the plans for a stealth entry into the lab. They just flew some planes over Jordan and bombed it. It was a good surgical strike. Admiral Raven of Navy SOCOM was disappointed his boys didn't do it. I called the Prime Minister of Israel and complained that this was not what we agreed to. He replied he couldn't wait for me to make up my mind. I played mad, but I understood. It's a whole different consciousness for the Prime Minister. Thank God, I don't have it. It would require some lunatic bombing a bus full of children in Maryland for me to have it. I flew back to Washington, D.C. right away.

Later in the morning, I ordered our aircraft carriers in the region to be put on full alert. The Jordanians were claiming this was an unjustified strike. The Israelis bombed a hospital. Freaks were jumping up and down in the streets burning American and Israeli flags. I feel like bombing them when I see them. I went on television this morning and spoke to the Press Corp. I told them that I knew the Israelis were contemplating this strike. I wished it could have been resolved without violence, but I can't blame the Israelis for wanting to defend themselves. I answered the expected questions. Two Israeli soldiers were killed when one of the planes flying by was shot down. They'll be forgotten by tomorrow. My approval ratings went up five points by the afternoon. Apparently, I looked Presidential talking about the military conflict.

DAY 14

I was up the whole night in the Situation Room. I felt guilty that I didn't move fast enough to do a stealth entry. Those two pilots. I don't know anything about them, except they are dead. Could I have changed the outcome? Would four others have died instead? Would I have put the USA in a bad situation? Would I have set off a war? With my guilt, I agreed to let Israeli planes land on an aircraft carrier in the middle of the Suez. I gave permission to let the planes bomb the homes of suspected Palestinian suicide bombers, and then land on our boat. "It's funny," the

Prime Minister said, that was "a nice consolation, but it's not enough."

DAY 15

Because U.S. troops didn't engage the Palestinians, I personally didn't have to engage the White House Press Corps. My press secretary did a great job. She reminded them that these suicide bombers are terrorists who don't belong to any nationality. They are evil. Language is very important. I swear I think one of the reporters called the suicide bombers commandos. Is a Palestinian state the answer to peace? I don't know. Should I help reward them for terrorism? Why don't I let the Mainland Chinese move into Texas and see how it goes?

Just became acquainted with some new technology: drones. Drones are unmanned aircraft that is coming along as an excellent surveillance and bombing tool. The pilot is sitting in a room in Nevada and goes home for dinner every night.

DAY 16

I've decided to make weekends a little more like weekends. I like to read on weekends, but the meetings have to be limited. Everyone wants to meet every day of the week. Everyone wants to claim, I meet with the President all the time. I'm going to try and only have Intelligence briefings on the weekend mornings. And then do little else. Oh, who am I kidding? I have more appointments and confirmation hearings. Everyone's hand is out. You would think every single person was important to my winning the Presidency. In this election, each and every person was, not to mention I told them so. You would think those people would let me do my job like I want to. No, they want their patronage.

DAY 17

I've become a part of something today that I feel could be helpful to me on the national security front. I decided to start having massages in the morning, and the masseuse asked me for a password. I didn't know what to tell him. So I said the CoInTEL password and he said that would be good enough for today. He then handed me a letter. Inside was a typed welcome and tomorrow's password. It wasn't a literal password. It was the key to a password. My second grade teacher's last name and the square root of the number of times I have travelled to Japan. Cole 1.414. I hope that's right.

It also warned me of how a certain faction outside the government wishes to end my honeymoon early by releasing a story that I had smoked marijuana in the past. It was signed, *The Receptionist*.

I didn't know what to make of the note, other than to wait and see if it was true. I suspected Peter Spark was behind the whole system. That would be his thing. But that would be redundant.

Peter does not have to secretly tell me anything, he can just tell me.

Today the White House released the Justice Department strategy. Incorporating more programs to help solve crime rather than just prosecute offenders. Law enforcement should be more social-worker oriented. That is, if we want to reduce crime, rather than just fight it.

DAY 18

Sure enough. This message center arrangement was right. *The Post* came out with a front page article that said I smoked pot in my twenties. Such a triviality. It is an attempt to thwart my momentum before I even get started. There was nothing I could really do about it. It was true. I said that I tried it once like I did. That should pretty much be the end of it. I didn't gum it, I inhaled it and enjoyed it. I don't think children should be doing it, but nobody's evil if they try it.

The good news is, I delayed the release of my economic package until the end of the week, so it would get the coverage in the paper that it deserves. I like this message center thing so far, whoever is behind it. Seems pretty reliable, but what's its spin? Relying on this system, and I'm ripe for an escort into a brick wall. Information is not about getting the truth; it's about getting what is probably true. I'll get facts, information, and what does it all really mean? People must be able to interpret the information, and decide what they want to do with it. I'm on my guard with this *message* system.

DAY 19

I decided to take a shot and turn the whole pot smoking scandal from past campaigns to my advantage. I've launched my new campaign about drugs that I felt the American people were not ready for. It involves a complete attack on cigarettes and now I'm considering taking the campaign to alcohol as well. I'm willing to compromise on the beer, where I'll get the most flak. I might as well plant the seed for the next President.

The Department of Justice announced today that the United States would realign our 'racist' policies in the Immigration Service. Medical screening will be the determining factor in most of these cases. I doubt if there will be much of a change in the numbers of immigrants. But at least it won't appear so racist on the books.

DAY 20

Peter came into the Oval Office at the end of the day. He asked me to go into the adjoining office where he works. There was nothing strange about his request, but his mood was unusual. He asked me to call the CEO of Symantec and have a friend of Peter's who "helped us with the campaign" appointed to the board. Who is it, I asked? Peter said, "his name is William, he's a professor at MIT. He'd be a good choice." When I asked Peter how he helped us, Peter didn't really answer. I'll bring it up again at another time. I said I'll make the call. "Put it on the call list."

DAY 21

It has been a real fashion show over in the residence. The First Lady is doing photo shoots and getting all sorts of designer outfits for all occasions. Her speaking tour is supposed to raise money for school literacy programs. I am very happy she picked that wonderful cause. I walked in her makeshift dressing room/ fashion runway, and she barely noticed I was there. All she did was tell me to check out the dining room, it should look like our Florida home. Sure enough it did. It was decorated exactly in the same way. My relationship with June is great when she's busy. When she gets bored, oh boy, I'm miserable. I think action around the White House should keep her occupied. If it can't, then nothing else will.

DAY 22

Eating at the dining room table was a pleasant, familiar experience this morning. The Vice President came in to join me for our first breakfast together as President and Vice President. He was upset we weren't having breakfast in the Rose Garden. It's amazing how everyone wants to have pictures like no one knows he's Vice President. Maybe no one does. All Vice Presidents have an inferiority complex. Jack is no exception.

DAY 23

I'm into my third week as President, and it occurred to me that I'm an only child with no parents. I'm feeling the loneliness of not having any family. My mother had a brother. Who knows where he is today. He could be dead. I remember him as a child. I remember caring about him. I remember being a good nephew with my fun uncle. But he let the vices of life destroy him. My mother told me that he succumbed to gambling. When he lost, he turned to alcohol and drugs. Then his wife left him, my aunt. I don't have fond memories of her. She was in it for the good times and not the bad times. She was gone when things got rough. My uncle was gone too, when my mother said he wouldn't give him any more money to destroy himself. He visited some ten years later, but that was it. I haven't seen him through my Senate campaign, or since I've been President. I half expected he would come calling. He didn't. I assume it's either he is dead or is too embarrassed to approach me. I feel lonely because I have no one, but I am not interested in resuming a relationship with him.

I enjoyed visits from relatives from June's side of the family, but she doesn't keep in touch with them. Truth be told she is embarrassed by her family roots. She never could accept what she calls her *white trash* family. She does everything to pretend that they don't exist. They send cards and photographs. June writes but does not call, and I've never heard her speaking to any of her relatives, except for one cousin, Cathy. She is coming tonight for dinner with her husband, Carl. Carl is a dermatologist. He lifted Cathy from the trailer to Park Avenue. So to June, she was acceptable. Carl is a boring dermatologist. He doesn't do cutting edge medicine, but makes a very good living. This makes him interesting to June, and uninteresting to me. Carl wants nothing from me. I invited the Surgeon General to dinner for conversation help. But Carl doesn't even want to serve on a Presidential Board for medicine. Thank God June will be so excited she won't stop talking. I can just eat and be quiet.

DAY 24

The dinner went better than expected. I brought up the opportunity of being on a Presidential Board of Medicine to Carl, and he accepted. He was falling over himself to accept. I guess Dr. Carl wanted a piece of the prestige. I keep learning that I can persuade people to do things I want them to do. It makes me feel pretty good. It's funny, I really didn't care if Carl was or wasn't. The point is, I asked. If I asked, then I wanted him to say yes. It perhaps is impetuous. I'm ego driven like anyone else.

DAY 25

So I decided to test drive my new found influence today. I signed a slew of new executive orders. Half of them were undoing the last administration's executive orders, and the White House staff came up with others.

Then over a nightcap with Peter Spark he told me how we really won the close election race in Florida. He told me why I have to make that phone call to Symantec.

DAY 26

It finally hit me. I'm depressed. I've felt this way before. It's not a sad event that touches me off, it's frustration, feelings of help-lessness. I am angry with Peter. I hate Peter. I wrote it. He wanted to win at all costs. He will be the ruin of me, if he hasn't done it already. I let him have too long a leash because I fell in love with the prospect of power. The idea that Peter can handle things on his own, and I didn't need to watch. Well, one day a special prosecutor will be watching, and he will see the crimes. No one will believe I didn't know. I didn't know! Or I didn't want to know. I let Peter do what needed to be done. I'm a loser. I am not the President of the United States. I didn't want to win. I don't want this job. I didn't want it. I dreaded waking up this morning.

What can I do? I can't be honest with this diary anymore. I can't be honest with myself. I'll have to act as if I'm President. I must be the President, even though in my heart I might not have won. I will resign the presidency. I will claim a heart problem, and I am putting the country before myself. How ironic?

DAY 27

Maybe I feel a little better today. I have a little more of a step in my stride. I'm thinking about being a professor. I will take a few months off, I know how to complain to the doctor about chest pains, and shortness of breath. You think a Naval doctor is going to tell me I'm crazy. I can't even tell the psychologist that I'm a fraud, and that's why I'm depressed. I've decided to talk to June tonight.

DAY 28

I was tense all day in my shoulders. Peter and I have been just speaking professionally. No real communication. We had an intimacy to our relationship, but it's not been that way. Maybe this is the way it's going to remain until I'm done. I really don't care. Peter lashed out once at some point in the day, "Do whatever the hell you want without a care for who or what brought you here. Be a Jimmy Carter!" "He was honest!" I shot back. I felt like saying, "You made me William Henry Harrison," but it was one of those great things you think of after the moment is gone. I guess I can't die of pneumonia anymore. I didn't see him the rest of the day. I just read for most of the day. June wasn't home at night. I forgot she was in New York with Melissa Spark. She'll be back tomorrow.

DAY 29

Well my anxiety was at a peak today. I raised my voice to the Secretary of HUD. She probably went home and cried. I'm not very focused. I went right in to see June as soon as I heard that she was in the residence. I told her I'm not feeling well, and the doctors said I'm having heart problems. She said get on medication. I said

I'm depressed from my heart too, the medication makes it worse. She said I should go see the psychologist. Resign? I could have said *suicide* and gotten the same reaction. There is nothing more important to June than being the queen of the country. I just have to breathe. Don't ever talk resignation again. I won't. My wife is like William Howard Taft's wife. She wanted me to be President. I just wanted to be a professor. One day, I can be like Taft. I'll be in a job I really want and forget I ever was President.

DAY 30

A Supreme Court position has opened. I will get to fill the seat. What a great honor. I know who needs to fill the seat. I need a thoughtful jurist. The staff I assigned is creating a profile. I also know how I have to go about doing it. I asked Professor Rob Popalizio to accept the nomination. He was a District Court Judge turned law professor. He will be an excellent choice. I hope he does. It will be a big favor to me. He's perfect.

DAY 31

Well, I was actually photographed making phone calls today. I called Senators all day asking for their support for nominations of assistant secretaries and other Cabinet positions. Of course the work to get the Supreme Court nominee is the most difficult. If I want the quality cabinet people I demand, then I need to get rid of Papalizio, and not nominate him. *Roe v. Wade* is going to stand or else. That's the big fear. I have these ultimatums thrust upon me, if Papalizio is out, then they'll vote for whomever else I want. I would shoot back that Bob Popalizio is one of your brothers. They shoot back: He's a brother in the Senate and a black sheep on the Supreme Court. The press and the Senate is going to give Papalizio a *full proctology exam.*

DAY 32

Bob Papalizio said that he will accept the nomination as a favor to me. He talked it over with his wife and she was for it. I was grateful and told him that I owed him one. True self sacrifice—an honorable man.

My son visited the White House for the first time since the election. It was the first time the East Wing residence felt like home. I missed him from the moment he left. Connie will be coming this weekend. Maybe my spirits will rise. President Lincoln had the hypos, a rich form of depression. So do I. I wish I could hang a lantern on my problem.

DAY 33

It's been very hectic strategizing over Papalizio. The meetings I've had with Senators. I think I might have to promise my son, Alan to get the Justice I want. I'm not promising too much. I think I know what I'm doing. See the problem is Papalizo is a strict constructionalist. Boy, the conservative and liberal columnists around the country are just cooking Papalizio for dinner. The internet is providing more and more avenues for loud-mouths to just write. People believe what they read. Like every blog is from the *New York Times*. The Silent Majority really know where he stood on issues it wanted to be outcome determinative. I wanted to invite Professor Pappalizio over for dinner one night, and Peter said that I couldn't. Word would spread and it would be spun negatively somehow. So I snuck him in on the schedule for a drink and game of chess. I beat him, of course.

DAY 34

This situation is wrong about Peter and this Symantec Board appointment. I don't know who this William Goode is. It is becoming more and more real why Peter is so hot for me to make a call and recommend Goode. What do I have to do for Symantec when this Goode is appointed? Peter slipped and said, "whatever they want." I've never seen him like that before. He's always so calculating and reserved. I demanded he get me a dossier on Goode before I make the call. I could see he was seething when I asked him for it. I'm getting bad vibes from the Goode appointment. I think Peter thinks the momentum of the hundreds of appointments I've been making, this one would just slip by me out of habit. I need to trust my instincts. Peter is resentful that I'm making him go through the motions.

DAY 35

I signed a bill today that expanded funding for research into a medical target research program at the CDC. A Democrat and a Republican sponsored the bill to earmark funding for target diseases: Alzheimer's, AIDS, and Anthrax. They nicknamed it the *Triple A Medical Research bill.* I think AAA was offended. Unbelievable? Anthrax for the war hawks who are completely freaked out about terrorism. AIDS for the Hollywood leftists, and Alzheimer's for me. Maybe I could do good until it's over. It will be over soon.

DAY 36

I just looked at June tonight, and she lashed out at me. Don't even think about being sick. Don't even think of that word Daniel Carlson. You are the President! Man up Pansy! That's what she called me. Who does she work for?

DAY 37

I spoke with the psychiatrist today. At least he is the first psychiatrist that I'm not 100 times smarter than. He actually was perceptive enough to say, "I don't think you're being honest about why you're having chest pains." I wished that he turned into Hannibal Lector and ate my heart out with a fine Chianti. He says I'll always have inferiority issues because of my father, but that's not really bothering me. He doesn't know why I have a *Peter principle* syndrome. I don't think I've been promoted to my level of incompetence. I have all the credentials to be President. I could be a good President. I'm just tired of dealing with morons. I'm tired of teaching morons of the Silent Majority which pretty much seems like most of America because they are unteachable. In my depression, I announced we should pretty much do nothing about a perceived economic downturn last quarter, and the stock market and my approval ratings went up. Maybe the Dow will save my Presidency? It just hit 13,000.

DAY 38

Well, word is out that I have chest pains. Someone in the press corps actually asked the Press Secretary, does the President see himself as a one term President if health issues continue to be a concern?" "We haven't even finished unpacking yet!" She replied. This ended the subject with a laugh. That didn't take.

DAY 39

I met with leaders of the EU today in the Blue Room. We had a discussion on a whole range of issues. These meetings are for getting to know each other. They are trying to get to know me. Some of the leaders are smarter than others. Overall, they're all servants to their parliaments. Then I had a two-hour meeting with the Prime Minister in England about the upcoming NATO conference. My goal is to reinvigorate NATO. When the U.S. goes in, then we should get help. That is expected to go over like a lead balloon. NATO is defunct. The CIA is defunct. Relics of the Cold War. We're afraid to reinvent ourselves. In a special meeting with the Prime Minister of France, I felt my depression lift and I was just infuriated with his arrogance. I actually said "remember World War II." I don't think we'll be friends.

DAY 40

I met with the French Prime Minister today. He's the only meeting that really stands out. We were supposed to talk about values. This getting to know you stuff is becoming incredibly boring. I can tell in twenty minutes what these heads of state are all about. I don't need days. It's easier to read these people than to play poker. No one is trying to bluff. The good news is that these leaders infuriate me, and that has helped my depression.

I've been speaking to a picture of Abraham Lincoln often. I don't speak out loud for fear some Secret Service Agent might think I'm flipping out. They should only worry if I think he's talking back to me. No such luck.

DAY 41

There is no time for depression, except for ten minutes in the morning before I wake up. I forced myself to sit with the psychiatrist again today. I felt compelled to take a nap, I felt so down. I bumped a meeting with a contingency from Spain to the late afternoon. I left a message that we shouldn't miss siesta. Word was they were tired as well, and were glad that I took a siesta. I came back to the meeting and told them that this was part of my new Zen diplomacy. Feeling the values and mores of our friends' culture and not just respecting it, but sharing it. They laughed, and we did share some good ideas for economic growth in the Union. Back to the grind of appointing a Justice tomorrow.

DAY 42

Senator Popalizio is drawing some criticism. The opposition is claiming he's a political person who never rendered a judicial opinion worth a damn in his life. Well that's true of most district court judges. They're trial level judges. They're claiming it's a political payoff by me and the party. Furthermore, the nonsense about him never paying a housekeeper's social security came out. He will have to answer questions about this matter if he goes to the Senate Judiciary Committee. I think this is going to work out well.

DAY 43

I figured out what the problem was today with Peter and William Goode. I'm completely depressed. I made the call to Symantec. Goode would be a good person to be on the Board, I told him. I looked at Peter with confusion, but I could tell that he was happy. He has power over me, not just influence. Now Peter knows it. This changes everything about the Presidency. He keeps saying I don't want to know, and even he doesn't know. I know that it doesn't mean something good, when Peter speaks in his cryptic vernacular.

DAY 44

I was expecting to get caught today. I waited all day long, but nothing. The optimism around the office was really in full swing. Everyone seems to be getting into their jobs and feeling good about it. Peter felt wonderful today. He was relieved, I'm sure. He wanted me to get Goode the position, and I'm sure he will since I made the call. That's the thing with Peter, he has no remorse. He needed to get a job done and he just did it. Problem solved. Terrence Bratton created this monster, and I have to live with him.

DAY 45

I got a note today, William Goode was appointed to the Board of Symantec today. He will get a million dollars a year and stock options that will be worth a lot more. There is nothing else of importance that occurred today.

DAY 46

I received another note from *The Receptionist* this morning. I get a sense it is a man writing these notes to me, but I can't be sure. I really can't tell who it is. It's the voice of prediction. The notes have been telling me things about important Legislative and Foreign policy issues. I'm starting to wonder if it is just one person writing.

The other day a message told me that the Slovakian Ambassador was going to ask the United States for twenty-five million dollars in aid. When he did, I had already had in place the three major banks that loaned the Slovakian government thirty-five million to extend an interest-free time window for two years. The Ambassador was disappointed, but not too disappointed. I told him that I wanted the Slovakian government to grow into a responsible democracy, not a dependent one. The stock market went up 200 points. The speed of growth is concerning. My approval rating went up seven points.

DAY 47

My popularity is rising with everyone except the CIA. Apparently, they don't like the changes I'm suggesting. They like to run their own show. Give them policy directives, that's fine, but don't have someone else tell them to share information outside the agency, and control its budget. *The Receptionist* told me that the real obstruction is coming from retired Army General Speiser who was hired at the CIA. I discussed the issue with Peter, who said he would look into it. He said it's a new administration and heads should roll. So I had General Speiser fired. It got a lot easier with Congress to get support for a new bill to consolidate the intelligence agencies. Another poll was taken, I'm up another seven points.

DAY 48

I guess that gaining fourteen points in popularity in a week is a historical Presidential first. A depressed, and soon-to-be questionable President, who won by a slight margin, has never turned a country around so fast. Every time I think I'm out, they pull me back in. Who is they? The Silent Majority again. The functional unit of democracy—the perception of what the people want from their government. I never forget that the Bill of Rights was written to prevent abuse by the government and tyranny of the majority.

DAY 49

I had just learned of the Rebbe and now I was going to meet him. The high honor was awarded to me. I, not even being an Orthodox Jew, have an honor, the privilege to meet the spiritual leader of the Hassidic sect. I found the background on the Rebbe so interesting I dreamed about the meeting before it happened.

I felt I should dress for the occasion. I must wear black; after all, which is what they, the Hassidim wear. I don't know where I got the black furry hat, which I of course wore with a yarmulke underneath. I walked into the room, which I took to be a place where nursery school children were playing. The walls were a pale yellow, but that did not mean much to me. Perhaps it was the same color of the room where I slept. I also noticed some of the children were playing and frolicking on a stage. Their motions I did not pay much attention to.

I stepped forward and saw two women speaking. I could tell immediately that they were Israelis. When one of them saw me, she walked toward me and the other woman disappeared. I announced that I was here to see the Rebbe, and she immediately recognized me.

I checked my yarmulke by lifting up my hat and feeling with my hand. I can't remember if she told me to see if I had one on. My breathing remained normal, but I could feel my cool blood race through me. The woman was wearing a dark colored outfit. She did not draw any attention to her sensuality. That's exactly the point. I think because of it I couldn't describe her or know her if I saw her again.

"You're here to see the Rebbe?" she asked. I nodded yes. She put her hand on her head and said a prayer, a blessing. She did not seem too excited for me, the blessing seemed required. Excitement juiced through my veins. How ordinary and perfunctory it seemed to her, I needed to see him. He was going to let me know something about myself, perhaps my future.

I do not believe that the Rebbe is the Messiah as some Hassidim do. But he is a very wise man and knows much about God. Excited by the idea that perhaps he would share a tale or two about God with me. He did not. I awoke before I could go see the Rebbe. A dream I regret ended, more than any other.

Dreams are a gateway to the unconscious. I wonder what my mind would have released to me. What great wisdom would I have revealed to myself? If dreams are a spiritual communication, what would have been communicated to me by God? There was no frustration or conflict in my dream. I could've screamed. I can't understand why I woke up. I will be chasing that dragon for a long time. I'm cracking up. I'm crying out. I need to meet this Rebbe.

DAY 50

I've been taking a Calvin Coolidge approach to the economy and it seems to be working. I just make statements about how great America is expected to do, and let's not tinker so fast with what's already in motion, and the stock market just has been going nuts. Research and development. Let's figure out how we can study and invest to do more to do well in the long term. The country is just eating it up. The popularity of Daniel Carlson is growing. Send D.C. to D.C. Because D.C. is good for America!

DAY 51

Went back to Camp David. I wanted to rest. I read most of the day, and hung out with the close staff. We were preparing for the next great economic summit. I hope and a push to do nothing, and then encourage research and development. Innovation! That's the key to an exciting future. I hate being bored.

DAY 52

I met the Rebbe today. He was willing to meet with me at Camp David, even though he rarely left his community in Brooklyn. He arrived early in the morning, but left to go back to Brooklyn. He didn't want to sleep outside of Brooklyn. We spoke for a while. I made him see me alone. I spoke to him under privilege, which took me a moment to make him understand. He politely said that he wouldn't repeat our conversation.

The Rebbe understood my frustration and pain. He told me that he too was a young appointed leader. Legend has it that his hair was straight and dark black when he became the leader of his Jewish community. He was only thirty-two when his father-in-law died and he succeeded him. For weeks he was tormented by the challenging and the lack of respect he received. He too had a dream. He went to visit his father-in-law. A woman greeted him and blessed him when he announced he was there to see the Rebbe. He was excited to see the Rebbe because usually that meant he would learn something about the Talmud, as he did several times before. In his dream he never spoke to the Rebbe, only saw him and touched his finger like Michelangelo's painting of Adam touching the hand of God. He woke up right at the peak moment in the dream. But as legend had it, he said his hair and beard turned gray overnight. From that morning on, he was respected as an elder leader. "Maybe, I need to go gray," I said. He answered: "Maybe you need to touch the hand of God, and that will bring you closer to light and grant you forgiveness so you can do something better, rather than repent and do nothing." I didn't ask how he knew. That was his message. Maybe I just need to touch the hand of God.

DAY 53

Well word got out that I met with a Jewish leader so I had to meet with a large Christian contingency. It went well. I was preached to about an agenda for an hour. Then they met with other staff members. They loved my selection of Popalizio. They were really sure he was a pro-life Justice. I'm sure he would be, even though I couldn't comment on such things publicly. He met the litmus test and that was good enough. But Popalizio was taking too much flak. That meant the White House was taking too much heat. I'll sleep on it, but I'm going to have to speak with Popalizio in the afternoon.

DAY 54

I told Bob Popalizio to withdraw his nomination. He agreed. He didn't like the whole process. I thanked him. I gave him lauds for his incredible sacrifice. He was offered a professorship at Columbia and believes it was because of the nomination. I had a feeling something good would come out of it for him. I am certainly jealous. Somehow, I wish our roles were reversed. He couldn't understand that. He always wanted to be President.

At a press conference, I announced that I had accepted the withdrawal of Bob Popalizio with great regret. He was a man honorable enough to serve and yet he was a victim of a vicious system that very few of us could survive. I think most members of Congress went 'whoop-de-do,' in response to me chastising them. Some resent that I didn't stick up for Bob hard enough. That's okay, I understand the system, I won, and it's still sad I had to play it like that.

DAY 55

Peter and I went for a walk. He did so at my urging. We walked like we did at the beginning of my campaign for Senate. It was the walk of candor. He told me he wasn't sure of what the outcome of the election in Ohio, Florida, and some New England States would be, so he made sure that it came out our way. The blood drained from me. I really had no idea, and if it ever came out, no one would ever believe that I didn't know. I didn't know what to say, but I said a lot. Peter had the nerve to say you have your secrets and I have mine. My secret actually helped Peter. I told him I'm surprised he didn't know the difference. Peter said it was called the Chad project and had been going on for about two years, right after I almost got stabbed.

"Did you set that up too, Peter?!" He didn't say, *no* when he stormed off either. I yelled back he's not getting away that easily. "Did you just turn your back on the President? We're finishing this walk of candor!" I went back to the *residence* and drank Glen Livet straight up. It mixes well with the Zoloft.

DAY 56

I had another sober late night walk with Peter. It was cold outside, and matched the way I felt all day. Peter assured me that there was nothing to a Florida *Sun Sentinel* investigation into the election. No one would believe I won an election by only several hundred votes. The counters had to be right. I confided in Peter I didn't know what the hell a chad was and had an intern look it up for me. Could I have won? I asked Peter. He said he honestly didn't know. We're going to get caught. He said he would get caught, if someone was going to get caught. But he's Peter Spark, and he's too good, and he won't get caught. And the *Geeks* they wouldn't talk under pressure. Peter said there was more than one group of *Geeks* and they all think they were the shadow group for the real *Geeks*. I guess I have to put them all on Boards of corporations.

DAY 57

Blackness struck the country today. It was a sorrowful day. I am in complete pain, now that I am focusing on what happened. A lunatic walked into a mall in Cherry Hill, New Jersey and killed twenty-two people, most of them children. I'm a leader of the Western world and I'm powerless to do something about crimes to humanity like this. What a freak! I'm exhausted. Any chance America is ready for real gun control? No, some gun-nut lobbyists will probably say that the reason the shooter got twenty-two was because the twenty-two weren't armed. Gun free zone = victim zone.

I got approval from my political affairs staff. Apparently, when I was told of the shooting, I stared down at the ground in what looked like deep thought, for fifteen seconds. It felt like a half an hour, but it wasn't. I looked up and apologized, but advised that an emergency situation came up and had to leave. Waved to the people who were around, and went back to the White House via Marine One.

I can't even write. I guess I'm President, and there is no election scandal that can undo that now.

DAY 58

The world seems dark to me. My whole administration has to be completely refocused so hard and fast that my stomach is sick and I have a stiff neck. The real tragedy of domestic terrorism. We have to focus on protecting ourselves against them and not educating our children, or anything else I'd rather was more important. On Maslow's hierarchy we were doing so well as a country. I got the country to self-actualize. I got the country focused on the important stuff. The Renaissance of a nation. I got this country excited about research and development, education and training, employment. The Arts! Now, we'll have to spend a whole lot of time building America's confidence to go back to a mall and see a movie! The Hawks in my party will be seizing the opportunity. They told us so. Deep down inside, I think they really are enjoying this whole thing.

DAY 59

My day has turned into one giant memorial service. I noticed my breathing is slow and shallow all day. I have to snap out of a trance just to speak to people. I received a phone call from the Prime Minister of Israel today extending his country's condolences. I snapped back: I have consciousness now! Don't worry, Mr. Prime Minister I'll be bombing some more Arabs soon!"

DAY 60

Today I announced my second choice for the nomination for the Court. It is Jose Rodriguez. He is a jurist's jurist. He clerked for Justice Stevens. He's been on the 11th Circuit Court of Appeals for fifteen years. He is left on most issues, and conservative on corporate law matters. I'm so pleased. More pleased than most will know. Senators from both parties were confident that he would be confirmed.

Interestingly, there were some rumblings about how Jose didn't pay a housekeeper's social security. Oh well, I guess that issue has already been done. It won't hinder his nomination at all.

Bob Popalizio called the White House today. I took the call. He was pleased. He couldn't believe our scheme worked. I thanked him for drawing the fire. Bob told me, so did Jose.

Picking a Supreme Court justice is a part of his legacy. A justice can serve for twenty to thirty years, long after a President is retired. This was a big opportunity to affect our nation's ethic. I had to win it even if it appeared I lost my first choice.

The world still seems dark to me. I wish I could blow something else up. I've never felt so helpless and angry at the same time. I have all the power in the world to blow something up, to start a war, and yet I don't know how to handle it. I'm supposed to feel strong, courageous, and self assured. With all the advice of the brightest foreign policy advisors, and between myself and this diary, I don't know what to do. The whole focus of my administration has to change. The terrorists have won. Ironic, they hate me, and now I have to stay.

CHAPTER 21

The Backroom

AT FIRST, THIS ASIAN guy seemed perfect. Just what everyone wanted. Even the man with the silver glasses like him, and he didn't like anyone. The Chinaman fit the profile. He spoke the right language. He was young and oddly handsome—even though that wouldn't be needed.

The blond man with silver glasses and a feminine voice said, "Are you good in the field of open law?" Which seemed to mean would he be willing to kill someone. Not that he even cared, he already had something planned for this boy.

"Yes, sir," the boy said, who was almost a man, barely out of college. He spoke both English and Chinese. His furry mustache was hair alone and not thick enough to be considered whiskers. The boy grinned. He sat up confidently waiting for the next question.

The man had chalk dust on the back of his blue blazer. It reflected the strangeness of the man with silver glasses. How deep does someone have to be not to realize he's leaning up against a chalkboard, and is getting the chalk all over him? What was even more strange was the board behind the man with silver glasses was a magic marker board, and there was no chalk anywhere.

"Tan, are you good with technical equipment and the likes?"

"Yes, sir." Then a gun came from behind this young man's head. The man with the silver glasses heard that chalk dust can disrupt the results of a paraffin that can determine whether someone has fired a gun or not in the past week or so. The man with the silver glasses blew some dust off his hands, and left the room.

The man wasn't even given the chance to enjoy the coolness of the weapon. Tan, did however notice the tattoo across the forehand of the man holding the gun. The tip of the man's pinky was missing. He put a bullet in his head. President Carlson read the entire transcript of this meeting, even though Peter didn't want him to know. The *Receptionist* gave Daniel the whole story in the *message room*.

★ ★ ★

"All rise for the President," someone said. The applause was loud. President Carlson bowed slightly, in jest, and exaggerated an indication for everyone to sit.

"Welcome to the White House, President Carlson."

"Thank you." President Carlson felt chills. "You all know the purpose of this meeting. I want to have these meetings to air out my feelings. But most importantly, to hear your feelings. After seven months in office and the terrible tragedy that has befallen this country, I need honest talk. You know the rules. No holds barred. Let it all come out. I'll throw out the topic and you all should start talking about it. First, I want to announce that I will be restructuring as well as renaming the following cabinet departments."

"Where's Peter Spark?" Eliot Marksman asked.

"He won't be joining us in these meetings," the President responded. Marksman was delightfully surprised. The new President thought that Peter's absence would send the knights of this round table a message that he truly was interested in what they had to say.

The President continued: "The Department of Labor will be renamed the Department of Employment and Labor. And the Department of the Interior now is the Department of the Environment. My Press Secretary will be releasing this information within the hour. Unless there are any strong objections from any of you." The President doubted that there would be. But he wanted to get the "backroom" sessions started with criticisms of ideas that were already decided on.

President Carlson looked around the room. No one spoke. He stared at each one of them. Some were older than the President. All of them were smarter—intellectually. Yet, these men were in awe of the power of the Presidency and dared not to stick their necks out so early in the term. What if they said something that made the President mad? They would have to suffer the resentment of the President for the next four years, if they lasted that long.

Most people who ask for constructive criticisms don't really want it. They want praise. Not with Daniel Carlson. He wasn't like ordinary people. He wanted desperately to keep in touch with the outside world. The White House can be a vacuum. Sunlight cannot be seen inside. It can only be described in reports and polls. These men cared enough about a Carlson Presidency to tell him how a situation really is. And they were reluctant to do so.

President Carlson looked at liberal Lawrence Thompson. No response from this brilliant attorney. He then looked to Austin Hesse, conservative and acting Director of Central Intelligence.

Clarence Terrell, a doctor, and the most pessimistic person in the room, likewise, had nothing to say. Daniel's personal accountant, Eliot Marksman offered nothing but a blank stare. Even the realist psychologist, Frank Curley was without advice. These men would have to be trained. Never had any president used the technique of open dialogue without hierarchy or formality.

After a moment of silence President Carlson said, "I tricked you, my friends. I thought you were smarter than that. What good would renaming the cabinets do? Just a name. Not the kind of thing a progressive President starts his presidency off with. Certainly, not to waste his honeymoon on such frivolities."

"Yes, what's in a name? I believe Shakespeare said," Marksman the accountant replied.

"Well, I think it's kind of neat. Why don't you name the Department of Justice to the Department of Law and Enforcement?" Thompson said. There was a murmur of laughter.

Again there was silence. They were waiting for the President's reaction. Were they doing what he wanted? Is this what the President wanted to hear?

"Goddamn it!" President Carlson yelled out. "If I wanted to have tea with the Elks I would've worn a buffalo cap on my head. I want raw language. I want interaction. None of you except for Austin is on the government payroll. And within a month he'll be off. I can't fire you. You're all my friends. Please let me know what you think. You don't even have to say what you think. Say what you think each other are thinking. Conservatives be liberals. And vice-versa. There's no media, no stenographers, and no one can speak of what we speak of in here under penalty of treason," he said in a calm and cool tone. A few eyebrows raised at the President.

"In all seriousness, I am changing the names of the Departments of Labor and Interior. As well as outlining some major changes that will occur within those agencies. I think it will psychologically prepare everyone in this country for the changes that are going to be made. So, on that note, I'm throwing out the topic of Drug Policy. Something juicy. Lawrence, what do you think Austin thinks about the American drug policy?"

Lawrence Thompson answered. "I think Mr. Hesse feels that we haven't a war but a program. We need more of a program that brings in the military. About forty billion dollars to start. I think, however, that steps need to be taken to make peace with drugs. Drugs are not something that one can fight like a man or a government. Education on a grand scale should be where the resources should be going."

"Everyone knows that smoking is bad for your health. They do it anyway. Tobacco is the largest cash crop in the U.S.," Dr. Curley chimed in.

"You haven't lived in an inner-city apartment complex. Where drugs are on every street corner. Violence is everywhere. You want to legalize it, you bleeder," Austin Hesse responded.

"I'm not a bleeding heart!"

"You're so left you busted an aorta when you graduated from Brandeis."

"I suppose you'd have the CIA help in the drug war. That would work. Hell, why don't we just have the CIA subsume the DEA." Thompson replied.

Daniel Carlson loved this dialogue. The conversation was on. This was just what he wanted. Brainstorming. He was listening to the static of the most intelligent and politically savvy men in the country. And he was not the center of the attack. He was in the eye of the storm.

"I have decided to propose a bill to restructure the Intelligence community entirely. The way we do it is to put one director of intelligence, and he has total budget control over all agencies. Then he's not just a figurehead, and no one can really get around this new director," the President said.

There was silence for a moment.

"Total budget control would be key to putting a new man in charge," Curley affirmed.

"He who has the gold makes the rules. Make sure the President approves the overall intelligence budget," Hesse chimed in.

"And I liked what you said about the CIA, Lawrence," the President said. "What do you think the role of the Agency should be in the future?"

"It should be strictly international in jurisdiction. If you give the agency overlapping jurisdiction in areas that might affect this country on a domestic level, you give the agency too much power."

"Not if you have the right leaders within the Intelligence Community," Hesse said.

"You need a long term policy that should set precedent for the country long after this administration's second term." A few of these knights of the round table snickered at the comment, which was a blatant attempt to suck up to the President.

"Now, now, Lawrence. Your flattery doesn't earn you brownie points." The other knights were relieved. They weren't fighting for established power or maneuvering for a higher position. They were, however, grappling for the affection and respect of the President, like jealous children.

"You watch Mr. President, the CIA will ask you in due time for a finding that will allow them to spy legally in this country in the name of drugs, terrorism, or some other hot business issue."

"I admit to you that I would like to see marijuana decriminalized—health inspected—and taxed. That way men like Steve Vann never would ever have crossed my path and it can reduce the federal deficit with the "grass tax," the President said with a laugh. "We can sell it to the American people as, 'make the deficit shrink—buy government weed.'" The laughter swelled. "Unfortunately, Congress wouldn't go for it and I don't think I should ruin my administration just so a few of us can get high. What will happen though is that monies confiscated on marijuana seizures will be funneled into programs to reduce cocaine abuse and other harsh stimulant drugs. I will send a finding to Drug Enforcement to de-emphasize marijuana enforcement."

The end of that statement was followed by some *hems and haws* but no one really argued with it.

"Watch how that goes to the press," Frank Curley warned.

"No pot amnesty, but definitely a new world order when it comes to intelligence," the President concluded. "Let's move on to domestic issues. And then, which country I need to bomb next." This comment seemed flip, even under these special circumstances. Not many gave it much thought, as even these older distinguished gentlemen were flattered they were being taken into the inner sanctum by the President of the United States. Dr. Curley considered the real possibility the President was depressed, but didn't dare suggest it. Perhaps another day he would. Curley knew Daniel Carlson for years. To the world Daniel seemed to be a simple do-gooder. The majority believes that the way things seem, are usually the way things are.

CHAPTER 22

China Doll's Revenge

T<small>HE ALARM CLOCK SOUNDED</small> early in the master bedroom of the residence. President Carlson turned off the alarm and looked over at the first lady. June appeared lifeless without any makeup on her face, but her hair remained flawlessly set from the night before. She sat up in bed tasting the emptiness in her stomach. She immersed herself in the joy her daily routine created. Daniel Carlson knew June well enough after these years. He knew she enjoyed the parades and the cocktail parties, and meeting foreign government officials; the necessary tours of mills, plants, and museum or library openings. She was looking forward to this morning's event, some *save the children of Cherry Hill event*. June would never admit it—that she didn't like children, but the President knew it and enjoyed the fact that he forged a better relationship with Connie and Alan than their own mother.

Carlson sat up with June. She grimaced at him. He groaned to communicate that he agreed it was too early in the morning to be awake.

"Every day, it seems to get earlier and earlier," she mumbled with her hands over her face.

"Every day, it's a new crowd of people that want to meet the First Lady for the first time. Today, it's little children. Children that have not much to live for other than to meet a woman like you. Someone who they think is a success."

Letting her husband's comment sink in, June says, "It's still the same thing to me every day. I own it! It's exhausting but I love it."

"What would you rather be doing?" the President asked.

"I would like to be younger. Just younger and have the ability to run for a third term." June reflected and saw herself as she was.

"You were my push, remember?" he said. She agreed. "We're doing good things. We're teaching America good things, and they're coming around to *our* way of thinking." Daniel had difficulty saying *our*. June couldn't help conceding to herself that it was Daniel's way of thinking and not hers. He was too tolerant and progressive for her. She pushed him to get into office and skillfully he turned her desire to his benefit. Now she was working for Daniel Carlson and his progressive cause. That had always been Daniel Carlson's gift—the ability to turn an enemy to his team. The stubborn enemies had a tendency to get ostracized by their resistance to DC's charm and logic.

"You like influencing others, June. Why don't you influence these children today? They're handicapped without parents; why not tell them they still have a life?"

June smiled slightly. She kissed Daniel on the cheek and got out of bed. As she disrobed in the bathroom, she began to think about what Daniel said. Her thoughts put her back to the place she was when she was first hungry for the power she now had. The trophy of power wasn't as good as the chase for it. Through his morning pep talks, she began to fantasize how she would influence the trade agreement with the Chinese government officials that would be dinner guests.

June slipped into a bathrobe and cracked the door to the bathroom. A billow of steam burst through the crack. The bedroom air-conditioner pushing the door open wider. The light coming from the bathroom forced Daniel to wake. He could smell the steam as it hit his nostrils. As he sat up, he could see the reflection of June in the steamy mirror that stood behind her. He'd seen the homely reflection many times before.

When June turned her back to the bathroom door, the back mirror showed her face. Under her nose, above her upper lip was a white cream. At a quick glance it looked thin enough to be a depilatory. At a closer scrutiny it was thick as shaving cream. As a ritual, once a week, June, with a thin pink-handled razor would remove the hair from her lip in three brisk masculine strokes. Even at this very moment, the sight of June in shaving cream made Daniel recoil in disgust. As liberal as he was, shaving was for men, and the sight of June doing this brawny task, tested the bounds of his framework of social equality.

It was if he had stared at the sun too long. Daniel squinted his eyes shut and laid his head back on the pillow slowly, waiting for the residual image to dissipate from the back of his eyelids. June saw Daniel do this and shut the door, protecting her privacy.

When June left the White House that morning, she was dressed to kill. She looked professional and stunning for the tour of a new children's handicap facility. Most of the patients in the facility were stricken with muscular dystrophy, but were mentally functioning. The vast differences that June foresaw, between her and the children, made her uncomfortable.

Bored on the trip to Cherry Hill, June picked up the car phone in the back of her limousine. June didn't like to fly when she didn't absolutely have to. She dialed Melissa Spark's number from memory. She felt calm and dull, not nervous to talk to her at all. Since the beginning of Daniel's Presidency, June and Melissa had grown separately. In June's attempt to overcome her success and feel accomplishment, and develop new reasons to have a zest for life, she became dependent on Melissa. To Melissa's surprise, she received at least three phone calls a day from the First Lady. Melissa expected they would grow apart from the lack of contact if anything; however, Melissa was pushed to a point where she felt she was smothered by June's need to have Melissa immersed in her life. Every thought June had she shared with Melissa.

Melissa, at one point said, "Stop complaining, or do something about it." June took the remark in jest, but June still called to feel better about herself. Melissa, after all, was still a school teacher, and the only act she ever did that was worthy of noting was marrying Peter.

"Melissa?" June said into phone when she heard someone pick up.

"Hello," Melissa answered.

"I'm going to a Cherry Hill school this morning."

"They still make you do those activities on Saturdays?" Melissa said trying to start a pleasant conversation.

"Oh, that's right, it's Saturday. The days seem to blend."

"How did you think you were going to get me if it was a weekday? I'm in school by this time."

"I thought maybe you'd've quit by now." Melissa became offended again when June dismissed her commitment to teaching. June resented that Melissa was doing something that Daniel took an unusual interest in, that is, for a President. That was the core of the special relationship that Melissa had with Daniel. June resented that also. The two friends became rivals. The reality that Melissa saved June from the tatters of a destructive marriage, and entered her into a world of excitement, has gone forgotten. Only long conversations between the President and Melissa in corners of banquet halls in the White House, which June considered a misdemeanor.

"Are you coming tonight for the Chinese visitors?"

"No, I don't think so. I want to work on my class plans and take it easy."

"Really? Peter shouldn't come unaccompanied."

"He doesn't care if I come or not. And I've met these people before. You remember the *Ambassador's daughter?*" Melissa said trying to get on the same side of an issue as June.

"The very one that screwed Terrence Bratton into the retirement home early?"

"That's right. I'd just as soon stay away," Melissa said.

"Oh, and trust Peter with her alone?"

"If he would want the slut, he can have her. He loves the game too much to fall into the same trap as Terrence Bratton. I guess she screwed her way to becoming the First Lady of China." That characterization, putting this woman in the same category has her, angered June.

"Well, if you change your mind, I'll see you there." June hung up, and contemplated who else she could call. She realized she could wake anyone this early if she wanted. June consequently enjoyed the rest of the ride.

Every arrival was festive and full of excitement to the people June visited. Smiling, eager faces greeted her at the entrance of the school of the special children. June had given up her Saturday morning for these children, and they gave up the morning cartoons. Some of the children felt sorrier for themselves than for the First Lady.

A tour was always a good way to speak perfunctorily with the staff of a foundation, than a general meeting with staff or members, in this case residents, to talk and answer questions. The new school wing was state of the art. June noted the fantastic equipment for the children to exercise with and a research wing as well. She never awoke for the tour.

A student read her letter to June. A letter that a little girl took all week to write. The letter was long for the first grader, about fifteen words. The girl in pigtails and silver wire glasses stood out of her wheelchair with special crutches with arm-braces, while an aide held the letter in front of her. Her mother died in the shooting at the mall, but the girl survived. The message was ordinary, if deciphered only through its plain meaning. That was all June was capable of. Therefore, she did not understand that this child sweated when she stood because it was painful, not out of nerves. A few seconds after she began to read, her arms shook with strain. Persistent, she stood tall. June didn't understand that this girl would someday have a hard time breathing because of her injuries.

June was not intimate with herself. She didn't feel she reacted. She lived in survival mode. She has done all she has had to do to survive—June has escaped from the ghetto, a small town mentality, and an abusive husband. She sought nothing from her spirit. Success was her biggest failure. Her zestful spirit was given the command to rest, and in response, it died. June was more pitiful then the little first grader in pigtails. The girl's goal was simple: stand and read for the First Lady. Tomorrow, her goal will be to stand and read for someone else. Every day that the little first grader could stand and breathe, was a good day. Each day was the same but a new challenge when you've lost both parents on the same day. The emotion the girl attached to standing was the same victory, the feeling of accomplishment never became jaded.

June thought the little first grader had tears in her eyes because she was nervous to meet the First Lady, and couldn't control herself. But that's how out of touch June was with her surroundings and with her own feelings. If she allowed herself to feel the joy of the little girl's accomplishment, she could wake the next morning at 5 a.m. and not complain. But June didn't know that the little girl felt special because she could stand for the television camera with a smile, and read her letter that took a week to write because her hands would not cooperate with her bursting wondrous first grade mind.

When the little first grader finished reading her letter, June was empty but the girl was full. Full of a lifetime of joy. The rules were different for this girl. She recruited the help of her friends by sharing the dream she had—to stand for the First Lady of the United States. If she could stand without falling, without anyone else's help, she would win. She did. The applause in the room was loud. June triggered a wide grin. The girl hugged the aide who then helped her back into her chair.

June was given permission to talk about gun-control. She gave a short statement that guns in the hands of mentally disturbed people are at the root of this tragedy. Guns will not solve the problem of mass murder with guns.

Daniel always wanted to know what June learned at these events. Daniel implored her to be another set of eyes and ears for him. She asked herself what she had learned, and without effort, she answered to herself, nothing. Her thoughts transferred to the evening's events.

June, as empty as she was, knew the importance of gun control. She said she made her statements as planned. Then June had her staff make sure that she had the proper dress, scheduled an afternoon nap and hair appointment.

The evening had arrived. The backdrop for this fiesta was again at the Anderson House. The building was preserved in the same manner as it was when Daniel and June first met. June admitted to herself that she felt the youthful excitement she once felt when she arranged parties for Senator Mathews. She remembered she met Daniel, the boy wonder, here. It was the place for romance. The leading tale rumored that Senator Bratton first met the then Chinese Ambassador's wife, and pursued their defeating affair. It amazed June that the wife had the gall to come back to the United States. Hadn't she ruined enough lives? June resented that the wife wasn't politically assassinated and Senator Bratton was her victim. Her resentment reminded her of a comment Daniel made when he told June that the Premier's wife would be coming to the United States.

June voiced her hostility for Cho, and again the President turned the negative around. "June," he said, "If Cho did not come to America when she did, I would never have been President." And he was right. Terrence Bratton would never have given up his seat. If he ran for President, Bratton never would've retired. While Daniel could turn a situation psychologically to his advantage, June didn't. She chose to resent Cho anyway, and it would be difficult to be around her this night.

June's first attack was to look good. June lightened her hair; there was no hint of gray. Her ears had carat diamond studs of an exquisite cut. A string of pearls supporting a five-carat diamond rock complemented her earrings. Her dress was black and silky. It was sexy, yet appropriate, not too low cut. June was daring, wearing red lipstick to match her nails. She emphasized her engagement ring by wearing nothing else on her hands.

The second attack was to learn some Mandarin. When the applause of the President's and her arrival subsided, she was formally introduced to the Premier and his wife. After shaking her hand, June said, in Mandarin, "I remember you." At first, June feigned a mistake and said, that Cho "still looked like a child," but then corrected herself by saying, "You're still young looking." The surrounding dignitaries smiled and grimaced at June's try at the foreign language. The mistake was intentional, and Cho knew it. Cho covered her disdain with grace, but she didn't forget. She just ran her two fingers over her top lip to send June a message.

June politely turned and walked away from Cho and her escorts. Only the shrewd eye and ear could detect the subtle cat scrap. Daniel had the ear, and he didn't like what June did. June was just an alley cat, Daniel thought. June had to stamp her point. It was her Christian way—never leaving one to one's own way.

President, with all his skill, attempted to turn the Prime Minister around to the importance of the trade issue, but he couldn't be convinced. He was offended for his wife. The Minister wouldn't think of the best interest for his people. The official word from the Chinese government was to delay signing an agreement because a certain faction of the government needed to discuss the agreement further. This effectively destroyed Daniel Carlson's hopes of having the agreement signed in his first term. It was a painful loss, considering Daniel thought this agreement would've put America in the 3.5% unemployment range. Daniel Carlson didn't even talk about June's misconduct. He learned the same lesson again about her. His enemies just tripled, and June was too stupid to understand why. But the President was resolved never to let her narrow imposing disposition affect his life or his presidency again.

CHAPTER 23

A Son of Abraham

IT WAS QUIET AROUND the White House this late morning. It was one of the few coveted lazy days around the West Wing. It was the Jewish Holiday of Yom Kippur, the day of Atonement. The President made sure that services for the Jewish staffers were available, for those who couldn't go home for the holidays. Daniel Carlson was always interested in the whole idea of reflection. Reflection made perfection, if the person was willing to look at his own flaws, and try to correct them.

Rabbi Schniarson drove all the way from Brooklyn with an entourage, to be the spiritual leader of the service. He had to drive days before the holiday, because the Rabbi would not drive on the eve of the Holy day. The Rabbi was the leader of the most religious sect of Judaism, the Lubavitch. He was called, Rebbe. Daniel Carlson was President of the United States, but the Rebbe was the leader of the Jews in New York. Even the non-Lubavitch Jews accepted that the Rebbe set the standard for Jewish tradition and decision-making. In times of desperation, when one goes toward religion, Jews turned toward the edicts of a Rebbe.

Because of the reputation of Schniarson, even some non-Jewish staffers did not leave the Beltway, in order to hear the Rebbe speak.

As President Carlson sat in the residence study in the White House, he reflected as he sat in his chair at his desk thousands of times before. He wondered if today was supposed to be a day of greater reflection. How do you make it a day of greater reflection? How much more critical do we have to be of oneself to meet the commitments of the Day of Atonement? It just isn't good to be so critical. He risked undercutting his own self confidence, which was as important as good judgment. It's part of good judgment.

The President's thoughts went on to how well he knew his own life. The media and his detractors raked through his life, and even made one false supposition after another to make for a good story. Still, there was so much that was undiscovered and President Carlson was thankful. Every day he was thankful. Selfish? Deserving? Yes, he felt he was deserving. No one deserves such scrutiny, not even the President.

Daniel Carlson looked on his desk and began to thumb through a family photo album. Mostly pictures of his mother and her family. They were from Kiev. Her grandparents came to this country after World War I. Anti-Semitism in Kiev was strong at that point in history. Jews hid their identities, if they could. One day when Daniel was sixteen, his mother told him that her grandparents were Jewish. She asked that he keep it a secret, and that even his father didn't know. Daniel wasn't sure how his father would react. His wife really was a Jew. Daniel asked his mother if she knew anything about being a Jew. She said she knew very little about being Jewish. Deep inside she felt she was Jewish. Right after Daniel learned about his great-grandparents, it explained plenty about how lukewarm of a Christian was Daniel's mother.

Daniel's mother was a Christian on Christmas and Easter. They seemed like more social events than religious events. It all made sense. Daniel's mother felt she still needed to be a Jew in the closet, like her grandparents. Which made him wonder about secrets.

So many secrets in Daniel Carlson's family. It was a wonder he ever spoke. A secret might fly out of his mouth. Daniel's father had some secrets he needed to keep from his mother. His mother had secrets she had to keep from his father. It was good to keep confidences, but what is the need for secrets. There was usually no explanation of why a matter was even a secret. Why couldn't his father know that his mother was Jewish? Was his father an anti-Semite? Daniel didn't even care to think about it. My mother may have thought my father would have loved her less. Just a lot of pent up anger from the secrets. He closed the photo album. He noticed the phone ring on his desk. He picked it up and the voice announced: it was time.

President Carlson walked over to the West Wing. He went into the conference room that was designated and converted as the temple. The Rebbe was about to give his sermon for Yom Kippur. The President put a yarmulke on his head out of respect for his religious environment. The crowd of Jewish staffers were amazed the President showed up for this private event. He smiled and shook the hands of a few staffers as he made his way up the aisle. Then he shook hands with the Rebbe's main assistant, and then the Rebbe. The President noticed the *machitza*—the barrier dividing the women and the men in the room. The barrier was supposed to force the men and the women to concentrate on God and not each other during this holy time. Daniel Carlson slipped from his political mindset, the one that makes him politically correct, and wondered if the *machitza* made the men and the women wonder what was going on over the other side, rather than concentrate on religion.

The Rebbe's assistant was also a rabbi. He was slender, wore glasses, and had red hair parted to the side. The Rebbe was sitting and had a long gray beard. He was wearing all white for the solemn holiday. He shook the President's hand and smiled, without standing up. The Rebbe was old and mostly got around by getting pushed around in a wheelchair. The President said a few words as an impromptu introduction before the sermon.

"The Rebbe needs no introduction. I'm so glad that he was able to make it to the White House this year. I want to welcome all of our friends from Brooklyn who escorted the Rebbe to Washington. The Rebbe is a man of peace. His words have always inspired values and caused to take time for reflection for all. Without judgment, his words offer guidance about how to be better. In our complex world of competing values and competing interests, the Rebbe explains a view on life that seems so simple, but based upon thousands of years of Judaic teachings. It is an honor that he is here, and I'm glad to be here to enjoy and learn from today's message. Rabbi, please . . ." There was no applause, as is the custom in a temple. The Rebbe stood at the podium. The President took an empty seat on the podium next to where the Rebbe was sitting. Everyone in the room, except the Rebbe and his assistant rabbi, thought the President was just being his usual cordial and articulate self. He wasn't. Daniel Carlson really meant it, and his words applied to him, specifically. The Rebbe spoke of kindness to animals, out of sake of pity, not animal rights. He explained the reason for kindness in the process for slaughtering animals for food. He explained the story of Jonah. The fear of the people who threw him into the water, since Jonah told them that he was the cause for the great storm. He asked can we all strive to believe in God the way Jonah did? Perhaps never, but we should strive.

After the sermon, President Carlson went to the Oval Office. An hour later, he went into a private office outside the Oval Office. There he met the Rebbe with his assistant. The President still had his yarmulke atop his head since the sermon. This meeting was not on the official Presidential log. The meeting was planned with the Rebbe. This was the second time that the President and the Rebbe had met. The first time the President mentioned in passing that he had some Jewish distant relatives. Candidate Carlson was in Brooklyn. He needed to meet with the Rebbe to get the Jewish vote in Florida. This was a political reality in New York. The one promise that Daniel Carlson made to the Rebbe was that he would be a friend to the Jews. The Rebbe insisted that the friendship must extend to this country, which at first bewildered President Carlson. Then he realized that the Lubvitch view on Israel is not the same as the conservative Jews' position. President Carlson assured the Rebbe that he would be a friend of the Jewish people. This was even before the Rebbe entered into a short and precise dialogue with the President. The precise dialogue is the trait that Daniel Carlson remembers most about the Rebbe. It was the Rebbe's ability to get precisely to the hidden point.

"God is a force, not a being to be reasoned with. You ask God for something, and even if it's bad, you will get it. If you are a man who can tap into the power of God, God will concede and give you what you want. For you it may be power. You have tremendous influence."

"Power is not what I asked God for, Rebbe. Freedom is what I asked God for," Daniel Carlson said.

"That you must save for Passover," the Rebbe said with a smile. Carlson nodded.

"I know who you are, Daniel Carlson. Daniel was a man from the Lion's den. You know we believe that a person's name has much to do with the luck he will have. You were destined to be alone in the den. With God's help you will be safe." Daniel felt tears well up in his eyes. The Rebbe hit a nerve.

"I'm not that religious. I'm not religious Rebbe," Daniel confessed.

"I know. You are confused. You are a Jew in your heart but you are raised as something else."

"Even with all the oppression the Jewish people have suffered, you are at peace with whom you are," Daniel said.

"I am what I am," the Rebbe replied.

"I am not what I am. My mother was a Jew. Her family was oppressed in Kiev. When they escaped, they gave up on their Judaism."

"Except you. You cannot?"

"I've studied quietly for years. I feel I am a Jew. But I can't, I really can't be a Jew."

"You mean you can't openly admit you are a Jew?"

"Yes," Daniel admitted.

"Then, I offer you this, Daniel of the Lion's den. Every Jew must do the minimum. The very minimum is: lay tefilin; keep kosher; and, observe the Sabbath. As President, we cannot reasonably expect to observe even the minimum. But there are three things you must do instead. You can: say the Shema in the morning, the anthem of our faith. *'Hear oh Israel the Lord our God, the Lord is One.'* Never eat pork. And lastly, you must tell your son that you are a Jew, before you die."

Daniel felt the tears build in his eye. This was doable. All that Daniel was, he wasn't who he really was suppose to be. Did his intelligence and his talent make the presidency a guarantee, his destiny? Daniel blessed the Rebbe to himself. The Rebbe gave Daniel a gift. He was given the chance to be a Jew in the only way that he could at this point, and for the man he was. The Rebbe then gave Daniel Carlson a dollar, as a sign of charity. It was a signature trait of the Rebbe, and signified the closing of the meeting. But even a perceptive man like the Rebbe didn't realize what pain the man Daniel Carlson really felt.

CHAPTER 24

A Presidential Auction

HIS ENEMIES MET IN the bright sun. Bright enough to illuminate all shadows of trickery, except for one. The one in Kingston, Jamaica. The streets teemed with natives. Only the brave locals dare to walk through the crowded downtown Kingston. Some carried machetes in hand for protection.

General Speiser (Ret.) was smuggled inside a sack in the back of a jeep. The jeep pulled down a narrow alley, and the General was delivered and removed from the sack inside of the building. Others followed moments later into the building, each allowed access through the warehouse door, steel reinforced and guarded by a large Jamaican man, standing about two hundred eighty, with no teeth, and wearing a plaid shirt untucked.

President Carlson didn't know about this meeting. Today, Daniel Carlson stood in the Oval Office wondering if he should go to an election party for the former Mayor of Washington, Harold Washington, who was seeking election after he was removed from office after spending time in prison for smoking cocaine. The invitation said, "Put Washington, back in Washington." That was his only qualification that President Carlson thought Washington had—a *good* name. Carlson thought his enemies would say that same thing about his initials and his campaign slogan. Washington still, very popular and unqualified, was caught wearing a toshiki earlier in the day. This outfit captured Daniel's thoughts all day. What an obvious ploy by Washington to associate himself with black America. As if the fact he weren't black enough. It would be tantamount to Daniel dressing in colonial attire for an election dinner. Daniel wouldn't go to the reception, it would be the right thing to do because the cameras would be there.

The steel reinforced doors slammed behind the last visitor. Inside the warehouse it was dark, and it didn't appear to be in a Caribbean country. Some light streaked through an easterly standing window. But the window sealed out all sound. Each member could hear the clacking and scuffling of the other shoes.

Everyone stood in a circle. They were all hot and tense. Even the two men standing outside the circle had shotguns resting on their shoulders facing up. Matumba was the organizer of the meeting. He was very dark skinned. He didn't live in Jamaica. He was raised somewhere on the Continent of Africa. He dressed in all white because it was so damn hot, it would've been stupid.

No one else wanted to identify themselves. No one expected anyone to either. The meeting wasn't exactly a power breakfast where the members were to make connections among themselves. It cost twenty thousand American dollars cash to get into this warehouse. Everyone turned over their envelopes filled with the cash to one of the men with a shotgun. When everyone anteed their amount, it was placed in a sack and brought to the other side of the warehouse.

"Welcome," Matumbo said. Everyone mumbled a greeting except for the General and the Italian. They caught each other's eyes when they realized they actually had something in common.

"How does this work?" The General demanded to know.

"I will explain," he said in a thick Southwest African accent. Pleasant, yet difficult to understand, until the ears got acclimated. "I have information. The information you've all been fighting for. As one of your American authors has said, General, 'Information is power!' And perhaps you'll be the one who gets it, to do as you please."

"*Como' conocere*'?"

"You'll know, because I'm selling a clue. And the clue leads you to the answer who lives on this island." Matumbo paused for effect. That's the way he liked it. He sought to increase the drama.

Matumbo was an intelligence broker. He obtained information and sold it. A mini-CIA salesman. Part of his love for the game was being a spectator; watching the mice scramble for the second clue. "That is the only way to ensure that the party that wins the *acumentelligence* will not be killed by the others ten steps after he leaves the auction."

"This is bullshit. You should've left it in another place. Buried it or something."

"You trust me enough to hand over cash and I'll tell you where to go?" Matumbo knew with confidence that this alternative when reflected upon would pose to be dangerous for all parties. The intelligencia doesn't stand a rung above living off of the well-paid information obtained by another.

"We barely know who you are, Matumbo. How will we know where to find you if we are unsatisfied with the product you produced?"

A smile greater than the one Matumbo painted on before shone, contrasted against his skin. "You all know my reputation. I've dealt with most of you before. But, if that doesn't satisfy a few of you, then I will give you this."

Matumbo accepted a six by eight-inch piece of clear plexiglass from one of his guards. He removed a handkerchief from his back pocket. Holding the plexiglass to the light, he wiped all smudges and debris from it. He placed the handkerchief back in his pocket. Matumbo held the object up for all parties to see, as if he were preparing a magic trick. He moistened the plexiglass with his breath, and then rolled his fingerprints on the glass. He kissed the glass, leaving his DNA. He placed that glass on an envelope sitting on the floor, in the middle of their circle.

"I assure you gentlemen that you'll be quite happy with the product my organization has discovered. You will have your President to control. He's idealistic, but is a self-preservationist like all leaders of the world. Or if he is not, then you can destroy him with the product. A product like that is worth $500,000."

"Five-fifty." The Italian said quickly.

"Who's the Italian going to sell it to, the President himself?" Some voice was heard.

"We have to worry about the General too. He's a goddamned American," another man stated.

"The President has a right to bid as well, gentlemen. But I don't think the General is bidding for the President." Matumbo replied.

"This is bullshit," the Palestinian said reaching down into his briefcase. Both guards lowered their guns toward the headdress.

"Six hundred thousand," the Palestinian operative said as he flaunted the cash in the brief case to all.

"Seven million dollars," the tiny Chinaman stated boldly. "End of negotiations." He paused for effect, and all attention was on him. "Did anyone bring that much?" No one answered. Matumbo was stunned with excitement. For a moment Matumbo was frightened the information wouldn't be worth that amount. But he proceeded confidently and did not let that thought slip into his mind again. After seconds of silence, Matumbo took the money from the Chinaman, and disclosed the location of his product. People would now die.

CHAPTER 25

Homicide

T HE ROOM HAD THE same feel to it. The eeriness, not apparent, kept Gina Rock moving forward. The office was bright; very bright, the light pointed outward toward her. As Gina neared, her eyes focused on the desk she bought her husband when he graduated from West Point Military Academy, and accepted his first job with the CIA more than twenty years ago. The desk was long with a light-colored wood. Chips of circular disks were configured under the heavy coat of lacquer that designed a picture of clouds into the desk. She looked up, not noticing Roger Rock sitting in the chair behind the desk. Hundreds of books were shelved neatly behind him. Some of them she noticed she had read years before. Reading what her husband read kept something in common in their marriage. She felt connected to a man that was all about creating and keeping secrets.

Gina Rock was proud of her husband. Living with him was adventurous. If Daniel Carlson were to win a second term in the White House, Rock would be assured a position anywhere he wanted. Reaching that goal was Rock's big struggle, and it was outwardly apparent.

Life in general was viewed as one big struggle to Rock. His mind's eye saw the despair and internalized angst with its view. His chest pained with each deep breath, when his mind questioned his worthiness to serve a president. He was Peter Pan, promoted to his level of incompetence. Gina knew all this, but never discussed it with her husband, for fear he might break down and not recover. Rock always would trick his mind to tread, and avoid drowning, but he could only tread so long. The damning of the follower who tried to lead.

Gina finally focused on the chair behind the desk. She couldn't deny any longer that Rock was sitting there, his head covered by a shadow, a gun inches under his hand. She knew he was gone. Tilting a lamp upward, his head fully illuminated, was painted and drenched with blood. Lifeless herself, she ignored her emotions.

Gina looked down on the desk and saw a note. She picked it up, and read it. After shaking her head for a moment, she opened the desk draw. Inside was a lighter. With a flick, the note was in flames. Disappointed with its content, Gina never wanted to read it again—nor have anyone else. The smoke, acute, thick, and black, rose to the ceiling. Gina waived her hand quickly to and fro. It got into her eyes, and they welled with tears. Gina wiped them away, reflected for a moment, and then kissed her husband on the forehead. Her job wasn't complete, however.

Gina dutifully ran into the bathroom, and grabbed a towel. She wiped away some of the blood that splattered around Rock's head—made the whole scene sinless. Gina retrieved the gun that lied inches underneath Rock's hand. She left the house, and called Peter Spark from a neighbor's house. As she waited at the neighbor's house, she was cold and numb. She didn't comprehend her loss. Staring into her lap, she wasn't dressed in business attire, she was slightly embarrassed. Crazy thoughts screamed through her mind.

Yesterday's conversation that Gina overheard from her husband in the study. Gina pictured him pacing, with the phone fixed to his ear. Rock yelled. He sounded desperate. Gina knew not to go down and hear better what was happening. She picked up the phone, and heard a voice she didn't recognize. Gina heard, "Get your message," before she clicked over to the second line to make a call. She did hear her husband answer distinctly from the study, "The next person that shoots me in the face will have to sew it up!" It meant nothing to her. He always spoke in some dark code.

Gina was acclimated to Rock's heady codes and political lingo in his Washington circle. She had no idea what he meant. Over and over in her head she picked apart each word. There was no doubt what she heard. Who would shoot her husband in the face? This could not be literal, as she thought then. Not completely.

Gina didn't understand who would shoot her husband in the face until she read the note by his dead body. She would never forget the words on the note, and she knew what she would have to do with them. A passive supportive political wife, she would be no more.

★ ★ ★

To Gina Rock's dismay, the initial investigation to the White House *revealed* a suicide. But she would have words with the President and out of respect she knew he would put the proper spin on her husband's death.

* * *

Alan Carlson sat at one of counsel's table as Brutowski walked in holding a briefcase. Alan's head turned toward him.

"How is it that it just so happens that you were the only guy available for this A.T.L.A. competition?" Alan said.

"You're lucky I signed up late, you could've been stuck with Satzman," Brutowski replied.

"I'm not complaining. I'm just wondering—we've been seeing a lot of each other lately and I want to know if it's by design."

"Shutup. Do you want to win this thing or not?"

"Yeah. Did you look over the case?"

"Yes. We're prosecuting, right?" Alan nodded in response.

"Let's see. David I. Jackson, accused of bank robbery with a weapon. He faces up to twenty years in jail and up to ten thousand dollars in fines."

"The problem is the robber wrote a note but the handwriting expert can't say that it was Jackson's handwriting," Alan said.

"He supposedly has an alibi witness too. Who's dead—committed suicide, but was deposed before he croaked himself."

"He's a lying sack of shit, who has an armed robbery conviction himself," Alan added.

"Speaking of that, what do you think of that guy, Rock?"

"Yeah, I'm totally depressed about it. He was a good guy."

"Are the papers right? Suicide?" Brutowski craftily directed Alan into revealing information.

"That's what they say."

"Yeah, but you know how it is. What does your father think?"

"He's not sure yet."

"Why? A man working his way up in the White House has no reason to commit suicide," Brutowski responded.

"It might have had something to do with an affair he was having."

"Really?" Brutowski sensed he was getting something he could use. "With whom?"

"It's just a rumor. I really shouldn't say."

"Oh just say."

Alan didn't know why he would say, but he trusted Brutowski. "Melissa Spark."

"No way. I don't believe that. The Chief of Staff's wife?"

"It's only what I heard. Don't repeat it."

Brutowski said he wouldn't. They continued to work on the case of *United States v. Jackson*.

That night at 2 a. m. Marcus Brutowski drove to a college bar hang out in New Haven. At a phone booth behind the bar he placed a call. It was pouring rain and it was chilly. Still Brutowski felt the call was urgent.

"Good morning, General."

"Go ahead."

"It's Brutowski, sir. He might have had an affair with Peter Spark's wife."

"That's excellent. How did he tell you that?"

"Just in passing. I believe him. You should check it out."

"Good work. I'll be in touch soon." The phone went dead. Brutowski put down the receiver with relief.

★ ★ ★

Daniel sat at his desk in the Oval Office two mornings after Rock's death by a gruesome bullet through the cheek. Daniel pulled out a piece of stationery and a pen, and began to write. He wrote a eulogy of tears. He felt pain and the mystery of Rock's death was a claw that clamped on his brain.

Daniel ate a rice paper message that morning which told him that Rock was in trouble. Daniel couldn't understand why the facts were not clearer. Rock had written something at his desk— there was fresh ink on his hands, and fresh pressings on the office blotter. But Gina swore there was no note.

The FBI initially told President Carlson that the angle of the bullet was inconsistent with suicide but the powder on Rock's shooting hand was consistent with a theory of suicide. President knew Roger Rock had problems, but he couldn't believe he would take his own life. Rock had an air of a desperate man, but he was a veteran of the Washington fray. He had a proper knowledgeable blend of legal and political issues necessary to be a White House fixer. He was just a guy in over his head, and under the thumb of Peter.

★ ★ ★

Gina Rock dropped her car off at the Metro station near her Virginia home. She wouldn't drive to the Hill that morning. The weather was hot and rainy. She wore a brown overcoat and dark glasses with large frames, and a scarf to protect her hair from the humidity.

Gina didn't know the man she called the night before. She dialed the number scratched by her late husband on the blotter at his desk. The person at the other end of phone. Nervously, she spoke. She was afraid that the wrong tone in her voice might destroy her plan.

The phone answered, "Yes."

"Do you know who shot my husband in the face?"

"Yes. I'm sorry, Mrs. Rock. I wish I could sew it up."

In that moment, Gina feared that she was talking to her husband's murderer. "I don't know what your husband was working on. I assume you know, since you're calling me. He must have told you about the Center." She lied.

"I need to meet you. Roger wrote a message before he died."

"How reliable is it? Was he murdered Mrs. Rock? And the note planted?"

"I thought you would know."

"Now how would I know! I've been nothing but loyal to the President and honorable to my country."

"I'm sorry, I didn't mean to imply anything."

"You really don't know as much as I thought, do you Mrs. Rock. Are you talking on your kitchen phone!"

"No! I'm in Roger's office," she replied.

"Good. Meet me at Abe's left-foot at six tomorrow morning. Can you wake up that early?" She wondered if he was kidding or was that a code of some kind.

"Yes, I'll be there. What about the FBI?"

"What about the FBI?"

"The President has assigned two or three agents to watch the house for my protection."

"My sweet Mrs. Rock, you have no idea what your husband did for the President, do you? The FBI works for us. You're not their prisoner. What time do they expect you to leave the house tomorrow?"

"Eight in the morning."

"Good, don't change it. Slip out and meet me there. Goodnight, Ms. Rock."

"Good night. Wait, what's your name?"

"Call me, Han."

* * *

The morning dew was on the grass. The sunlight was white and could not be seen so early. The weather was becoming hotter as the sun rose. Gina Rock was tense as she slipped out the back of her home. She felt she was doing the right thing. She didn't know what she was doing.

Gina didn't take the car parked in the garage. She took Roger's car that was on the street and slipped into the car, from the passenger side. Crouched down she slipped the key into the ignition. Slowly she rotated the key, as if the car would make less noise that way. Louder than she expected, the engine roared.

Gina slipped the car in drive and drove half way down the street before she lifted her head up in a normal position. She parked her car in the Metro station and got out. Looking left and right, she saw nobody suspicious following her. She adjusted her frames as she walked onto the platform. The train pulled up as she stepped onto the platform, and she was consciously grateful for not having to wait for it to come. The train was not terribly crowded at a few minutes after five.

As Gina sat on the train, she had wished she brought a newspaper to cover her face. She was uneasy. She dreamed about how involved Roger was in this whole network for the President. It had to be that. He didn't kill himself. He was a soldier who went down in service to his President. Moments away from the Lincoln Memorial she resolved, that if the person who met her at Abe's left leg wasn't Chinese, she would hand him an alternate note, and run.

★ ★ ★

Han, in black, stood at the left leg of Abraham Lincoln. He was almost alone except for a couple of early morning tourists jogging by the steps of the Memorial. Han was a thin man with a strong wiry frame, wore sun glasses, and was in a pissed off mood.

Han was smoking a cigarette and pacing when two men approached. One man approached from behind, and the other head on. The man in back grabbed Han around his biceps, and said, "Sir, you're coming with us." Han stepped forward and threw the man off him. Immediately, the man in front drew a .357 snub nose revolver, and pointed it at Han's face. "Hey, cut the karate shit. FBI." Agent Brad Lefkel lowered his gun and showed Han his FBI credentials. "See?" Han was enraged, but knew they had his number. Four more agents walked out from behind Lincoln. One directed him to a four-door sedan on the street. Han took a step, and the agent on the ground came up with his fist to Han's groin. Two agents grabbed Han by the arms, and escorted him to the car.

Once Han was ushered away, another Chinese male with a cigarette and dark sunglasses appeared at the left foot of Lincoln. He paced and had a smile on his face—and he was waiting for Gina Rock. Moments later Gina Rock approached the man who stood at the left leg of Lincoln.

"Hello," Gina said.

"Hello, Ms. Rock," he responded with a slight feigned Chinese accent.

Gina pulled a .38 caliber gun from her handbag. "Tell me who you are."

Startled. The man said he was Han. She relaxed and put the gun back into her handbag. "Here is the message." She had written it down before the meeting. "I can't believe it is literally true."

"We'll figure it out. Don't worry about it."

"My husband worked for you?"

"No, we worked for him."

"And he worked for the President?"

"Yes, ma'am."

"Then I'm proud of him."

"You did the right thing, Ms. Rock. Goodbye." He turned and stepped quickly away.

★ ★ ★

After the third meeting Daniel had in the morning, he scribbled on a pad in the oval office. Daniel Carlson had difficulty breaking the melancholy he felt over, what had become a national scandal—Rock's death.

Scratching circles on the morning paper that said, Rock's Suicide Over Affair, Daniel asked himself what was good about the situation. The only answer his mind could come up with is that this crisis would be his last before the election.

Daniel stopped, glanced upward, and pressed the intercom button.

"Lynn, call Alan please." A moment passed and Alan picked up his extension.

"Hello?"

"Hello, Alan?"

"Hi. Thanks for calling me back so soon."

"What's up?"

"You've read the papers about Rock today."

"Sure," Daniel replied.

"I've got a feeling I'm responsible."

"How?" Daniel wondered.

"I was joking, but I told a friend that Melissa Spark was having an affair with Rock, and the next thing I know is the papers are repeating it, and you are responsible for not stopping them."

Daniel would ordinarily have dismissed the concern, but at the morning's meetings no one could figure out where the leak about Melissa Spark and Rock came from. It was because it was not a leak, it was a lie.

"Who did you tell?"

"One person—Marcus Brutowski."

Daniel wrote the name above the newspaper headline.

"Hold on."

"Daniel clicked on the intercom, "Lynn, get Director Stone on the phone."

"Director Stone?"

"Mr. President, what can I do for you?"

"We're on the phone with my son, Alan. He tells me that we might have a spy following my son. Alan and a few friends were sitting around having pizza and someone blurted out that Melissa Spark and Roger Rock were fooling around and all the nonsense that followed.

"What's his name?"

"Marcus Brutowski."

"What year is he?"

"Alan?"

"Third year," Alan said. "He's from Deerlick, Indiana."

"Hmm. Like General Speiser," Stone said. "I'll call you back, Mr. President."

"Will you see Brutowski again?" Daniel asked.

"Probably."

"Mention that Rock will have a memorial in Guantanamo. And Alan, don't mention my name until this election is over."

"I'm sorry."

* * *

Director Stone lifted the phone receiver. He summoned his assistant.

"What did the President say," Greenberg asked.

"He wants us to check out someone who is investigating the Presidency through his son, Alan."

"Do you think it's true?"

"It might be," Stone replied. "Did the Rock thing go together okay?"

"Yes. Very smoothly. We're interviewing Han who's giving us the whole breakdown of the auction. You'll probably want to talk to him yourself."

"Where's the message that Gina Rock gave us?"

"It's right here, sir." Greenberg handed Director Stone the note.

"It's literal, isn't it?" the Director asked.

"It can't be, sir."

"Oh it is, unfortunately." After looking at it again.

Greenberg hesitated for a moment and then cleared his throat. "Don't we owe it to the President to let him know what he should be expecting? Or, is this a code for a physical attack on the President."

"We do owe the President. Make it obvious. Send the message over a NASA satellite. Make it easy enough for a junior aide to pick it up. When Peter Spark gets wind of it, he'll call here. Then I'll level with him. In the meantime, tell the Secret Service and everyone else, we have a threat." Director Stone said.

"With all respect, sir, why don't we just do the President a favor and speed the whole thing up and let him get it personally through the center?"

"Because the President might get the wrong idea if it goes through the center. He may think we're leveraging him. This way is the best way. I hope he survives it. This is the dirtiest I've ever seen. And, it sounds like it's true."

CHAPTER 26

Chess & Checkers

THE SEVEN O'CLOCK ALARM beeped quietly but loud enough to wake the President. President Carlson sat up in his bed and turned the alarm off. When he pulled the sheets and cover off himself, his maroon silk pajamas were exposed. June quickly snatched up more than her share of the blankets. Immediately, upon rising, the President went to his closet and put on a robe. Then he went to his bathroom and brushed his teeth.

The President leaned down to the intercom by his night-table and pressed, "I'm ready for my session," he said to the Secret Service man outside his bedroom door. The President's day began the usual way.

★ ★ ★

"Hello, Zulu, this is Yankee," the voice said into the phone.

"Go ahead Yankee, the line is sterile."

"Drag is coming to a peak. The muscle has been provided. The trainer will confirm. The ink will tell all tomorrow morning."

"Good. So much for an invulnerable President. The ignorant will be educated. The silent will be heard."

"I just hope the ends justify the means, Zulu. Yankee out."

The President's day concluded in the usual way.

* * *

Peter Spark sat in his office pondering about the next four years in the Carlson Administration, over a brandy. Peter was going to ask for State and probably get it. The election was in the bag.

His thoughts went to a long winter vacation skiing with Melissa. She deserved a break from politics. What a great wife she turned out to be. Always supportive, even though Peter thought he didn't deserve it. Her career was supporting Peter's. The luncheons, the dinners, the museum openings. Peter remembered that Melissa had aspirations to be a teacher. She loved kids. He denied her both, a career in teaching and children of her own. Peter never discussed her wants and desires, not in her realm of desire. It was either, do you want to go to the library opening or the Senator's birthday party?

Peter felt neglectful of Melissa at this moment. He contemplated retirement after the second term. Life would get better. There are less social obligations in a second term—his President couldn't run again. But State, that's not a job with less time constraints. It was a job that would extend Peter's influence abroad. It would mean leaving Melissa at home for days, sometimes weeks at a time. Perhaps he would suggest she should be a teacher now. She would need an activity that she could fall in love with, while he was away. He would definitely discuss the option with her. Hopefully, she would be pleasantly surprised at the unexpected support.

There was a knock on the door.

"Come in," Peter said not moving from his desk. It was one of Peter's aides working late.

"I just got an interesting transcript that may relate to national security, Mr. Spark."

"Where's it from," Peter asked, taking the sheet from his aide.

"Would you believe NASA was doing some weather experiments and didn't know what to make of it?"

"Hmm. Let's see what it says." Peter put on his reading glasses and stared at the page intently, but wasn't taking it too seriously. What's the chance NASA came up with something pertaining to national security? "Hello Zulu, this is Yankee. That means there are two parties involved. Drag has come to a peak. Drag must be the name of an operation and it must be coming to a close. The muscle has been provided. Must be some type of enforcement or strong arm tactic. The trainer will confirm," Peter thought for a second. "I take it back. Muscle must be another source because, trainer is backing up what muscle is saying or doing. The ink will tell all tomorrow. That must be the newspapers. Something will be in the paper tomorrow. You got this when?"

"The call seemed to be made two hours ago, sir."

"So much for an invulnerable President. The ignorant will be educated. That's barely a code. The people will learn of some critical information. The silent will be heard. Either that means someone will also shed light on what this information is all about, or people won't like the information they're going to read about. I just hope the ends justify the means. Wonderful, that means the information can be fiction. All right, good work. I'll look into it."

"Good night, Mr. Spark." The aide left the room.

Peter knew it could be the one thing he and Daniel had feared for years, but it was improbable. The other thing it could be is some manufactured evidence that implicated the President in some wrong doing. A last minute scandal to sway a mass of voters to go the other way. Peter hoped it was the latter. It would be much easier to deal with the fiction than with the truth. No matter what it was.

The phone rang and Peter answered it on the first ring.

"Mr. Spark? It's Kensington at the *Post*. I think tonight I'm going to earn my money." Peter was worried. He had a feeling it was related to the intercept he just received.

"Good, because I've been paying you since the Bratton scandal."

"I don't know how much this is going to help. This article has been under wraps for months now. I just found out about it tonight. O'Brady is writing a story, and I don't know if you know this sir but it claims something unbelievable about the President."

* * *

The President went into his bedroom and changed into his bath-robe for a late night massage. He walked into the massage room and greeted Bruce.

"Missed you this morning, Bruce," Daniel said.

"Sorry, sir," Bruce seemed a little disturbed about some-thing. Perhaps personal family life, so the President didn't want to intrude.

"I have that pain in my neck again. Will you do that thing you do? Thanks." Moments passed and Daniel spoke again. "Ying is strong for a little woman, but I really got a kink."

"How's your son coming along in therapy?" Daniel asked.

"Fine. Much better every day. He wants to get back to work," Bruce replied. His voice connoted that Daniel hit a source of pain.

"That's understandable. Car accidents can do that to someone. He'll be back to normal soon."

"I hope so."

"You know you seem to brood all the time lately," Daniel said.

"I know. It's Catherine. She's going through one of her life changes again. She wants to travel."

"So go travel with her, Bruce."

"She wants to travel by herself," Bruce replied.

"Oh, I understand why that might be difficult for you."

"You know how it is with wives like ours, sir."

"Too well," Daniel replied and then remained silent as his thoughts drifted to the situations of the day.

The effects of the massage seemed to be setting in, and the President relaxed as his mind drifted to other ideas besides American politics on the Hill. Ten minutes into the massage there seemed to be a ruckus outside the door.

"I must see the President immediately!" The voice was heard clearly through the door.

"The President sees no one!" There was a loud thumb against the wall. "Post 3. . . ." Instantly, a dozen Secret Service men with rifles and automatic weapons teemed the hall.

"Mr. President, get under the table, sir," Bruce said. He seemed to reach into a bag. The President wondered what he was grabbing.

"No, wait a second." The President recognized the voice through the door. He put his robe on quickly and then opened the door. "What's the problem, Jasper?" All the President saw was two men pressing another man against the back wall.

"I'm the Goddamn Chief of Staff!" It was Peter Spark.

"Let him go," the President ordered. The Chief of Staff fixed his suit. "Couldn't this wait until our nightcap?"

"Sorry to disturb you, Mr. President." The formal approach from Peter struck the President as odd. "I know no one is supposed to interrupt your massages. But they know. They know, Daniel. We have a crisis on our hands." The two men locked eyes. "This will probably turn the whole election around. We're in deep trouble." Daniel Carlson knew what had happened. The Presidency had just become a nightmare. The election road, a gauntlet of embarrassment and explanation. After all these years, President Carlson never would have believed that it would ever be known—it was—and now he would have to deal with the impending scandal.

★ ★ ★

Peter and Daniel worked furiously into the night. Who knew what? What would be released? All of Peter's aides were called in at home. Peter ran his investigation strictly like an Intelligence group—highly compartmentalized. No one group knew what the other was doing. Twenty phones were installed next to each other in the three rooms surrounding the Oval Office. Everyone was sitting at a large table in one of the three rooms. None of the top people in the Cabinet were notified in order to prevent premature leakage. No one could be trusted at this point. Peter bounced from one room to the next. Peter was executing his plan to obtain *intelligence*, but D. C. planned his own strategy. After four hours of work it was 3:00 a.m. Fatigue had set into Peter's face as he approached the President and closed the door.

"It was what we expected. I think we should wait until the story is released and then categorically deny it. The election is in a couple of days. There will be enough loyal supporters to just squeak by, then it won't matter. You can't be impeached for this. Some of our agenda on health care may fall through," Peter said.

"That is a chance I'll take. I resolved a long time ago that I would come clean if it ever came to be known."

"You're the President. You owe it to this country. You're the most idealistic man I know. You became President for the country, not for the party, or yourself. We can win this."

"I want to win it my way. If I can't, then this country doesn't deserve me as President. Call it egotistical. I won't serve a country that won't accept me."

"Please be reasonable, Daniel! Give me just a few more hours and I'll be able to figure out how this all started and I'll squelch it. I'll make whoever is the responsible person pay."

"What if it's a conspiracy? The Palestinians? The Chinese? The CIA? How are you going to punish them? Start another war? I owe the people honesty, not a fancy story."

Peter acutely remembered the feelings he was having at this moment. Another betrayal. His muscles seized up. "Daniel, don't be an asshole! You've worked too hard. You're twice the man Bratton ever was. I can't let you do what he did to himself. He fucked it up for himself. Don't do it Daniel! I'm begging you. For your sake. You can fire me, but I have to say this. Don't be such a pansy! You have to handle this job with a cloak and a dagger—not diplomacy. You can't handle the people, here. You can't persuade the silent majority; they vote in two days! We're dealing with vicious animals here. You're in no position to make this decision. Please, this is my area of expertise. You've taught me things about dealing with people and being diplomatic. And I know this isn't the time to be anything like that. I respect your judgment on everything, Daniel. But you must listen to me. You're too emotionally involved! I will handle it."

There was silence. The two friends stared at each other. Then the President spoke in a calm and low tone:

"Peter, I would never fire you for telling me your feelings, no matter how strong they were." The President stood and approached

Peter. "You're my closest friend and confidant. But this decision is a *me* decision, so I will make it. I know it could affect everyone in this country. I'm going to tell them that it doesn't have to."

"You're being too ambitious," Peter said softly. "You have too much faith! The Civil War wasn't won in two days. Desegregation wasn't won in two days. Pulling out of Vietnam didn't happen in two days."

"Then it will be the last mistake I make as President. Set up an address to the nation, at the end of the day tomorrow. I'll make a speech from this office. I will write it myself. Notify Directors Stone and Yates and tell him to start an investigation to the cause of the leak. I'll do that for your sake, okay? That's all. I'm going to sleep. Goodnight."

★ ★ ★

The Director of Central Intelligence briefs the President, who was briefed by CNN, that violence breaks out in the Middle East. Some Israeli villages on the West Bank, victims of several air strikes.

What Director Yates knew that CNN didn't, was that, in effect, this was an Arab response to the news that President Carlson's days as President were numbered. Assurances would be lost. The Arabs having the perfect opportunity to cause disruption while the President's career brutally dies. The Director of Central Intelligence, following the President, demands to know why. The President turns to Yates, and said, "You will find out in a matter of moments."

It required President Carlson himself to ask the network executives to set aside five minutes of uninterrupted air time for a presidential candidate a day before the election. They wanted to know why. They didn't want to be seen as partisan. It was a shoe-in for Daniel Carlson, but why should a candidate get presidential time.

* * *

President Carlson sits at the edge of his desk in the Oval Office and he stares into the camera's eye as the red light turns on. A host of media people and Presidential advisors look on with anticipation to what would be, win or lose, a historic speech given by a President. His future, too, depends on what the cameras see. A director from the White House Press Office points to the President.

"My fellow Americans. It is my privilege to be invited into each one of your homes on the eve of the nation's most important election. My faithful companions explained to me that I may need to regain the confidence of the American people, in light of the most recent discovery about my personal life. My true friends have worked tirelessly to neutralize and protect me from the potentially adverse effect that a discovery of this type might have on this administration. Over some objections, I'm speaking to you tonight. I'm going to speak to each of you and share with you the way that I feel. I want each and every one of you to remember that we, as a nation, have been through some bad times, and have overcome them together. Tonight, I know we'll be able to overcome again.

"As Americans, we know the Bill of Rights ensures us all of certain protections from governmental abuses and the tyranny of a vocal majority. One of these protections is the right to privacy. The government, without just cause, cannot infringe upon our personal lives. This is our right."

There is silence. The President looked into his hands folded in his lap. He looks up. The sadness is unmistakable. Through the television, curiosity and empathy swell in the hearts of millions. Most pray that whatever the President is about to say, they and he can overcome with time. With confidence, the President resumed. "I'm an American. Personal privacy is also my right. However, my enemies have picked apart and drilled into my political affairs searching for some evidence of indiscretion. When they could find nothing, they attacked me personally. Certain unsavory characters pressured, through blackmail, a member of the White House domestic staff to add credibility to the personal campaign of destruction. The people involved in this are counting on you, the American people, to condemn me as an American leader. It will work, if we subscribe to their value system.

"If the Declaration of Independence were written today, the Framers would demand that privacy be included in the list along with fundamental rights of life, liberty, and the pursuit of happiness."

The President takes a deep breath. He runs his fingers through his natural, non-gelled, graying hair.

"The great philosopher, Plato, gave his most famous speech which was later titled an apology. Traditionally, an apology means that one exercises sorrow for an action—when, in fact, the Greek translation is an *explanation*. My friends, I do not ask for your forgiveness, I request your understanding as I offer an explanation." The President took a last deep breath as an undetectable sweat broke out at his hairline.

"My fellow Americans—I am a homosexual." There are no other words for the moment. The President stares directly into the camera. The sadness has vanished. He is confident, poised, and calm. He continues to wait as though he knows. He hears the raucous disbelief of millions of Americans in their living rooms. He knows, too, when to continue, his timing, as always, is impeccable.

"Now I ask you to examine the implications of such a characterization. You will hear many arguments and justifications. The news media will cite the father of modern psychotherapy, Sigmund Freud, as evidence of a noted psychologist who believed homosexuality to be a psychological abnormality. I encourage you all to research Freud. Listen to those who quote, interpret, and cite him. Read Freud and articles pertaining to his work, philosophies, treatments, and psyche. Then decide how relevant Freud is to today's issues.

"Proponents wanting to argue my case will tell you about Abraham Lincoln, his greatness, his achievements, his political accomplishments. Then they will also tell you about his severe bouts with depression and other theories.

"There will be others from the past who will be analyzed and used to strengthen arguments for both sides. You will hear about William H. Taft's mannerisms, poor speech, and obesity, about Thomas Jefferson, being a slave owner, and John F. Kennedy's alleged infidelities. Listen carefully to the arguments and justifications, then seek answers for yourself. These men of history lived through many crisis situations, politically and personally, yet remained leaders who were able to advance our country."

The President breathes again and wonders which President would've met the Silent Majority's standards. As the fleeting thought passed with acute resentment, he continued with care, a delicately poised delivery.

"As you evaluate, consider the man, his performance, his intentions, his motivations, and his commitment to the nation. Do personal choices made in privacy for one's personal life influence the actions and policies of a political leader? Does human compassion, understanding and tolerance apply to a President?"

Again, the President's eyes search the audience as if he is personally speaking to each of his listeners. So unnerving visual intensity that, spontaneously, the camera people as viewers at home, look away.

He knows it is time to change the pace and lighten the message. The President stands and places his hands in his pockets. His voice is calm and filled with steady optimism.

"Serving you as President has been both an honor and a tremendously rewarding experience. I have been blessed with a talented, dedicated, and diverse group of people working together as my staff. We have shared the power of a presidency with each other and with you in order to strengthen the fiber of this country. We are one nation shared by millions. For this reason, I have come to you, before the vultures who are my enemies, spread nasty little secrets with dirty intentions. I hide nothing tonight. And tonight nothing has really changed from this morning other than that you all know of my sexuality before I was married. Yes, before. In the twenty-five years that June and I have been married, I have remained faithful to our vows. My opponents wish to create a scandal from a long-ago past.

"Homosexuality is not something one cultivates or develops. It's a part of the whole of who one is. It is a personal part that does not have to cloud one's professional judgment any more than heterosexuality. I want, as Dr. Martin Luther King, Jr. said, '. . .to be judged by the content of my character.'"

"It is my pleasure and honor to serve as your President. I'm proud that the polls have shown that I'm the most popular fourth-year President in history. You've given me your trust.

"One fact most people don't realize is that all of my cabinet has remained with me throughout my term. I think it's because I've let each and every one of them realize that I appreciate them. Even on the occasions that my cabinet members disagree, their viewpoints are always listened to and considered. If you ask them, they will tell you I'm a man who gives away power rather than collects it. My power serves me, so I can serve you. I've never collected power for the sake of collecting it." The President again pauses for effect.

"What am I really asking from you my fellow Americans? What is the real purpose behind my speaking to you tonight? I don't need the American people to vent my feelings of frustration. I've known about my preference for some time. My purpose—to tell you our relationship remains the same. I'm still your President, still your leader, still your representative and friend. In a few weeks is the election. You must cast a vote of confidence for my political abilities. Yes, I want to be reelected so as to continue to actualize the policies, programs, and ideologies that have been the foundation of my campaign and administration. There is a lot of work and growth yet to be accomplished. I want to serve this country and its people.

I want you to believe the successes of the past four years as proof that your vote for me can mean results. What the others are selling is based on leaked information designed to damage success, a smear campaign of deceit, and intangible rhetoric without policy to bolster the words. You have a say about how this government is run. You have had this power for four years. I am no different now than I was two hours ago or for the four years I have served you thus far. I have the confidence that you will do that which is best for this nation. Do vote. Tomorrow I will thank you, each of you, for your support." He steps forward, closer to every viewer. "All of you. Good night."

As with every other address to the nation, the President steps out into the audience and shakes the hands with the technicians, camera crew, make-up personnel, prompters and news media gathered in the Oval Office. The television cameras remain on until he has made his rounds, then, he exits turning one final time to wave goodnight. The cameras turn off and the few people in the room begin to clap.

In the private Presidential office quarters on the second floor, Peter Spark slouches down on the family's couch. His Ralph Lauren pullover is drenched with perspiration and his left ear is crushed to the phone receiver as he listens to the first reports from pollsters.

★ ★ ★

"Did you hear what political analysts are calling the Carlson Era at the White House," the comedian asked his audience. "Well it ain't Camelot." Laughter was heard throughout the club. "No, seriously, some noted historian on 'Nightline' tonight called the Carlson presidency, the Gay millennium." Laughter emanated throughout the room. A waitress had to stop in her tracks because she thought she was going to spill her drinks, she was laughing so hard. "I also heard that Paramount just signed Robert Redford to star in a movie based on the life of Daniel Carlson called, *All the President's Men*." Loud applause was heard. The crowd whistled at the shrewd witticisms of the comedian. "I guess by now the guys at the *Washington Post* realized that Bob Woodward's contact, Deep Throat, was actually Daniel Carlson." A 'bada-bum' was heard from a drum set in the background. "Goddamn, can you believe it? The Goddamn President, a homosexual. He was a great guy too. I guess Richard Nixon doesn't seem like such a bad guy after all? Richard Nixon got on television. and said, 'I'm not a criminal. 'I thought Carlson was gonna say, 'I'm not a faggot,'" the comedian said raising his hands and shaking his jowls in a Nixon-like imitation. "Seriously folks, the guy was the most popular President in history. Raise your hands if you voted for him in the last election." The comedian paused and only saw a couple of hands raised. "Sure, sure, come on folks, it's not like you're admitting you're a communist. I mean this guy did wonderful things for the country. He helped the economy, improved foreign relations. Yes, not everyone realized the President had a good foreign policy agenda. Especially with Greece." Laughter erupted. "Come on, honey," the comedian pointed to a girl in the front row who didn't get the joke. "You don't get it? The Greeks like it up the ass. She gets it now. I can't believe it. This girl never heard the one about the Greek quarterback and the scared Center." The girl was now in tears of uncontrollable laughter. "So now the truth comes out. Now we know why he could pass almost any bill through Congress. I mean every President had closed door sessions, but this guy must have been giving champagne and blow job parties." The comedian paused. "It's just the beginning folks. I'm just getting started—"

A heckler in the audience yelled out, "Hey, that's the President you're talking about!"

"You were laughing too, pal."

CHAPTER 27

Rats

THE PRESIDENT FELT NUMB this morning, just going through the motions. Lynn was talking to campaign coordinators on the phone, and tried to keep them motivated. Her makeup couldn't hide the swelling under her eyes from a night full of tears. She didn't need an explanation even though Daniel said they would talk after the election.

The polls, the cameras, were illustrating a decline in Daniel's approval rating. As Daniel walked by her desk Lynn smiled and waved robustly. She felt he wasn't feeling very well. He smiled at her, but she could see past the grin, and for that moment could see the world through his eyes. What she saw was a depressed and desperate man. A man she had never seen in Daniel before.

A whole lifetime goes into making an American leader, it was not just a job. Daniel devoted his life into being the best he could be, honorably. He rode the magic carpet ride of success, now it was being pulled out from under him.

Daniel looked down at his desk and saw the FYEO (confidential) file from the Director of the FBI. Inside, it contained the name of the person who leaked the information about his homo-sexuality to the press. Curiosity peaked. He wanted to know who betrayed him. Who made his life a hell?

Daniel studied the design of his desk. He noticed the book shelves and the pictures of Washington and Jefferson. He saw them peering down at him, as if to say, 'Now what are you prepared to do?' He viewed the room like a child whose parents decided to move and he was seeing his childhood home for the last time.

Powerless. That's how he felt. Like a rat in a cage who sees the red light go on and knows he'll be shocked— and there's nothing he can do. As he looked down, he reflected on the scandal that forced Senator Bratton into early retirement. Daniel didn't quite understand at the time what Senator Bratton meant when he gave his soliloquy years ago in his office. Now he understood the point about the irrelevancies of the job requirements. He felt bad for Senator Bratton, but always felt that if a man betrayed his wife, someone who he's supposed to have a sacred trust with, how difficult would it be to forsake the trust of the people he isn't so intimate with?

Daniel was a man of integrity, and he was gay. He was gay in first term, and the most popular President in the history of this country. What had changed? He was still the same man. It was true what Peter said all those years, from the days of Senator Bratton to the Presidency. It's all about imaging. Truth is irrelevant. Competency is irrelevant. Do you appear truthful and competent? Straight and mainstream?

He picked up the file and stopped as he was about to open it. What happens if it's Peter? Could it be? For whatever Peter was or wasn't, one thing for sure, he was loyal. Everything he did was to protect the person he worked for and the ideals he stood for. He never served a cause higher than the person he served or worked with. Yet, on the other hand, that is the nature of the deep cover spy. The Talbots, the Yuris, the Sashas, the Woo Tai Chins, they all had the implicit trust of the people they worked for. They knew how to hide well. The best cloak was hiding above the heads of the people you were acting against.

The irony had come to a head at this point. Daniel felt from time to time that he was destined for the Presidency, yet never considered himself above anyone else because of it. The Silent Majority allowed him to be the king on the throne. Will it take it away? A man like Peter, his scar was on the outside. Daniel's scar was on the inside. The Party didn't want to support Peter because of that scar. Jealousy? What better motive for Peter. Yet, the real question was, would the Party have supported Daniel Carlson if they had knows he was gay before the election?

After all is said and done, Daniel thought, what would be the point of knowing who started this mess? Would it change the minds of the American people? Would it prevent a scandal like this from happening again in the future? Then he looked critically at his philosophy and values system. It was bad management to figure out the cause of a crisis when the situation demanded a solution. What a way to vent anger. Lynch the man who started the whole damn thing.

Daniel picked up the file, nodded his head, and threw it in the garbage. Lynn got on the intercom and reminded the President that it was time to meet Charles Mathews for the final election day run-down.

The strategy was to go back to the core of his support. Hit the Universities, starting with Yale and a quick stop by helicopter at Harvard, and turn the tide back to him before the end of election.

The President brushed himself off. With the whole investigation over, he was willing to give the American people a chance.

As futile as it may have seemed, Daniel had forsaken the polls, which cited massive undecided, and was determined to finish the final days of the campaign in strength.

As the President was leaving his office, Lynn buzzed in and said Peter Spark was on the line.

"Hello, Peter. What's happening?"

"Never mind me. How are you doing?"

"I'm hanging in there."

"Please, Daniel, make it a good day. You can't afford to be down," Peter said sincerely.

"I'm giving my best effort."

"Good. Did the Director finish the report on the leak?"

"Yes, Peter, he did."

"And—Are you going to tell me what it said."

"I don't have time to explain my motives, but I didn't read it and I don't plan to." Peter suspected that he might not read it. He knew Daniel well.

"What do you plan to do with it?"

"I just threw it out, Peter. All I can say is the person who's responsible should be the next Vice President," Daniel joked.

"Ah, I really don't agree, but, okay. Keep your eye on the ball. I'll speak to you in a couple of hours." Daniel was about to hang up and to start the long day, but Peter interrupted with one last comment. "By the way, Mr. President. The *Receptionist* is none other than our friend Eugene Hawkins. Your messages in the *message room* were from a friend. I guess he liked what you stood for." Daniel didn't know who was a friend or what was a friend.

* * *

Peter made his way up to the office suites in the White House. He was wearing a dark pin striped suit with a dark black tie. In his right hand he had a large shipping envelope. He walked past the Secret Service man standing outside the Oval Office. He waved at Lynn who was on the phone and said that he wanted to drop his file on the President's desk. She absent mindedly waved him in.

Peter slipped over to the President's desk. He looked down at the waste basket and saw the FBI report sealed in the shipping envelope. He switched envelopes. Quickly, Peter opened the envelope and started to read the report. He scanned the first few paragraphs and then turned the pages quickly. It was about a ten page report. Then he just skipped to the last page and read the last sentence very slowly. *The Fedral Bureau of Investigation, on special assignment in service to the President, find that the individual who leaked the personal and private information about the President's homosexual nature was Bruce Porter, White House domestic staff.*

Peter was in shock. His suspicions were with someone high up in the Administration. After all, what about the Chinese and the CIA? It was Bruce Porter—the President's masseur. Peter asked the question: Who was Bruce working for? The answer to that question, Peter knew, could never be answered fully. It was also quite apparent that Bruce Porter didn't know that he was found out. The investigation was strictly, hush, hush.

Peter picked up the President's telephone.

"This is Mr. Spark. Set up a massage for me in the President's massage room in an hour. Oh, and I would like the President's masseur. What's his name? Yeah, Bruce, great!"

As Peter hung up, he noticed the Secret Service agent standing at the doorway. Peter smiled as he folded the report and tucked it in his jacket pocket.

"Sorry, I took so long," Peter said to the agent. He waved at Lynn, left the Oval Office, and went on his way to his office.

Behind closed doors Peter read the FBI's analysis. The analysis backed up by an interview substantiated the fact that the President spoke with members of the Republican party six months after the election. The President would discuss the complications of being homosexual and having a family. Bruce, a homosexual himself, would discuss problems and joys of raising a family, and being a husband. This whole account made for fascinating reading for Peter. He couldn't believe Daniel was discussing something so sensitive with a domestic staff person. No wonder he was never to be disturbed when he was having a massage. Everyone thought it was because of the messages. Daniel really had everyone fooled.

According to the report Bruce admitted that he never had any sexual relations with the President. It was strictly therapeutic discussions. Bruce was pressured under blackmail, either he finds something the opposition could use, or his family of Czech descent would be deported. A host of other threats were used, like IRS audits for the whole extended family that would make them all broke or serve a term in jail. Unbelievable, Peter thought.

Peter stood up, unbuttoned his jacket, and began undressing. As he finished dressing in casual clothes for his massage he picked up the FBI file and ran it through the shredder. He told his secretary to call and say that he would be going to the third floor for his massage. She thought that was odd considering it was days before the election. She then assumed it was a meeting Peter Spark didn't want to talk about.

Peter approached the massage room. He said to the Secret Service agent, "Like the President, I don't want to be disturbed— for any reason." The agent wondered what the Chief of Staff was doing getting a massage on what should be the busiest day of his life, even if he had little to do with the campaign management.

Peter stepped in the room and saw Bruce setting up the table. The spa jets were on heating up the water.

"Hello, Mr. Spark."

"Hello," Peter said.

"Have you ever had a massage before, Mr. Spark?"

"No, I don't think I have. Well, just from my wife."

"Well, just take off your clothes and lie face up on the table." Peter disrobed and adjusted himself on the table.

Bruce draped a white towel discretely around Peter's hips. As Bruce rubbed the oil into Peter's body, Peter thought it felt pretty good. He understood why the President enjoyed them once or twice a day.

Peter turned over and felt his muscles relax and his disks in his back slip into place. He was amazed. It was wonderful. Several minutes later Bruce remarked:

"Why don't you slide into the tub, Mr. Spark?"

"Hmm, I will." Peter enjoyed the hot-tub as well. He told himself to remember to tell Melissa to buy one for their home in Maryland.

"Would you like some of the President's orange juice, Mr. Spark?"

"Yes." Bruce was suspicious of Mr. Spark's congeniality. Peter had the reputation of being somewhat of a tyrant. If a massage and hot-tub doesn't loosen up a tyrant, nothing would.

"Any of the President's rice paper in the fridge?" Peter wanted to see if Bruce would break security protocol. Bruce just smiled politely pretending not to understand what Peter meant.

Bruce admired Peter's body. He thought for a man in his early sixties, a man a few years older than the President, Peter had stayed in great shape. He looked good.

Peter stepped out of the tub and dried off. He began to dress quickly as Bruce said, "I have to leave, Mr. Spark. I have to work out with the Vice President's wife in a couple of minutes. Anytime you want to have a massage, let me know. I mean, I hope that we'll be able to do this again. I know the President enjoys the massages." Peter tensed up again.

"Oh, just another second, Bruce." Peter adjusted his shirt and looked in the mirror and saw he was acceptable. Peter walked toward the door and put his hand on the knob. He was a few feet from Bruce, and leaned over as to only be inches from his face. "Bruce, I'm going to have you killed," he said a matter of fact. Bruce smiled in disbelief.

"What?"

"I'm going to have you killed. You see, I know you're the one who leaked, that the President is gay, you fucking faggot. You ruined the presidency, you fucking fudge packer," Peter said as he poked his index finger into Bruce's chest. "You ruined a great man. I'm going to fuck your world if it's the last thing I do as Chief of Staff. You have two weeks to move some place where I can't find you. One week, if you don't resign at the end of business day today."

Bruce gulped and said he was threatened. They already knew.

"Didn't you think I would protect you if you'd have told me they were threatening you? You chose to deceive the President. Well, now you're going to have to pay for your stupidity. Have a nice fucking life. Two hours. If my people find you after two hours, you're dead!"

Peter turned the door knob and left Bruce standing with his mouth opened and his knees shaking.

CHAPTER 28

Existential Aloneness

A N HOUR AFTER HIS telecast, on the President's desk was one letter informing him of Carl Wills' resignation. Of all the people to resign, Carl Wills. It was not that he was the most valuable person on the Committee to Re-elect, but he was a known homosexual. Daniel was sure he, like Peter, once had political ambitions, but knew that he resigned to a life behind the scenes because their scars were visible or were known.

Daniel didn't think about Carl very long before Lynn ushered in Daniel's old college buddy, Scott Witherspoon. Lynn opened the door and smiled. She was excited about the reunion until she saw Scott stagger in slowly. The *Times* was supposed to come in and take a photo of the two. Two war buddies reunite—that kind of theme. It would be for the morning edition. It became a hot news day so the papers wouldn't cover it. Only the White House photographer would be covering it now.

The whole election was a shoe-in for the incumbent President. Now every ten minutes somewhere in the country every political advertisement on President Carlson was focusing on the strength, power, and leadership he'd offered. The Committee to Re-elect was piecing together films it never thought would be necessary. Action shots of him playing tackle football with a group of ex-football players on the lawn of the White House. A total shift in campaign strategy was started on the day of the election. Military issues were being discussed on the radio and television. Generic strength in foreign policy was being bolstered and tagged with President Carlson. Fox News was just repeating segments of President Carlson's speech stating he was a homosexual. Commentators were getting personal and mean. They referred to the most effective President in the history of the country as Danielle. The talking points were all the same: homosexuals are weak, indecisive, and ladylike. Operatives from the campaign have fanned out on the news networks defending President Carlson. He's the man you all know. He's the same man, the operatives pled. Do you care who brought you this strong economy?

Scott Witherspoon still looked the same, but older. He even looked a few years older than Daniel, although they were the same age. Scott walked with a cane as a result of being near a freak explosion on a Marine base in Lebanon. Scott served in the Marines as an infantryman. President Carlson stood up to greet him, but detected that Scott was uncomfortable. His first clue was that Scott didn't bring his family along with him.

Scott was different. He wasn't the guy's guy he was in college. He was an alcoholic, and instead of being jovial and fun he became uptight and surly. His raspy voice spotlighted the last shadow of doubt that he was occasionally sober.

"Hello, Scott." Daniel patted Scott on the shoulder.

"Hello, Mr. President. How are you?"

"Could be better my Phi brother." Daniel couldn't lie.

"Hmm." Scott adjusted his position and looked down at the floor.

"Why don't you sit down, Scott?"

"I'd rather stand because of my hip and all. You knew about that. Besides I can't stay very long. I'm taking the grandkids to my wife's parents in Maryland. It's kind of a long ride." It occurred to President Carlson that this was the first time in almost four years that someone said to him, 'I don't have time for you, Mr. President.' Daniel didn't note this as a matter of arrogance, just as a plain fact. People don't dismiss the President. As President, Daniel was instinctively angry. Who was he to dismiss the President? Daniel had such a flash of anger. Peter Spark wouldn't dismiss such an idea as quickly as Daniel did.

"Oh, why didn't you bring the grandkids?" Daniel asked even though he knew the real answer.

"Well, the little one is sick from the trip. And Mary wanted to stay with him. You know, I think about our trip to Jamaica all the time. That was the best time of my life." Not a bad side-step. Scott should've been a politician.

"Yeah, I loved that trip too."

"Daniel, why didn't you tell me you weren't interested in girls. I wouldn't have pushed so hard." Daniel wasn't surprised with Scott's bluntness. They were very old close friends. Haven't been close for a while. Then it occurred to Daniel, had he ever been close with anyone? Daniel then wondered about Elana. Didn't she know him the best? Didn't she know he was different? She realized they were not destiny in her first stolen kiss in her car in Miami. In the Oval Office. President Carlson was enraged with Scott's disappointment.

"Scott, in the Oval Office, I prefer to be called, Mr. President. I don't know. I'm not sure I really knew."

"All those years I thought you made it with that beautiful woman who wanted to be your first. I just figured out that it was that big guy, Bob. Yeah, was that his name?" All those years of one or two minute phone calls to Scott and Daniel never realized that Scott lived vicariously through him. It was the only way to explain Scott's exceptional recall of the situation.

"Yeah."

"Goddamn, I never would've thought that big guy. He worked out, he had a tremendous body. He was magnificent. What a handsome guy he was."

"Watch it, someone might get the wrong idea, Scott." Scott gave a short laugh. A sudden serious look swept over Scott's face.

"Tell me, Mr. President, did you really believe you could've led a platoon into battle, like you wanted?" Daniel wondered where Scott had been for the past four years. He opened the door to his office and said, "Yes, Scott, I think I could have."

* * *

On the plane ride to a weekend in Star Island, Daniel phoned Peter. Melissa answered the phone and spoke to Daniel only long enough to say that Peter had a hangover from the last night, and was sleeping it off. He understood but didn't like it. Peter was drowning in alcohol and tears because it seemed he kept investing his life's energy in losers—first Bratton, now Daniel. If only he didn't have that damn scar. Some inspirational support from Peter was necessary for what Daniel was about to do— talk to his family, some of whom might not have learned of the scathing disclosure in the media.

Daniel poured himself a "D.C." with vodka. If Peter wouldn't help then perhaps the Russians would. What was this weekend going to be like? The reason he scheduled this weekend off was because he had a sizeable lead that a weekend with the family would advertise confidence and continue the family man image. Now the only thing it advertised was that he was hiding. For the rest of the trip he played cards with a Secret Service agent that was assigned to the flight.

★ ★ ★

The first person Daniel had to see was his wife. He had grown to love June in a brotherly way. The only romantic moment he ever had was on his wedding day. As the marriage went on June became disgusted with sex. Daniel never tried to satisfy her. He wondered if she was involved in an affair. It was a thought he never really investigated. Because he didn't care. The relationship sustained itself because she was disinterested and became mildly repulsed by sex with Daniel. He came to terms with his nontraditional relationship with June and after all the years of marriage the best moments became simply cordiality. June grew into the part. To the outside world, she became a traditional wife. She loved the power and the glory of being the First Lady and was the perfect wife in public. She had the whole world fooled.

Daniel made his way to the master bedroom.

"June, I want to talk with you." Daniel paused for as long as he did after he announced he was homosexual a few hours ago in his speech. "I'm sure you heard the news." She was shocked all over again, but inside she knew it could happen one day. June had hoped it was way after the presidency when the world wouldn't care. Why wouldn't the world care at that point, but it cared now?

"Oh, Daniel," she gasped. June put her hands to her mouth. "How?" Instantly her dreams shattered. Her way of life was destroyed. She comprehended what she suspected throughout their marriage. Her heart sunk and she began sobbing. Her instinct was to respond like Terrence Bratton's wife years ago, when he had the revelation of a scandal of another woman. At that moment, June couldn't believe that was even a scandal. Today, it would be ridiculous. Not even considered by the public as a factor in character. Or would it?

"I can't believe it," June sat on the bed. "It can't be true. All we've worked for. All I've done."

Daniel was a little surprised June didn't even question if it were true. Even this fact, as in all of politics, the truth is a relative and arguable thing. "I'm sorry it's going to change our life for a while."

"Can you still win? You can't back out now." Her head was spinning and desperately she said, "Deny it! I'll get on television and say you're a great lover. I'll be convincing. We'll figure something out."

"Perhaps it won't matter," Daniel said in desperation.

"Oh, but what about our friends, Daniel?"

Daniel wondered, 'What about me?' June released some of her tension with a laugh.

"Listen, I already made the address to the country. The world knows." It took a moment to sink in. He made such a monumental decision without asking her. How did Peter let him get away with it?

"How dare you?" She said with demonic scorn.

"I didn't consult you because I wanted to come clean with this. I wanted to defuse the scandal. I didn't want my enemies to destroy me. I wanted to give the American people a chance. The benefit of the doubt. I didn't want the Silent Majority to win, for once. I know after all I've done they will be able to handle it. And if they can't, I can become the professor I always wanted to be."

"You fool! I knew this would come to an end someday. What did I do to deserve such a thing? I became a good Christian. God.

It was Tom. I betrayed my husband. I let him get involved in the sinful world of drugs. . . ." Daniel's temper rose quickly.

"Oh shut up, June. I'm sick and tired of your bullshit! The Lord can't help us now. We have to help ourselves." There was silence. June stared at him with an intensity that said that he was blasphemy.

"This is what I get for marrying a man who is a sinner against nature."

Daniel took a deep breath and sighed. He stared into the mirror on the wall. He saw the wrinkles on his face. He turned and saw the hate in hers.

"I'm going to talk with my daughter."

"Remember, she's my daughter. You didn't have the desire to make your own. All those times you tried to pleasure me." June contrived a laugh. "Thanks for the favor."

"Thanks for your support." Daniel said disdainfully. He turned to leave and June left him with a final thought, "I'll pray for your soul, Daniel." Strangely, she said it with sincerity.

Daniel walked to the other end of the house to find their daughter laying face down on her made bed. Paul was in the room and excused himself.

"Connie. Hello, kitten." Daniel sat next to her on the bed.

"Hello, Daddy." He rejoiced in hearing her address him as, "Daddy." Connie turned over because it was uncomfortable to lean on her baby. She turned over and covered her eyes with her hands.

"I have something to tell you."

"I know, Daddy. And I don't want to talk about it. Tell me it isn't true. Please!" He wished it weren't. For a fleeting moment he tried to will himself into being a heterosexual.

"I'm sorry, darling, it is. It's been true for a very long time. I was . . ."

"I don't want to hear it! I don't want to hear it!" Connie kicked and screamed like a child.

"I'll let you be," Daniel said as he left to go to the bathroom.

He admitted to himself that this would be tough for a child of any age to accept. Probably the older, the harder, because children design a certain schema their parents fit into. If they violate it in any way, it's a shock to the psyche. Daniel never intended for his children to ever find out. It wasn't a secret. No parents should really talk to their child about their sex life. It's none of their business. In this case too.

The downtrodden Daniel Carlson again stared at himself in the mirror and sobbed into his hands. He had no one. No one to share his pain in this time of misery. Everyone was making their own misery. No one was comforting Daniel. Daniel had another drink before he went to visit Alan. He figured that Alan would take it the worst.

Daniel entered Alan's room and saw that Alan was studying for semester exams.

"Hey, Dad."

"Hi."

"Is something the matter, Dad? I've never seen you drink in the afternoon."

"Actually, the drink's for you, Alan. I have something to tell you that's going to upset you." Alan braced himself emotionally.

"Did somebody die?" He asked solemnly. Daniel sat on Alan's bed and Alan turned his chair to face him.

"Maybe me."

"You're sick?" Alan said in a nervous tone.

"No. I was just trying to make light of the situation. Alan, you sometimes grow up and you think certain things about certain people. For instance, a son thinks that his father is the strongest man in the world. Can do no wrong. Is the best father in the neighborhood?" Alan didn't quite follow his father's point but didn't interrupt. "When the son finds out something different about his father, the boy may feel differently about him. To get to the point, I'm going to tell you something about myself that you don't know. It may change what you think about me. And I hope that one day you'll think of me as the hero I once was to you."

"Dad, are you involved in some type of Watergate scandal?"

"No, Al." Daniel stood up and touched his son on the shoulders. "The media is going to release that I'm a homosexual."

Alan laughed, "Get the hell out of here, Dad. I'm trying to study. Go bother Connie."

"I'm serious, Alan." It took a moment to sink in. Al shifted and broke free from his father's touch. There was complete silence for a few seconds.

"But, you're married to Mom." Alan realized that logically what he just said didn't necessarily make sense.

"Some homosexual men are married, Alan."

"I can't believe it. Cut the shit, Dad. You got me." If it were a joke, Daniel would be taking it a little too far. The absence of a response made Alan finally believe. He began to take his shirt off. He felt very hot and it was hard to breathe and sweated profusely. "I . . . I, this is true?"

"Yes. I can turn on the TV."

"Jesus!"

"Please talk about it with me. I need help dealing with it myself."

"How long have you known?"

"Since I was a young adult."

"What am I supposed to say? I thought my father was a man and today he's not." Alan began to cry. "I make fun of gay people, Dad. I don't get it. What did we do to make you gay?"

"You did nothing. Who knows what makes people heterosexual or homosexual? But I'm still your father. You're still my son. This is information I never wanted to tell you about."

"So have you been having sex with Mom all these years or what?"

"I'm not going to . . . It's really not your business to know."

"No, but it's okay to know you're a fag!" Daniel's anger welled up inside of him and he struck Alan with his open hand. The blow tossed Alan to the corner of his room. Alan was in shock. His father never hit him before. He was confused; he didn't know how to react.

Alan charged at his father and tackled him into the opposite wall. Daniel recovered and broke his arms free. As he smacked Alan, Daniel screamed, "I'm still your father! I'm still a man! I can still kick your ass like I did when you were a little boy." Alan fell to the ground and just laid there weeping.

"Am I going to be gay?" Alan asked. Daniel began to cry again into his hands. He turned away from Alan so he wouldn't see his father weeping. Again he saw himself in a mirror on the wall. He looked away.

"I don't think it's something that is taught, or runs in the family."

"You'd rather be with a man than with Mom?" Daniel actually found humor in that question. It would be tough for anyone to be with his mother. If there was a theory that claimed that a man could be driven toward homosexuality, she'd be the best case study.

"I haven't had a male relationship since my early twenties."

"How did they find out?" He turned and let his son see that he was crying. Alan remained on the floor.

"Who knows? But I made a speech asking the American public to understand."

"I know this is pretty selfish, but, how am I going to take the bar exam now? I've been looking for an excuse to do poorly on it." Both men smiled at each other. Alan sat up and wiped his tears.

"I'm going to leave you alone. We'll talk later. I know it's going to be a difficult time for you. It's a lot to deal with. Most importantly, Alan, I love you." Daniel left the room, and Alan said nothing.

* * *

The President went into his private study and looked around. He sat in silence for a long period of time. He noticed the books on the shelf and remembered reading almost every one. He looked at his watch and discovered that dinner would be served in about an hour. It would be a solemn and silent supper.

Daniel always loved the Ivy League look to the library. With the leather seat and mahogany desk with the green shaded lamp attached to the desk, it reminded him of his Yale and Harvard days. Daniel sat behind his desk, opened the drawer, pulled out his presidential stationery, and placed a fountain pen on top. As he opened another drawer, he saw the glint of the metal gun in the corner. The gun was always loaded. The President's attention turned to the pictures and awards on the wall. He stood with great men who respected him. He wondered how many would respect him when they read the papers.

Perhaps he wasn't giving the cameras enough credit. Maybe there was an ounce of decency in someone's bones who had the power to stop the destruction of a great man's career, and his family life. He laughed at the thought. It was the camera's job to tell all that was factual and interesting to the reader. All in the name of the First Amendment, the right to know.

Alan decided to look for his father. He had thought of something to ask him. He himself was still shaken up over the whole idea of it. He went into the kitchen, but Daniel wasn't there. Daniel picked up the loaded automatic weapon and placed it on his desk. Picking up the fountain pen, he began to write some notes on the sheet of paper in front of him. Alan looked in the family room. His father always watched television before dinner. He called it the *journal hour*. He would sit in silence watching a blank television screen.

Daniel wrote and wrote, taking only a second to caress his gun with his left hand. He squeezed it, then wrote another sentence. Squeezed and wrote. He pointed the barrel in his direction. He squeezed then wrote.

Finally, Alan figured that his father must be in the study to sit in silence. Daniel looked at himself in his mind's eye. Everyone he told about the upcoming catastrophe was asking, 'What about me?' 'Look how it's going to affect me.' That's what Daniel's job had been throughout his life. He answered everyone's question, 'What about me?' When his mother died, his father asked it. When Peter was dumped by the party, he asked. The one time he really asked for help, no one would even listen. They only wanted to talk about what they wanted to talk about. He wished someone would talk about what he wanted to talk about, instead of running for cover in a shield of selfishness. 'Me. Me. What about me?' He squeezed then wrote. It occurred to Daniel that this was the third time he really cried in his life. Once for his mother, another for failing the army physical, and now.

Alan opened the door forcefully. Alan stood at the door still without a shirt. His eyes were red from tears. "Dad, I just wanted to say I love you too." Daniel quickly slipped the gun back into the drawer. He rose and walked over to the door. The two men hugged and cried. "I love you, Dad. It's going to be okay. We'll stick it out together. Me, you, the whole family."

"You don't know how good that makes me feel," he said between sobs.

"You weren't going to kill yourself with that gun?"

"No. I thought you and me would go out and kill some members of the press. Good idea?"

The sanctimonious Silent Majority might have wanted it, but Daniel chose life instead.

"Hmm. Can you do that?"

"Of course I can. I'm the Goddamn President." The two smiled at each other. Daniel held Alan's head in his hands and kissed him on the lips. "You really turned out to be a great kid."

"Well, I take after my dad." Daniel let that comment sink in, and he smiled.

"Well, while we're talking, I might as well tell you my mother was Jewish." Alan looked at his father and tilted his head in bewilderment.

★ ★ ★

The election day arrived. Usually excitement and anticipation filled the air like Christmas Eve to a child. Daniel was flying around the Northeast getting out the vote. The crowds he spoke to were of course friendly ones. He could scarcely tell at all that he had a cloud hanging over his head.

Daniel reconsidered the repercussions from his speech. He feared that he asked the American people to radically change their thinking toward acceptance of an idea too quickly. The American mind is like changing the direction of a large ship—even when the wheel has turned, it takes many miles before it turns around. And what a shame. What a great President Daniel Carlson had become. Today, the unemployment rate for the previous quarter, three percent unemployment, the lowest in the country's history.

* * *

It was Election night and the polls were closed. Daniel asked that his family come to Washington and stay in at the White House. He wasn't going to attend any parties no matter what the results of the election. He also told Peter not to prepare "winning" or "losing" speeches. He sent a message to the Chairman of the Committee to Re-elect, stating that he would neither accept congratulations nor defeat until the following day. Peter had the speeches written anyway. Peter knew that he would convince Daniel that a concession or acceptance speech must be given.

Connie still had pain. Pain of being kept in the dark through all those years. But Daniel was her father, a loving and caring man since the day she met him—unconditionally. But even with his family home on the East Wing of the White House, Daniel knew he was alone, and always was alone —when he was a hero and in his moment of disgrace.

Peter Spark was on the phone the last few hours with the campaign advisers in key states and the *Geeks*. The *Geeks* were uppity. They were rich, powerful, and arrived. Peter was too grateful and gave them so much. Bradford said Peter didn't give them enough time to learn how to break the encryption of touch screen voting machines in Ohio, Texas, Arizona, and Pennsylvania. Peter realized he didn't need the *Geeks* because President Carlson was too far ahead in the polls just a few months ago, and he wasn't desperate for them. Boy, did he want them now. Yesterday, winning the election fairly was an easy promise Peter could keep to his President and friend. Today, the counting in Florida and California were closer than expected. Both sides were saber rattling about litigation for recounts.

Daniel pulled out the bed in his office, knowing that he wouldn't sleep with June. He took off his jacket and tie, wrapped himself in a robe and turned out the lights, going to sleep, perhaps the last night as the President. But as he went to sleep as a great leader of the nation, he knew he would awake as the same man. The Silent Majority having won.

ABOUT THE AUTHOR

Robert Buschel was born in Brooklyn, New York. He grew up in South Florida. He flies compassion missions for the medically needy as a private pilot. He practices as a trial lawyer in Florida and California.